Oscar set aside ████████████ notepad, and picked up a ballpoint pen. His handwriting was large and overblown, like the man himself: *Someone is trying to kill my grandson's wife. Help us.*

I blinked at the message, then stared at Oscar. He motioned for me not to speak out loud. *Who?* I scribbled.

Don't know, he scribbled in reply.

With a sigh I leaned back in my swivel chair. It would do me no good to urge Oscar or any other Nyquist to go to the sheriff. Rapidly, I considered the previous problems the family had encountered. All of them were petty, probably pranks. Young people in Alpine didn't have enough to do, especially in the winter. My initial reaction was to dismiss Oscar's fears as part of a persecution complex.

Except that we already had two dead young women. Was it possible Bridget Nyquist might become number three?

Also by Mary Daheim
Published by Ballantine Books:

THE ALPINE ADVOCATE
THE ALPINE BETRAYAL

THE
ALPINE
CHRISTMAS

Mary Daheim

BALLANTINE BOOKS • NEW YORK

Copyright © 1993 by Mary Daheim

All rights reserved under International and Pan-American Copyright Conventions. Published in the United States of America by Ballantine Books, a division of Random House, Inc., New York, and simultaneously in Canada by Random House of Canada Limited, Toronto.

Library of Congress Catalog Card Number: 93-90512

ISBN 0-345-38270-6

Manufactured in the United States of America

First Edition: November 1993

Chapter One

FATHER FITZ HAD lost it. That didn't come as a surprise to those of us who were his regular parishioners, but it knocked the socks off my brother, Ben. Luckily, Ben has enough poise as a person and experience as a priest that he didn't fall off the altar.

On holy days of obligation, Father Kiernan Fitzgerald always managed to keep mass under forty minutes. Since December 8 commemorates the Immaculate Conception of the Blessed Virgin, I attended the eight o'clock service on my way to work at *The Alpine Advocate*. Ben was concelebrating the liturgy while on vacation from his job as pastor to the Navajos in Tuba City, Arizona.

It is always with a sense of pride that I watch Ben say mass. Like me, he is dark and brown-eyed; he has the same round face (but more nose), and an extra six inches of height. He is not handsome and I am not beautiful, yet—as our late parents used to say—we make a very presentable pair. When we try. Certainly Ben looks most impressive in the vestments that some of his female parishioners made for him, complete with Navajo symbols of sun, earth, and sky.

The fifty parishioners and one hundred schoolchildren from St. Mildred's sat huddled together in winter coats and heavy-duty footgear. At the left of the altar, two purple candles burned in an Advent wreath fashioned from fir, cedar, and pine. The remaining candles, one pink and the other

1

purple, would be lighted on the last two Sundays before Christmas.

Outside, three feet of snow covered the ground. As usual, winter had arrived early in Alpine. At over two thousand feet above sea level, we were not only in the mountains, we were part of them. I turned my attention to Father Fitz as he stood to give the final blessing.

"I have some announcements," he said in his low, mellifluous voice with its trace of County Cork. Father Fitz's legs might be crippled by arthritis, his hearing may be poor, but there is nothing wrong with the way he speaks. "Last week's Christmas bazaar brought in $1,185.37. Half we'll be giving to the school, the other half to the families of unemployed loggers. God bless you for your generosity and hard work." He paused, peering at his notes through thick trifocals. "The school Nativity pageant, *Elvis Meets the Three Wise Men*, will take place Thursday, December 17th, in the school hall at seven P.M." He gave the principal, Mrs. Monica Vancich, a glance of disapproval. Mrs. Vancich smiled serenely, then tweaked the white shirt collar of Joey Bronsky, a notorious fidgeter and my ad manager's son. Joey snapped to.

Father Fitz continued: "Finally, we ask you all to pray for the repose of the souls of the thousands of brave Americans who died in yesterday's attack on Pearl Harbor in the Hawaiian Islands. Monstrous cruel it was, and our president will be needing your prayers as well. May Almighty God keep Mr. Roosevelt." Father Fitz turned to his breviary. "The Lord be with you."

"And also with you." The congregation's response was a little wobbly. I caught Ben's eye. He was staring stonily ahead, his face tight. It was a sure sign that he was trying not to laugh.

Father Fitz bestowed the last blessing and dismissed us. Annie Jeanne Dupré pumped away at the old organ as the congregation launched into an off-key rendition of "Immaculate Mary.'' Father Fitz and Ben left the altar, the school-children began to file out in a disorderly fashion, and little clutches of worshippers buzzed in the aisles, presumably about Father Fitz's unfortunate lapse. I edged off to a side altar where the statue of St. Joseph seemed to wear a bemused air. I was waiting for Ben and didn't want to get caught up in controversy just yet. I faced enough of that every day in my job as editor and publisher of *The Advocate*.

It wasn't unusual for our officially retired pastor to operate in a time warp. His sermons often reflected an era of bootleg liquor, creeping Communism, or family life lived only by Andy Hardy. This, however, was the first time he'd enlisted his parishioners' prayers for a event long past.

Except for Mrs. Patricelli, who was lighting enough votive candles to bake a ham, the church had grown empty. I could feel the cold come through the stained glass windows and hear the wind stir in the belfry. It was going on nine in the morning and very gloomy outside. The heavy gray clouds had been hanging over Alpine since early November. We might glimpse the sun before May, but we wouldn't see the ground. Only seven miles from the summit of Stevens Pass in the Cascade Mountains, the four thousand residents of Alpine knew winter far better than most Pacific Northwesterners. Eighty miles away in Seattle, I suspected it was fifty degrees with a seventy percent chance of rain.

Ben came from the sacristy just as Mrs. Patricelli ran out of matches. On her way out, she beamed at my brother, a gap-toothed, maternal smile, befitting the mother of nine and grandmother of eighteen. Maybe they were the reason for all the candles. The last I'd heard, her oldest was president of a bank in Yakima and her youngest was doing time for embezzling. Not, I guessed, from his brother's bank.

Ben had planned on taking himself to breakfast at the Venison Eat Inn and Take Out after mass. ''I'd better skip the ride downtown,'' he said in his crackling voice that could keep even the sleepiest parishioner awake during a sermon. "Father Fitz is pretty shaky and the housekeeper is upset."

"Mrs. McHale? Really?" Teresa McHale had been the housekeeper at the rectory for a little over a year, but she struck me as having a cast-iron disposition. "Is Father Fitz sick or just daffy?"

"He went through his usual routine this morning: up at six, got dressed and showered, devotions in his room, heard confessions at seven-thirty for the holy day, then readied for mass. He seemed fine, but Mrs. McHale wants to call Doc Dewey." Ben steered me down the aisle toward the main entrance. "She thinks Father may have had a little stroke."

"Oh, dear." I pulled on my driving gloves as we stood in the vestibule. At eighty-nine, a stroke couldn't be a surprise. Still, in the second week of Advent, Father Fitz's timing was lousy. Or, I thought, glancing up at Ben, maybe not. "Could you take over?"

Ben rolled his eyes. He was back in his street clothes, thick navy sweater, blue jeans, and knee-high boots. He was very tan from his assignment in the desert. "So there goes twenty days of my twenty-one day vacation? Hell, Emma, I just got here day before yesterday."

"Ben . . ." I sounded reproachful. "You're a priest, after all. . . ."

"A *tired* priest," he put in, looking unwontedly grim. "After twenty years, I finally got things halfway organized down on the Mississippi Delta, then I get shipped to the Navajo reservation a year ago and have to start all over. To make matters worse, the Mormons got to Tuba City first— over a hundred years ago. And the Hopis have been plucked right down in the middle of the Navajos. No wonder they hate each other. The federal government's relocation in the Seventies still causes hard feelings. Now D.C.'s got a new plan, but who knows if it'll work. It's rough out there on the fringes of the Painted Desert. I'm almost forty-five, Emma.

I have this dream of a well-heeled, well-oiled parish in the suburbs. Alpine ain't it, Sluggly.''

I grinned at the old nickname, a cross between Sluggo and Ugly. "You'd last about two weeks in the suburbs, Stench," I asserted, retaliating with my childhood moniker for him. "You thrive on adversity and you know it. Besides, it may be only a few days. Think not of your vacation, but of your vocation.''

"The parishioners might resent my stepping in." Ben rubbed the thatch of brown hair that he combed off a side part. "On the other hand, I *am* here. . . ." One of Ben's flaws is his indecisiveness. He always sees six sides of any issue. I have a similar tendency, which I regard as journalistic objectivity. But with deadlines to meet, I can't often indulge myself. Conversely, Ben's propensity for equivocation has grown more pronounced over the years, perhaps as a result of two decades spent in the slow lane along the Mississippi Delta.

We argued briefly, and at last he gave in as I knew he would. "I'll have to check with the arch," he said, referring to the archbishop in Seattle. "But first we'd better see how bad Father Fitz really is. I don't want to usurp his authority. You know how proprietary these old pastors can be, especially the ones from Ireland.''

I was about to concur when Teresa McHale entered the vestibule from the church proper. She gave me the briefest of nods, murmured "Mrs. Lord," and then addressed Ben: "I called young Doc Dewey. He's in surgery, but that new man, Peyton Flake, will be over as soon as he finishes cleaning his guns.''

Teresa McHale had replaced Edna McPhail, who had served in the rectory for over thirty years. Edna had died the previous year, suffering a heart attack while cleaning the bathtub. Since Edna was some ten years younger than Father Fitz, he had presumed she would outlive him. When she didn't, he had a tizzy and put an ad not only in the church bulletin but *The Advocate* as well. Except for a well-known alcoholic and a woman whose wits could be most kindly described as lacking, there were no takers.

Alpine is predominantly Scandinavian, and there are only about seven hundred registered Catholic parishioners in the vicinity. Since half of these are either too young or too old, and half of the rest are men, that doesn't leave a large labor pool of would-be housekeepers on which to draw. Father Fitz had called the Chancery in Seattle for help. He got it, in the form of Teresa McHale. I suspected he viewed the replacement of McPhail by McHale as a minor miracle.

Teresa did not look like a typical parish housekeeper, being rather chic, at least for Alpine, sporting dyed red hair, considerable makeup, and a plump, unbridled figure. She had strong features and shrewd green eyes adorned with long false lashes. Yet from all accounts, she was very efficient, and Father Fitz had not been heard to complain, though naturally some of the parishioners did.

"I'll go sit with Father," said Ben, giving me a punch in the upper arm. "Later, Sluggly."

I took my cue and headed out into a world of white. My green Jaguar was the only car in the lot between the church and the school. St. Mildred's had been built shortly after World War I, a white frame structure that would have been right at home in New England. The rectory, which was connected to the church by a covered walk, was of the same vintage, a one-story frame house with a basement, and enough room for two priests as well as a housekeeper. The parochial school was much newer, from the early Fifties, with a beige brick facade, an even newer gymnasium, and a school hall that also served as a lunchroom. The convent had stood behind the church, approximately where my car was now parked. About twenty years ago, when the shortage of nuns forced the school to hire lay teachers, vexed parishioners refused to pay for renovation of the convent. The archbishop had gotten a bit vexed as well, and had ordered the convent razed. Any nuns who taught at St. Mildred's were forced to live elsewhere. At present, there were two, Sister Clare and Sister Mary Joan, who shared an apartment in a three-story building across the street.

The Jag started immediately, and I drove carefully into the drifting flakes, hearing my chains grind and crunch. Alpine is built on a mountainside, which makes for very dicey driving in the winter. I eased my way down Fourth Street, past the Baptist Church, Mugs Ahoy, the local bank, and finally, the intersection at Front Street. The newspaper office was across the street, repainted a tasteful light blue after its brief passage of egg-yolk yellow during a film crew's location shoot the previous summer.

Ed Bronsky's station wagon was pulled up to the curb, as was the white Buick sedan that belonged to my House & Home editor, Vida Runkel. My sole reporter, Carla Steinmetz, had probably walked to work, as had our office manager, Ginny Burmeister. Carla had owned a car of sorts when she first arrived in Alpine after graduating from the University of Washington a year and a half ago, but she had turned it in last September for a motor scooter. Naturally, it didn't work very well in the snow, but neither did Carla. In fact, Carla didn't work very well under any conditions, but at least she was enthusiastic.

Vida was playing the trombone. Badly. I winced and put my gloved hands over my ears. "Stop!" I shrieked. "Why are you doing that?"

Vida gave one last toot and put the trombone down on the empty chair next to her desk. "It was stolen from the high school last night. Somebody broke into the band room. My nephew Billy found it this morning at the base of Carl Clemans's statue in Old Mill Park." She rummaged under her desk. "There's a piccolo, too. And a pair of drumsticks."

Bill Blatt was not only Vida's nephew—as I sometimes thought half of Alpine was—but also a deputy sheriff. "So why didn't Billy take the instruments back to the high school?''

Vida, who is in her early sixties, and exudes an aura of rumpled majesty, shrugged her wide, multilayered shoulders. "He intended to, but he got a call from the sheriff, so he left them here. For the time being.''

"Milo was having a cow," said Carla, bouncing up from her chair and looking like a Christmas elf in her red parka. "He raised his voice on the phone. I actually *heard* him.''

I gazed at Carla. Excitement did not become Sheriff Dodge. Carla, I felt, must be exaggerating. "I thought Milo was taking the morning off to go steelheading.''

Ed looked up from a dummy ad for Barton's Bootery. He was wearing an old overcoat that was two sizes too small for his ever-expanding girth. "Why bother? Fishing's terrible around here these days. I haven't gone out in five years.''

An eternal pessimist, Ed probably wouldn't have hit the Skykomish River if a twenty-pound steelhead had flopped onto his desk. "Milo caught two last winter," I remarked, taking off my purple car coat and discovering that the news office was freezing. "What happened to our heat?''

Ed gave me a doleful look. "It broke. The Public Utility District's having problems. They're going to try to fix it by this afternoon.''

"Great." I gazed down at the baseboard that ordinarily would be emitting comfortable waves of warmth. Stubbornly, I refused to put my car coat back on. I might not be a native Alpiner, but I wasn't going to give in to a spate of twenty-degree weather. "Okay, so what's with Milo?" I inquired, getting back to the sheriff's uncustomary state of excitement.

But Ed was picking up the phone, Carla was rocketing off to the front office, and Vida was typing sixty-to-the-dozen on her battered old upright. Vida, however, had the courtesy to eye me over the rims of her tortoiseshell glasses. "Milo was disturbed. He didn't tell Billy why." She kept right on typing.

A car wreck, I decided, and no wonder, what with the compact ice under the fresh snow. Even with four-wheel drive or chains, there were plenty of accidents not only in town, but out on the pass. I went into my office, which felt like a deep freezer. Trying not to let my teeth chatter, I wished for once that I didn't have a fear of portable heating units. But my career as a reporter on *The Oregonian* had included too many gruesome stories about people who had died in fires caused by plug-in heaters. I'd rather watch my breath come and go in little puffs while my knees knocked together under my desk.

The best cure for freezing, I decided, was work. It was Tuesday, after all, and our deadline for the weekly edition of *The Advocate*. Despite a sagging economy and Ed Bronsky's best efforts to discourage advertisers, we were putting out a thirty-six-page paper, crammed with holiday specials. It was a good thing, since we were running light on real news. This was the season for Vida to shine, with plenty of party coverage, charity functions, and how-to holiday articles. I'd allotted her six pages this week, but of course they were all inside. The front page was unusually bland; Carla's lead story recounted the city council's decision to allow a ten-foot plastic Santa Claus to tower over Old Mill Park.

"It will blow away," said council president and ski lodge manager Henry Bardeen.

"It will detract from the memorial to our town's founder, Carl Clemans," said council secretary and apparel-shop owner Francine Wells.

"It will be the target of every snowballer and potshot artist in town," said council member and building contractor Arnold Nyquist.

"It will be an appropriate seasonal reminder, and a compromise in response to criticism of the manger scene that has stood in Old Mill Park every Christmas since 1946," said

Mayor Fuzzy Baugh. "Let it not be said that the City of Alpine is insensitive to those who do not share basic Christian beliefs. No matter how misguided, these fine folks still vote." Fuzzy was your basic Baptist.

He was also a savvy politician, but his quote needed pruning. I was about to exercise my editor's pencil when the phone rang. It was Milo Dodge. He didn't sound excited so much as disturbed.

"Emma, can you come over for a minute?"

I started to fabricate an excuse, then realized that Milo's office might have heat, and said I could. The Skykomish County Sheriff's office was only two blocks away, after all. "Shall I pick up some doughnuts?" The Upper Crust Bakery had recently moved into the space formerly occupied by the hobby and toy shop, which had graduated to the Alpine Mall. The town's original source of baked goods had dried up three years earlier when its current owner had left Alpine to dry out and had never come back. The Upper Crust was owned by a pair of upstarts from Seattle who had a yen for the wide open spaces—and cheap real estate prices. Their baked goods were fabulous.

But Milo declined. "Just come over, quick as you can," he said, then hastily added a word of warning: "Be careful—it's slippery out there."

I agreed not to turn cartwheels on Front Street. After putting on my car coat, I trudged over to the bakery, which was closed. No heat, I supposed. No ovens, no doughnuts. The marzipan reindeer in the window display looked as if they were seeking shelter in the gingerbread house. Next door, Parker's Pharmacy was open, but I noticed that the clerks were wearing heavy sweaters and the fluorescent lighting had taken on a jaundiced tinge. Across the street, the Burger Barn was completely dark.

Luckily, Milo isn't afraid of space heaters. He had a large one going full tilt next to his desk. I sat down opposite him and cozied up to the glowing coils. Milo asked Bill Blatt to bring me a cup of coffee.

"At least the lights work," I noted, though they gave an ominous flicker even as I spoke. "What happened?"

Milo thought I meant him, rather than the PUD. He shook his head slowly, incredulously. "Emma, it was the damnedest thing. I hit the river above Anthracite Creek, six miles down the highway. I got there just before first light. Jack Mullins got a twelve-pounder in that hole Saturday morning," he went on, referring to another of his deputies. "Within the first fifteen minutes, I had a couple of bumps. I was sure it was going to be my lucky day."

Milo paused as Bill Blatt brought my coffee. I could visualize the scene, the river rushing among big boulders, the leaden sky overhead, the freezing air, the wind cutting to the bone, the snow swirling everywhere. Perfect steelheading weather. Only a true masochist could love the sport.

"And?" I encouraged Milo after Bill had made his exit.

Milo leaned on his elbows. He was a big shambling man in his mid-forties, with sharp hazel eyes, graying sandy hair, and a long face with a square jaw. It was a nice face, even an attractive face, though I made a point of not usually acknowledging the fact. When it came to the male-female thing, Milo and I had our own agendas. Or so it seemed.

"Then something really hit," Milo continued, his high forehead creasing. "It didn't feel like a fish, but it didn't seem like a snag, either. I let the line play out a little, but there wasn't any fight. So I started to reel in. I damned near died when I saw what I had." Milo gulped, blanched, and gave a shudder. Impatient, I stared at his stricken expression. He'd been the sheriff of Skykomish County for over eight years. Surely he'd seen it all.

"Well, what was it?" I demanded.

He passed a big hand over his face. "It was a leg, Emma. A human leg. And it was still wearing a tennis shoe. With no sock."

Chapter Two

I FELT A bit pale, too. For a long moment, Milo and I stared at each other across the desk. Finally, I spoke, my voice a trifle weak: "What did you do with it?" I clutched at my Styrofoam cup, feeling the warmth, but not benefitting from it.

Having related his grisly tale, Milo sat back in his chair. His color was returning, but he was shaking his head again. "I had a big garbage bag in the Cherokee Chief, so I got it and put the thing in it. Then I came back here and called Bill and Jack to come over quick. Doc Dewey will do the rest. I tell you, Emma, it's the damnedest thing I've ever seen in twenty-five years of law enforcement."

I sipped my coffee and reflected. We could get the story on page one, but it wouldn't run more than a couple of inches. Later, when and if we knew more, we could do a detailed article. Over the past two or three years, several body parts had been hauled out of rivers in Snohomish and King counties. This, however, was a first for Skykomish.

"So it's all up to Doc?" I inquired. Gerald Dewey, M.D., known locally as young Doc, had recently taken over not only his late father's practice, but old Doc's coroner's duties as well.

Milo nodded. "It's pretty routine. Try to make an ID, figure out time and cause of death. If foul play is suspected, then we go to work." Draining his mug with its NRA emblem, Milo seemed to have regained his composure. He actually chuckled. "Weird, huh? Except for a couple of those Snohomish County cases, nobody's been able to figure out if we've got another serial killer or a lot of accident-prone people in western Washington."

"Or too many nuts living in the woods and playing with their Skilsaws," I remarked.

"Always a possibility," agreed Milo. "City people don't realize how many goofballs take to the high country. Recluses who were strange to start with and keep getting stranger."

"Transients, too," I pointed out. "Either as victim or as hermit. Or both. Do you figure this was a man?"

Milo turned serious again. "My guess is that it was a woman, or maybe a kid. It had been in the river a long time. I'll spare you the decomposition details, but judging from the sockless tennis shoe alone, I'd say maybe two or three months."

I was grateful to be spared. One of my flaws as a journalist is my squeamish stomach. "Will you check out a list of missing persons?"

Milo gave a grunt of assent. "It won't do much good. Nobody I know of is missing around here, except for the usual wandering husband or fed-up wife. If it's a juvenile, we'd have a better chance—most of them are on the National Crime Information Center computer. After the Green River killer investigation, there was a move to report missing prostitutes on a national basis, but the truth is that the people who first miss them usually aren't anxious to get tangled up with the law."

I had taken my notebook out of my handbag and was writing swiftly. Maybe the story could run at least six inches if I included the background Milo was giving me. I could dump all of Carla's quotes about the plastic Santa and cut the last two grafs of my latest spotted owl piece, which was merely a rehash of the most recent plan to resolve the environment-logging industry controversy.

"Let me know if you find out anything more," I requested as I stood up, loath to leave the space heater. "We've got the rest of the day to get the story in this week's edition."

Milo grimaced. "Don't make me look like a damned fool."

I cocked my head to one side. "Have I ever?"

The sheriff looked the other way. "No—I can probably manage that on my own."

"Can't we all?" I gave him a wave and headed out through the reception area where Arnold Nyquist was pounding his fist on the counter and griping at Jack Mullins. Nyquist was a large, bluff man in his fifties, with a fringe of gray hair and a ruddy complexion. Known to most Alpiners as Arnie, but to some as Tinker Toy, he was the biggest building contractor in Alpine. The nickname had been coined by some wag who didn't consider Nyquist's residential dwellings up to snuff. Since three of the thirty homes in the Ptarmigan Tract west of town had collapsed during the early 1980s, the criticism might have been justified. Of late, Nyquist was concentrating on commercial construction.

". . . couldn't find a two-by-four up your butt!" Nyquist was saying to Jack Mullins.

Mullins, who had a reputation for drollery, turned his head to look down at his backside. "Golly, I don't see anything. Do you?"

Nyquist banged his fist again, causing ballpoint pens to jump and papers to flutter. "Don't be a wiseass, Mullins! That stuff cost close to a grand. And the fountain pen belonged to my granddad. He brought it over from Norway in oh-seven."

Standing at the bulletin board, I pretended to scan the various announcements and notices. Arnie Nyquist stormed out, with a parting shot for Jack: "This isn't the first time I've had problems with theft and vandalism. That moron of a sheriff and the rest of you dumbbells couldn't arrest anybody if they broke into the county jail. I'll expect to hear from you or Dodge by five o'clock this afternoon. You got that?''

Jack nodded his shaggy red head. ''I'll put it with the two-by-four,'' he said after Nyquist had made his exit. ''Hey, Mrs. Lord, isn't old Tinker Toy a world-class jerk?''

''He can be,'' I conceded. Luckily, I hadn't dealt much with Arnie Nyquist. The kind of news he generated usually came through cut-and-dried building permit or zoning council stories. I had, however, dealt with his father, Oscar, who owned The Whistling Marmot Movie Theatre. At one time, in the 1920s, Oscar and his father had owned the entire Alpine block where the theatre was located, kitty-corner from *The Advocate*. Although Lars Nyquist had chosen *Gösta Berling's Saga* with Greta Garbo for the opening of his new picture palace in 1924, his son had refused to show foreign films for decades. Oscar asserted that they were all obscene, obscure, and anti-American. He had been tricked into presenting *Wild Strawberries* because he thought the Bergman involved was Ingrid, not Ingmar. According to Vida, at least four people in Alpine noted the irony of one Norwegian getting confused by two Swedes.

''What's the problem?'' I asked of Jack, sensing another late-breaking, if minor, story.

Mullins pushed the official log my way. ''Somebody got into Nyquist's van last night and stole a bunch of stuff. Portable CD player, half a dozen CDs, some tools, a box of Jamaican cigars, a couple of fancy photographs . . . whatever. Nyquist left the van unlocked. It serves him right.''

It probably did, but people in Alpine still have a tendency to trust each other, at least with their belongings, if not with their spouses. ''Could it be the same thief who stole the band equipment up at the high school?''

Jack shrugged. ''Maybe. But Nyquist's van was parked at his son's place on Stump Hill. That's a good mile or so from the high school.'' The implication was that Alpine's crooks were too lazy to cross town to commit a second burglary. Especially in the snow.

I jotted down some more notes, just in case Carla had forgotten to check the log. I recalled some other incidents involving Arnold Nyquist. Last December, a display of Christmas lights at his home on First Hill had been swiped; his second floor office in the Alpine Building was egged in the spring; a load of garbage had been dumped on his front lawn in July; a small fire was started at his construction site for the new bowling alley across the river. Nyquist was right about one thing, though—if memory served, no one had been apprehended for any of the mischief. I supposed it was only natural that Arnie would take it more seriously than the law enforcement officials did. Indeed, the family's string of minor bad luck was ongoing.

"How is Travis?" I asked, referring to Nyquist's son, who was recovering from a broken ankle suffered in a skiing accident over the Thanksgiving weekend. Until the theft of last night, Travis's mishap on Tonga Ridge had been the most recent Nyquist calamity.

Jack grinned, which always seemed to make his teeth sparkle and his freckles dance. "If I had that wife of his to take care of me, I'd break a leg three times a year. Trav's doing fine, and why shouldn't he? There's a guy who's got it all."

On the surface, at least, Travis Nyquist had attained many a young man's dreams before he was thirty. A graduate of Pacific Lutheran University in Tacoma, he had gotten his M.A. in finance at the University of Washington, gone to work for a big brokerage house in Seattle, met his future bride, Bridget, and moved back to Alpine to mull over his stock options. The young Nyquists had been married for a little over a year. They now lived in a handsome Pacific Northwest version of a Cape Cod on Stump Hill, otherwise known as The Pines. The house had been built six years earlier by Arnie Nyquist on speculation, but this time he'd spared no expense. When the well-to-do commuter family from Everett had gotten fed up driving back and forth on Stevens Pass, Arnie put earnest money down and held onto the place until his son carried his bride over the threshold.

"Trav and I went to high school together," Jack was musing, his freckled face now wistful. "He never seemed to work that hard, but he always got good grades. The other guys and I used to say that he charmed his teachers, at least the women, but I guess Trav is really smart. He must have gotten his brains from Mrs. Nyquist. Old Tinker Toy's IQ isn't so hot, if you ask me. My dad says it's a wonder Arnie didn't flunk out of UDUB in his freshman year."

Briefly, I considered Arnie Nyquist's wife, Louise, a meek ex-schoolteacher who had reputedly jumped out the window of her seventh-grade classroom during a particularly arduous social studies session. Fortunately, she was on the first floor at the time and landed virtually unharmed in a rhododendron bush.

With some reluctance, I left Jack Mullins to his musings about The Life and Times of Travis Nyquist, and headed out into the snow, which had turned fairly heavy. Through the curtain of white, I could barely make out the Christmas decorations along Front Street: golden strands of tinsel, big red shiny bows, and tall amber candles that covered the regular streetlights.

Back in the office, I found Ginny Burmeister distributing the mail. There was nothing much of interest: only the usual press releases, bills, promotions, and a couple of letters to the editor and/or publisher. The first missive was in response to our front-page article about cutting Christmas trees on state lands, an activity that was permitted in certain areas every year from the last week of November until mid-December. The irate correspondent, Ruth Rydholm, asserted that such plundering of the forests was unnecessary and even dangerous. Since Mrs. Rydholm's son Cliff owned a Christmas tree farm in Snohomish County, I figured she was a bit biased.

The other letter, also tree-oriented, chided me for my previous spotted owl story. A week without a spotted owl letter was like a week without a Monday. Alpiners, except for the recycled Californians, were generally anti-owl and pro-logger, which befitted a town founded on the timber industry. Even though the original mill had closed in 1929, logging was still an important, if severely jeopardized, source of income. Most of the locals viewed efforts to protect the endangered spotted owl as no more necessary than saving the pterodactyl. The longer I lived in Alpine, the more I tended to agree, but I hoped, in my fair-minded journalist's way, that a compromise could be reached.

What I could not reach was my son. Adam was taking a final. He was due to arrive at Sea-Tac Airport Saturday from the University of Alaska in Fairbanks. Although I'd spoken to him by phone, I hadn't seen him since he'd spent two days with his father, Tom Cavanaugh, in San Francisco. It was the first time Adam had met his dad. My son indicated that all had gone well. Young men—most men—aren't much for relating intimate details. Wish I'd been there. Wish Tom were here. Wish my life away. That's what I'd done for over twenty years. . . .

Just as I was entering Milo's fishing incident on my word processor, the phone rang. I hoped it was Adam, returning my call, but the voice at the other end of the line was equally pleasing to me.

"Hi, Sluggly," said my brother. "I'm at the hospital. Mrs. McHale was right: Father Fitz has had a small stroke. Dr. Flake wants to keep him for a couple of days. I'm wondering if I should move into the rectory."

I was torn: Ben was currently staying in Adam's room, but had insisted he'd take up residence on the living-room sofa once my son got to Alpine. I had argued that I would sleep on the sofa—Ben was on vacation. But maybe the rectory was a good idea. Someone besides the housekeeper should be there during Advent.

"Have you called the Chancery?" I asked. Ben had. The archbishop—or an underling—had given my brother a green light. Priests were scarce; priests were needed. The Chancery office was only too glad for someone who had actually taken holy orders to run St. Mildred's. Otherwise, we might have been stuck with liturgical services conducted by Helga Wenzler, parish council president and manic-depressive—or worse yet, Ed Bronsky, eucharistic minister, who would immediately change the Good News to the Bad News. Or no news at all . . . Such was Ed's morbid style.

I made the proper sisterly noises about having Ben sleep away from my cozy log house, but ultimately we agreed that he ought to stay at the rectory, if only until Father Fitz was released from the hospital. I thought of telling him about Milo's dreaded catch, decided to wait, and said I'd see him for dinner around six.

"Make it eight," said Ben, sounding apologetic. "I've got to say a seven o'clock mass for the Immaculate Conception."

Having done my duty at eight A.M., I'd forgotten about the extra mass for a holy day. "No problem. We'll have T-bone steaks."

"Maybe I should stick around at the rectory," Ben mused. "Somebody might wander in after mass."

This time, I made up Ben's mind for him. "Tell Mrs. McHale to make an appointment for the lost soul. You want your steak medium rare, don't you?"

Ben did. Shivering from the cold, I hung up and returned to Milo's account of the leg. Now that I had recovered from the ghastliness of the incident, I began to wonder where the rest of the body was. Halfway through the story, I dialed Milo's number.

"Hey, Milo," I said, my fingers on the keyboard and the phone propped between my shoulder and my left ear, "will you and your deputies go looking for the missing pieces?"

Milo uttered a heavy sigh. "With the river up the way it

is? Hell, Emma, I'd be lucky to catch a steelhead, let alone find a spare arm. What's the point?''

I made a little face of exasperation into the receiver. How typical of Milo, to be only as curious as circumstances permitted. On the other hand, it wasn't up to me to tell him his business. "Just curious," I said. "Bye."

"Emma—wait. What are you saying in the paper?" Milo sounded faintly alarmed.

I almost never offered copy on approval. My readers had to trust me, while I, in turn, worked hard to earn that trust. But Milo was a friend as well as a news source. "What's it worth to you, Dodge?"

There was a slight pause. "Dinner at King Olav's?"

I'd had worse offers. The lights flickered; so did my computer screen. "What would Honoria think?" Milo's current lady love was Honoria Whitman, a transplanted Carmel potteress who lived in Startup and got around in a wheelchair.

"Honoria wouldn't mind," said Milo. "She likes you."

The feeling was mutual. Still, I was a bit chagrined. Milo's trust was fine when it came to my writing efforts. Honoria's trust was an insult when it came to my feminine wiles. I read the three paragraphs I'd written aloud to Milo. He quibbled over a couple of words, but I ignored him. The sheriff wasn't any more qualified to meddle in my business than I was in his.

I'd just finished the piece when Henry Bardeen made his brisk way through the newsroom. Trim, slim, and ever-dapper, Henry ran the ski lodge with great efficiency. His brown toupee, gracefully etched with just a touch of silver, rested naturally on his well-shaped head. Henry had come to confer with Ed Bronsky, and was not pleased to learn that Ed was out.

"I wanted a final look at that ad about the sleigh ride to the restaurant," said Henry in his dry monotone voice. "We've decided to keep doing it after New Year's, maybe until ski season is over."

"I can find it for you." I led Henry back into the larger office. Ed was more organized than either Carla or Vida. Under a double-truck ad for Safeway, I found the mock-up Ed had created for Henry. It was tastefully done, with an original illustration of a horse-drawn sleigh going through snow-tipped evergreens. "This is very nice," I remarked. "How did you talk Ed out of using his odious clip art file?"

Henry was mulling over the copy. The promotion had its charm and was practical to boot. Diners heading for the new King Olav's restaurant could park on the far side of the bridge near the highway and ride a horse-drawn sleigh for two miles up to the ski lodge. While the gimmick was primarily an advertising promotion, it was also aimed at out-of-towners who didn't mind traversing the pass in winter weather but weren't keen on making the final leg up a steep, narrow, winding stretch of road. The last quarter-mile was through trees decorated with fairy lights, and ended in front of a Christmas scene straight out of Dickens. Like many Alpiners, I was anxious to take the sleigh ride, too.

"Can we say *through February* instead of *until January 3*?" Henry inquired. I told him we could, and made the appropriate changes on both the dummy and Ed's computer. Henry, who had left his sense of humor in the nursery, was actually smiling, albeit thinly. "That's Evan Singer's art work. He's the one who drives the sleigh."

The name rang no bells, sleigh or otherwise. After almost three years in Alpine, I was still lost in the maze of names. Small-town residents love to toss out names, as if testing newcomers. They assume everybody knows everybody else. It's a form of snobbism, making the new arrival feel even more like an outsider. As the editor and publisher of the local newspaper, I was supposed to know all—but names were still my nemesis.

Henry noted my blank expression.

"Evan's new in town, what you might call a free spirit." He wrinkled his aquiline nose. "As a rule, I'm not in favor of hiring that sort of person, but this sleigh driver's job was hard to fill. The Dithers Sisters volunteered to take turns since we're using their horses, but you know what *they're* like." This time, Henry not only wrinkled his nose, but wiggled his eyebrows. The Dithers Sisters were a pair of middle-aged horse owners who had been left a considerable amount of money by their parents. It was probably the greatest misfortune ever to befall them, since neither had ever had to work, except to keep the farm going. That should have been sufficient to instill a sense of responsibility, but they'd had enough wealth to hire help. Judy and Connie Dithers spent their days pampering their horses and their nights watching TV. They were said to be eccentric, miserly, reclusive lesbians. As far as I could tell, they were none of the above. Occasionally, they played bridge in the same group I did, and the worst that could be said of Judy and Connie was that they were unmotivated and dizzy. Still, I had to agree with Henry—I wouldn't want them pulling my sleigh, either.

". . . how fussy some people can be," Henry was saying in his flat delivery. I realized I was wool-gathering, thinking not only of the Dithers Sisters, but admiring Evan Singer's art work. "And don't I know it, running a resort. But what I say is that Video-to-Go's loss is my gain."

Hastily, I tried to reconstruct the conversation. "Evan was there . . . how long?" I took a wild guess.

"Just a month," said Henry, initialing the mock-up with his silver ballpoint pen. "He came to Alpine in October, one of those city boys who thinks the grass is greener in a small town." The glance Henry shot me implied that such beliefs were quite right. I could have argued the point, but didn't.

"Dutch Bamberg fired Evan, but he gave him a recommendation anyway," Henry went on earnestly, as if he needed to justify the hired help with me. "Dutch said Evan not only knew movies backwards and forwards, but that he'd waited tables, driven a cab, done some retail, and worked at a riding stable near Issaquah. That was good enough for me. Then I found out he could draw, too."

I gave Henry an encouraging smile. "Evan sounds like a real Renaissance man. Who did Dutch get to replace him at Video-to-Go?"

"He hasn't found anybody yet," replied Henry, looking troubled. Even though it appeared that Evan Singer had been dismissed for reasons I hadn't quite grasped, Henry, in his typical self-flagellating manner, seemed to blame himself. "By the time Dutch let Evan go, most of the folks around here had taken seasonal jobs. The only people out of work right now are loggers, and they wouldn't fit in at Video-to-Go." Henry looked very somber, as if the idea of a former logger discerning between Woody Allen and Woody Woodpecker was impossible.

Henry lingered long enough to grouse about the Forest Service's recent decision to reject expansion plans for the White Pass ski area near Mount Rainier. Supposedly, the project would endanger the habitat of the spotted owl, the grizzly bear, and the gray wolf. "I've been considering adding two downhill runs and a warming hut below Mount Sawyer, but I'll never get approval now. If one of those grizzlies ate a couple of environmentalists, I wonder if they'd change their tune?"

Still grumbling, Henry left just as Vida returned with Bridget Nyquist in tow. It might seem coincidental that I could run into two Nyquists in less than two hours, but Alpine was small enough to make such occurrences unremarkable. Indeed, I had seen Bridget the previous afternoon at the Grocery Basket, and on Sunday she had passed me in her cream-colored Mercedes on the bridge over the Skykomish River as I headed for Sea-Tac to meet Ben.

Vida shrugged out of her tweed coat, yanked off her kidskin gloves, and adjusted the ties of her black gaucho hat. "Bridget has volunteered to be Santa's Little Helper for the Lutheran Retirement Home's Christmas party," said Vida, shoving her spare chair at our visitor. "Fuzzy Baugh is going to be Santa."

Gingerly sitting down, Bridget gave me a charming smile. She was in her early twenties, tall, slim, auburn-haired and blue-eyed. Her skin was flawless and her clothes were expensive, if casual. A russet fox-lined raincoat was worn over a cashmere sweater and wool slacks. Her hand-tooled boots came almost to the knee and matched her shoulder bag.

"This will be fun," said Bridget in a breathy little voice. "I used to visit old folks' homes when I was a Girl Scout in Seattle."

"Then you've had lots of practice," said Vida, whipping out a ballpoint pen. "Just remember: you'll never run out of old people, but someday you'll be one of them. Now—give me the program, in order of events."

As usual, Vida seemed to have the situation well in hand. I returned to my office just as the phone rang. This time it was Teresa McHale, the parish housekeeper. She went straight to the point, expressing her displeasure over Ben's decision to move into the rectory.

"It was one thing with Father Fitz being almost ninety," she asserted. "But this is quite different. People will talk. Your brother is very close to my age."

I figured Ben was probably a good ten years younger than Teresa McHale, but if she wanted to kid herself, that was okay with me. It wasn't okay for her to interfere with the clergy, however.

"Sorry, Mrs. McHale," I said cheerfully, "but this isn't the Chancery. Ben's a big boy, and while I'd just as soon have him stay on with me, I understand why there ought to be a priest available at the rectory. As I'm sure you realize, people undergo more spiritual crises at this time of year. They need to know somebody's there to help."

Teresa McHale emitted a snort of contempt, probably aimed at me rather than the spiritually depressed. "So what if he's six blocks away? You live on Fir Street, don't you?"

I acknowledged that I did, then started to say that the distance between my home and St. Mildred's was beside the point.

Teresa interrupted: "Have it your way." She huffed as if I were indeed a Chancery official rather than merely the sister of a visiting priest. "But don't blame me if something happens."

I gave a little sniff of my own as she banged down the phone. *Dream on, kiddo,* I thought to myself. If anything happened, it wouldn't be Ben's fault. Women weren't a weakness with my brother, at least not one that he hadn't been able to overcome. Teresa McHale was looking for trouble that didn't exist.

But of course it was already there.

Chapter Three

BEN HAD BORROWED Father Fitz's aging but still reliable Volvo to transport his few belongings up to the rectory. He had come and gone while I was at work, but left a message on my answering machine asking me to pick him up after seven o'clock mass. It seemed that Teresa McHale, who had no car of her own, had commandeered the Volvo so that she could visit Father Fitz in the hospital.

Ben and I had a leisurely dinner, prefaced with two bourbons apiece. The steaks were excellent, the conversation mellow, and the Viennese torte divine. The Upper Crust, along with the rest of downtown Alpine, had gotten its power restored just after lunch.

Ben talked at length about the challenges of his assignment in Tuba City, how tough it was for the Navajos to keep their pride, to pass on their culture, to not lose their children to the wider world while at the same time preventing them from falling into poverty and alcoholism. I talked about the differences between general assignment reporting in a metropolitan area such as Portland and running a weekly in an isolated community like Alpine. My problems seemed trifling compared to Ben's. As usual, I came away from our one-on-one session feeling as if his role in life far surpassed my own. He, of course, always insisted that this was not so.

"You're the community's conscience," he told me over coffee. "You not only inform, you serve by example. A newspaper is a watchdog, a catalyst. Especially in a small town. Don't shortchange yourself, Sluggly.''

I appreciated his words. Indeed, they were mine, too. But I still felt trivial by comparison. Circulation was up by a small percentage in Alpine, yet elsewhere it was generally down, and newspapers were dying across the country. People didn't read any more; they relied on TV. The print media might go the way of the dinosaur, but there would always be souls to save. If I hadn't had to drive Ben back to the rectory, I'd have poured us a double brandy.

Ironically, the only business that is more precarious than print journalism is logging. While Alpine hasn't been a one-industry town since Carl Clemans's original mill closed in 1929, forest products still provide a major source of income. There are three mills, two of them on the small side, and several independent logging companies. The threat of the spotted owl looms large over the entire Pacific Northwest, but nowhere does it flap its wings more ominously than in towns like Alpine. Ironically, the ski lodge, which had saved the local economy during the Depression, was beginning to suffer from the endangered species fallout. Sooner or later, I had to come to editorial grips with the issue. As a city girl, I tended to side with the environmentalists. But since moving to Alpine, I was beginning to realize that simplistic solutions don't solve multifaceted questions. Ben agreed, citing the differences he had discovered not only on the Delta, but also on the reservation. Issues, like people, were never simple. And, as my brother pointed out, I was the community's conscience.

By morning, we had another six inches of snow. The plows were out early, while a sanding crew blemished the pristine new fall along Front Street, Alpine Way, and the third main artery in town, Highway 187. I crept down Fir Street to Alpine Way, taking the long route to work. The current issue of *The Advocate* had been hauled off to the printer in Monroe, but there was a good chance it would come out late. Our driver, Kip MacDuff, had broken his chains on the newly-laid gravel and had gotten off to a bad start.

Vida, however, was beginning the day with a burst of creative energy. "I think I'll do a feature on Bridget Nyquist," she announced after I'd poured a cup of coffee. "For a young bride, she's done oodles of charitable work since she came to Alpine. I doubt that she has a brain in her head, but I ought to give her credit for a kind heart. Besides, this old folks' home story is a dud unless I perk it up with something personal. I'll be a sap six times over if I write another word about that old blowhard, Fuzzy Baugh. He refused to carry a pack because of his lumbago and wouldn't pad his stomach because he wanted to show off the ten pounds he lost at TOPS. Take Off Pounds Sensibly, my foot! They should have drained Fuzzy's brain!"

Having dismissed our mayor's role as Santa with a slashing gesture of one hand, Vida turned to her battered typewriter. "I got the impression you weren't wildly warm about Bridget," I commented, perching on Carla's desk.

Vida shot me a look over her shoulder. "I'm not, but you know I like to be fair. The girl hasn't had an easy time of it, I gather. Don't you remember the wedding?"

I didn't. Vida swiveled around, took off her glasses, and rubbed furiously at her eyes. "Of course you don't, you weren't here. It was last November—a year ago, I mean—when you went to Portland for the weekend to visit your friends."

I recalled the trip, to a former *Oregonian* colleague's home in suburban Tigard. Mavis Marley Fulkerston had worked on the editorial page while I toiled as a reporter. She had married a sportswriter from the paper, given birth to three children, won a Pulitzer, survived cancer of the cervix, and retired early. I had attended her fiftieth birthday party the previous November, a gala affair at the Benson Hotel.

"Bridget didn't have anybody on her side." Vida was gazing at me without her glasses. Her face always looked so naked, yet never really vulnerable, without those big tortoiseshell frames. "Doesn't that beat all?"

"You mean—no family or friends of the bride?" In Alpine, wedding etiquette was still observed to the letter.

Vida nodded solemnly. "That's right. Oh, the Lutheran church was packed—the Nyquists know everybody in Skykomish County—but there was nobody there for Bridget."

Ed was lumbering into the office, shaking snow off his overcoat. "There's no end to it," he grumbled. "Some of those dopey merchants in the mall want to have a pre-Christmas sale. Imagine!" Under the brim of his wool cap, Ed rolled his eyes.

"I guess there's no stopping them," I noted in mock sympathy. It was a wonder Ed hadn't tried to persuade the local retailers that they didn't need to advertise in the paper because people would shop for Christmas anyway. As Ed heaved himself out of his overcoat and muttered under his breath, I turned back to Vida. "I thought Bridget was from Seattle. Why didn't anybody come up for the wedding?"

Vida gave a shrug of wide shoulders covered with a print blouse, a suede vest, and a plaid muffler. Apparently she wasn't taking any chances on the heat going out again. "There wasn't anybody to come. That's why they had the wedding in Alpine, instead of Seattle. She's an only child," Vida continued, settling into one of her favorite sports, Family History. "Her father died about six years ago of a heart attack. He owned a small trucking company. Her mother committed suicide shortly before the wedding. As for friends, I couldn't say." Vida made a little face, as if she were disowning responsibility for Bridget's lack of sociability.

"Poor Bridget," I remarked, watching Ed discover we were out of coffee. His galoshes made dark marks on the floor as he went out to give Ginny the bad news. "Has she made friends since she got to Alpine?"

"I don't know," Vida admitted. "She's trying, I'd guess. I think that's why she does so much charity work. But let's face it, Emma, there aren't very many young women in her age group who have much in common with her. More to the point, she'd make them feel inferior with her lovely home and beautiful clothes. I suppose that's why I feel sorry for her."

It was, I reflected, typical of Vida to lament the plight of someone who appeared to have everything. A successful husband, material possessions, financial security—on the surface, envy would be the emotion Bridget would elicit in most people. But Vida would go straight to the heart of the matter and see that somebody like Bridget was lacking a lot.

"Why did her mother commit suicide?" I had worked with Vida long enough not to question her sources. Bridget's background could have come from any number of Vida's friends or relations.

"She had cancer, poor thing," Vida replied as Ginny tended to the coffee maker while Ed watched. "I heard that she didn't want to do something embarrassing—like die—about the same time Bridget got married. So she threw herself off the Bainbridge Island ferry."

I winced. "Poor Bridget!"

Vida inclined her head, then flipped open her phone book. "I think I'll set up an interview at her house. I wonder how they've decorated the place. The Lovells went Amish."

The Lovells were, of course, the previous owners of the house on Stump Hill. I suppressed a smile, wondering if Vida's desire to do the story on Bridget wasn't motivated as much by curiosity as by sympathy. It didn't matter; Vida would turn out a first-rate profile. In the process of talking to her subject, she'd also dig up material that she wouldn't be able to use in the paper. Vida had a knack for unearthing the darkest secrets, which she usually kept to herself.

Hearing my phone ring, I went into my office and grabbed the receiver. Milo Dodge had Doc Dewey's report.

"This is pretty sketchy," he warned me. "Subject was female, aged fifteen to twenty-five, about five foot six, a hundred and twenty pounds, probably Caucasian, reasonably well-nourished, dismembered after death. Oh, and the tennis shoe is a Reebok, size seven and a half."

"It doesn't sound so sketchy to me," I said, making notes. "What's this *dismembered after death* bit?"

I heard Milo's sigh. "You don't like gory details, right?"

"Right. Oh, dear." I steeled myself for the worst. "You mean . . . ?"

"Sawed up. Just like you said."

Somehow, it sounded worse coming from Milo than it had from me. But maybe that was because I had been guessing. Milo's verdict—or rather Doc Dewey's—was official. "Foul play?" I asked in a faint voice.

"We can't rule it out," said Milo. "That's obvious. Right now, we're checking the missing persons file, but as I told you . . ."

"What about the tennis shoe?" I didn't care to hear Milo's missing persons lecture a second time.

"It's pretty ordinary," he replied. "It'd take forever to track it down. In fact, we probably never could."

I fiddled with my ballpoint pen. It would be almost a full week before we'd publish again. Maybe Milo would learn something else by that time. If he didn't, I might as well relegate the item to next week's back page. In this case, no news wasn't good news, but it was no more than a follow-up.

After I hung up from talking to Milo, it occurred to me that Evan Singer, Jack of All Trades, Master of Some, might be worth a feature. I went into the newsroom and offered Carla the assignment. She balked.

"Evan is weird," she declared. "I was in Video-to-Go a few times while he worked there. He was always trying to push X-rated films off on me. All I wanted to do was chill out with Mel Gibson or Dennis Quaid."

Since Carla rarely balks at anything and enthusiasm is her major asset, I capitulated. "I'll do it myself. I need to keep in practice." It was true—I hadn't done a feature in six months. My last interviewee had been a U. S. Senate candidate who'd made a swing through Alpine. The quotes were platitudes, the pictures were dull, the background was bland. The would-be senator had lost in the primary. It served him right for making such lousy copy. Yet it had occurred to me that maybe I was losing my touch as an interviewer. I would try to do better by Evan Singer.

But I had another task slated for that afternoon. It was December 9, the traditional day I bring home my Christmas tree. When Adam and I had lived in Portland, we'd always bought one from a lot, made a two-inch cut off the trunk, and stuck it in a bucket of water outside for a week. Sometimes the trees stayed fresh and fragrant through New Year's; other times, their branches drooped and needles dropped by Christmas Day. Since coming to Alpine, I had cut my own trees, not on designated forest service lands, but wherever I happened to find the perfect Douglas fir during the course of the year. Last June, I had discovered my tree, eight feet tall, bushy, virtually symmetrical, just below Alpine Falls. As always, I'd checked with Milo to make sure I wasn't trespassing or poaching or whatever I might be doing if caught in the act of hacking down a tree with somebody else's name on it.

"That's state land, so don't tell me about it," Milo had said as he did every year. "It's not strictly legal, and if you get caught, I've never seen you before in my life."

About eleven-thirty, I called Ben at the rectory to see if he wanted to have lunch and accompany me to Alpine Falls. Teresa McHale answered the phone and sounded pained when I asked for my brother.

"I thought he'd be spending the days with you," she said in an irritated voice. "I don't see any need for him to go through yesterday's collection. Father Fitzgerald can handle that when he feels better."

"It's probably wise to get the cash to the bank," I said in a mild tone. "It may be a few days before Father can cope."

"He's coming home tomorrow, Friday at the latest," Teresa went on in her irritable manner. "Knowing him the way I do, he'll want to get right back to work. Speaking of which, why doesn't the city get off its lazy backside and plow Cedar Street or Cascade? It's very hard for our older parishioners to get to mass in all this snow."

I sympathized, though I was confident that most of Alpine's senior citizens had probably been dealing with snow all of their lives. Maybe it was Teresa who was having problems. I made commiserative murmurs, then asked if the Volvo had four-wheel drive. It did, she assured me.

"That's not the point," Teresa went on, sounding increasingly cranky. "I've been here over a year and I can't believe how backward this place is. Half the streets don't have sidewalks, the power is unpredictable, you can't get decent TV reception without one of those ugly satellite dishes, the growing season lasts about four months, the Seattle Sunday paper has to be trucked in on Saturday. There's only one dress shop, two decent restaurants, no public swimming pool, no espresso carts, no live entertainment unless you count the drunken loggers throwing each other through the windows at the Icicle Creek Tavern. I feel marooned in this town!"

Again, Teresa McHale struck a sympathetic chord. After almost three years, I often felt the same way—cut off, isolated, cast adrift. I, too, missed the opera, the theatre, major-league sports, vast shopping malls, and high-rises. But most of all, I missed the energy of the city. Despite the demons that drive urban dwellers to despair, there is no other atmosphere that has such vitality. But I wasn't about to say so to Teresa McHale.

"Dear me," I sighed in mock anguish, "why ever did you move up here from Seattle?"

There was a faint pause. When Teresa spoke again, I heard a defensive note in her voice. "I wanted a change. I thought

I'd be doing some good, taking this job. I never figured I'd be bored to tears in the bargain."

"I wouldn't think you'd be bored, what with all the help you could give Father Fitz in the parish," I pointed out, genuinely trying to exercise compassion.

"He's got plenty of lay people to do all that," asserted Mrs. McHale. "That's another thing: this town has more busybodies than we had in the whole north end of Seattle. I'm talking about spare time activities. Instead of passing that bond issue for the new swimming pool in the last election, these backwoods dodos voted it down because they're getting a bowling alley. Now who in their right mind would rather bowl than swim? No wonder everybody is about fifty pounds overweight!"

Again, Teresa had a point. Alpine, like many other small towns, seemed to churn out a greater proportion of people with greater proportions. On the other hand, Teresa wasn't exactly wasting away. "There is a gym," I said, a bit sharply. Teresa and her gripes were spoiling my festive tree-cutting mood. "Has my brother shown up yet?" *Like in the last ten minutes while you were bitching my ear off,* I wanted to say.

"He just walked in." Mrs. McHale was obviously not appeased by my suggestion of working out at the gym.

The next voice I heard was Ben's, faintly amused. "I haven't cut down a Christmas tree since we were kids," he said in response to my invitation. "The parish council meets tonight. I wonder if I should prepare for it."

"Why? It's not your parish." Exasperation tainted my voice.

"True." He hesitated. "Father Fitz probably doesn't hear half of what goes on anyway. He's pretty deaf. Do you want me to bring the axe from the rectory woodshed?"

"I've got Dad's old Swede saw already in the trunk," I said. "And some ropes and clippers, in case we see any good greens for a swatch."

Ben emitted a little sigh. "Dad's old Swede . . . I didn't know you kept that, Emma."

I knew Ben was picturing our dad sawing up the cord of wood we had delivered every fall to our home in Seattle's Wallingford district. Dad never started cutting the wood until it had stayed on the parking strip for at least three days. Mom would nag at him, insisting that it would rain, or that somebody would trip over it and sue us, or that kids would steal it. I still remembered the smell of the freshly cut wood, usually hemlock with just enough cedar to provide some snap, fourteen-inch chunks, to fit our small fireplace.

"I wonder if the big maple is still there," I said, my mind staying in a tree mode. "We used to rake leaves until we dropped."

"Mom and Dad made us take down our tree house," recalled Ben. "We never should have dropped water balloons on Mr. and Mrs. Peabody."

"That wasn't so bad," I noted. "What really riled Mom and Dad was when we threw Brewster Baxter out of the tree."

"It was Baxter Brewster," corrected Ben. "Hell, he landed in one of those big piles of leaves. He wasn't hurt— just rustled around and got dog poop in his hair."

We both laughed. I wondered if Teresa McHale was lurking in the rectory, listening to our reminiscences. I told Ben I'd pick him up in fifteen minutes. Nostalgia is best when shared, but it's sometimes painful. The memories Ben and I had of our parents were wonderful, but there weren't enough of them. They had died together, when a semitrailer jackknifed in front of them on the way home from Ben's ordination. Dad was fifty-two; Mom was forty-nine. In the usual scheme of life expectancy, we could have had another thirty years to make memories.

After lunch at the Burger Barn, it took us only five minutes to get to Alpine Falls, which is just up the highway from the town. The tree I had selected was about twenty yards from the river's final cascade—far enough not to get drenched, though close enough to impair our hearing. The snow had stopped, but the air was chill and damp. I struggled over the rough ground in my boots, gesturing for Ben to watch his footing.

"Here!" I yelled, pointing at the stately Douglas fir I'd adopted half a year ago.

Ben sawed, while I clutched the trunk. When he finished, I sniffed euphorically at the cut he'd made. But before he could hoist the fir and carry it up the bank to the car, I motioned at a couple of small cedars. Ben waited while I attacked them with my clippers. There was no pine in sight, but I could pick up a couple of branches off the Christmas tree lot in town. Maybe some holly, too, I decided, and even a bit of blue spruce. That always made a cheery combination for a swatch.

Gathering up a half-dozen branches, I saw Ben at the river's edge. The waters roiled past him, the churning falls at his left, the snow-covered ground under foot, the great stands of evergreen marching up the mountainside. How different this must be for him from the hot, dry plateau in Arizona. Or the humid, lethargic delta of the Mississippi. How much did Ben really miss his roots here in the Pacific Northwest? My brother and I were city children, but never far from the forests and mountains and rivers and sea.

Ben was bending over, presumably digging around in the rocks at the river's edge. I smiled fondly. When we were young, he was always looking for a flat pebble that he could skip across whichever body of water we were visiting. I waited, expecting him to reach back and pitch. Instead, he turned to look at me, and his face had gone pale under its all-year tan.

"Don't come any closer, Emma," he yelled. "Go up to the car."

Puzzled, I stared at him. But his stunned expression, more than his words, urged me to flee. Clutching the greens and the clippers to my breast, I scurried up the bank. I slipped

twice, swore, dropped the clippers, retrieved them, and finally reached the Jaguar. A minute later, Ben appeared,
dragging my beautiful Douglas fir.

"What's wrong?" I gasped, out of breath.

Ben righted the tree, shaking snow from its branches. His
color was beginning to return, but his face was very grim.
Suddenly, I thought of Milo and let out a little squeal. "Ben—
what did you see down there?"

He shoved the tree into the trunk of my car. "Shit." His
gloved hands dangled at his sides. "It was an arm. I swear
to God, Emma, it was an *arm*." He gazed at me as if he
didn't expect to be believed. Along with my shock came the
realization that Ben didn't know about Milo's ghastly catch.
The paper wasn't out and I hadn't thought to tell him.

I stuffed the greens into the trunk and began to wrestle
with the ropes. "We have to tell the sheriff," I said, hearing
my voice crack. Abruptly, I began to laugh. Ben stared at
me, the horror on his face replaced by mystification at my
reaction. I waved a weak hand at him. "It's okay," I gasped.
"It's just that . . . somebody has gone to pieces!"

Ben didn't laugh. There was nothing indecisive about my
brother as he pushed me into the passenger side of the car
and took the wheel. I was still semi-hysterical when we
crossed the bridge into Alpine.

Chapter Four

FOR OVER TWENTY years, I had relied on nobody but myself. I took great pride in my independence, my resourcefulness, my competence. On the short ride into Alpine, I chided myself for falling apart. Was it because I had Ben at my side, the older brother who had shielded me from all harm unless he was the one perpetrating it? Or was I genuinely shattered by the discovery of various body parts along the Skykomish River? I didn't know. But I wasn't about to go on being such a weak sister, as my mother would have put it. Giving one last sniffle, I showed Ben where the sheriff's office was located. He pulled the Jaguar into the slush at the curb just as Milo came down the street, presumably from lunch.

After listening to our recital, Milo looked as if his lunch had rebelled. "Damn," he breathed, then gave Ben an apologetic nod. "Sorry, Father. I didn't mean to offend you."

"Shit," said Ben, "I didn't know that you'd already found a leg. What the hell is going on around here?"

Milo looked askance at Ben, apparently shocked by my brother's salty language. Milo had been brought up a Congregationalist, which explained his amazement, as well as a few other matters. Milo said he'd get Sam Heppner, then take his deputy and Ben up to the falls in a county vehicle. Having regained my composure, I insisted that I should go along, too. After all, I was the press.

"Here comes more of the press," said Milo, indicating Vida, who was marching briskly down the street, her tweed coat flapping around her boots. "Why don't the two of you have a press conference?"

"What is all this?" demanded Vida, forthright as ever, but testier than usual. Her boots crunched on the rock salt the city had used to melt the ice and snow on the downtown pedestrian walkways. "Well? Did you find the other leg?"

Milo had gone into his office to get Sam Heppner. "It was actually an arm," said Ben, reaching out to hug Vida. He knew how fond I was of my House & Home editor, and although he had met her on a previous visit to Alpine, this was the first time he had seen her on this trip. "How are you, Mrs. Runkel? I hear you're converting from Presbyterianism."

"Aaaaargh!" Vida shuddered in Ben's embrace, then stepped back a pace. "I'd rather be burned at the stake! Or have you people stopped doing that by now?" She didn't wait for an answer, but jabbed Ben in the front of his down jacket. "Don't you ever wear a collar, Father Lord? That old fool of a pastor up at St. Mildred's has been seen in long underwear."

"He was wearing *pants*," I pointed out. "Anyway, that was a stupid story from Grace Grundle. She also reported that the Episcopal rector was seen kissing a woman. Which he was, but it happened to be his wife."

"Never mind." Vida retreated, almost stepping in the slush. Obviously, she didn't want to hear any more scandal spawned by a fellow Presbyterian. "An arm? What sort of arm?" Again, she didn't wait for an answer, but turned to me. "Shall I get a camera?"

I started to tell Vida that I wasn't sure we were wanted. Just then my Christmas tree fell out of the trunk. In his haste, Ben apparently hadn't secured it very well. The ride home must have jarred it loose. At that moment, Milo reappeared with the dour Sam Heppner. A small crowd was beginning to gather in front of the sheriff's office: Cal Vickers from the Texaco station; Dr. Bob Starr, the dentist; Heather Bardeen, who worked for her father, Henry, at the ski lodge; and a half dozen other people I recognized but couldn't name.

"All right, everybody," ordered Milo, as if he were dispersing an unruly mob, "let's move along. If you want a show, go down the street to the Whistling Marmot." Somehow, he'd managed to include Vida and me with the riffraff. Before Vida could do more than shriek at Milo over Cal Vickers's head, the sheriff, the deputy, and my brother were off in the squad car, lights flashing, siren squealing.

"Well!" Vida was miffed. "Doesn't that beat all!" She gave me a dark glare. "You're the newspaper publisher. Don't you have any clout?"

"If you want to know the truth, I'd rather rescue my Christmas tree." I pointed to the Jaguar.

Vida started to join me at the curb, but the little crowd surged around her, asking questions. Typical, I thought, they would seek out Vida as the font of all knowledge. Even after almost three years in Alpine, I was still regarded as a newcomer. I tugged and hauled at the Douglas fir, finally managing to get it back in the trunk.

"Let's go," Vida shouted, at last making her way to the Jag. She got in on the passenger's side, grumbling all the while.

I turned on the ignition. "I'm not sure we should follow . . ."

Vida heaved a sigh of annoyance. "I don't mean Milo; I mean your house. You'd better get that tree home before you ruin it."

Vida was right, though her attitude struck me as wrong. It wasn't like her to abandon the trail of a juicy story. But it would take only a few minutes to deposit the Douglas fir. I shifted into first gear and waited for a UPS truck to pass before I pulled out.

"I don't like all these spare parts floating around," Vida declared as we headed up Fourth Street. "Milo's got trouble on his hands."

"Is that why you didn't want to go to the falls? Are you afraid he might screw up and we'd have to report it?"

"Oh, no! He and Sam and your brother will dig and delve and measure and put samples of this and that into little plastic bags and well nigh freeze to death in the process. Men like to do stupid things like that, but the rest of us have more sense. We'll find out everything in good time and have hot cocoa while we do it." Vida paused, pointing at the windshield. "Be careful, Emma, there's Averill Fairbanks, skiing across Cedar Street."

Alpine residents on skis in town weren't a rarity. On certain days, Seventh Street was barricaded from Spruce to Front to provide a free ski run. Henry Bardeen didn't approve, but the lodge made plenty of money off the tourists.

"On your left," Vida noted. "Mother with child on sled." She took a quick breath. "Meter reader, the Whipps' grandson, not looking where he's going. Dunce."

"Stop!" I braked for a school bus that was heading out to collect its afternoon load of middle-school children. "Vida, what's wrong with you? You're driving me nuts."

From under the brim of her knitted cloche, she shot me a penitent look. "I'm annoyed. It makes me edgy."

I was passing St. Mildred's. "Annoyed about what?"

Vida heaved another sigh. "Bridget Nyquist. I set up an interview with her for one forty-five, but when I got to the house, she'd changed her mind."

"Why?" It was starting to snow again.

Wriggling in the bucket seat, Vida mimicked Bridget's wispy voice: " 'I don't think it's right to draw attention to myself. I like to help others. It's the way my mamma raised me. Tee-hee, simper, simper.' *Ugh!*" Vida's lip curled.

I turned onto Fir Street. "Don't worry about it. Say—what happened to that idea you had about an anniversary story for the Whistling Marmot? Isn't that coming up January first?"

Vida emitted a snort. "Oscar had the wrong year. His father started showing movies in the old social hall during

World War I. So either we've missed the seventy-fifth anniversary, or we'll have to wait a couple of years for the official opening of the theatre commemoration. Personally, I don't care. Oscar probably won't talk to me, either. Even when he does, he never has much to say. He told me once that when he was young he thought silent pictures had to be that way because people in California hadn't yet learned how to speak. Moron.''

I turned into the driveway. My log house looked particularly charming with snow on the roof and icicles hanging over the little porch. It would be wonderful to have a painting of the house as it looked in December and another to show the way it was in June. I'd had a hanging fuchsia then and window boxes full of red geraniums, white alyssum, and purple ageratum. If Evan Singer could draw, maybe he could also paint. I'd ask him when we did the interview.

Vida helped me haul the tree out back, where I put it in a bucket of water. Maybe it wouldn't freeze if I kept the tree close to the house. Vida recommended the carport, but there wasn't room.

Fifteen minutes later, we were back in the office. Vida was still grousing about Bridget Nyquist. I asked Ginny and Carla, who were about the same age as Bridget, if they knew her very well.

"I met her once during Loggerama," Carla said. "She seemed okay, but too much into herself."

"The first time I saw her," Ginny explained in her usual carefree manner, "was at Dr. Starr's. She was coming out just as I was going in. We said hi." Ginny's fair brow furrowed under wisps of auburn hair. "I've seen her a couple of times at the Grocery Basket and once at the Venison Inn, but we didn't speak. They only other time I saw her up close was about a month ago when I picked up some pictures for the paper at Buddy Bayard's Picture-Perfect Photo Studio. Bridget was there with Travis. They were having a first-anniversary portrait taken. Travis was friendly—he usually is—but Bridget sort of hung back.''

Carla flounced around her desk, long black hair flying. "Low self-esteem. Imagine, with her money and looks. Maybe she's dumb."

Vida eyed Carla over the rims of her glasses. "She behaves as if she might be. But I doubt it. Travis Nyquist wouldn't marry a *nincompoop*." She uttered the word with emphasis on all three syllables, still looking meaningfully at Carla. Vida and I were at odds in assessing *The Advocate*'s reporter. My House & Home editor thought Carla was definitely stupid; I felt she was merely dizzy. Unfortunately, the result was often the same.

When my phone rang, I figured it was Milo or Ben. But it was neither. Adam was on the line, calling from Fairbanks.

"Hi, Mom," he shouted over a bad connection. "You okay?"

"Sure," I shouted back. "How are finals?"

"I could do them in my sleep," said my son so breezily that I assumed he had. "Hey, I may not get in until Tuesday or so. To Alpine, I mean."

"Why not?" I felt a pang of disappointment pierce my maternal breast.

"What? Wow, is this phone screwed up or what?"

I heard a clicking sound which might have been the cable but more likely was the drumming of my son's nails on the mouthpiece at his end. "Why not?" I repeated.

"Wow, I can't hear you—we've got about a hundred feet of snow. I'll call you when I get to Seattle."

"Hold it!" Vida, Ginny, and Carla were all watching me. I'd taken the call at Ed's desk. I tried to ignore my staff members. It was impossible. "Adam, where are you going if not to Alpine?"

"Erin asked me to spend a couple of days in Kirkland." Though Adam had lowered his voice and semi-mumbled, I still managed to catch the words.

"Erin who?" Or was it Aaron? Either way, I didn't know the name.

"Erin Kowalski. She lives in Kirkland. With her family. Right on Lake Washington. She's into animals." Now Adam was speaking more clearly. I could never keep up with his girlfriends. They seemed to exist on a monthly rotation. Even as he spoke, I was rummaging through Ed's out-of-town phone directories. I found Seattle, but that wouldn't do. The suburbs east of the lake had their own phone books. I rummaged some more. "We're going skiing," he added.

"You can ski in Alpine. Right in town, as a matter of fact," I pointed out.

"That's for pussies, Mom. We're going up to Crystal Mountain. I'll call you from Kirkland, okay? How's Uncle Ben?"

I'd finally found the Kirkland listings. There were two Kowalskis, a Leonard C. and a Douglas L. Kirkland, like the rest of Seattle's Eastside, had grown so much so fast that the addresses didn't mean anything to me. "Ben's fine," I replied, deciding to give Adam a dose of his own medicine. "Right now, he's out on a limb."

"Huh?"

"Call me as soon as you get in. Bye." With a smirk, I hung up the phone. My staff applauded me.

Ben, Milo, and Sam Heppner still weren't back at four o'clock. Worried, I called the sheriff's office, but Dwight Gould, another deputy, informed me that he'd been in touch with Milo as recently as three-thirty. They were heading back into town with the ambulance, stopping first at Doc Dewey's.

"Ambulance?" It didn't make sense.

"Right," said Dwight in his rumbling bass. "For the body. Young Doc'll do an autopsy."

"On . . . what?" I had an awful feeling I knew.

"The body," repeated Dwight. "It wasn't just an arm, Mrs. Lord. It was a whole body."

I put a hand to my forehead, for some irrational reason thinking of Safeway's ad in today's paper: WHOLE BODY FRYERS, 89 CENTS A LB. Maybe that was better than thinking of the previous week's CUT-UP FRYERS, $1.19 A LB. But of course I thought of both and feared my hysteria was returning.

I got a grip on myself. "Do you mean that literally? About being whole? Nothing missing—like a leg?" I winced as I spoke.

"Nope," rumbled Dwight. "All of a piece, at least near as I can tell from over the radio phone. Excuse me, Mrs. Lord, Bill Blatt and I are here all alone. Arnie Nyquist just came in, steamin' like a smokestack."

I passed the news on to Vida. She, too, was shaken, albeit briefly. "That means two dead bodies. My, my." Her face was grim as she looked up to see Kip MacDuff come through the door with the latest edition of *The Advocate*. He was only two hours late, which wasn't bad, considering car troubles and the weather.

By five o'clock, I'd had six phone calls inquiring about the leg item. Three asked if there was any further identification. Two reported they thought they'd hooked onto something strange, maybe an arm or a torso, maybe near Anthracite Creek, then again, maybe closer to Sultan or Index or Gold Bar or in their dreams. The last caller wanted to know if Milo got any fish.

All my staff had left by ten after five. Vida had been reluctant to go, but was committed to her round of festive holiday parties, this particular gala sponsored by the Burl Creek Thimble Club at the Grange Hall. Just before five-thirty, I closed up shop and walked over to the sheriff's office.

Milo, Ben, and Sam had just returned, not directly from Doc Dewey's, but from Mugs Ahoy. None of them were feeling any pain.

Exasperated, I turned my ire on my brother: "You jerks! I've been stewing and squirming all afternoon! You might have at least called!"

Ben grinned lopsidedly and punched me in the arm. The crackle in his voice had turned into a cackle. "Knock it off, Sluggly. You sound like Mom. Why didn't you get off your duff and look for us? We were a whole block away."

Sam Heppner had managed to slip off quietly, but Milo was lounging against the front counter, looking vaguely sheepish. "Ben's right, Emma. We just went into Mugs Ahoy to steady our nerves. You think it's fun freezing your unit off while you try to thaw out a stiff? Hey, that's good—frozen stiff!" He glanced at Ben, and they both broke into unbridled laughter.

I was grinding my teeth. I hadn't been this mad at Ben since he filled my strapless bra with Elmer's Glue the night of the Blanchet High School winter ball. I'd never been this mad at Milo, period. Where was Vida when I needed her? And the hot cocoa? If I'd had some, I would have poured it over Ben and Milo's heads.

"I need news, not a pair of drunken sots!" I railed. "What's this about a body? A *whole* body?" The image of a chicken hopped through my mind. I started to laugh, too. "Oh, good grief!" I collapsed onto a chair, shaking my head, but still laughing.

"Hey, Emma," said Milo, trying to lean his elbow on the counter, but missing, "your brother's okay, especially for a priest. And I'm okay, too. I'm off-duty. It's after five."

I stopped laughing. "A priest is never off-duty," I said, but my voice didn't convey much indignation. "What will Mrs. McHale think?"

It was Milo, not Ben, who answered: "That old broad? Who cares? She tried to put the make on me at the Labor Day picnic. Maybe she's the one who gave Father Fitz his heart attack."

"It was a stroke, you boob," I replied. "Do either of you two rollicking goofballs know how Father is doing?"

"As well as can be expected." It was Ben, this time,

giving me a skewed look. "We saw Doc Dewey, remember?"

I narrowed my eyes at my brother. "I sure do. But do you remember *why* you saw Doc Dewey?"

Ben ran both hands through his thatch of hair and turned around in a little circle. "Oh, yes. We remember. Why do you think we were drinking to forget?"

"But we didn't," put in Milo. He was patting himself down, as if searching a suspect for weapons. "Hey, where's my beeper? Did I leave it at Mugs Ahoy? Shit!"

I realized that Ben couldn't return to the rectory in his inebriated condition, nor could Milo drive home. I wasn't making much progress in getting to the facts, but if I stuffed them both with food, they should be able to tell me what I wanted to know. With the lure of beef stroganoff, I led them out of the sheriff's office to my car. The snow was coming down quite hard, with another two inches on the ground since mid-afternoon. I drove home cautiously, while Ben and Milo told each other perfectly dreadful jokes.

"I'm divorced," Milo announced to Ben as I pulled into my driveway. "Do you care?"

Ben responded with more laughter. "Joke's on you, Dodge. In my church, you were never married. Ha, ha!"

Milo's jaw dropped. "You mean . . . my kids are . . . Whoa! That's great! If I turn Catholic, can I stop paying child support for the little bastards?"

"You're only paying for one of them as it is," I said, pushing the car door open. "The other two are over eighteen. Besides, we're talking church, not state. Get out of the car, you two bozos. The first thing I'm going to do is make coffee."

My beef stroganoff takes only about twenty minutes to cook. By the time I was ready to serve, Ben and Milo had downed three mugs of coffee apiece and were almost themselves again. I suspected that neither of them—or Sam Heppner, for that matter—had drunk as much as it appeared.

There hadn't been time for them to down more than two or three beers apiece. Rather, I surmised, my brother and the sheriff were reacting to the horror of their find down by the falls.

My guess was verified when Milo announced that we'd wait until after we finished eating to discuss the afternoon's occurrences. Ben agreed, but almost blew it by saying grace and offering a prayer for the repose of the soul ". . . of the unfortunate young woman who met a violent end in Alpine." My curiosity further piqued, I ate very fast.

Clearing away the remnants of stroganoff, rice, and green beans, I offered Ben and Milo the rest of the Viennese torte with more coffee. I love food, but am not a big sweets freak. While they tackled the torte, I remembered Vida's words and heated some cocoa.

Milo was the first to broach the subject that held our minds hostage. "The body apparently had been dumped in the river, but the current had pushed it toward the bank. Snow had drifted onto some big boulders where the body was wedged. All you could see was the arm." He paused, looking at Ben for confirmation. "When we got there, we realized there was more than just an arm. It took us some time to dig her out. She probably hadn't been there very long." Milo's voice had grown subdued. Ben's mouth twisted at the memory.

"Was she naked?" I asked, and wondered why the question had sprung into my mind. I hadn't seen the arm, but if it had been clothed, surely Ben would have said so.

"Right," nodded Milo. "She was young, early twenties, pretty, I'd guess, hair about the color of yours, but longer. She had a tattoo."

I arched my eyebrows. "Where? What?"

Milo touched his backside. "Here. It spelled C-A-R-O-L, then B-A-S or something like that, then I-O-B-F, all in small letters. It was hard to read."

Finally, I was managing to set aside personal feelings and follow the story. "Not a last name?"

"I don't think so." Again, Milo turned to Ben. "You agree, Father?"

Ben inclined his head. "The B-A-S or whatever it is was under the name Carol, but smaller and centered. Then the I-O-B-F beneath that, also centered and even a little smaller."

"I-O-B-F doesn't spell anything," I said, getting up to put another log on the fire, "unless it stands for something like International Order of whatever. Are you sure that's what it said?"

"No," Milo replied flatly. "Doc Dewey will use one of his high-powered microscopes on it. We'll get a full report tomorrow."

I sat back down on the sofa next to Ben. The living room was cozy, with its comfortable, eclectic furniture, stone fireplace, forest green draperies, and the wonderfully warm, stained log walls. So far, the only Christmas decorations I'd put up were the first ten pieces of my Nativity set—one for every day of Advent. It was a tradition I'd started when Adam was a toddler. Tonight I would add another sheep.

"I suppose," I mused, "there's no way to connect this corpse with the leg?"

Milo gave me a wry glance. I made a face. There didn't seem to be any way to discuss this case without uttering something that sounded like a bad joke. "No. Two different parts of the river, probably a time frame of three or four months' difference. It's probably just a coincidence."

"Probably." I had to agree, yet I wasn't much of a believer in coincidences that didn't mean anything. "But you've got to admit that there *could* be. What about foul play?"

Before Milo could answer, the phone rang. It was Vida. "I'm almost out the door," she said in a rush, "but Marje Blatt just called from Doc Dewey's office." Marje was Vida's niece and Gerald Dewey's receptionist. As such, Marje walked a fine line between strict patient confidentiality and her aunt's mighty badgering. Her aunt usually had the edge. "Marje worked late tonight, so she was still around when young Doc started the autopsy. He practically had a fit—that body Milo and your brother dug out of the snowbank had been frozen!''

I pulled back, staring at the receiver. Had Vida lost it, along with Father Fitz? ''I should think so,'' I said calmly. ''It's been getting down to about ten above zero the last few nights. You'd be frozen, too, if you were lying under a snowbank in the Skykomish River.''

Vida's tone was not only rushed, but impatient. ''I mean frozen beforehand. She'd thawed a bit, maybe the other afternoon when it got up to thirty-six. Monday, wasn't it? Think about it—I've got to head out to the Grange Hall. By the way, Doc can't find Milo. He doesn't answer his beeper.''

Milo called young Doc right away. Yes, Doc figured the victim had been left to freeze, judging from the internal organs, then somehow had been partially thawed. Definitely, foul play: signs of trauma, a blow to the head. Blunt instrument, no idea what, brick, bat, or bowling trophy—that was Milo's department. When? Hard to tell, given the frozen state of the corpse. Maybe, said young Doc, four or five days, possibly longer. No, there was no sign of sexual assault or of recent intercourse. As for the tattoo, Doc hadn't gotten around to that yet. Ever the man of science, young Doc was more interested in the medical post-mortem than in such superfluous details as who he was performing it on. Milo looked very unhappy when he hung up.

''Now the rest is up to us,'' he sighed after relaying Doc Dewey's multiple messages. ''You wait and see, everybody will jump on that spare leg and figure we've got a serial killer loose. Damn.''

The Burlington Northern whistled in the distance, a mournful sound. Outside the window, I could see snow piling up, drifting against the small panes, obscuring the rest of the world. The train whistled again. Irrelevantly, I thought of the avalanche, over eighty years ago, that had caved in the Great Northern Railroad tunnel on the second switchback up the line at Tyee. Ninety people had died, buried under a mass of snow. There had been only a handful of miners and loggers living in Alpine at that time. The disaster had served as a reminder that death lurked even in the most remote, beautiful settings.

Trying to shake off such grim thoughts, I made an attempt to encourage Milo. "You ought to be able to find a match with missing persons. If this poor young woman has been dead for going on a week, she'd be reported by now."

Milo refused to be consoled. "Not if she was a prostitute. Or if she's from out-of-state. Or on the run from some guy who was trying to beat the crap out of her. You'd be surprised. People can lose themselves pretty easily. At least on a temporary basis."

Ben had gotten to his feet and was toying with my manger scene. He set the three shepherds in a row, as if they were queuing up to get into the small wooden shed. "She must have worn clothes. What happened to them?"

Looking mildly affronted that Ben would raise such a point, Milo shrugged. "How do I know? According to Doc, it wasn't a sex crime. At least not rape. Maybe the killer is trying to hide the victim's identity."

Putting the two sheep in line behind the shepherds, Ben turned to Milo. "Do you mean she had her name stitched in her clothes?"

"Not necessarily," replied Milo. "Labels, maybe, that would narrow down where the clothes came from. You know, like some fancy designer store." He glanced at me. "Isn't that right, Emma?"

I nodded. "Some boutiques put their own labels in their merchandise. But it seems a little strange to me that the killer would check something like that." I played the scenario through in my head: violent murderer bashes in skull of victim, then calmly looks to see if clothing came from other than off the rack. It didn't make much sense, and I was sure that Vida would agree with me. It also didn't strike me as likely that a young woman with a tattoo on her rear end would buy her apparel at an exclusive shop. But people were unpredictable.

The discussion wound down. Ben finished putting the cow and the ox on the top of the stable roof, then announced that he had better get back to the rectory. I volunteered to drive both men, but they insisted on walking. St. Mildred's was half a mile from my home; Milo's house in the Icicle Creek development was about twice as far. I didn't press either of them, figuring the cold air would do them both good.

After they left, I cleared away the remnants of our meal and played around with possible ways of handling coverage of the latest murder victim. I had almost six days to write the story. A lot could happen between now and then. Still, it was a mental reflex on my part to take any news item and run with it. Two decades on daily newspapers was habit-forming. Often, I still found myself unable to adjust completely to the slower pace of a small town. I also found it impossible to adjust to murder.

I rearranged my Nativity set, added the new sheep, and tried to focus on other, more pleasant concerns. It was Advent, my favorite liturgical season. Hope. Joy. Peace. Those were the emotions I should be experiencing. Year after year, I had vowed to seek more quiet in the weeks before Christmas. But as a single working mother, there had been little time for anything but my son and the job. As Adam grew older, I figured I'd have extra hours to myself. Yet every December had brought a new, unexpected crisis: for example, the gingerbread house for German class which Adam had wanted to resemble Mad Ludwig's castle in Bavaria, but which, after forty-eight hours of shared toil, looked more like an overturned Dumpster. Adam knew he wouldn't get extra credit when his teacher had to ask, *"What is it?"*

When Adam went off to college, I was already an editor-publisher. Free time, let alone quiet time, was hard to come by. This year was proving no different. In a flurry of activity,

I hauled out a half dozen boxes from the storage room off the kitchen. Candles, wreaths, figurines, garlands, colored lights, ornaments, tinsel—it was all there, most of it mine, some of it my parents', and a few treasured items passed on from my grandparents. I set aside all the decorations for the tree with the remainder of the nativity pieces, then began to drape artificial pine over the doorways. I arranged candles on the mantel, hung a trio of wreaths, and put the rest of the Santas, Madonnas, angels, reindeer, and elves on whatever spare places I could find. Weary, but content, I surveyed my handiwork. My log house looked festive, warm, welcoming. When the tree was up, it would become sheer magic. I smiled with pleasure.

The tree. I had thought about it in the abstract, almost as if it were the same tree, from year to year, as artificial as the pine garlands. But the perfect Douglas fir that stood in a bucket next to the house had been witness to a murder. Or at least to a murder victim.

It was not a thought that brought hope or joy or peace. In fact, it was a damned rotten thing to happen to me during Advent.

But of course it was even worse for the victim.

Chapter Five

OSCAR NYQUIST, OWNER of the Whistling Marmot, had started going bald in his early twenties. He was, like so many older people in Alpine, a living legend. One of my favorite bits of Oscarana, as I called it, concerned Alexander Pantages, famed West Coast theatre entrepreneur. When the great man took his final curtain call in 1936, Oscar wanted to pay homage to a fellow impresario. Either out of respect for this icon or vanity for himself, Oscar was compelled to cover his half-bald head. His neighbor, Millard O'Toole, had butchered a cow that very morning. In a fit of inspiration, Oscar had cut off enough hide to make a toupee. It didn't match his remaining hair; it didn't fit his large head; and it wouldn't stay put—but Oscar wore it anyway. He drove off to Seattle in his Model-A Ford feeling respectable and looking ridiculous. When he bent over Pantages's coffin, the makeshift hairpiece fell off. Humiliated, Oscar left it there, and all Alpine assumed that the famed impresario was spending eternity with a little bit of local lore.

At eighty-two, Oscar had long since become completely bald. He was still a big man, an inch taller than his son Arnie, and probably thirty pounds heavier. On Thursday morning, he lumbered into the *Advocate* office behind his grandson, Travis, who had graduated to a walking cast, but still leaned on a pair of metal crutches.

"I want publicity!" boomed Oscar, standing in the middle of the room and somehow making the walls suddenly appear

54

to close in on all of us. Ed looked up from his copy of the *Seattle Post-Intelligencer*. Ginny pivoted in the act of handing me some phone messages. Carla jumped so violently that she spilled latte on her desk. And Vida gave the newcomer a tight-lipped glare.

"Oscar, you old fool," she railed, "how many times do I have to tell you—and fifty other idiots in this town—that we don't do *publicity*. We do news or ads. After sixty years of running that movie theatre, you ought to know the difference. Either get yourself arrested or plunk out some money. Which is it you want?" She stopped long enough to cock her head to one side and smile warmly at Travis. "You're up and about, I see. How's your leg?"

"Dr. Flake put the walking cast on this morning and it feels . . ."

"Like hell!" interrupted Oscar, barging in front of his grandson. "If I say publicity, I *mean* publicity! Isn't this a newspaper? Isn't it printed for the public?"

"Oooooh . . . !" Vida whipped off her glasses and frantically rubbed at her eyes, the telltale gesture that indicated she was highly agitated. "I give up! Emma, you deal with this crazy old coot. He's impossible!"

So far, my dealings with Oscar Nyquist had been limited. Ed handled his weekly ads; Ginny did the billing; Carla had written a little news story the previous spring when a new Dolby sound system had been installed; and Vida, of course, covered any social events connected with the Nyquists. I knew Oscar only by sight—and sound, since his presence in the office was always unmistakable. To get my further acquaintance off on the right foot, I invited Oscar and his grandson into my inner office. Travis, however, demurred and sat down at Carla's desk. With a shrug, I followed Oscar and closed the door. It wouldn't prevent the others from hearing him, but at least it might muffle the roar.

"Have you seen my marquee?" he demanded, sitting across from me with his elbows on my desk.

"I saw it yesterday, I guess. You have your special annual showing of *It's A Wonderful Life*. I'd like to see it again. . . ."

"Today!" He pounded on the desktop, rattling objects and shivering timbers. "Yesterday I was showing *It's A Wonderful Life*, this morning I'm showing *It's A Wonderful File*! Who's the culprit, I ask you? Who's persecuting the Nyquists? That stupid sheriff of ours does nothing! We want you to help us. It's your duty, right?"

My brain was still dealing with the switch of letters on the marquee. It was simple enough, no doubt the nocturnal effort of some kids. It was also kind of funny, but I didn't dare say so to Oscar.

"Frankly, Mr. Nyquist," I said in a serious voice, "I'm not sure *publicity* would suit your purpose. That only calls attention to this sort of thing and invites more trouble. As long as there's no damage to your . . ."

"Not yet," bristled Oscar, taking a briar pipe out of his lumber jacket. "Not to the Marmot, I mean. But damage, yes, oh, yes, we've had plenty of that. Theft, vandalism, passion pits—what next? Where does it end when there's no police protection in this town?"

Oscar Nyquist was shaking his pipe. He had gotten very red in the face, which in his case meant all over his skull as well. His jaw jutted, and there were deep furrows in his forehead. Fleetingly, I wondered if he were about to have a stroke, like Father Fitz.

"Wait a minute," I urged, keeping calm. "Back up a bit. I heard about the theft and some of the vandalism. That's happened mostly to your son, Arnie, right?" I saw Oscar give a jerky nod. "What's this passion pit business? That's news to me. Are you talking about necking in the movie theatre?" I phrased the question in the old-fashioned terms Oscar understood.

"Sheesh!" breathed Oscar, arching his eyebrows far up into his dome. He settled down enough to extract an oilskin pouch of tobacco from his jacket. "Not in *my* theatre, you don't. I still got ushers, remember? But I can't say exactly in mixed company," he murmured, lowering his voice as well as his head. "It's the new bowling alley site. Immoral acts. You know what I mean? My son has proof of it. That's not all, either." His voice began to rise again. "Somebody punctured the tires of two of Arnie's construction trucks. And then there's that Peeping Tom at my grandson's place."

"Has all this been reported to Sheriff Dodge?" I asked, still trying to keep my tone mild.

"Why bother?" exploded Oscar. "I tell you, he hasn't done anything! Oh, Arnie went to see him about the break-in the other day, but this new stuff—what's the use? That's why I'm here."

A single knock sounded on my door. I called out.

Travis Nyquist poked his head in. His words were for his grandfather: "Popsy, what did I tell you?" Travis's blue eyes narrowed slightly, distorting his otherwise appealing, all-American face.

Oscar turned slightly, then banged the desk again. "You're soft, boy! This is persecution, I tell you!"

Travis, however, stood firm, if slightly unbalanced on his new walking cast. "For Bridget's sake, Popsy. Come on, she asked nicely, didn't she?"

"Nyaaah!" Oscar made a scornful gesture, taking a swipe at the framed Sigma Delta Chi Award from my days at *The Oregonian*. "She's a baby, still wet behind the ears. . . ." But he caught the warning stare from Travis and began to simmer down. "Okay, okay, but those tires—do you know what they cost?"

"The tires don't bother me," agreed Travis, his face regaining its usual pleasant aspect. "Just remember what you promised." He winked, then closed the door.

"Maybe," I suggested, having racked my brain for a way out of this awkward situation, "what we need to do is look into the matter of the sheriff's office. That's what you're really complaining about, right?'' I saw Oscar give a little shudder that passed for assent. "Perhaps I could assign one of my staff to investigate how the sheriff handles complaints. We might do a series, you know, in-depth, and in the process, goad Dodge and his deputies into taking complaints such as yours more seriously.'' It sounded exemplary, even though I had absolutely no intention of following through. Over the years, however, I have learned that most unreasonable requests made to journalists can be put off by the promise of *in-depth*. The average layman is impressed by the idea, and when nothing comes of it, the explanation is easy: *in-depth* takes time. Most people's attention span is only slightly longer than that of a bug's, so eventually the crisis dries up and blows away.

Oscar, however, was looking dubious. Instead of protesting, however, he set aside his pipe and pouch, reached for my notepad, and picked up a ballpoint pen. Apparently, Oscar was incapable of whispering. His handwriting was large and overblown, like the man himself: *Someone is trying to kill my grandson's wife. Help us.*

I blinked at the message, then stared at Oscar. He motioned for me not to speak out loud. *Who?* I scribbled.

Don't know, he scrawled in reply.

With a sigh, I leaned back in my swivel chair. It would do me no good to urge Oscar or any other Nyquist to go to the sheriff. Rapidly, I considered the previous problems the family had encountered. All of them were petty, probably pranks. Young people in Alpine didn't have enough to do, especially in the winter. None of the Nyquist complaints would lead me to think that they could be connected with a killer. My initial reaction was to dismiss Oscar's fears as part of a persecution complex.

Except that we already had two dead young women. Was it possible that Bridget Nyquist might become number three?

I found a fresh piece of paper and invited Oscar to come over to my house around six. He mulled over the request, fidgeted with his pipe, then gave a nod of assent. "Okay," he said out loud. "You promise to help?"

"Of course." It felt like an empty vow, but at least I could hear the man out. He was on his feet, heavy shoes tramping on the floor. "What about Travis?" I murmured. "Would he like to come?"

The bald head gave a sharp shake. "No." Oscar started for the door. "He needs to rest." The remark was an afterthought.

Out in the news office, Vida and Ed were gone, Ginny had returned to the front desk, and Carla was deep in conversation with Travis. She giggled, which Carla often does, a decidedly unmusical sound. Travis was laughing, too. They were head-to-head, and I noticed that Oscar stiffened at the sight of them.

"Let's go, boy!" bellowed Oscar, barreling through the newsroom like a tank. Startled, Travis looked up from his tête-à-tête.

"Sure, Popsy," he said, appearing to struggle with the crutches. He slipped, caught himself on the desk, then allowed a wide-eyed Carla to brace him. "Thanks, I needed that." Travis beamed down on Carla, who actually blushed. I was refreshed and at the same time annoyed. Carla's private life was none of my business, but flirting with married men was dumb. After all, look where it had gotten me. . . .

I waited by the window to make sure Oscar and Travis had taken off in a brown Range Rover. Throwing my purple car coat over my shoulders, I turned to Carla. "What's with the bridegroom? I thought he had a nurse at home."

Carla giggled and blushed, blushed and giggled. "Travis Nyquist is just a friendly kind of guy. You know, the type who makes you feel like a *woman*."

"So how come you're acting like an idiot?" The response was more cutting than I'd intended. Immediate remorse set in, and I gave Carla a crooked smile. "Sorry, Carla, but someday I'll tell you the story of my life. It'll cure you of friendly men who wear wedding rings."

Carla sobered suddenly, and her complexion returned to its usual smooth olive hue. "Do you mean Adam's dad?" If nothing else, Carla was direct.

With a resigned sigh, I perched on her desk. "Yeah, that's right." So far, I'd confided only in Vida about my ill-starred love affair with Tom Cavanaugh. But with Adam due home for Christmas break and no doubt headed back to the Bay Area to visit his father over the holidays, my secret was about to come out. "It wasn't just a flirtation, though. It was the real McCoy. But that hasn't made it any easier for the past twenty-plus years." I lifted my chin, attempting dignity. Carla frowned. "Hey," I went on, shaking her arm, "I don't mean to deliver a lecture. I'm overreacting. But Travis reminds me of Adam's dad—on the surface, that is. Smart, good-looking, charming, ambitious, talented—and married. Seeing the two of you together at your desk brought back those days at *The Seattle Times* when I was an intern and Adam's father was a copy editor. I was just about your age, maybe a year or so younger. Do I sound sappy?"

Carla considered. "A little. Gosh, Emma, it's tough up here in Alpine. Most of the unmarried guys have grease under their fingernails or have lost a few digits in the woods. Where do you find a guy who isn't married and who uses good grammar?"

My brown-eyed gaze met her black-eyed stare. "Good question. Where, Carla? Where?"

Carla giggled. But she didn't blush.

The one man in Alpine who might have qualified, as far as I was concerned, was sitting in his office with the phone propped up against his ear and his long legs stretched out on his desk. The problem with Milo Dodge was that there was no chemistry between us. Then there was Honoria Whitman, his current woman of choice. Also, he was divorced, and I was Catholic. But most of all, there was Tom Cavanaugh. As long as I remained stupidly, stubbornly in love with Tom, Milo's flaws and virtues counted for naught.

Milo gestured for me to sit down, then went on with his monosyllabic side of the conversation. Whoever was at the other end was monopolizing the call. With a promise to see to it ASAP, Milo rung off.

"Dot Parker," said Milo with a sigh. "Durwood bought a snowmobile."

Durwood Parker, retired pharmacist, and unarguably the worst driver in Skykomish County, had been grounded by Milo for six months. Obviously, he was chafing at the bit and had discovered a new way to make mayhem. I clapped a hand to my head and gave Milo an incredulous look.

"Where is he?" I inquired, hoping it was nowhere near civilization.

"Somewhere up the Icicle Creek Road," replied Milo, rubbing his temples. "He got Averill Fairbanks to give him a lift as far as the ranger station. Ave saw a UFO land near the campground up there this morning."

"Oh." I marveled that Ave hadn't called the paper to report his latest sighting. He usually did. In fact, we could have kept a standing headline for Averill Fairbanks and his alien spacecraft. "Is Dot worried?"

"Yeah, a little. She wants Jack or Bill or somebody to go check on him if he's not back by mid-afternoon. You had lunch?"

Since it was only eleven-thirty, I hadn't. But breakfast had been meager: cinnamon toast and coffee. Tired out from my decorating efforts, I'd slept in, almost twenty minutes later than usual. I decided that if we could find a discreet table at the Venison Inn, it would be as appropriate a place as any to tell Milo about Oscar Nyquist's concerns.

Since we had beaten the usual lunch crowd to the restaurant, we had our choice of seating. I steered Milo to a back booth, next to a window. Red paper bells hung from the ceiling, with silver tinsel looped wall-to-wall. Springs of holly stood in slim white vases and red felt stockings were hung over the fireplace at the rear of the main dining room. "Rudolph the Red-nosed Reindeer" was prancing along the restaurant's music track.

"What's up?" Milo inquired after he'd ordered a steak sandwich medium-well and I'd opted for the beef dip because I could get it rare this early in the lunch hour.

I relayed Oscar's complaints, as well as my empty promise. Milo looked mildly exasperated. "Jesus, those Nyquists think they own the damned town. Old Lars used to face off with Carl Clemans about once a month. Luckily, Carl usually won," said Milo, referring to the fair-minded mill owner who had been Alpine's unofficial founder. "Oscar followed in his father's footsteps, then Arnie, and now Travis, I suppose. I wouldn't bother myself with that marquee crap—kids have been doing that for years around here. Remember *The Mail and Louse*? Then there was *Lethal Peon 2*. We found the extra letters in the litter can. Same with *The Prince of Ties*. My favorite, though, was *Silence of the Lamps*—they turned the *b* upside down . . ."

"Yes, yes," I interrupted, for Milo was starting to chuckle himself into a small fit. "But that's definitely kid stuff. Stealing isn't."

"Arnie didn't lock the damned van. . . ."

"It's still stealing. Did you even bother to get prints?"

Having recovered from his bout of mirth, Milo gave me an irked stare. "Sure. We got a bunch of smudges. In this weather, who isn't wearing gloves?"

I paused as the waitress brought our salads and poured more coffee. "Okay, let's skip the silly stuff," I said, a trifle tight-lipped. Reaching into my purse, I took out the note Oscar had written to me. Milo's long face twisted in what might have been dismay, but more likely was disbelief.

"Hunh. So the old fart thinks he can get us moving by

making a claim like that?'' Milo tossed the sheet of notepaper back.

"Can you disregard it entirely?'' I asked. "Especially with dead bodies floating down the Sky?''

With a wave of his fork, Milo guffawed. "Now how the hell can you tie in one spare leg and an unidentified girl with the Nyquists? If the body was one of ours, okay. But nobody's missing from Alpine. I've checked. The only person unaccounted for as of this morning is Durwood.''

"Okay, okay,'' I said hastily. "But I promised I'd talk to Oscar about it tonight after work. I think I'll ask Vida to come over, too.''

Milo rolled his eyes, then stuffed his face with salad. "Don't you have enough to do with Ben in town and Adam on his way and the paper and all?'' At least that's what his remark sounded like through the lettuce.

"Oscar Nyquist isn't exactly the fanciful sort. And he's far from senile.'' I speared a piece of tomato and gave Milo what I hoped was a steely stare. "I'll hear him out. Vida thinks Bridget is behaving a bit oddly. Maybe the reason is because she feels her life is threatened.''

"Vida!'' Milo chuckled again, though he spoke the name with affection as well as scorn. "By the way, those weren't letters on that dead woman's body.''

"What?'' I held my coffee cup poised in mid-sip. "What do you mean?''

"They were numbers. One-Nine-Eight-Seven. The year, maybe, 1987. And it was B-H-S, not B-H-F, or whatever we thought it was at first. Doc Dewey used his microscope.''

"BHS?'' I gave a little start, spilling some of my coffee. Quickly, I mopped it up with my napkin. "That means Blanchet High School to me. I went there. The *1987* could be the year she graduated. Well, Milo?''

An unsettled look came over Milo's long face. "Is that right? In my line of work, it stands for Bushy-Haired Stranger. You know, the suspect who wasn't there,'' he said in an unusually tentative voice. His gaze fixed on the remainder of his salad. "You're right, it could be a high school. But why Blanchet? What about Bellevue? That's where my kids have gone since Old Mulehide and I split up. Or Ballard or Bremerton or Bellingham or . . . hell, any place in the country with a high school that starts with the letter B."

"That's true. It's just that those initials mean Blanchet to me," I pointed out. "Had you figured that it might stand for a high school?"

Milo looked a trifle sheepish. "No. I was thinking more of a person. A guy, maybe." He finished his salad, shoved the plate to one side, and nodded at a couple of loggers who were going into the bar. "There are about six missing women in the state who fit her description, but none of them are named Carol. If we could access a data base for high schools beginning with a B, then we could narrow it down to any Carols from the 1987 class. At least we'd have some place to start."

"Then what?" I asked as the waitress removed the salad plates.

Milo lifted his hands in a helpless gesture. "Then we'd try to find out if any of them are missing. That's assuming the dead woman's name is Carol. It would be one hell of a job. I doubt that we could do it out of this office. If we found out that there are no missing Carols from Blanchet, Ballard, Bellevue, or any of the other *B* high schools in the state, then maybe we could get the FBI to come in."

"For starters, I could call Blanchet," I offered. "Mrs. Hoffman is still in the tuition office. She's very helpful."

"I could get my kids to check out the Bellevue annuals," said Milo. "In fact, my oldest daughter graduated in 'eighty-seven."

The waitress returned with our entrees and more coffee. There was still no one sitting directly across from us, though I'd seen four men move into the booth at my back. I couldn't hear them, so I assumed they couldn't hear us. I decided it was time to reopen the subject of Oscar Nyquist's biggest worry, but I'd do it in a roundabout way. I started by asking Milo if any of the Nyquists had reported a Peeping Tom incident.

"Not officially," said Milo, drenching his meat with steak sauce. "But Arnie mentioned it when he was in with one of his numerous other complaints. Bridget Nyquist is a knock-out. It's no wonder some guy felt an urge to watch her undress. She should have pulled the shades."

"Do you know who it was?"

"Hell, no. Sam Heppner tried to pin Arnie down, but he suddenly became vague. It makes me wonder if Bridget didn't know damned well who the peeker was, but got skittish about saying so." Milo wiggled his sandy eyebrows at me.

"You mean she knew the guy?"

"I mean she sure did, and maybe he thought he had a right to be there, but her husband wouldn't have agreed." Milo chewed his steak complacently.

"But they're still newlyweds," I protested. Then I thought of Travis, apparently flirting with Carla. I also remembered Travis's warning to his grandfather. Had Travis been trying to keep Oscar from saying anything more about the Peeping Tom? I tried a different tack. "So you wouldn't tie this peeker in with a threat on Bridget's life?"

Milo gave a little grunt of a laugh. "If it's what I think it is, the only danger she's in is from Travis. In fact, the most likely victim would be the peeker. But if there's something going on between this guy and Bridget, Travis is the type who'd want to save face. He's got a big reputation in this town as an all-around success story. Four years on the job and he retires. Hell, why couldn't I have found a boondoggle like that?"

"Luck," I noted. "In my opinion, playing the stock market isn't much different from betting on the horse races. You might as well pick out the corporate logo you like best, just like choosing a horse by the jockey's colors."

"He sure knew how to pick them," said Milo. "Travis knew how to pick women, too, or so I thought until the so-called Peeping Tom showed up. If she's playing around on him, he's not so lucky after all."

I wasn't as ready as Milo to dismiss the peeker as a love-struck suitor waiting for Bridget to give the all-clear. In fact, I was beginning to get the uneasy feeling that the Nyquists weren't entirely wrong in their criticism of the sheriff's department. I was getting anxious to hear what Oscar would have to say when he came to my house.

"How's Saturday?" Milo was watching me expectantly. I'd been wool-gathering, and hadn't heard the first part of the question. Judging from Milo's quirky smile, he knew he'd caught me unawares. "For dinner at King Olav's? Paging Emma Lord, paging Emma Lord . . ."

"It's fine," I said hastily. "Adam won't be in until early next week. Ben will have the Saturday evening mass. What about Honoria?"

"She's going to spend Christmas with her family in Walnut Creek," said Milo. "She leaves Saturday morning." His expression grew wistful.

"Do you want to have Christmas dinner at my place?" I asked.

"I'll have the kids." Milo didn't seem thrilled by the prospect.

"So bring them." His son, Brandon, was almost the same age as Adam; Tanya was a couple of years older, and Michelle was a high school senior. My brother related beautifully to young people. We could have a real family gathering. I rocked a little in my seat, excited at the idea.

"I don't know. . . ." Milo was still looking uncertain. "They'll be driving up from Bellevue Christmas morning. Tanya is probably bringing that five-star jerk she lives with. It'd be a lot of bother, Emma."

"No, it won't. I'd love to have you. The jerk, too. Honest." Impulsively, I put my hand on Milo's. "I'll get a twenty-five pound turkey. Stuffing, mashed potatoes, gravy, cranberry sauce, green beans, and mince pie. Oh, rolls, too— I've got the Clemans family's potato roll recipe. Vida gave it to me." As far as I was concerned the matter was settled.

"It sounds good." Milo was weakening, enticed by the vision of a groaning sideboard. "I could bring some wine."

"Ben's doing that. You can get sparkling cider or pop. And maybe some rum so I can make Tom and Jerrys." I was very pleased. It would be the first big holiday dinner I'd fixed in years. In Portland, Adam and I had spent the first three Christmases by ourselves. I had been absolutely miserable.

Putting his free hand over mine, Milo gave me a surprisingly diffident smile. "It could be fun, huh?"

"It *will* be fun," I assured him. "We can play board games and act goofy. We can have a snowball fight. We can eat ourselves into a big fat fit."

"It's been a while since I've done that," Milo mused. "Had a big family-style Christmas, I mean. Last year the kids and I ate at the Venison Inn."

"Vida asked you to come to her house," I reminded him. Adam and I had gone there, joining Vida's three daughters, their husbands and children, and Carla. It had been lively, it had been lovely—but it hadn't been my own.

"It would have been too crowded," Milo asserted. Slowly, he removed his hand. I did the same. Our gazes locked, just for a moment, then fell away. "How about those Seahawks?" said Milo.

We returned to the outside world, once again firmly closing the door on our inner emotions. If we had any. I could never be quite sure.

". . . So it could be Blanchet or Bothell or Burnaby, up in B.C., or any—"

Vida stared at me, her eyes wide behind the big round lenses. "Don't you remember my wedding story?" She gave a swift shake of her head. "No, probably not, you weren't here, you were out of town. Bridget Nyquist went to Blanchet. And if memory serves, she was in the class of 'eighty-seven."

Chapter Six

I HAVE SEEN the mountains scarred by logging; I have seen the loggers scarred from living. The great gouges along Mount Baldy and Tonga Ridge speak to me. But so do the men who made them, and their voices keep me awake at night. I have heard the cry of the spotted owl. I have seen tears in the eyes of rough-and-ready human beings whose pride has been destroyed along with their livelihood.

In early September, when newly restricted logging activities were further curtailed by the danger of forest fires, I'd interviewed several loggers and their families. The image I'd carried in Seattle and Portland of two-fisted, hard-drinking, poorly educated louts armed with chain saws and no brains had begun to change. In its place, a new portrait began to emerge, not in bright red and green plaid, but in more somber colors. Despair, discouragement, depression were etched in the worried faces of the men, women, and children who depended upon the woods to make their living. A logger is a logger, and can't—not won't—think of himself as anything else. In Alpine, as many as four generations in one family had worked in the timber industry. Some had lost a leg or an arm, many were missing fingers and toes, a few were paralyzed, and the death toll was too high for any business. But the risks didn't scare off these gutsy woodland knights. What frightened them was the possibility of losing their livelihood—and their pride. The threat of shutting down the forests hovered over these people like an axe. I decided it was time to take my stand.

Culling my research from a number of sources, I started to outline my piece for next week's issue. After returning from lunch with Milo, I had called Blanchet High School in Seattle, but Mrs. Hoffman wasn't in. Supposedly, she would call me back.

"Look," Vida said, not exactly appearing out of nowhere, since I could hear her coming from a mile away. "I put together a Nyquist family tree."

Sure enough, Vida had scrawled a genealogy of sorts on a sheet of typing paper. Lars, the Norwegian emigrant and founder of the dynasty as well as of the Whistling Marmot Theatre, had married Inga Fremstad in 1909. Oscar was born a year later; his sister Karen came along in 1917. Oscar had taken Astrid Petersen as his bride in 1932. Karen had become Mrs. Trygve Hansen in 1938. Astrid Nyquist had passed away three years ago. Two children had been born of that union—Thelma, who married a man named Peter Nordoff and moved to Spokane, and Arnold, whose wife, Louise, had been born a Bergstrom. Their son, Travis, was an only child.

"I've met Louise Nyquist but I honestly don't remember the woman," I mused. "What does she look like?"

Vida was scanning my owl editorial on the computer screen. "Good for you, you're taking a stand. You've got spunk, Emma. I've always said as much. Which," she went on without missing a beat, "is more than I can say for Louise Nyquist. No wonder you don't remember her. She fades into the woodwork, like an unnecessary coat of varnish. Mousy creature, your height, plump as a pigeon, and about the same coloration—gray and more gray. She's never stood up to Arnie, but how many people have where the Nyquist men are concerned? They don't even stand up to each other."

I couldn't place my encounter with Louise Nyquist. Not at bridge club, not from the library, not in passing at the grocery store, not as a member of any of the civic groups I came into contact with through the newspaper. "Does she ever leave the house?"

Vida gave me a scathing look. "Well, of course! She's not a recluse, and she's no dope—she's just a mouse. She still occasionally substitutes as a teacher. She taught all the time Travis was in high school. Then she decided to get her M.A. about three years ago. Now that was something, I'll admit. She had the gumption to live in Seattle and take classes at the UDUB and come home every other weekend. I heard Arnie was fit to be tied."

I admired Louise Nyquist's determination. "At least she's tried to establish her own identity," I remarked.

Vida nodded. "It's taken some doing. But when she isn't subbing, Louise keeps busy as a homemaker and does her share for the Lutheran church. She and Arnie take trips now and then. Arnie's always asking me to write them up, but they never go anywhere interesting. Arizona, Palm Springs, Hawaii—you know, all the places that everybody else goes and is sick to death of hearing about. Do you really think we need to run a photo of Louise Nyquist standing next to a cactus? Or Arnie cavorting around Konopali Beach in Bermuda shorts? Ugh!"

I smiled agreement, then again studied the Nyquist family tree. "They sure stick to their own," I noted. "These are all Scandinavian names except for Bridget. I see she was a Dunne." Irish, maybe. And, if she had graduated from Blanchet, possibly Catholic.

Vida picked up on my wavelength. "If Bridget was R.C., she gave it up. She married Travis in the Lutheran church, remember? Don't think the Nyquists would permit anything else. In college, Arnie was crazy about some Catholic girl. Oscar put a stop to that, I can tell you!" To my dismay, Vida didn't look entirely disapproving. I was still having trouble adjusting to the narrow-mindedness of Alpiners when it came to people of different races and creeds. Alpine might be only seventy miles from Seattle, but it was seventy years behind the times in terms of social integration.

"So he got stuck with the mouse?" I remarked innocently. "Or is Louise a pigeon? I forget."

"She's both," Vida replied, a bit testily. "So was Arnie's first love, for all I know. I never met her. He wanted to bring her home from the University of Washington to meet his family, but you can imagine how Oscar reacted to that. And old Lars, too. He was still alive then. Karen's first husband was killed early on in World War II. She married again," Vida noted, pointing to Oscar's sister on the makeshift genealogy. "He was Jewish. You can imagine how *that* stuck in the family's craw!"

Vida exited my office just as Ben came through the outer door. He greeted my House & Home editor warmly, but I could tell from the drawn expression on his face that he was upset. Either as a measure of trust in Vida or an acknowledgment of my friendship with her, Ben didn't bother to shut the door behind him. Vida, however, appeared to be absorbed in her typing. I knew better. Vida could have overheard whispers on game day in the Kingdome.

"Dr. Flake is sending Father Fitz to Everett for tests," Ben announced, sitting down in one of my two visitors' chairs. "He's not responding as well as he should. His speech is impaired and he's partially paralyzed on one side. Flake thinks he may have had a second stroke."

"Oh, dear." I wasn't sure who I felt more sorry for—my pastor or my brother. "Are you stuck at St. Mildred's for the duration?"

Ben grimaced. "I can't be. I've got my own parish. I have to be back in Tuba City on January second. You know that."

"I mean are you going to have to take over for the holidays?" I gave Ben a look of genuine sympathy.

He sighed, reached into his pocket, and pulled out a huge cigar. "I suppose so. Dr. Flake went over to Everett to see Father Fitz. The poor old guy has been trying to give Flake instructions to pass on to me. He's sure St. Mildred's will collapse without his guidance, I guess. He can't speak very well and he can't write, so it's very frustrating. All I can do is have Flake tell him everything is under control. Technically, I'm not under this archdiocese's jurisdiction, but my conscience wouldn't let me walk away. With the shortage of priests, I doubt very much if the arch can spare anybody, especially during Advent and Christmas.''

For a moment, we were silent. Ben was lighting the cigar; I was trying to make the best of a disruption. St. Mildred's was a self-sustaining entity. The parish council, the school faculty, the various committees would hold the parochial fabric together. Given Father Fitz's advanced age, he wasn't the most active priest in the archdiocese. Ben would be stuck for daily and weekend masses, a couple of weddings, maybe a baptism, and, if he had time, visits to the sick. Except for the fact that he'd probably have to stay on at the rectory, he'd still have plenty of free hours to spend with Adam and me.

''Where'd you get that cigar?'' I inquired as my office grew hazy with smoke. ''Your old drinking buddy, Milo?''

Ben shook his head. ''Peyton Flake. He says they taste even better over a fifth of Wild Turkey. Ever see a Desert Eagle?''

''I've got enough problems with the spotted owl. Does the Desert Eagle hang out with the Wild Turkey?''

''You got it, Sluggly.'' Ben grinned, clenching the cigar in his teeth. Apparently, he'd faced up to his unexpected responsibilities, acknowledged his pastoral duties, and made peace with himself. Ben was like that—he went through agonies of indecision, but once he'd made up his mind, he put all doubts behind him. ''A Desert Eagle is a gun, in this case, a .357 Magnum. They're made in Israel. Dr. Flake just bought one. He may be able to solve the spotted owl controversy single-handedly. Right now he's threatening to practice on the religious statuary up at St. Mildred's. I told him he'd better not, or I wouldn't lend him my Browning high-power nine-millimeter semiautomatic.''

"You've got a *gun*?'' I shrieked. Vida, I noticed, paused in her typing, but briefly.

Ben gave me a disgusted look. "Of course I've got a gun. Do you think I'd wander all over the Mississippi Delta or the Arizona desert without a gun?''

I was flabbergasted. Of course our dad had owned guns, and had done some hunting before he decided that too many of his fellow hunters couldn't tell a cow from a deer—or each other. "What are you afraid of,'' I demanded, "the Ku Klux Klan and the Mormons going after your parishioners?''

"I'm more afraid of my parishioners.'' Ben chuckled, then shook his head. "No, it's not people that worry me so much as animals. Snakes, mainly, in Arizona. Anyway, Dr. Flake asked me to go shooting with him. He's quite a guy. Not what I'd expect to find in Alpine.''

I'd met Peyton Flake twice, and had to agree with Ben. The new doctor in town was not much over thirty, and a graduate of the University of Chicago's medical school. Flake was a lanky six foot three with a ponytail, rimless glasses, and a careless beard. His professional uniform seemed to consist of faded blue jeans and a rumpled denim work shirt. His untidy appearance, not to mention his somewhat flamboyant personal habits, had aroused a good deal of criticism, but his medical expertise was slowly starting to win people over. Doc Dewey sang his new partner's praises.

I was still reeling from my brother's revelation that he roamed the reservation with a cocked and loaded handgun when I saw Ginny and Carla come into the outer office carrying a couple of cartons. I recognized them as containing *The Advocate*'s official Christmas decorations. They were, I recalled from my previous Alpine Yuletides, a pathetic lot. Marius Vandeventer, who had founded the newspaper almost sixty years ago, had been many things. Most of them were admirable, but he hadn't been overly keen on Christmas. I cringed as Ginny pulled out a two-foot-high tree made from aluminum foil.

The phone rang. It was Mrs. Hoffman, calling from the Blanchet attendance office in Seattle. As we caught up with each other over a gap of almost twenty-five years, I scrawled a note to Ben.

He nodded, then made a notation of his own: *BHS chaplain—Bill Crowley—fellow seminarian.*

Mrs. Hoffman and I finally got down to business. Offhand, she recalled two or three Carols in the class of '87. I could hear pages turning. Maybe it was easier to look through the yearbook than to rely on computer records.

"Here's Carol Addams, tall, blond girl—it helps to look at their senior pictures—got a scholarship to some school back east, graduated in biology, got married last summer, and lives in Maine. Or is it Vermont? It's so hard to keep track of these kids, but her youngest brother is a junior this year. . . ."

It occurred to me that—at least as far as Blanchet High School was concerned—Clarice Hoffman was almost as valuable a resource as Vida was for Alpine. But of course it was Mrs. Hoffman's job to keep track of students, at least while they were attending the school. It was she who took the calls from parents reporting on sick, tardy, or otherwise absent teenagers, and she who had read—and heard—every excuse in the book.

"Janovitz," she was saying, "but she spelled it Carole, with an *e*. You said this one doesn't?"

"Uh . . . right." I hadn't told Mrs. Hoffman why I was trying to track down a 1987 graduate named Carol. If there was no connection between Blanchet and the body by the river, then there was no need to unduly alarm the attendance office or the rest of the faculty and staff.

"Neal," she said. "Let me think . . . Carol Neal . . . Her parents weren't as well-off as some." Which, I assumed, meant that they were often behind in their tuition payments.

"St. John's? Or St. Catherine's? I can never remember home parishes. North end, though—she took the bus. That is, until she got a car in her junior year." The sound of more pages being riffled came over the line. "Winters, but that's Carolyn." Mrs. Hoffman paused, presumably finishing up the alphabetical listings. "That's it, Emma. Do you think you're looking for Carol Neal or Carol Addams?"

"Neal," I replied. "Addams doesn't live around here, right? By the way, was that the same year Bridget Dunne graduated?"

"Bridget!" Mrs. Hoffman's voice took on an edge. "Now there was a piece of work! I could never figure that kid out. Say, didn't she marry somebody from up your way?"

"She did. A local named Travis Nyquist." Ben was watching me closely through a cloud of cigar smoke. Ginny and Carla were putting cheap plastic ornaments on the aluminum-foil tree. Vida had given up all pretense of typing and was standing in the doorway of my office.

"Funny girl," mused Mrs. Hoffman. "You never knew where you were with her. One minute, she'd be sweet as candy; the next, she'd be a real little snip. Of course she lost her father when she was a sophomore. And I heard Mrs. Dunne committed suicide. I guess I'd better go dig into my bag of Christian charity and spare a bit for Bridget."

"Do you remember if Bridget and Carol Neal were friends?" I asked innocently.

Mrs. Hoffman hesitated. "That whole class was even more cliquish than some of the others. I'm not sure. They may have been. But it seems to me that Bridget in particular palled around with girls from other private schools. Holy Names. Forest Ridge. Even some of the non-Catholic ones. I told you: she was odd."

I didn't know if Mrs. Hoffman's judgment of Bridget was based on the girl's unpredictable personality or her choice of companions. It didn't matter. I had a link between Bridget

Dunne Nyquist and Carol Neal. If, of course, that was Carol Neal's body lying in Al Driggers's mortuary.

"Have you got a mailing address for Carol Neal?" I asked, giving Vida and Ben a high sign.

"The alum office would have it. Should I transfer you?"

Briefly, Mrs. Hoffman exchanged pleasantries about our reunion via telephone. Just before she rang off, she wished me luck in finding Carol Neal. I mumbled my thanks.

I didn't recognize the female voice that answered for the alumni association. She sounded young, eager, and efficient. Maybe she thought I wanted to give money. But she met my request with a buoyant spirit. As I waited for her to look up Carol Neal's address, my gaze shifted from Ben to Vida and back again. Vida was waving both hands, not at me, but in an attempt to disperse Ben's cigar smoke.

"Filthy," she muttered. "What kind of vices do you priests have?"

The lively voice came back on the line. "We have an address for Carol Neal in the University District, on Fifteenth Northeast. But that was four years ago. She moved after that and apparently left no forwarding address. We have her listed as inactive."

That, I thought, was an understatement.

Chapter Seven

THE ALUMINUM-FOIL TREE with its plastic ornaments, the ragged red and green paper streamers, and the Styrofoam snowman with his missing nose and mangled top hat didn't do much to cheer up the editorial office. I flinched when I remembered what Ginny had to work with in the reception area: three cardboard Magi, a Star of Bethlehem that had lost half of its pasted-on gold glitter, and a Holy Family fashioned from bread dough. The array was depressing.

"Nice decorations," Ed Bronsky commented as he lumbered through the office. "I really like the tree. It's like the one we have at home, only smaller. We put homemade stuff on it, like cranberries and popcorn and hard candy."

Ben had left for the rectory and Vida had returned to her desk. "What a stupid idea," she declared, narrowing her eyes at Ed. "I've seen your tree. By the day after Christmas, it's bare. Your children have eaten all the decorations." The accusing stare she gave Ed indicated that she thought he and his wife had probably helped.

I didn't give Ed time to defend himself. "Here," I said to Ginny and Carla. "I'm writing a check to Harvey's Hardware and Sporting Goods Store. Go get something decent, and keep it under fifty bucks."

Ed stopped removing his heavy overcoat. "Harvey Adcock! I was supposed to see him fifteen minutes ago! Wouldn't you know it! He wants to double the size of his usual ad next week just because he thinks men like to get tools and sports stuff for Christmas! Why can't they be happy with a tie? I am." He plodded out of the office behind Ginny and Carla.

Vida rolled her eyes. "Honestly," she breathed. "It isn't just that people are jackasses, Emma. It's that there are so many *kinds* of jackasses!"

"I'm afraid so." I poured a cup of coffee and sat down in Ed's chair. "I've got to go see Milo and tell him about Carol Neal. Then he can start tracking her down and find out if she's really missing." I paused, waiting for Vida to respond. But Vida was doodling on a notepad. "If she's the same Carol," I went on, "then she must have known Bridget. Blanchet's not that big—under a thousand students at the time, I'd guess." Vida kept doodling. "I should have asked Mrs. Hoffman who Carol's friends were, assuming she and Bridget weren't buddies. Maybe Ben can call Bill Crowley. He's been the chaplain there for almost ten years."

At last, Vida looked up. "Who was your best friend in high school, Emma?"

I blinked. "I had two. Chris Sullivan and Ursula Guy."

"When was the last time you saw them?"

My brow furrowed under bangs that needed a trim. "I had lunch in Seattle with Chris last summer. The Fourth of July weekend. Ursula lives in Houston. I owe her a letter. She sent me a Thanksgiving card and enclosed a note."

Vida nodded slowly, while I gazed at her in puzzlement. "You keep up. Even though you live a whole county or half a continent away. Now if you and Tommy"—I made a face as Vida called Tom Cavanaugh by the nickname only she dared to use—"had taken the trouble to get married, I imagine you would have invited these dear high school chums to your wedding. Oh, stop looking like you swallowed a dill pickle! I know it wasn't your fault you didn't get married, and he may be Tom to you, but he's Tommy to me. And he's a very fine man, not nearly as big a lunkhead as most. But don't get me started on *that*. What I'm saying is that it's very strange Bridget had no friends at her wedding. She's only twenty-two or twenty-three. At that age, they couldn't possibly have all moved to Timbuktu. So what is wrong with Bridget Dunne Nyquist?''

I was taken aback by Vida's question. "How do I know? More to the point, what's Bridget's lack of social expertise got to do with Carol Neal's dead body? If, that is, the corpse turns out to be Carol?" I saw Vida's expression of exasperation and grabbed the phone. "That does it! I'm not waiting to go over to Milo's office; I'm going to call him right now!"

As I vigorously punched in the sheriff's number, Vida sat back in her chair, wearing a smug look. "It's about time. I thought you were going to sit there all day and slurp coffee, just like Ed."

I gave Vida a wry glance. At the other end of the line, I was put on hold. Before I could say anything more to Vida, Milo's laconic voice sounded in my ear. He was mildly interested in the information I'd gleaned from Mrs. Hoffman. One thing that I've learned from dealing with law enforcement agencies is that their representatives in general—and Milo Dodge in particular—rarely get excited over what the average lay person would consider a hot lead. They deal only in facts. Guesswork is anathema.

But Milo agreed to get on Carol Neal's trail. He'd call the King County sheriff's office in Seattle right away. My so-called tip was the only lead he had, after all.

Vida had resumed her doodling. Six circles and an evergreen silhouette later, she put the pad aside. "I'm going to do the Whistling Marmot story after all," she announced, just as I was heading back into my private office. "Oscar is eighty-two. He might not be around by the time we get to the Marmot's official seventy-fifth anniversary. Oh, I know, Lars lived to be ninety-three and still had all his faculties, such as they were to begin with, but I don't want to take a chance. As far as that goes, *I* might not be around."

That didn't strike me as likely. Vida seemed about as indestructible as any human being I'd ever met. She had a point, however. "What's the hook?" I asked.

"The Capra movie," Vida answered promptly. "Oscar has shown *It's a Wonderful Life* every Christmas now for going on twenty years. I want to ask him why he thinks people keep coming back to pay for something they know by heart. He won't have any answers because he's never thought about it, but it's a feature story and I can speculate. It also gives me an excuse to be at your house when he comes over tonight."

"Crafty," I remarked. "By the way, I'm leaving early. I want to go to the mall and do some Christmas shopping."

On my way out, I met Carla and Ginny, who were each carrying a rather small paper bag. "Didn't Harvey have any decorations?" I asked.

"Sure," Carla replied, rustling about in her paper sack. "Look, isn't this adorable?" She pulled out a six-inch figure of Santa Claus, or more precisely, Father Christmas, since he was decked out in a nineteenth-century satin suit of blue trimmed with white fake fur.

"It's charming," I said in admiration, as the wind blew snowflakes before my eyes. "But I was thinking more of—"

"See this," Ginny interrupted. Her paper bag held a pair of candlesticks shaped like angel heads and two green tapers. "We can put them on the reception desk instead of those crummy Wise Men."

Somehow, I'd been thinking more in terms of evergreen garlands, tasteful plastic holly wreaths, even a small artificial tree with a few handsome ornaments. "These are very nice," I said with a weak smile, "but they don't make much of a display. Maybe we could get a couple of other items. How much did these cost?"

Ginny dug anew into her paper bag. "Here's the bill. They came to $53.73. We kept it under fifty dollars, but of course there's the sales tax."

I clenched my teeth. It was no good criticizing my staff members for their ill-chosen method of eroding my finances. I had, as Vida and other Alpiners would say, sent a boy to the mill. Or a couple of them, in this case. They'd gone, they'd seen, they'd purchased. Ginny and Carla simply weren't up to the task. A veteran Christmas decorator had been required, and neither of them qualified.

I brushed snow off my nose. These two pieces were at least a start toward improving the quality of our holiday de-cor. Maybe I could find some other decorations on sale after Christmas. But for now, I wasn't about to deplete my check-ing account any further.

At least not on behalf of *The Advocate*. I was, in fact, about to make a large dent in my current balance by filling some of the gaps on my Christmas list. The parking lot at the mall was full of slush, with big piles of plowed snow around the outer edges. I'd taken care of most of my shopping on two weekend trips to Seattle during October and Novem-ber. But there were still a few presents I wanted to buy for Adam and Ben. And Vida. It wasn't so much that she was hard to please, as that she never seemed to want anything. I took a chance on bedroom slippers and headed for Barton's Bootery.

The Alpine Mall isn't very large by big city or suburban standards. There are only fifteen stores and two restaurants, though Ed has been trying to track down a rumor that Fred Meyer and Starbuck's Coffee plan to open in the coming year. We've heard other such stories, usually concerning big chains, but so far nothing has come of them. In my dreams, I see an honest-to-goodness department store, with three or four floors of merchandise. But I don't think that will happen soon in Alpine. Too many people are out of work. Even now, so close to Christmas, the large parking lot was only half-full. A couple of cars looked as if they had been sitting there for a week or more. Snow was piled high on their roofs, hoods, and trunks. If their owners had suffered from mechanical problems, I wondered why they hadn't pushed the cars across the street to Cal Vickers's Texaco station.

The merchants at the mall had done their best to make their shops look festive. The light standards in the parking lot wore gold garlands and sprigs of plastic holly. Inside, more garlands hung from the ceiling with more holly and clusters of shiny colored bells. The display windows were jammed with Santas, reindeer, angels, snowmen, trees, wreaths, fireplaces, and candles; at Tina's Toys, Snow White and the Seven Dwarfs were dressed in holiday finery.

In Barton's Bootery, I saw several people I knew, including Annie Jeanne Dupré, music teacher and the organist at St. Mildred's; Heather Bardeen, Henry's daughter; and Charlene Vickers, whose husband Cal owns the Texaco station. I had just made my purchase of turquoise blue high-top slippers with little bows when Arnie Nyquist came into the store. At his side was a plump middle-aged woman who I realized must be Mrs. Nyquist. Yes, I probably had met her, but on closer inspection, I realized that not only was Louise Nyquist mousy; she was the type of person who looks like everybody else; a bit under medium height, a bit overweight, a bit of gray in her brown hair, a bit of this and a bit of that. She was utterly average, though I suspected that in her younger years, she had probably been pretty.

Arnie was prepared to breeze by me, but I executed a quick step in my fur-lined boots and barred his way. "Hi, Arnie," I said cheerily, then beamed at Mrs. Nyquist. "Louise, right? We've met . . . uh . . . ah . . ."

"At Doc Dewey's funeral reception," Louise replied with a diffident smile. "I poured."

The senior Doc Dewey had died of cancer the previous month. His funeral had been held right after Thanksgiving. Less than two weeks had passed. I felt like a fool. I couldn't believe Louise Nyquist could be so forgettable. I must be having a memory lapse.

"Everyone was so upset about poor Doc," Louise murmured, as if excusing me for my obvious gaffe. "If it isn't one thing, it's another."

I'm never sure how to respond to that particular cliché, especially since I've never figured out exactly what it means. I gave Louise a weak smile and turned to Arnie, who was all but tapping his foot in his impatience to move on.

"Any luck with the sheriff?" I asked brightly. "We'll be running your complaint in the weekly log. You don't happen to have a description of the guy who's been lurking around Travis's house, do you?"

Arnie Nyquist bristled. "Ask Travis. I got problems of my own."

Louise was obviously embarrassed by her husband's manner, and not, I figured, for the first time. She patted his arm and gave me an apologetic smile. "Arnie is so upset by all these incidents, and who can blame him? Really, there's not much to say about this person, whoever he may be. Very ordinary: medium height, stocky, a working man, mid-thirties, perhaps."

Arnie looked fit to spit. "Mid-thirties! How the hell could Travis or Bridget figure that out? They've only seen him two or three times, and never up close. What a bunch of bunk!"

Surprisingly, Louise Nyquist held her ground. "By the way he moved. Or so Bridget told me. And he wore workmen's clothes, like a logger or a millworker. That's not much help, I know."

She was right. In Alpine, that description could fit at least two hundred men. Not wanting to further annoy Arnie, who would probably take his anger out on his wife, I wished them a pleasant shopping trip and made my exit from Barton's Bootery. Arnie didn't exactly heave a sigh of relief, but he did relax a little. Louise, however, looked as if she was sorry to see me go. As I headed for SportsWearWorld, I wondered why.

Ninety minutes and two hundred dollars later, I was loaded down with parcels and heading back to the Jag. Two sweaters for Adam, a lightweight jacket for Ben, the slippers for Vida, and, as an afterthought, a little something for Milo. If, I reasoned, he was coming for Christmas dinner, I ought to have a token gift for him under the tree. I opted for a trio of alder-smoked sockeye salmon, rainbow trout, and kippered king salmon, then added a bag of Ethiopian coffee beans. I was at the Jag when I suddenly thought about Teresa McHale. Would she be alone at the rectory for Christmas dinner? It was possible that Father Fitz would be out of the hospital by then. As the snow drifted around my inert figure, I debated the matter: Teresa had been in town for about a year and should have made some friends among the parishioners. If memory served, this would be Teresa's second Christmas at St. Mildred's. But Alpine was slow to accept newcomers. On the other hand, surely someone in the parish would remember what Christmas was really all about and take her in. I decided to bide my time. Ben would find out about Teresa's plans, if any.

I was at the arterial on Alpine Way when I realized that the one person I hadn't bought anything for was *me*. If Milo and I were going to dinner at King Olav's Saturday night, it would be nice to have a new dress. It was after four o'clock and already quite dark. I hadn't planned on going back to the office, but Francine's Fine Apparel was only two blocks away, across Front Street. I parked the car in my usual slot and cautiously walked over to Francine's. Even though the main byways had been sanded that morning and rock salt had been put down on the sidewalks, the below-freezing temperatures and the new snowfall made footing hazardous.

The apparel shop was deserted, except for the owner and one customer I recognized as Roseanna Bayard, wife of Buddy Bayard, the photographer we use for our darkroom work. Like Francine, the Bayards were fellow parishoners. Roseanna greeted me with a friendly wave.

"I *love* your brother," she declared, her wide-set blue eyes dancing. Roseanna was an enthusiast, a grown-up Carla, but intelligent and well-grounded. When she wasn't helping Buddy run the photography studio, she tutored children with reading disabilities. Roseanna was a tall woman, rather rangy, with short blonde hair and incongruous dimples. "Not that I don't think the world of Father Fitz, but let's face it: he's been gaga for years. I don't care what that old bat up in the rectory says, it's great to have a priest who's got all his marbles."

My proud smile endorsed my brother. But I had to ask Roseanna about the old bat. "You mean Mrs. McHale? What's she got against Ben?"

Roseanna sniffed. "She's a typical parish housekeeper. Remember Mrs. McPhail? She thought *she* ran the church, and Father Fitz along with it. That's why those women take those jobs. They're on a power trip."

Francine Wells's carefully plucked eyebrows arched. "That's true, Roseanna," Francine said in her amiable retail manner. "They don't have a vocation, but they want to be involved with the Church. So they become housekeepers. What do you think?" She held up two tweed skirts, one in soft tones of heather, the other in creamy browns.

Roseanna seemed caught off-guard. I'd watched Francine in action before and knew some of her tactics. This one involved forcing a customer to choose between two garments, rather than rejecting a single item out of hand. It was a trap, and both owner and customer knew it. But like most women, Roseanna would prefer to have than have not. She merely needed a little coaxing.

"The heather," she said, giving me a rueful smile. "I haven't a thing to go with it. Now Francine will sell me a new sweater, a blouse, and some damned scarf I'll never take out of the drawer."

We all laughed, but Francine was shaking her head.

"No, I won't. I'll wait for Buddy to come in here looking hopelessly baffled. Then I'll whip out the blouse and the sweater. Buddy will practically kiss my feet in gratitude, and you'll end up with something you really want for Christmas. Your kids can give you the damned scarf.''

We laughed some more. After Roseanna had gone out into the dark late afternoon, I told Francine what I was looking for. She led me not to the rack of moderately priced dresses, but back up front to the display window where three mannequins stood on a sparkling snow-covered floor and huge crystal snowflakes were suspended from almost-invisible wires.

''The dark green is you, Emma. You've got a nice figure and it will emphasize your height.''

I gazed at the green wool crepe with its surplice bodice and gently draped waistline. In my head, I also translated Francine's comments: *Your bust's okay, your hips aren't bad, you don't have much of a waist, and you're kind of short. This dress will make for good camouflage.*

''I'll try it on,'' I said, ''but I hate to have you wreck your window display.''

Francine was already heading for the back room. ''That's an eight. I've got a ten out here. I was saving it for Dr. Starr's wife, but she didn't think the color looked right on her. She got purple silk instead.''

The last words were spoken from behind a mauve velvet curtain. I looked around the shop, marveling as always that Francine could make a go of it in Alpine. Her clothes were in what retailers laughingly call the *moderately priced* designer range, which meant that anything under a hundred bucks could be found only on the clearance sale rack. Vida once told me that Francine had made out like a bandit ten years earlier when she'd divorced her alcoholic attorney husband from Seattle. Apparently, she had taken the money and run—back to her hometown of Alpine, where she'd opened Francine's Fine Apparel. It was the only store within sixty miles where a woman could buy clothes that didn't look as if they were designed primarily for spilling beer down your front at the bowling alley. Despite the dearth of customers on this dark December afternoon, Francine obviously did enough business not only to keep going, but to make a profit.

"Roseanna Bayard's off-line, of course," Francine announced as she emerged from the back room. She held the green wool crepe up for my inspection, not unlike a wine steward proffering a bottle of champagne. I wondered if I should ask to sniff the sleeve.

"About what?" I finally inquired, coming out of my shopper's daze.

"Teresa McHale. I don't think she's spent her life as a parish housekeeper. She applied for a job here first."

I'd already stepped inside one of the two small dressing rooms. They were also curtained off by velvet draperies. "She did? You mean after she moved here?"

"No, before that." Francine's voice was slightly muffled by the curtain. "She'd worked at a couple of apparel stores in Seattle. Nordstrom's, I think, and then some place in the Westlake Center. But I don't need anybody full-time. Gerry Runkel fills in whenever I have to be out of here."

Geraldine Runkel was one of Vida's numerous in-laws. She was married to Everett, Vida's husband's youngest brother. Or so I recalled from the complicated and extensive Runkel-Blatt family tree.

I stood back a few paces. More than my bangs needed a trim; I realized I was at least two weeks overdue on a haircut. Most of my makeup had worn off during the course of the day and the harshness of the elements. Still, I looked good in the dress. Or did the dress look good on me? I peered at the price tag: Francine's dollar amounts were always printed in round numbers and so smashed together that it practically took a magnifying glass to decipher them. Two hundred and fifty dollars, the tag read. I gulped, and visualized my rapidly sinking checking account balance.

"Let's see," Francine called.

Dutifully, I walked out of the dressing room. Francine beamed at me. "I was right. What a difference—Carrie Starr couldn't handle that color. It's great with your brown eyes and that almost-olive complexion. Here, Emma, let me show you something.'' Francine dashed over to the display case where the cash register was located. She whipped out a single strand of pearls set with random dark green oval beads. ''Put this on. There are earrings to match. It's going to be dynamite.''

It was. I guess. In fact, after I left Francine's Fine Apparel, I felt as if I'd been blown up by a ton of TNT. The dress, necklace, and earrings had set me back three hundred and forty-seven bucks, sales tax included. I'd had to use my bank card.

As I drove home through the swirling snow, all I could think was *Did I do this for Milo*? The answer was *No*. I'd done it for me.

And, just in case he might show up over the holidays, I'd done it for Tom Cavanaugh. It occurred to me that if Alpine had a contest for the Christmas Fool, I could win it hands-down.

Chapter Eight

Vida arrived ahead of Oscar Nyquist, stamping snow off her buckled boots and shaking out a long plaid muffler. Her black hat looked like the sort that Italian country priests are supposed to wear, but in this informal, global era, I suspect they lean toward Mets baseball caps.

"You didn't come back to the office," she said accusingly.

"I didn't say I would," I countered, taking her coat.

"I thought you might want to check in with Milo." She plopped down on the sofa and gazed around my living room. "Now this looks very nice," she said approvingly. "Why is there a camel on your Nativity stable's roof?"

I stared at my cherished set. Sure enough, the standing camel, as opposed to the other two which were seated, appeared to be stalking across the stable. "Ben," I muttered. "He must have come by to get the rest of his stuff. The camels don't go up until this weekend." I whisked the little figure away, putting it back in the desk drawer.

"Milo didn't call," Vida remarked, apparently willing to excuse me for my truancy.

"He probably won't know anything until tomorrow," I said, going out into the kitchen to fetch us an eggnog. "Rum or not?"

"Half milk," Vida called back, and I winced. I like my eggnog pure and simply fattening. I only put liquor in it when I figure I need to cut my cholesterol count. Happily, I rarely gain weight. I have too much nervous energy.

I told Vida about my encounter at the mall with Arnie and Louise Nyquist. Vida was mildly interested in Louise's description of the so-called lurker. She had been more intrigued by Milo's suggestion that Bridget knew the man's identity.

I was putting another slab of wood on the fire when Oscar Nyquist arrived. He looked like a snowman, having walked—uphill—the six blocks from his home on Cedar Street. Snow was caked to his overcoat, his stocking cap, his boots. I practically had to pry him loose from his outerwear. Yet at eighty-two, he seemed none the worse for his exertion.

"I been here all my life," he said, easing into the beige armchair. His voice bounced off the walls, but he wasn't operating at full bellow. "You get used to the snow. The rain, too. The weather's good for the movie business." He nodded sagely, as if he'd invented the climate.

"Good," Vida retorted. "We're going to talk about just that in a minute. Meanwhile, tell us about this pest and what's worrying you."

Oscar squinted at Vida. "You think I'm nuts?"

"Of course I do. Most people are." Vida sounded impatient. "But why are you so concerned about your granddaughter-in-law?"

Oscar didn't respond immediately, but gazed into the flickering flames and barely seemed aware that I was shoving an eggnog at him. Absently, he took the mug and sipped. I'd laced it lightly with both rum and milk. I had a feeling that Oscar Nyquist could have drunk Drāno and had neither a reaction nor a complaint.

"She's an odd girl," he finally said. "Different. Maybe that's because she comes from the city." His gaze lighted briefly on me, as if I, too, might be pretty odd. "She's up, she's down. You never know. She seemed so scared the other day, then she's happy as can be. I figure it's this fellow, hanging around and making her nervous. He can't mean any good."

It was time for me, the official interviewer, to speak up. "Has Bridget expressed a fear of this man?"

Oscar's bald head tipped to one side. It seemed that he never answered any questions impulsively. "Not outright. But she's scared. No doubt about it. When she isn't being happy, she acts like she's scared to death."

Scared to death. Vida and I exchanged swift glances. Two young women, approximately Bridget Nyquist's age, were already dead. Was there a connection? If Carol Neal was missing and Bridget knew it, she had a right to be scared. To death.

But her erratic behavior was strange. I kept thinking of Milo's explanation. "Do you think Bridget has any idea who this person is?" I asked, hoping to sound casual.

Oscar shook his head. "Why should she?"

I was sitting on the sofa next to Vida. I leaned forward, trying to gauge how far I could go without riling Oscar. "Travis said Bridget didn't want you to talk about this. Why? Is she embarrassed?"

Oscar made a stabbing movement with his right hand. "Nyaaah! She's silly! She's a kid, she still thinks everybody's decent! She's a city girl, she ought to know better." His voice dropped to a rumble.

"You should give Sheriff Dodge a description," Vida said crisply. "You and Arnie may not think much of Milo, but most people agree he's a good lawman. It seems to me you're making a mountain out of a molehill with all these petty complaints, and in the meantime, ignoring the mole. The deputies cruise around town all the time. They should know who to be on the lookout for."

Oscar all but sneered. "I did tell them, this afternoon. Tall, skinny fellow, young. Big jacket, jeans. Maybe jeans; I forget. Bridget told me."

I gave Oscar a skeptical look. "But told you not to tell?"

Oscar's chin jutted like the prow of a Viking ship. " 'Don't bother, Popsy,' " he mimicked in a girlish voice. " 'This is such a little town. What else do people have to do but look in other people's windows?' Pah!''

Bridget wasn't entirely wrong. Since moving to Alpine, I'd gone on a few evening strolls with Vida. While I admired the sunset or commented on the gardens, Vida's eyes fixated on windows. Her usual long-legged stride always slowed when we came upon a house where the drapes hadn't been pulled. ''Daleys—new picture above the mantel, a Maxfield Parrish,'' she'd murmur. Or, ''Eversons have company—out-of-town plates. Seattle, I'd guess.'' She didn't consider it snooping, merely doing her job of keeping up with the local news. I suspected that a lot of Alpiners did the same, but weren't in a position to give their curiosity such a noble name.

Again, I glanced at Vida. She was frowning into her egg-nog. ''This is all very vague. I hope Bridget uses good sense. If you're worried about her, it's up to her to see to her own safety.''

With a grimace, Oscar nodded. I felt it was time to make some sort of professional commitment. He had trudged through the snow to unburden himself and not received much in return.

''I'll tell you what,'' I said, darting a quick glance at Vida. ''We're going to do an article on the Marmot. If we slant it so that it's as much of a family story as it is about the theatre, then we can work in some of the problems you and Arnie have had with vandalism and such.''

I couldn't tell if Oscar Nyquist was alarmed or mollified. Something sparked in his blue eyes, but his only verbal response was a grunt. Vida was regarding me with a vexed expression. I knew she thought I was compromising myself.

''We'll need photos,'' she said, and it was my turn to feel a sense of relief. ''Old ones, as well as new ones. We have some, but yours might be better.''

Oscar nodded again, this time with more assurance. ''In the basement. At the Marmot. Come by tomorrow around nine. I can show you a lot of old stuff. If you're interested.''

Vida didn't respond, but I did. "That's wonderful," I enthused. "If I have time, I'll come with Vida. I like old movie mementos."

Now on his feet, Oscar gazed at me as if I were a bit lacking. "It's junk," he asserted. "We should have thrown it out a long time ago. But we didn't."

Visions of lobby cards from *Casablanca* and *Rebecca* and *Gone with the Wind* danced in my head. Publicity stills of Chaplin, Pickford, Gable. Souvenir programs from blockbusters such as *Ben-Hur, 2001: A Space Odyssey, The Godfather*. I am not a movie buff in the true sense, but I definitely appreciate the art form.

"What have you got?" Vida asked dryly. "W. C. Fields's false teeth?"

Oscar Nyquist took Vida seriously, but at least his denseness averted bloodshed. It was probably a blessing that I intended to visit the Marmot the next morning. My House & Home editor's lack of respect for the movies and their local purveyor might land her—or him—into trouble.

I never thought to include myself in that equation. Foolish me.

There were compromises to be made. In the summer, a University of Washington professor had devised a plan to thin out or prune almost two million acres of ten- to thirty-year-old forests in Washington and Oregon. The process would not only increase quantity, but would also enhance quality. If the trees were not cut, their density would choke out animal life and create a sterile environment.

That was just one of the proposals I included in my editorial. Naturally, we had run the story when it first broke in *The Seattle Times*. The article had elicited enthusiasm—and criticism. While most Alpiners are pro-logging, there are quite a few people who have moved to town because they love the wilderness. They would just as soon melt every chain saw in the Pacific Northwest as prune a limb from an evergreen.

I typed away, trying to balance my editorial, while at the same time taking a stand. I noted that one of the problems was that the spotted owls were—and I phrased this more gently—screwing themselves by not screwing each other. The birds had resorted to miscegenation, mating with different owl species. While that might not be a bad method to resolve racial tensions among human beings, it wasn't good news for the owls.

"Ready?" Vida stood in my doorway, muffled to the eyebrows. It was two minutes to nine.

Out on Front Street, Oscar Nyquist was furiously shoveling the walk in front of the Marmot. The snow had finally stopped for a while, but during the night another eight inches had fallen on Alpine. Walking carefully over the frozen patches, Vida and I wished him a good morning.

"What's good about it?" demanded Oscar, a big scowl showing under his stocking cap. He waved the shovel up at the marquee. "See that? More mischief!"

It took some effort not to laugh or even smile. The letters of *It's A Wonderful Life* had been rearranged to read *Saw One IUD Triffle*. Vida, however, was up for the occasion.

"I like it," she said. "It might be a science fiction movie about birth control."

Oscar looked mystified. "What's a triffle? What's IUD? Is it like Averill Fairbanks and his goddamned UFOs?"

It was now Vida's turn to hold back a smirk. "Well—not exactly." She gave me a puckish glance. "Let's say that it certainly beats rhythm, which is the Catholic version of science-fiction birth control. Speaking of which," Vida went on as I raised my eyebrows, "was that what Arnie found at the bowling alley site? Birth-control devices?"

Oscar Nyquist looked shocked. He was of a generation and a disposition that did not discuss such matters, especially between the sexes. Vida's frankness embarrassed him.

"Nyaaah," he replied, shaking out rock salt in an almost frantic manner. "It was clothes, women's clothes. A sweater. Slacks. Shoes. Underwear." He mentioned the last item as if he shouldn't know that women wore underwear. "Come inside, see the pictures."

The exterior was not what I'd call typical Alpine architecture. While less flamboyant and much smaller than many of its urban kin, the Marmot's turrets and dome were nonetheless more evocative of the Middle East than the Central Cascades. For all the grief it was causing Oscar, the marquee was a handsome affair, running across the front of the theatre and set off with row upon row of lights. The double-deck *Whistling Marmot* sign stood above the marquee proper, with a carved stone marmot at each side, like bookends.

In the lobby, Oscar flipped some switches, flooding the area with light. The concession stand had been modernized, but the Middle Eastern/art deco interior had been left mercifully intact. A wide, green carpeted staircase swept up to the auditorium, giving an illusion of vastness, despite the fact that there were a mere six steps in the ascent. Briskly, Oscar led us into the empty auditorium, down the wide aisles, and past the comparatively modern seats that had been installed in the 1960s and reupholstered two years ago. I glanced back at the balcony and the darkened projection booth. The frieze that ringed the ceiling showed a series of whistling marmots—running, jumping, sitting. On the walls, scatterings of silver specks set off dark green, three-dimensional scallop patterns, giving an impression of trees clustered in the rain. The recessed sounding board in the high arch of ceiling above the stage was dappled with silver stars and snowflakes, buffeted by the west wind at one side, caught by a crescent moon on the other. The chandelier that depended from the ceiling held tiers of petal-shaped lamps. Metallic scallops ringed the stage with its heavy midnight blue curtains edged with silver bars. I appreciated the decor anew, realizing that if Lars Nyquist wasn't blessed with artistic taste, he'd had enough sense to hire someone who was. And Oscar Nyquist hadn't been tempted to modernize. The Whistling Marmot was a little gem of a theatre, a reminder of the days when the movies not only had faces, but places in which to show them.

We went out through the exit at the left of the stage, then down a flight of stairs. The air immediately turned damp and musty. Oscar turned on more lights, revealing an awesome hodgepodge of equipment, storage boxes, and just plain junk. The heating system was on our right; the old prop room used in the days of vaudeville lay dead ahead. Dressing rooms, or more precisely a changing area with a divider for males and females, could be entered by edging around a stack of discarded theatre seats, a life-sized pasteboard cutout of a zebra, a bear suit, half a dozen buckets of paint, and a large wooden barrel filled with film cans.

I paused by the barrel. "Are these old movies?" I asked, pointing to the big tins.

Oscar, who was clearing a path for us through the debris, looked over his shoulder. "Nyaaah. When I was a kid, my father would save any extra cans for my mother. She stored cookies in them. At Christmas, she baked so many that she gave them away, wrapped in those tins. Now, we keep little stuff in 'em." He lifted the top tin out of the barrel and pried up the lid. Nuts, bolts, screws, rubber bands, and paper clips rested inside. "It's the barrel I like best. In the old days, my father kept it outside the social hall, where he first showed the movies. It'd fill up with rain water. Sometimes the fellas would come by after they'd been fishing and throw their trout in there to keep while they went to the movies. 'Course, during the winter, the water would freeze. One year, after the thaw, we found a ten-inch rainbow in there. It was still alive, swimming like crazy."

Vida apparently had heard the story before, but I exclaimed and laughed. Oscar, however, didn't seem to find the anecdote all that remarkable. It was merely part of Alpine's lore, neither unusual nor amusing.

Inside what was the real storage room, we were confronted with stacks of boxes, trunks, and grocery bags as well as shelves piled high with notebooks, ledgers, and files. Oscar scanned the boxes, finally choosing a battered cardboard container that had once held Crisco. A smiling half-moon and stars looked vaguely familiar, a logo I had seen in my childhood or perhaps in old magazines.

"Here," he said, opening the top, which was secured with ancient tape that had lost its glue. "You'll find the pictures of the old social hall in there, then the ones while the theatre was a-building. Opening night, too, with Carl and Mrs. Clemans and a bunch of other old-timers who were the guests of honor."

Vida, who knew *The Advocate*'s morgue far better than I did, took over. The pictures were all in albums, black imitation leather with tasseled cords. But like the tape that had held the box together, the hinges had come unglued, causing many of the photos to fall out of place. Flipping through them quickly, Vida selected five.

"I've never seen these," she said, holding up an eight-by-ten sepia print documenting the early stages of the Marmot's construction. In the background, I could see the original Methodist Church, so new that its wooden spire was still surrounded by scaffolding. At the edge of the photo, another structure was just getting underway. It was the Clemans Building, I realized, which stood directly across the street from *The Advocate*.

"What was on the site of the newspaper office then?" Oddly enough, I'd never asked Vida—or anyone else—that question.

Oscar's endless forehead furrowed. "The Dawsons' house. Mr. Dawson worked in the mill. He liked to act. Sometimes the townspeople put on plays, first in the social hall, then here. Mr. Dawson especially liked to play bums. His brother-in-law, Mr. Murphy, was a wonderful singer. One of them Irish tenor fellas."

I nodded, gazing at the photo, thinking about Alpine's early residents with their propensity for hard work and their proclivity for home-grown entertainment. Except for Lars Nyquist and his movies, what else was there to do, particularly during those long winters? There were no radios, no TV, no electric lights in that first decade of Alpine's existence. If Alpiners wanted to be amused, they had to amuse themselves. Obviously, they did.

We left Oscar to fix his marquee. But Vida wasn't inclined to return to the office. Rather, she stood at the curb, her attitude alert.

"Travis," she said, nodding her padre's hat in the direction of the Venison Inn. "That's him at a window table with Rick Erlandson. You know, Rick, with the orange sideburns, at the bank? Travis and Rick went to high school together."

"So?" I replied, trying to match Vida's long strides across the sanded street. "Is Rick a lurker?"

"Of course not," huffed Vida. "He's a most respectable young man, even if he does have comical hair. Especially for a loan officer. The point is, Travis is over there, and not at home. Let's go see Bridget." She pounced on my car. "Come on, come on. What are you waiting for?"

It took less than five minutes to drive from *The Advocate* to The Pines, otherwise known as Stump Hill. The gracious homes that nestled among the evergreens were situated between the mall and the ski lodge, with Burl Creek running through the west end of the property. Colonial, Tudor, Spanish, and Cape Cod architecture, all with a Pacific Northwest twist, somehow managed to avoid aesthetic conflict. Maybe it was the half-acre on which each house stood; maybe it was the buffer of tall trees; maybe it was the hilly ground that permitted the homes to sit on different levels. Whatever it was, it worked—and Arnie Nyquist had been responsible. It occurred to me that Tinker Toy wasn't a complete dunce.

We didn't attempt to get up the steep drive, but parked behind a PUD truck across the street coyly known as Whis-

pering Pines Drive. Even with the chains, I'd had a bit of
trouble negotiating the narrow road through the development. Residents of The Pines neither sanded nor shoveled.
Maybe it meant they all had four-wheel drive. Or that they
didn't have to worry about getting to work. They were too
well-heeled to care.

Travis and Bridget's Cape Cod looked picture-perfect in
the snowy landscape. The firs that had been left standing
formed a semicircle around the house, as if cradling it in
their snow-covered branches. Off to one side of the sloping
front lawn, a single old cottonwood lifted angular limbs up
to the sky. Lower down, someone had hung out suet for the
birds. A huge silver wreath with a bright red bow clung to
the front door, while a matching garland wound its way up
the mailbox post. The two front windows, presumably in the
living room, sported smaller versions of the front door
wreath. The younger Nyquists' home could have posed for a
Christmas card.

And Bridget could have posed for *Playboy*, I thought nas-
tily, as she warily opened the front door and revealed just
about everything in a skintight plum-colored leotard.

"I'm exercising," she said, somehow managing to beat
Vida to the verbal punch. "Excuse me." She started to close
the door.

Vida was not to be bested. Sticking her galosh inside the
door, she managed to kick it open. "Now, Bridget, you don't
want us to go away mad, do you?"

Bridget pouted. "I just want you to go away. I've got a
video running."

Vida barged right in. "We'll wait."

Bridget glared at both of us. "You're trespassing. I'll call
the sheriff."

"Fine," Vida replied, taking in the handsomely appointed
living room with its French country accents. Pickled pine
finishes, woven rush chairs, delicately painted wood, and
wrought iron proved that money could buy class. I wondered

who had chosen the furnishings. Not Bridget, I fancied. Maybe she and Travis had hired a decorator.

The TV, which was encased in a beautiful armoire, did indeed show a vigorous young woman leading an equally vigorous group of enthusiasts in an exercise routine. Such displays make me queasy.

"Well?" demanded Vida, looking over the rims of her glasses at Bridget. "Are you going to call Milo or just stand there and perspire?"

Bridget shot Vida a rebellious look, but marched over to the TV and shut the set off. "What do you want? I told you, I'd rather not be written up in your paper."

"We don't intend to," Vida responded, admiring the painted faux marble walls. "We're doing a big piece on the Marmot. And we're curious how it has affected your life as a Nyquist." Vida never took notes; her memory was prodigious.

"The Marmot?" Bridget wore a baffled expression. "What do you mean, *affected* my life? I've seen some movies there. So what?"

"So it's the original family business," Vida said, tilting her head to one side. "The theatre, along with your father-in-law's construction business, has helped pay for all this." Vida waved a hand, taking in the living room, and presumably the entire house.

"No, it didn't." Bridget had turned smug. "Travis paid for all this. He made a fortune in the stock market."

I wasn't sure why Vida had been so insistent about calling on Bridget Nyquist. It was too soon to ask Bridget about Carol Neal. There was no point until the dead woman was identified—or Carol turned up missing. This particular line of inquiry on Vida's part baffled me. So did Bridget's attitude. Her initial hostility had dwindled into inertia.

"How did he do that?" Vida inquired, now moving to the mantel, where half a dozen gilded cherubs dangled from a golden holly garland.

Bridget blinked, then looked vague. "Stocks. Bonds. You know—investments." She shrugged, muscles and curves rippling under her leotard.

"My, my." Vida chucked one of the cherubs under the chin. "How clever. Did all his clients get rich, too?"

"Of course." Bridget's jaw was thrust out.

So was Vida's bust under the tweed coat. She had deftly moved across the living room's flagstone floor to stand directly in front of Bridget. "And his partners? Which brokerage house was it, Bridget? My nephew works in one of them. Piper something-or-other, I think."

I'd never heard of Vida's nephew the Stockbroker, but that didn't mean he didn't exist. Given her extended family, Merrill, Lynch, Pierce, Fenner & Smith might all be related to the Runkels or the Blatts.

Bridget fingered an arrangement of pine and cedar boughs in a terra-cotta container. "Sampson. Or Frampton. I forget. Travis had already quit when we got engaged." Bridget didn't look at either one of us.

The names meant nothing to me. But I hadn't lived in Seattle for years. And even if Bridget was referring to a national firm, I'd never been in a position to get cozy with brokers. If they didn't advertise on network TV, I probably wouldn't have heard of them.

Vida pushed her glasses back up on her nose. "Cramden's?" she offered. "Very reputable, old-line Seattle."

"That's it." Bridget nodded energetically.

"Very good." Vida started for the entry hall. I trailed along, feeling about as useless as Rudolph without his red nose. "You like movies?" She threw the question at Bridget over her shoulder.

"Sure," Bridget replied, coming along behind me. "Popsy gives us free passes."

"I should think so," murmured Vida. "By the way, have you seen that pest lurking around lately?"

Bridget almost ran into me as I stopped next to Vida on

the threshold. "The pest? You mean that guy? No. That is, not this week."

Vida's eyes were keen as she peered at Bridget. "What did he look like?"

Bridget shifted from foot to foot. "I'm . . . not sure. Ordinary, I guess. It was always dark. And snowing," she added hastily. "He was just a form."

"Of course he was." Vida started down the front steps, which had been swept clean of snow. "Thank you, Bridget. Generally speaking, you were courteous."

We had started down the walk, which had also been cleared. "You should have pulled into the driveway," Bridget called after us. "The Amundsons across the street have been having trouble getting their car out with that PUD truck parked there."

I decided it was finally time for me to stop acting as if I were Vida's mute stooge. "Did you lose power out here the other day?"

Bridget shook her head. "No. We were lucky. G'bye." She closed the door before we got to the Jag.

"Liar, liar, pants on fire," muttered Vida as I turned on the ignition.

"What?"

"Bridget." Vida was resettling her hat. "There's no such investment house as Cramden's."

I gave Vida a sly smile. "Well, well. And there's no such thing as a PUD truck parked where there isn't any problem."

Vida gave a faint nod. "It's been an interesting visit."

"So it has." I steered the Jag carefully down the little hill that led away from The Pines. "But to what purpose?"

Vida made a face. "I wish I knew."

So did I.

Chapter Nine

CAROL NEAL HAD disappeared. According to Milo, she wasn't missing; she had merely dropped out of sight.

"There was a forwarding address after she moved out of the apartment on Fifteenth Northeast in the University District," he explained over the phone. "It was for another apartment just a few blocks away, on Eleventh. But my Seattle source tells me she hasn't lived there for the past two years."

"What about a work address?" I asked, looking up at Vida and shaking my head.

But Milo hadn't dug that deep yet. His theory was that Carol had probably moved in with a roommate, male or female, which might account for the lack of more forwarding addresses. "Let's say she had another girl living with her on Eleventh, then they moved together but put the new address in the other girl's name. Maybe Carol was avoiding her creditors. Or escaping from some guy who'd made a pest of himself."

"What about parents? Relatives? Friends?" I was unwilling to let go of the possibility that the dead girl was Carol Neal.

"We're checking on it," replied Milo at his most laconic. "We need someone to ID her, after all."

I almost suggested that Milo ask Bridget. But that was a ghoulish idea. The victim might turn out to be a stranger. Why put Bridget Nyquist through such an ordeal?

"The thing is," Milo continued, "if this is Carol and Carol had a roommate, why hasn't said roommate reported her missing? It's probable that she's been dead for almost a week."

"Maybe she can't," I replied with another glance at Vida. "Maybe the roommate is dead, too."

Evan Singer lived in a cabin two miles out of town off the Burl Creek Road. I decided against maneuvering the Jag up his winding, snow-covered drive and parked in a small turn-out some fifty yards down the road. Although it had stopped snowing, the gray clouds hung low, almost touching the tree-tops. The temperature seemed stuck in the mid-twenties.

Cabin was probably too extravagant a term for Evan's dwelling. The one-story frame shack might have been a sum-mer retreat at one time, or more likely a hermit's lair. Tar paper stuck out from under the uneven cedar shakes, the tin chimney was crooked despite being wired to the roof, and several panes of glass in the two front windows were pock-marked with BB pellets and bullets from a .22.

Evan Singer met me at the door, standing on the top step that also made up the entire front porch. He was wearing a loosely woven slate-gray sweater, paint-stained khaki pants, and workmen's shoes, laced halfway up his calf. A bandanna was tied around his red-gold hair. The reek of marijuana wafted from the cabin.

"This is truly remarkable," he announced, ushering me inside. "Everyone gets to be famous for ten minutes, right?"

"Something like that," I replied, taking in the single room that made up the entire cabin. Happily, the interior was an improvement over the exterior. A Franklin stove stood in one corner and a Christmas tree in the other. Several sketches and a movie poster for *Patriot Games* were held up by thumbtacks on the unfinished walls. There were candles ev-erywhere, including on the tree. The shapes were both exotic and erotic, no doubt fashioned by Evan himself. He had clearly put his stamp on this ramshackle old place, and I marveled at his hardiness. A Murphy bed was folded into the far wall. There was an icebox and a sink but no pipes for running water. Two Coleman lanterns hung from nails, but only one of them was lit. It was extremely cold, and I wondered how Evan kept from freezing to death at night.

"Have a seat," he urged, pulling out one of the three chairs that circled a small wooden table. "This is amazing. Why me?"

For the first time, I took in Evan himself. He was probably in his late twenties, with an angular face and a few freckles. His nose was slightly hooked, his blue eyes seemed to be in constant motion, and his entire lanky body appeared to be charged with a set of powerful batteries. I couldn't tell if he was nervous, exhilarated, high or merely wound too tight.

"You're new in town," I said, getting out my notebook. Unlike Vida's, my memory is flawed. "Our subscribers like to read about newcomers. They're always particularly interested in why anyone would exchange city life for a small town. I suppose they want their own attitudes reinforced."

Evan, who had been drumming his long, thin fingers on the knotty pine tabletop, stopped. "Is this like *The Visit*? You know, the movie that Anthony Quinn and Ingrid Bergman starred in? Am I going to die?" The question seemed rhetorical, but given recent events in Alpine, I wasn't about to make false promises. Evan apparently didn't want any; he didn't wait for an answer. "You know where I'm from? How?"

"How?" I tried to gauge his expression. Alarm? Pleasure? Curiosity? I hadn't the foggiest notion. That constant motion of the eyes made it difficult to read Evan Singer. "Somebody told me, I guess. Henry Bardeen?"

"Oh, Henry." Evan rolled his blue eyes. "Henry's a case, huh? People like him can never die."

"Really." I waited for Evan to explain.

"That's right. They've never lived. So how can they die?" He gave the table a light tap with his fist and grinned at me.

I couldn't disagree completely with Evan Singer's assessment of the dour ski resort manager, but I felt a need to defend him all the same. "Henry has given you a job," I reminded Evan.

"Right! He's wonderful, he's caring-sharing-daring—and wearing. But up your nose, if you think he's got blood in his veins." Evan was still grinning and wagging a finger at me. The ill-fitting sweater slipped a notch in the sleeve, revealing a Rolex watch. I tried not to stare. "People always give me jobs," Evan went on blithely. "I can do a lot of things. I'm the stranger in their midst, like Alan Ladd in *Shane*. And if I've never done something before, I'm willing to try it. Ever skinned a snake?"

"Alas, no." It was time to gain control of the interview. "Where did you learn to drive a sleigh?"

Evan sobered and stared straight into my eyes. "Saudi Arabia." He waited for my startled reaction, got it, and burst out laughing, slapping his knee all the while. "Ha-ha! You almost believed me! Henry Bardeen did!"

I doubted it, but decided to forge ahead. "What do—"

"It's not driving a sleigh that takes any training," Evan interrupted, growing more serious. "It's the horses. I've worked at a couple of riding stables outside of Seattle. Tiger Mountain. You know it?"

I did, vaguely. In my youth, the area east of Lake Washington had been a sleepy Seattle suburb. But no more. Bellevue, Kirkland, Redmond, Issaquah, even North Bend were rapidly becoming congested, overdeveloped bedroom communities. For all I knew Tiger Mountain was laced with condominiums and shopping malls.

"You grew up on the Eastside, not Seattle?" I inquired.

Evan stomped on the floor with his workmen's shoes. "I grew up in the world. We moved a lot. Chicago. Paris. Cairo.

Philadelphia. Toronto. Rome.'' He shrugged, then grinned again and leaned across the table. ''But not . . . ?''

''Saudi Arabia?'' I tried to keep a grip on my patience.

''Right! Never been there. In this lifetime, anyway. I used to be a toad.''

And I used to be a newspaper reporter, I thought through gritted teeth. This interview was out of hand. Should I humor him? His fancies could make a sprightly feature. As long as he didn't sue me.

''When did you start to paint?'' I held my breath, dreading the answer.

But Evan had turned serious again, his jaw resting on one hand. ''I always made pictures. It runs in the family. The visual arts, that is. But it's not a career with me. You have to please too many other people, especially the ones with lots of money and absolutely no taste. I do what I do for myself.'' Jerkily, he pointed to a large sketch of a gnarled tree. An oak, maybe. Its bare branches appeared to shelter mistletoe, its twisted roots hunched into the earth. ''You see that? I call it 'Lost Love.' Stripped bare, yet still alive. Are you moved?''

''It's very forceful.'' That much was true. More to the point, I could tell what it was. I'm not a fan of abstract art. At least Evan Singer had painted a tree that looked like a tree.

''I make jewelry, candles, some sculpture. I can sing and I can dance. One summer, I was a mime at Lake Tahoe.'' He plucked at his upper lip, suddenly acquiring a brooding expression. ''It was a bad idea. Those holiday gamblers only care about this''—he made yanking motions with his right hand. ''I should have dressed up as a bowl of cherries. You know, like on the slot machines . . .''

I gave him a faint nod. I was well acquainted with cherries, as well as plums, lemons, watermelons, and Harold-in-a-barrel. There had been a gang of us at *The Oregonian* who had made an annual pilgrimage to Reno or Vegas. It wasn't any riskier than listening to advice from the paper's business editor.

I complimented Evan on being so versatile, trying to bring him around to his educational background. He was vague about high school, dismissing those years as "an abyss." College was another matter.

"I liked Reed," he remarked, referring to the somewhat unorthodox private school in Portland. "Stanford was okay, so was USC. And Pepperdine. But give me Baylor or give me death!" He rolled his eyes again.

"Is that where you got your degree?" My head was spinning from his whirlwind of higher education.

"Degree? *What* degree?" He laughed so hard that tears filled his eyes. I waited, not too patiently. Even in my heavy car coat, I felt chilly. If there was a fire going in the stove, I wasn't benefitting from it. But Evan Singer didn't seem to be suffering in the least. "A degree . . . is just a . . . waste of . . . paper," he said between gasps for breath. "What's . . . in a . . . diploma? All it says . . . is that you have completed the required courses as stated by a specific institution. Now what does that mean?" He had recovered himself and was gazing at me in an imploring fashion.

For me, it had meant a great deal, including my passport onto a daily newspaper. But it was pointless to argue with Evan Singer, who was probably a candidate for Averill Fairbanks's UFO collection.

I steeled myself for the final, and perhaps most important, question: "Why did you come to Alpine, Mr. Singer?"

His gaze traveled to the sketch of the gnarled oak. The long pause made me wonder if he'd ever considered his own actions. But of course he had. I waited some more, my eyes drifting to the Christmas tree with its eclectic ornaments. I'd noticed only the traditional glass balls and fantastic candles earlier. Now I saw some unusual objects dangling among the fir branches: an ivory skull and crossbones; a tiny, shiny pistol; a dagger with a carved hilt; a small Kewpie doll in a body cast. I had a fervent desire to get the hell out of Evan Singer's cabin.

Apparently, Evan wasn't quite as self-absorbed as he appeared. "You're admiring my ornaments?" he asked with a big smile. "You find them odd?"

"A bit." I tried to smile back.

He nodded sympathetically. "Of course. I'm not a Christian, you see. The original trees were a pagan rite. I put together the best of both worlds, though I belong to neither. Intriguing, huh?"

"Very." My voice was a little faint. "Now about your decision to . . ."

"Oh, yes." He sounded wistful. "Can't you see it?" He inclined his head toward the sketch.

"The tree?" I frowned at the picture. "There aren't any oak trees around here."

"That's not the point!" He seemed positively shattered by my response. Or perhaps he was disappointed in my lack of perception. "Consider that tree, in all its ramifications."

"I will," I promised, getting up a bit awkwardly. "I don't suppose you could give me a hint?"

Evan Singer had also stood up. He threw his hands high above his head. "A hint? It's all there! Everything! My whole life!"

"Yes," I agreed, making for the door. "Thank you so much."

It was just as well that I couldn't run through the snow. It would have been undignified. But I was ecstatic to reach my car. All but jumping inside, I locked the doors before I started the engine.

A glance in the rearview mirror showed no one in sight. Of course Evan Singer wouldn't follow me. He was nuttier than a Christmas fruitcake, but probably harmless. Then again . . .

I decided against asking him to paint my house. Photographs would be cheaper. And safer.

* * *

Milo Dodge was coming out of his office when I pulled up in front of the bakery in the block between *The Advocate* and the county sheriff's headquarters. My usual parking spot had been usurped, presumably by one of the holiday shoppers taking advantage of the lull in the weather. I paused to gaze at the display of Christmas confectionery, which, appropriately for Alpine, leaned toward Scandinavian delicacies: Berlinerkransar, fattigmand, sandbakkelse, spritskransar, yulekake, rosettes. The breads and cookies looked wonderful, but as an old family friend from Bergen, Norway, had once told my mother, "The bakery is well and good, but never like homemade." She might have been right, but The Upper Crust's offerings looked pretty tempting to me.

"Emma!" Milo called from the opposite curb. "Got a minute?"

I was debating between stuffing myself on Scandinavian goodies or going to the Burger Barn for something a shade more wholesome. It was well after one o'clock, and I was famished. Fleetingly, I wondered what Evan Singer cooked for himself. Bat wings and puppy dog tails came to mind.

"I need some grease," I said, gesturing across the street. The Burger Barn's roof exhibited a fake red brick chimney with a jolly Santa waving with the hand that didn't carry a packful of toys. "Have you eaten?"

Milo met me in the middle of the block, both of us jay-walking. A couple of cars, a flatbed truck, and a Jeep slowed to avoid running us down.

"Yeah, I had lunch with Sam and Jack," Milo replied, "but I wouldn't mind another cup of real coffee. Jack waters it down at work."

Milo also had pie—apple, with a wedge of cheddar cheese on the side. I dug into a burger, fries, and a small salad. Ben was coming to dinner again, but probably wouldn't make it until after seven. I didn't worry about spoiling my appetite.

"We got some background on Carol," Milo said after we'd been served and I'd finally wound down in my recital of the interview with Evan Singer. "Parents are divorced, mother remarried and living in the L.A. area, father somewhere in central Oregon, which is where he came from. Probably a rural type who never adjusted to the urban jungle, but I'm guessing. There was a brother, but he died when he was about ten, some kind of accident on a bicycle."

I looked up from my hamburger. "Where did you get all this? Did somebody clone Vida for the SPD?"

"Actually, it's out of the King County sheriff's office, but my contact got hold of a neighbor who still lives next door to the Neals' old house in Greenwood. That's close to Blanchet, right?"

"Sort of." Blanchet is just a few blocks from Green Lake. The neighborhood that bears its name borders on the Greenwood area in the north end of Seattle.

"Anyway," Milo went on between bites of cheese and pie, "the house was a rental. The Neals didn't have much money, but somehow they managed to send Carol to private school. By the time she was a junior, she had a nice car, expensive clothes, a fancy CD player that had a bass loud enough to cause earthquakes. Or so said the neighbor." Milo raised an eyebrow. "Interesting, huh?"

"Very. Did she have a job?"

"She did, at least for a while. In a place like this." He waved a big hand, taking in the Burger Barn with its rustic decor and paper cutout Christmas decorations.

"Hmmmm." I was gazing at a cardboard angel with blonde dreadlocks. "Minimum wage, probably. Not enough to buy nice cars and clothes and CD players."

"Not enough to *pay* for them," Milo noted. "Carol left home right after graduation. I gather that Dad left before that. Mom headed south a few months later."

"And?" I looked up expectantly.

"And nothing." But Milo was looking smug. "Except

this." He reached inside his heavy jacket, pulled out a piece of paper, and handed it to me.

I studied the words carefully. It was a faxed copy of a complaint, filed the previous day by Stefan Horthy, owner/ manager of the Villa Apartments. The complaint stated that Carol Neal and Kathleen Francich had defaulted on their rental agreement and vacated Unit #116 without giving proper notice. Horthy wished to confiscate their belongings, which had been left behind, to cover the outstanding monthly rent payment of $1,025. The damage deposit would not be refunded.

I looked at the address, which was on Capitol Hill, south of the University District and east of downtown Seattle. "When was the rent due, I wonder?"

Milo shrugged. "The first, I suppose. Why?"

"Because most apartment houses in Seattle—and Portland—ask for first and last months' rent, in addition to a damage deposit. It's only December twelfth. This Horthy is covered for the last month. His tenants must have owed for November, too." I pushed the complaint back at Milo. "More to the point, they left all their belongings. Doesn't that suggest they intended to come back?"

"Sure." Milo gave me a wry smile. "If you want to stretch it, you might say it suggests they were murdered. First Kathleen, then Carol." His expression turned bleak.

"Damn all," I breathed, though I'd already had a whiff of this particular fear. "Any chance to find out about Kathleen Francich?"

Milo shook his head. "No. I'm wondering if we should get Horthy up here to ID our victim."

It was better than my brief brainstorm to ask Bridget. I didn't know Stefan Horthy; I wouldn't feel any responsibility for him if he turned blue and passed out. "Did you learn where Carol worked?"

Again, Milo hadn't had the opportunity to make further inquiries. "Horthy should know. I'm afraid he's our pigeon.

We can't force him to come up to Alpine, but it would be in his best interests."

I agreed. Milo's revelations had driven Evan Singer into the shadows. As we paid our respective bills, I realized that I still had to write a feature article about the strange young man with his baggy sweater and Rolex watch. I hadn't the vaguest idea how to approach the story.

Indeed, I was still mulling over a lead when Ben called. To my mild dismay, he informed me that on an impulsive Christian whim, he had invited Teresa McHale to join us.

"What?" I yipped into the phone. "Shall I ask Milo? Is this a double date?"

"Listen, Sluggly," my brother admonished me, "you're the one who was thinking about having her over for Christmas dinner. This will let you off the hook. And me. Father Fitz either fasted a lot or didn't have a big appetite. Teresa's been cooking up a storm since I got here. She won't let me near the stove or the fridge or anything resembling a frying pan. You give Teresa a meal and finish up Advent with an extra star in your crown."

"Bull," I replied. But Ben was right: including Teresa was an act of charity. And possibly of endurance. I told him I'd pick up a small salmon at the Grocery Basket. "They've got some silvers in this week. Naturally, Ed Bronsky wanted to keep it a secret."

Vida was amused by my brother's invitation. She was also vaguely alarmed. "If I were you," she cautioned, "I'd drive over to the church and pick them up, then take them home. I don't trust that woman an inch."

"You don't know her." It was true: Teresa had kept herself to herself, as they say, at least as far as non-Catholics were concerned. For once, I had the upper hand with Vida.

"I've seen her around," Vida muttered, giving me her gimlet eye.

"So? She and Ben are all alone at the rectory. What's such a big deal about them driving back and forth to my house?"

Vida's eyes narrowed behind her big glasses. "Cars. They're always dangerous when it comes to sex. Cars liberated Americans, giving them an opportunity to become promiscuous. I'll bet you've never seen a rumble seat."

"Of course I have!" I countered. "Don't you remember the Classic Car Rally last June?"

Vida ignored the remark. She was pounding on her typewriter when my phone rang. It was Milo.

"Durwood's been found!" he announced, evincing more animation than was customary.

"Huh?" I'd forgotten that Durwood was lost. "Where was he?"

"He took Crazy Eights Neffel for a snowmobile ride up Mount Baldy. Crazy Eights hopped off halfway to the top and Durwood had to go looking for him. He found the old nut making snow angels and talking to a goat."

"Swell." I put the phone down. Durwood and the town loony weren't a news item. In Alpine, they were merely a way of life. As my father used to say, you can get used to anything, including hanging. After three years, I was obviously getting used to small-town ways.

Teresa McHale wore a gold charmeuse blouse with a black and gold wrap skirt and matching shawl. Her dyed red hair was carefully coiffed in a side part that curled just under her ears, her makeup was flawless, and at the door, she exchanged her sensible boots for a pair of sling platform pumps. She did indeed look as if she were on a date.

By contrast, Ben wore an Arizona State University sweatshirt over blue jeans and kept his boots on. I was determined to watch Teresa like a hawk. At the first coquettish glance, I fully intended to smack Teresa in the kisser with the silver salmon.

But as we chatted amiably through cocktails, Teresa McHale's demeanor was irreproachable. The hard edges I had observed earlier were now softened. Maybe it was the vodka. Or the sociability. Perhaps Teresa really did lead a lonely, isolated life as the parish housekeeper.

Still, there was a girlishness about her that struck a discordant note. Her ensemble was smart, perhaps expensive. It might have flattered a woman who was ten years younger and twenty pounds lighter. As it was, the shimmering gold and black made Teresa McHale look like a large Christmas bauble.

Up until we served dinner, Ben had dominated the conversation, not out of a desire to seek the limelight, but at Teresa's urging. He recalled his years on the Delta. His new life on the reservation. The three trips to Rome in two decades. The life and times of a priest in the home missions. Teresa never ran out of questions. I had to assume that she and Ben didn't talk much at the rectory.

"Father Fitz must know these people inside and out," Ben remarked after giving the blessing. "How long has he been at St. Mildred's?"

Teresa looked at me. I looked blank. "Years," I finally said. "Fifteen? Twenty?"

Teresa lifted one shawl-clad shoulder. "I guess so. Someone said there was no regular priest in Alpine before he came."

"Probably not," Ben said. "It would have been a mission church, served out of Monroe or even Everett."

"And will be again, I'm afraid." Teresa sighed over a forkful of salmon. "I doubt that he'll be back. At least as pastor. He can't possibly resume his duties."

Ben was slapping butter on his baked potato. "You may be right. Dr. Flake isn't too optimistic about the prognosis."

I hadn't thought beyond Ben's stay at St. Mildred's. It was so wonderful having him here in Alpine, with Adam due to join us shortly. I didn't want to look beyond the holidays to the New Year when I'd have to wave goodbye to both my brother and my son. Regrettably, Father Fitz hadn't been preying on my mind. It hadn't occurred to me that I might have seen the last of our pastor.

"He *is* up there," I commented, "and has certainly served the Church well. What will you do if he doesn't come back, Teresa?"

The housekeeper's green eyes avoided my gaze. "Oh—I don't know. I take one day at a time."

Ben had added sour cream, chives, and onion bits to the butter. His potato looked like Mount Baldy. "Have you considered going into pastoral administration?" he asked. "With the shortage of priests, parishes need more lay people to staff the rectory."

Teresa gave a sharp shake of her head, the red locks flipping this way and that. "No, that's not for me. Too much politics. It's hard enough being a housekeeper."

"There aren't a lot of jobs in Alpine just now," I noted. "The economy is bad everywhere, but especially in a logging town like this one."

Teresa's green eyes now met mine head-on. "As I said, I'm not going to worry about it. Something will come along." She gave Ben a smile that was more coy than coquettish. "We have to trust in the Lord, don't we, Father?"

Ben smiled back, albeit crookedly. "It makes more sense to trust in the Help Wanted columns."

I passed Teresa the bowl of buttered baby carrots. "I take it you want to stay in Alpine?"

Again, she avoided my eyes. "I like it here. It's a beautiful town." Then, as if she suddenly remembered railing against the rural life earlier, she continued on a more breathless note: "That is, the scenery is beautiful, even if there isn't much to do. But location can make up for a lot, isn't that so?"

Ben agreed, though he immediately launched into what evils could lurk behind the scenery in, say, Tuba City, Arizona. I'd already heard Ben talk about snakes and scorpions and small dinosaurs or whatever else crawled and slithered in the desert. My mind drifted, engaging itself in debate over whether or not to ask Teresa why she'd moved to Alpine in the first place. But I'd tried that once already that day, with Evan Singer, and received a wildly enigmatic answer. I decided to refrain from putting the same query to Teresa McHale.

My guests departed shortly after ten. It had been a pleasant enough evening, with the conversation turning again to Ben's adventures. Teresa had led him down the garden path with more questions, reserving a few for me regarding my newspaper background. But a full work day, dinner preparations, and playing hostess had drained me. I was not in top form as a *raconteuse*. It was only after Ben and Teresa had driven off in Father Fitz's Volvo that I stopped marveling over Teresa's interest in others and wondered if the truth was that she didn't want to talk about herself. Did Teresa have a dark secret in her past? It's amazing how many people do. Or *think* they do.

I was affixing an angel to the roof of my Nativity stable when I noticed that one of the shepherds was smoking a cigarette. Ben had rolled up a small piece of paper and taped it to the figure's mouth. Funny Ben. Naturally, I laughed. Not for the first time, I thought how essential a sense of humor was to Christian faith. Or to just plain getting through the days that spin out over a lifetime. While I giggled at my brother's puckish stunt, there were people suffering and dying out there in the winter landscape. There was nothing funny about that. But if I couldn't laugh, I couldn't live. It was that simple. I turned out the lights and went to bed.

Chapter Ten

"THE RENAISSANCE MAN has come to Alpine."

It was the worst kind of overstatement, but I couldn't think of any other way to write the story about Evan Singer. I spent Saturday morning working at home on my word processor, trying to fill a two-column by six-inch space about the bizarre young man with the erratic emotions and multifaceted personality. It was easy to make him sound interesting; it was damned hard to make him sound sane.

And I'd forgotten to take my camera. Ordinarily, I could send Carla to cover for me. When she remembered to use film and take off the lens cap, she was a better photographer than I was. But Carla wasn't keen on Evan Singer, so I decided to bring the camera to dinner at King Olav's. I could get a picture of Evan driving the sleigh up to the ski lodge.

The afternoon was devoted to cleaning house for Adam's arrival Monday. Not that my son would notice if I had a Dumpster parked in the living room, but it made me feel like a proper mother. I even ventured into my son's room, something I usually did only under duress or when certain odors threatened to drive me out of the house. He had left his belongings in no worse condition than I'd feared, which meant I could probably apply for Federal funds under the National Disaster Act.

At five o'clock, I emerged, feeling virtuous and weary. But the prospect of a good dinner and relaxed companionship buoyed me.

My companion, however, looked as if he'd been beset by Vandals and Huns. Or spent a week in Adam's room, pre-cleaning. Milo Dodge was far from his laconic self when he arrived on my front porch. His long face was far longer than usual, his sandy hair was disheveled under his ski hat, and his long mouth was set in a thin, angry line.

"I'm going to kill him," he announced, stalking into my living room.

I had been prepared to twirl about to show off my new green $250 dress. "Who?" I demanded, planting my feet firmly on the floor.

"Arnie Nyquist, that son of a bitch." Milo started for the Scotch, thought better of it, and turned around to jab a finger in my face. "Arnie's going around town saying you told old Oscar you were going to investigate me! What the hell is going on, Emma?"

I was abashed. "I told . . . Oh!" Enlightenment dawned. "Hold it, Milo. I told Oscar no such thing. Sit down, relax, take a break." I all but shoved Milo onto the sofa. Giving him a moment to collect himself, I lighted a pair of big red spiral candles on the mantel, turned on the CD player, and let Bing Crosby dream of a white Christmas.

"You may have one short Scotch," I announced, heading for the liquor cabinet that was actually part of a big bookcase. "You are a law enforcement official, though off-duty. I hate it when you have to arrest yourself."

Milo was now pouting. "I wasn't drunk the other night. Neither was Ben. We were just . . . upset."

Milo and Ben may not have been drunk, but they hadn't been exactly sober, either. I refused to argue the fine point. "Here," I said, shoving a Scotch and soda at Milo. "Oscar is muddled. I stalled him with a promise of an in-depth study of the sheriff's department. You know what that means—nothing. Then I placated him further by letting Vida do a story on the Whistling Marmot—and the Nyquists. If that doesn't make Oscar forget, then you'll have to pour him full of these.'' I hoisted my glass of bourbon and water.

"The Nyquists don't forget *anything*," Milo lamented, but he suddenly looked a bit less miserable. "Emma, do you realize how long memories are in this town?"

"Not as well as you do," I admitted. "Take it easy. You got re-elected by an overwhelming majority last month. And I'll bet the Nyquists all voted for you."

Milo looked askance. "I've got a murder investigation that's going nowhere. I don't need distractions like the Nyquists."

I had sat down in an armchair opposite Milo. I'd given up expecting him to notice my new dress. Or how nice the house looked, with all the Christmas decorations. Only the tree was missing. Briefly, I visualized it standing in the corner between the bookcase and the window next to the carport.

"Speaking of Nyquists," I said, hoping to steer him a bit off course, "I'm puzzled about their peeker. Oscar and Louise gave two different descriptions. Bridget is vague."

"Bridget is brainless. Travis didn't marry her for her mind." Milo tugged at his polka-dot tie. He hated getting dressed up. His concession to King Olav's dress code was a herringbone sport coat, flannel slacks, a pale blue dress shirt—and a tie. "You ought to know that eyewitnesses never see the same event."

"This is different," I persisted. "Louise said the guy was medium height, stocky, in workman's clothes. Oscar described him as tall and skinny, wearing jeans. They were both relaying what Bridget said, and when Vida and I asked her, she insisted she only saw an outline. What's the official rundown on this bird?"

Milo sipped his drink and shrugged. "As I said, people aren't good at giving descriptions. It can make us law enforcement types crazy, especially when they testify in court. Or at a lineup. Now there's the worst possible scenario. About four years ago last summer, Darla Puckett filed a complaint about some guy who'd broken into her house and stolen some money and a watch and a berry pie. Shaggy hair, a beard, big son of a gun. We actually threw together a lineup and . . .''

I have never considered Milo Dodge loquacious, not even after a shot of Scotch. He's a good conversationalist—direct, candid, humorous. But he never runs on. I half-listened to his elaborate account, which I'd heard a long time ago from Vida. I knew the punch line, which was that Darla Puckett had fingered a visiting state law enforcement official from Olympia, she'd given the money to the milkman, the watch had fallen into the garbage, and the berry pie had been eaten by a bear. It was amusing, it was cogent, it was very Alpine. But it wasn't like Milo to talk my ear off. I suspected him of fobbing me off.

''. . . And the bear had left the empty pie plate out by the woodshed!'' Milo chuckled richly.

''And you're dodging me, Dodge.'' I stood up, glancing at my watch. ''We've got a seven-thirty reservation. Let's go. You can tell me all about it over dinner.''

Milo was still protesting his innocence when we got to the turnout for the ski lodge. The Overholt family owned the property bordering the county road that took off from Front Street at the edge of town. The big old rambling farm house was ablaze with Christmas lights, and a Star of Bethlehem glowed on the barn roof. The Overholts were close to ninety, but their son-in-law, Ellsworth Griswold, still actively farmed the land and kept a few cows. The family had leased the big rolling front yard to Henry Bardeen to allow diners to park their cars before getting into the sleigh.

Milo and I weren't the only customers waiting for Evan Singer. Neither of us recognized the other two couples. From their excited talk about the snow and treacherous driving conditions, we guessed they were Seattleites. Milo regarded the quartet with bemusement. He clearly considered them effete.

The sound of sleigh bells jingled on the cold night air, signaling Evan's approach. Sure enough, the sleigh pulled off the Burl Creek Road, with Evan at the helm and two giggling young women passengers. They looked vaguely familiar, and Milo nodded to them both after they allowed Evan to assist them in alighting from the horse-drawn conveyance. Evan was dressed in a Regency coachman's costume, complete with a tall black felt hat. He looked quite imposing, especially when he flicked his long whip.

The two other couples got in first, then Milo and I squeezed in. There were lap robes to ward off the chill and a tub of popcorn to alleviate hunger pangs. Evan had greeted me politely, if indifferently, as if he'd forgotten I'd spent part of yesterday in his rude cabin. Maybe he had. It wasn't easy to figure out how Evan Singer's mind worked.

Discreetly, I clicked off a few frames of 35mm black and white film. Evan must have been used to having his picture taken. He paid no attention to the camera.

Our companions were exclaiming about the quaintness of the sleigh, the endurance of the horses, the beauty of the snow-covered wonderland. Indeed, for a man whose imagination usually seemed to be set at simmer rather than boil, Henry Bardeen had come up with an enchanting idea: the small bridge that crossed Burl Creek halfway up the hill to the ski lodge was decorated with tiny white lights and big green wreaths. Lamp posts, also of the Regency period, stood at each end. As our route wound through the trees, more fairy lights twinkled among the branches. The effect was magical, a charming mesh of Old World beauty and contemporary commercialism.

The sleigh glided ahead; our fellow passengers chattered on. Evan cracked the whip, but spared the horses. Milo and I remained silent. This was hardly the place to discuss a brutal homicide.

Evan Singer stopped for the arterial at Tonga Road, which was well traveled, since it hooked into Alpine Way over by

The Pines. A single car went by, perhaps heading for Arnie Nyquists's Ptarmigan Tract west of town. The horses plodded on across the road, their big hoofs making comfortable clip-clop noises that seemed to provide a bass note for the jingling bells.

Through the trees, we could hear the rushing sound of Burl Creek as it tumbled down the mountainside. There were more fairy lights, and somewhere a discreet speaker sere-naded us with a choir singing "It Came Upon a Midnight Clear." I couldn't resist grinning at Milo.

"This is the best thing to hit Alpine since Vida," I said in a low voice.

Milo grinned back. To my astonishment, he took my hand under the lap robe. "You're a Christmas nut, Ms. Lord. Whatever happened to your hard-bitten newspaper cyni-cism?"

I was about to reply that I put such negative emotions on hold every December, but the sleigh was suddenly zipping along at a surprisingly rapid speed. We were almost to the ski lodge; perhaps the horses sensed it and picked up the pace. They weren't exactly galloping, but my guess was that they were executing either a canter or a very fast trot. The two other couples had finally shut up. I tightened my grip on Milo's hand and gave him an inquiring look.

Before Milo could say anything, a car came down the road from the opposite direction. It moved slowly, since the ac-cess was narrow and had been cleared of snow to allow pas-sage of only one vehicle at a time. I noticed the familiar Mercedes symbol first, then recognized the occupants: Bridget Nyquist was driving; Travis was at her side.

Evan Singer let out a howl, and the horses both reared up, pawing the freezing air. The Mercedes rolled past us. Instead of getting his steeds under control, Evan turned around and stared at the car. With a shudder, the sleigh sprang forward, then sideways. The horses were making for the trees. We hit the piled-up snow along the roadside with a jolt. The sleigh tipped over, and we all fell out. The horses kept going.

I was still clinging to Milo's hand when I tumbled into the snowbank. One of the other women was screaming, while her male companion cursed a blue streak. Now hatless, Evan Singer sat wide-eyed, virtually dumbstruck. The horses had stopped a few feet away, balked by the deep snow and the heavy underbrush beneath its surface.

Milo sat up, pulling me with him. "You okay?"

I wasn't sure. I felt stunned, battered, and bruised. Otherwise, I decided I'd live. My main concern was that I hadn't ripped my new dress. "Yeah, except that black and blue aren't my favorite Christmas colors. How about you?"

Milo was shaken, but also unharmed. The couple that hadn't been screaming and swearing had descended upon Evan Singer, berating him and threatening lawsuits. The other two were also on their feet, still making nasty noises. Milo hesitated, then finally let go of me and approached the city folks.

"Excuse me, I'm the sheriff. If you have a complaint, file it with my office," he told the quartet of strangers. "However, I'll testify that there was no negligence involved. It was an accident. If you're going to go for a sleigh ride in the mountains this time of year, you'd better be prepared for just about anything."

Our fellow passengers didn't exactly look mollified, but at least they stopped yapping at Evan Singer. He had retrieved his hat and appeared indignant. He didn't bother to thank Milo for intervening, but made straight for the horses.

"You'd better walk the rest of the way," he called without turning around. "Enjoy your dinner."

The parking area for the ski lodge was just around the bend in the road. Of course Milo and I knew that, but the others didn't. They were still bitching when we turned the corner and saw the lodge in all its yuletide glory.

The slanting roof with its dormer windows was decked out

with yet more fairy lights. Garlands of evergreens hung from the eaves, tied with huge red bows. Off to one side at the parking lot entrance was a miniature Dickens village, complete with rosy-cheeked carolers, a gaunt lamplighter, frolicking children, and a terrier wearing a green scarf. The photo that Carla had taken didn't do the decor justice. I found myself smiling again. Indeed, even the out-of-town foursome was beginning to pipe down and cheer up.

Inside the lobby, a huge spruce soared up into the high beamed ceiling. There were smaller trees placed in various spots, all touched with fake snow and trimmed with blue and white ornaments. The restaurant continued the color theme, but highlighted Scandinavian traditions: St. Lucy with her crown of candles; a sheaf of grain tied with a blue and silver ribbon; Jul Tomten, the tiny old Swedish Santa, with his hunk of bread and bowl of milk; a Danish horn of burnished brass; the Norse god, Baldur, holding a sprig of mistletoe; a small evergreen hovering over silver straw to commemorate the manger. Henry Bardeen—or his decorators—had done their homework, casting a Christmas spell from out of Europe's northern reaches.

Milo and I were shown to a table near the massive stone fireplace. The restaurant itself might be brand-new, but the design had taken up where the original lodge left off. More high ceilings with great beams, natural pine, and a Swedish floor gave the room a spacious, open look. The Indian motif which was featured in the other public rooms had been discarded in favor of a Viking theme. The longboats, horned helmets, furs, and spears now took a backseat to the holiday decorations. However, I imagined that once Christmas was over, the old Norse decor would fit the dining room just fine.

We started with cocktails and an hors d'oeuvre of pickled herring in sour cream. I didn't badger Milo until he was halfway through his drink.

"You're holding out on me, Sheriff."

"No, I'm not. I won't hear from the folks at King County until Monday."

"I don't mean about the Seattle angle," I said, noting that the quartet from the sleigh now seemed to be happily draining wineglasses at a nearby table. King Olav's cellar was rumored to be an improvement over the Venison Inn's limited stock of domestic red, white, and rosé that could be purchased for a third of the price at Safeway. "I'm referring to Bridget's lurker. You know something you're not telling me."

Milo looked faintly exasperated. "And if I do? I'm the sheriff, for God's sake."

I gave him my most wide-eyed stare. "You want Vida and me to muck it up for you?"

"You two . . ." Milo speared another piece of pickled herring. "Okay, let me clarify one point. Just one." He tapped his index finger on the linen tablecloth. "There may be two men hanging around the Nyquist house. I don't know much about the tall, skinny guy in jeans. But the so-called workman is from the PUD truck."

I made a face. "The PUD? Why? Are the Nyquists wasting electricity?"

Milo slowly shook his head. "I didn't say he worked for the PUD, I said he was from the PUD *truck*." His hazel gaze fixed on my face. I had the feeling he thought I was being stupid.

"A cover? Are you talking about a stakeout?"

Milo hummed an offkey tune and looked beyond me to the sextet of high school students who were dressed à la Dickens and singing "I'll Be Home for Christmas" to a table of eight near the bay window.

I wiped my fingers on my napkin and leaned my elbows on the table. "Okay. To what purpose? Who is this man watching? Bridget? Or Travis?"

Milo kept on humming. I was getting annoyed. He was playing a game, supposedly keeping his confidences while forcing me to guess what was going on. This was not like Milo. Which, I realized, meant he was out of his mind or out of his league. I opted for the latter.

"FBI," I asserted. "Or some such Federal agency. Keeping an eye on . . . Travis." I had a fifty-fifty chance. Usually, I make the wrong choice. But this time, I could tell from Milo's swift glance of approval that I was right. "Why?" I demanded.

Now Milo stopped humming and ended the game. "I'm not sure. We've been asked to cooperate, but only to give these guys permission to maintain surveillance. If we need to know more, they'll tell us."

"Travis," I murmured, recalling Vida's attempt to pin Bridget down about her husband's former place of employment. "Have you checked him out?"

Milo made a dour face. "What for? As far as we're concerned, he hasn't done anything except break his leg."

I had to admit that Bridget's uncertainty was no indictment of Travis. Still, I persisted. "Do you know where Travis worked in Seattle?"

"Sure, Bartlett & Crocker. Jack Mullins went to high school with Travis. They weren't best buddies, but they kept in touch."

Bartlett & Crocker struck only the dimmest of bells. Or half a bell, since I remembered Bartlett, but not Crocker. "Local?" I asked.

Milo shrugged. "You mean in Seattle? I guess so. Not one of the big international houses, but well established. What are you driving at?"

I didn't know. Our waiter, whose name was Vincent and who looked like a ski bum, stopped to ask if we'd had time to consider the menu. Milo had—and ordered the Danish roast loin of pork, which went by the name of Stegt Svinekam. I scanned the entrées swiftly, choosing the Norwegian duck stuffed with apples and prunes.

The conversation turned to Evan Singer. Milo dismissed

my idea that the unexpected appearance of Bridget and Travis Nyquist had anything to do with our crash landing.

"You've got Nyquists on the brain," he chided me. "Evan Singer's a terrible driver. He's already been picked up by us three times, once for speeding, and twice for illegal turns."

"Drunk?"

"No, just out of it. He's not a world-class driving disaster like Durwood, but give the guy some time. Evan isn't thirty yet." Milo wore a pained expression. If there was one thing his deputies didn't need, it was a contender for Durwood Parker's reckless driving crown.

"He's weird," I asserted as Vincent showed up with our beet salads. "Very weird." The high school chorus was coming closer, now serenading the next table with "The Twelve Days of Christmas."

Milo made no further comment on Evan Singer. Except for exceeding the speed limit and turning out of the wrong lane onto Alpine Way, the multitalented, mega-bizarre Mr. Singer didn't seem to trouble Milo. Yet I knew the sheriff had something on his mind, and it didn't take a swami to figure out what it was.

"You've been getting calls about the bodies?"

Milo sighed and put down his fork. He had gobbled up all his pickled beets, which was more than I could manage. "You bet. Winter's a bad time to have a murderer loose. People feel trapped, especially the old folks. On the face of it, we've got two dead young women. There may or may not be any tie-in—except for their youth and gender. But try to convince an eighty-year-old arthritic woman living alone up on Icicle Creek that she's perfectly safe, and you might as well talk to a Norway spruce. Of course there are the calls from worried parents who have daughters in that age group. That makes more sense."

I thought of Carla and Ginny. My spine tingled. Between Ted Bundy and the Green River killer, we of Western Washington weren't strangers to serial murderers. "Do you really think these women were killed by the same person?"

Milo's hazel gaze was steady. "I don't know. Hell, I don't even know who these women are. We may never figure out who the first one was if we don't find more than that damned leg."

It wasn't the right moment for Vincent to bring Milo's loin of pork and my carved duck. Milo sucked in his breath; I regarded the drumstick with dismay.

But I ate it anyway.

It was delicious.

After Milo polished off his lingonberry mousse and I devoured my egg flip with a side of macaroons, we climbed back into the sleigh and headed down the mountain. Evan Singer seemed subdued, even glum. There were three other couples crammed into the conveyance, two from Alpine, though they were merely nodding acquaintances to Milo and me.

Milo walked me from his Cherokee Chief to my front door, but declined my invitation to come in. It was just as well. We had talked ourselves out over dinner, and one—or both—of us might feel compelled to do something foolish. I suspected that we didn't want to ruin a beautiful friendship. Or that we were chicken.

Virtue cannot dispel loneliness. In the cold quiet of my living room, I set a Wise Man up next to one of the camels in my Nativity set. I should be accustomed to being alone, I told myself, or at least used to not having a male companion. Oh, there had been men in my life since Tom Cavanaugh, but only a few, and never for very long. A single working mother has to give up many things. Intimacy is only one of them, but it may be the greatest sacrifice. Raising a child alone takes time and energy. As the only parent who can drive, clean, cook, cheer, chastise, teach, nurture, and listen, you discover there aren't many minutes of the day left to yourself. And even after that child has gone away, the mold in which life has been cast for almost twenty years has grown virtually unbreakable. After all, it's a safe haven, with those thick, high walls, like the womb that put you there in the first place.

But Ben was close by, and Adam was coming home in less than forty-eight hours. No doubt my son was within driving distance, somewhere in Kirkland, snug in the bosom of Erin Kowalski's family. As for Tom, he was probably in San Francisco, surrounded by his unstable wife and insecure children. I could imagine their beautiful home, their lavish decorations, their expensive presents. Graciousness and good taste would flow from their holiday festivities. Mr. and Mrs. Tom Cavanaugh's photographs would grace the pages of the Bay Area newspapers as they attended a whirlwind of parties, galas, and candlelight suppers. To the casual observer, it would look like a fairy tale—until Sandra Cavanaugh got hauled off for trying to eat the plastic grapes in an I. Magnin display window.

Poor Sandra.

Poor Tom.

Poor me.

Chapter Eleven

BEN GAVE A terrific sermon Sunday morning, transforming St. Luke's account of the barren fig tree into a clear-cut forest on Mount Baldy. *Patience*, my brother urged; it takes time to grow a stand of Douglas fir, but even longer to live a fruitful life. Logger or lawyer, don't just stand there, but reach, stretch, *grow*. Ben's words could be taken on a couple of levels, which may have been lost on some of the parishioners, but they seemed appreciative all the same. At least they weren't being called upon to drive out bad thoughts or avoid suggestive entertainment.

Ben was going to entertain himself by joining Peyton Flake on an excursion to Surprise Lake. I didn't ask if they would be armed. It was scary enough to think that it might snow before they got back.

I spent the day wrapping presents and catching up on Christmas cards. I'd had mine ready to go the previous weekend, but had held off mailing them. As usual, I'd already heard from several people who weren't on my list. I'd ship the whole batch off in the morning on my way to work.

By late afternoon, the snow began to drift down again. I baked spritz cookies, squeezing camels, dogs, trees, wreaths, flowers, and every other imaginable shape out of my copper pastry tube. Adam loved spritz. So did I. By the time I'd finished, I'd already eaten about a quarter of the dough. My original intention to take a couple of dozen cookies to the office went by the board.

I was beginning to worry about Ben when he called just before seven o'clock to say that he and Dr. Flake had returned. I asked my brother if he'd like to pick up something and eat with me. But Ben had been invited to join the ecumenical celebration of St. Lucy's Day at the Lutheran Church. I had attended the previous year, enjoying the Scandinavian custom of crowning a young girl with a wreath of candles and serving strong hot coffee and piles of pastry. Carla was covering the event which would star a thirteen-year-old Gustavson, yet another shirttail relation of Vida's. I've always secretly questioned the wisdom of allowing an awkward teenager to waltz around with burning tapers in her hair while pouring out quantities of steaming liquid, but, I must admit, I've yet to hear of a St. Lucy Wannabe incinerating herself or scalding her family to death. Still, I decided to conserve my resources and stay home.

Monday would be a busy day. We were publishing twenty-four pages, to capitalize on holiday advertising. Naturally, Ed Bronsky was in despair. He had scarcely recovered from the thirty-six pager the previous week. Gleefully, I warned him that we wouldn't get back to sixteen pages until the second week of January. Promotion had been Tom Cavanaugh's key advice when I'd consulted with him about making *The Advocate* more profitable. While he'd insisted that a special edition could be published almost every week, I'd been too timid to try. Once, maybe twice a month was the extent of my ambition—except for wonderful, lucrative, dazzling December. Of course it would have helped if my advertising manager hadn't preferred to sit around on his dead butt and drink coffee.

Twenty-four pages, however, doesn't require more work only from Ed. It also means that Vida, Carla, and I have to produce enough news copy to carry the non-advertising part of the paper. Consequently, we were all busy banging out stories first thing Monday morning. I polished the Evan Singer piece, Vida pried information about the Marmot from

Oscar Nyquist, and Carla concentrated on a Russian Christmas customs feature. Although she'd plagiarized most of it from a library book, she'd taken the trouble to interview a family who had recently moved to Alpine from Minsk via Vancouver, British Columbia, and Bellingham.

I was getting back to my editorial when Milo called. He'd heard from his contact in the King County sheriff's office. Stefan Horthy said that Kathy Francich worked as a cocktail waitress in a bar near the Kingdome. Carol Neal was a table dancer at a seedy nightclub on the Aurora Avenue strip. They'd moved into the Villa Apartments in July. He had never met Carol or Kathy, so he wouldn't be coming to Alpine to identify bodies. Horthy also managed the Riviera Apartments two blocks away, which was where he lived. He would certainly like to know if his tenants were dead or alive.

So, of course, would Milo. I was about to ask if he intended to send someone to talk to neighbors in the Villa Apartments who might know Carol and Kathy, but Ginny Burmeister rushed up to my office door, signaling that I had another call, long distance. Reluctantly, I hung up on Milo and pressed line two. Adam's voice sailed into my ear.

"Mom! I missed the bus! Can you come get me?"

"What bus?" There was no bus service from Seattle to Alpine, only to Everett, with a change for Monroe.

"Huh?" Adam sounded amazed. "Hey, I remember a bus. You know, last summer. It came right up Front Street and stopped at Old Mill Park."

I gritted my teeth. "That was a tour bus. Where are you?"

"Kirkland." Adam had regained his aplomb. I envied and despised the resiliency of youth. "You need directions?"

I did. Like the rest of Seattle's Eastside, Kirkland is a suburban maze. Indeed, my son's proposed route so confused me that we finally settled on a landmark, rather than the Kowalski residence. At one P.M., I would meet Adam at the carillon bell tower by the lake in downtown Kirkland.

My day was virtually shot. It was now after ten, and the

round trip would consume almost four hours. What had I been thinking of? That Erin or her parents would drive Adam to Alpine? That Ben would volunteer to collect his nephew? That Durwood Parker and Crazy Eights Neffel would zip down Stevens Pass on the snowmobile?

As usual, the burden fell on good ol' Mom. I abandoned the editorial, not wanting to rush through the conclusion, and instead devoted what remained of the next hour to a few local news briefs and reading proofs. As usual, Carla had made several typos, including the fact that Alpine had been blanketed with four feet of *snot* and a reference to the Episcopal *rectom*. If necessary, I could start working on the layout in the evening. Meanwhile, it occurred to me that as long as I was going to be in the Seattle area, I might do a bit of sleuthing on my own. As ever, Milo seemed set on going through channels. That could take forever. Or at least until our deadline had passed. I very much wanted to get an ID on one of the nameless victims before we went to press.

It was snowing fitfully as far as Sultan, but the trees along the highway were bare and the ground was visible. I was in a green world again, with the temperature climbing into the forties. I actually rolled the window down an inch or two. The rain pattered steadily on the windshield, but I didn't mind. As a native Seattleite, I was used to it. The snow was another matter. When I was growing up, there were winters when we never saw a snowflake or even a hard frost. The same was true in Portland. Yet after almost three years in Alpine, I thought I was growing accustomed to a seemingly endless world of white. Twenty miles down Stevens Pass told me otherwise. I definitely preferred rain to snow.

I arrived at the appointed spot almost ten minutes early. The wind was coming off Lake Washington, and its sharp damp chill cut to the bone. I didn't mind too much. Unlike a lot of people who can't wait to spend part of winter on a sun-soaked beach, I prefer clouds to sun. Gray days invigorate my mental processes; heat smothers them. I sat on a bench, admiring the modernistic cluster of bells in the carillon and the whitecaps on the lake. A few hardy souls hovered about, sipping lattes and nibbling on muffins. As the bells chimed one o'clock, Adam crossed the square, a pair of skis slung over one shoulder and his hands clutching three large vinyl bags.

We hugged—briefly, since Adam is still young enough to be put off by excessive displays of affection. Indeed, our latest parting had been of a remarkably short duration. Adam had been home for Thanksgiving, just two weeks earlier. Tom's generosity had guaranteed the airfare for frequent trips between Fairbanks and Alpine.

After the requisite questions about Erin, her family, and the Sunday ski trip to Crystal Mountain, I informed my son that we were heading into Seattle. I half-expected him to be excited at the prospect of detecting, but he was surprisingly indifferent.

"As long as we're going up to Capitol Hill, could we stop at REI? I need to get some new ski bindings."

"You could do that in Alpine," I replied as we headed for the Evergreen Point Floating Bridge across Lake Washington.

But Adam shook his head. He was a confirmed believer in REI, the sporting goods co-op that serves not only as a provisioner of outdoor gear but as a fashion guru. Seattleites are known not for their tailored three-piece suits, but for plaid flannel shirts, all-weather pants, and Gore-Tex jackets. In fact, most big city inhabitants would, in terms of apparel, fit nicely into Alpine's woodsy milieu. And that goes for men *and* women. REI may be the mecca of unisex clothing. Seattleites wouldn't have it any other way.

I, however, am an anomaly. I prefer fitting rooms with classic covers of *Vogue* and sales clerks who tell monstrous lies to bolster the customer's ego and pad their commissions. In Alpine, Francine Wells suits me fine. And in Seattle, I still lament the demise of Frederick & Nelson, one of the world's great department stores until greed and mismanagement got the better of it.

Consequently, I dropped my son off to wander in the wilds of REI while I drove north on Broadway to the Villa Apartments. Located above downtown Seattle, Capitol Hill is only eighty miles from Alpine, but demographically it's a world away. The land that climbs above the city center reaches to the ship canal on the north and the fringes of the International District to the south. The neighborhood is made up of large, stately homes and bunker-like condos, legendary watering holes and trendy boutiques, old money and new drugs, college students, artists, panhandlers, lawyers, punk rockers, homosexuals, chiropractors, philanthropists, and every hue of the ethnic rainbow. It's the big city in a nutshell—crazy, colorful, vibrant, and depressing. I love it and yet fear it. But after almost three years in Alpine, my first spotting of a transvestite startled me as much as the sight of a black man and a white woman pushing a baby stroller made me smile.

The Villa Apartments, a block off Broadway, wore a tawdry air. The four-story brick facade had none of the charm of its English Tudor neighbors, and the once-sweeping view of Elliott Bay and the Olympic Mountains had been obliterated by a block of new town houses.

I pressed the buzzer for number 116, next to a strip of paper that read K. FRANCICH/C. NEAL. As I expected, there was no response. I tried R. Littleriver in 115, then D. Calhoun in 119, and finally, V. Fields/T. Booth in 117. Nothing. I got back in the Jag and drove over to the Riviera Apartments, two blocks away. The building was about the same vintage as the Villa, but larger and better maintained. I found S. HORTHY—MGR. at 101 and buzzed some more. To my relief, a woman answered, her voice heavily accented.

After identifying myself, I launched into fiction, stating that I was a friend of Carol Neal, over at the Villa Apartments. I had lent Carol some photographs of my family reunion. They were the only copies I had and they meant much to me. My tone hinted that though I knew Carol, I realized she was irresponsible. I, however, was an honest, if sentimental, fool. "I understand Mr. Horthy plans to confiscate Carol's belongings. Could I please get my pictures back?"

There was no immediate reply. I wondered if the woman had understood what I was saying. A scratchy sound emanated from the small wire speaker; then I heard muffled voices in the background. They weren't speaking in English. Hungarian, maybe, judging from the manager's name.

The woman spoke again into the intercom: "Wait," she commanded, and the speaker shut off.

A moment later, the front door with its wrought-iron grille swung open. A gaunt man of middle age and medium height eyed me warily. He introduced himself as Stefan Horthy but didn't offer his hand. He, too, had an accent, but not as pronounced.

"You know where are these pictures?"

"No." I had trouble meeting his stern gaze. I was a lousy liar. "But they shouldn't be hard to find. They were in a big manila envelope."

Stefan Horthy shifted from one foot to the other, scowling into the rain. Traffic moved cautiously up and down the hill. A trio of black teenagers in Starter jackets walked by, drinking pop out of big plastic cups and eating onion rings from a small cardboard container. Across the street, an elderly woman hunched under a drab wool coat pushed an empty grocery cart into an alley. Nervously, I waited for Stefan Horthy's response.

"Come on." Horthy stalked off in the direction of the other apartment building. I wondered if he would mention being contacted by the sheriff's office.

Stefan Horthy, in fact, didn't mention anything. I hurried to catch up, deciding not to mention my car. He unlocked the Villa's front door, led me up a short flight of stairs past an ungainly Douglas fir that was adorned with bubble lights, and down a stale-smelling hallway. Horthy opened number 116, and stepped aside.

Whoever and whatever Kathleen Francich and Carol Neal were, they would not have qualified as conscientious housekeepers. My initial reaction was that the place had been ransacked. But I'd had some experience covering crime scenes for *The Oregonian* and I could recognize the aftermath of an intruder. There is a certain method to such madness. Unit 116 was merely a slovenly dump.

Even if I'd really been looking for something specific, such as the nonexistent family reunion pictures, I wouldn't have known where to start. Dirty clothes, fast food cartons, wine bottles, magazines, pop cans, grocery sacks, and even a rotting jack-o'-lantern were strewn about the room. My eyes fastened on a bunch of unopened mail lying helter-skelter on the shabby carpet. It all seemed to be addressed to Kathleen Francich.

Stefan Horthy was watching me like a hawk. Casually, I picked up one of the empty grocery bags. "Do you mind if I take this mail? I understand they didn't leave a forwarding address. Is there any more downstairs?"

"Maybe." His ambivalent answer could have referred to either my request or my question. Horthy scowled at the litter of brochures, bills, and mail order catalogues. He might have been considering the legal implications, but I suspected he was calculating monetary value. "Go, take that much. But all else is mine."

I gave him a flinty smile. "Except my photos. Let me check the bedrooms." I was already heading for the hallway, staving off Horthy's anticipated protests. He said nothing, however, but followed me as far as the first bedroom door.

I tried to overlook the chaos, zeroing in on the dressing table with a framed picture that was almost obscured by cologne bottles, cosmetic jars, and underwear. A young, pretty face gazed out at me from under dirty glass. Curly dark brown hair, brown eyes, a disarmingly self-conscious smile. The subject was posed in a high-backed rattan chair. A typical Blanchet High School senior photo. Was it Carol? I didn't know what the victim looked like. I grabbed the picture and put it in the grocery bag.

"Hey!" Stefan Horthy growled. "You're not taking that!"

I gave him a steely look. "Yes, I am. I'm sure you know something terrible may have happened to Carol. I'd like a memento."

Horthy made a face, but didn't argue. I opened drawers, perused the closet, even looked under the bed. I didn't know what I expected to find, but if Milo Dodge could ID our victim from the photo, he could get a search warrant for the apartment. I brushed past Horthy and went into the other bedroom. It was only slightly less of a shambles. There was no graduation picture, but a dozen snapshots had been tucked around the mirror on the dresser. They featured a fair-haired young woman with dancing eyes and a dimpled smile. I selected three of the pictures and put them in the grocery sack, too.

"No luck," I called to Horthy, who was standing in the hallway, hands jammed into his pants pockets. He turned away just as I tripped over a tennis shoe. On impulse, I snatched it up, then followed Stefan Horthy back into the living room. Next to the battered, tattered sofa was a small table where the telephone stood. The table had a little drawer. I opened it and sucked in my breath. A square, blue spiral address book was too much to resist. My back was turned to Horthy.

"Here are the pictures," I said in triumph, allowing him to hear but not see the address book join my little collection. Inspired, I picked up the phone, grateful to get a dial tone. I'd half-expected it to be disconnected.

"Hey—what you doing now?" Stefan Horthy leaped across the room, no mean feat, considering the obstacle course he had to overcome.

Waving Horthy off, I hit the redial button. A female voice

answered on the second ring. "History Department. This is Rachel Rosen. How may I help you?"

"Oh!" I made flabbergasted noises. "What number is this?"

Rachel told me. I recognized the prefix as belonging to the University of Washington campus. "I'm sorry," I apologized. "I misdialed."

Stefan Horthy's patience, which I judged to be chronically on the thin side, finally snapped. "Hey, you—get out of here now. You got your pictures. You waste my day."

I smiled, this time more amiably. "You're right. I just wish I knew what happened to Carol."

Stefan Horthy obviously didn't share my concern. With another scowl, he closed and locked the apartment door. When we reached the foyer, he indicated a row of brass mailboxes. "Letters may be inside or in that pile by the stairs. People are careless pigs." He selected another key from his big silver ring and unlocked the slot for 116 with a show of grudging condescension. "Let yourself out," he said abruptly, and then banged the door as he made his exit.

Five minutes later, I put my stash in the Jag and headed back to collect Adam. He was standing in line to pay for his purchases at the cashier's counter.

"Nick o' time," he said with that engaging grin so like his father's. "I can pay cash for the bindings, but I need some of your plastic to cover the gloves and the boots and the ski wax."

"Adam . . ." The motherly lecture died aborning. With his six-two stature and his once-boyish features sharpening into Tom's chiseled profile, I knew I was sunk. Nor was it just the resemblance that turned me to jelly. This was my baby, my son, the only man who had been a real part of my life for the past twenty-one years. I produced the plastic; Adam offered a pat on my head. It was, I suppose, a fair exchange.

* * *

I hadn't planned on serving dinner for five, but that was the way it worked out. Adam and I had stopped for a late lunch at the venerable Deluxe Tavern on Broadway, so it was going on six o'clock by the time we reached Alpine. We swung by the newspaper office, where I discovered that Vida was still working. I invited her to join us for dinner, at which point she informed me that Ben had called and said he'd be able to come, too. My brother was anxious to see his nephew.

I was anxious to show Milo the photos I'd filched from the Villa Apartments. I took a chance that he was also still on the job and asked him to eat with us. No arm-twisting was required. Adam and I rushed off to the Grocery Basket, where I tossed chicken breasts, French bread, cauliflower, two bottles of Chardonnay, and a frozen lemon meringue pie into my basket. Dinner would be late, but, along with the rice I already had at home, it would be ample.

Milo and Ben studied the framed photograph with somber expressions. At last Milo looked up, his hazel eyes showing pain. "It's her. She looks different here, but I'd swear to it in court."

Milo didn't need to explain that his memory was based on Carol Neal being at least four years older and maybe three days dead. Ben concurred with Milo's opinion.

For the first time, my son evinced interest in the case. "She was a mega-babe," he murmured, looking over Ben's shoulder. "What a waste! Who'd do something like that?"

I eyed Adam carefully. He'd turned pale, and it occurred to me that in Carol Neal, he had come face-to-face with his own mortality. Twenty-two-year-old women shouldn't die. Neither should twenty-two-year-old men.

"The worst of it," put in Vida between mouthfuls of trout pâté and crackers, "is that there are two of them. Let's see that tennis shoe again, Emma."

I handed it to Vida. It was an Adidas, but, like the Reebok Milo had found, it was a size seven and a half. Vida looked up at Milo, who was now on his feet by the fireplace, fiddling with a candle in the shape of a choirboy. "Inconclusive?"

"Of course. But suggestive, if nobody knows where Kathleen Francich is. The King County people will be on this first thing tomorrow. It's their case now, too." Milo wore a faint air of relief. The law enforcement officials in Seattle had far greater resources than he had in Alpine. Indeed, Milo was still smarting over the failure of a bond issue on the November ballot that would have allowed him to hire two more deputies and acquire more sophisticated equipment. Skykomish County voters had also turned down a proposal to expand the fire department. My editorials urging passage of both measures had gone for naught.

I went into the kitchen to turn the chicken breasts over. Vida was perusing the address book. I'd only had time to glance through it. I wasn't sure if it belonged to Carol or Kathleen, but whichever it was, she had certainly jotted down a lot of masculine names, and strange ones at that. Corny. Stitch. Porky. Big Wheel. Diver Dan. Shaft. I was curious to know what Milo would make of it.

The cauliflower was aboil, the rice was steaming nicely, and the buttered bread loaf was heating along with the chicken breasts. I returned to the living room, where Vida was tapping the open pages of the address book.

"Prostitutes," she asserted. "These names are clients. Disgusting. But part of life. What else would you expect of a table dancer and a cocktail waitress?"

"I don't know about cocktail waitresses . . ." Ben began.

"You don't know about prostitutes," interrupted Vida. "At least I hope you don't. You're a priest." She whirled around on the sofa to give Adam a sharp look. "I hope you know better than to get mixed up with that sort of woman. They'll take your hard-earned money, give you a dreadful disease, and tell you you've had a wonderful time. Men are silly enough to believe them. Oh! It's maddening!"

Milo, either out of professional duty or in an attempt to

ward off his turn on the spit of Vida's tongue, ventured that prostitution was a good guess. "Which means we may have a typical serial killer on the loose. Most of the Green River victims were hookers, or at least runaways who turned a trick to make survival money."

On the face of it, Milo's argument made sense. But the Green River ran its course near the Sea-Tac airport strip, a bit of real estate notorious for its vice crimes. The Skykomish River was far removed from the sins of the city. I had to disagree with Milo.

"If Carol and Kathleen are both dead, and even if they were both part-time hookers, they still had something else in common," I pointed out. "They were roommates. That means they were probably also friends. They had more in common than just turning tricks."

"An excellent point." Vida nodded vigorously, then carefully turned the pages of the address book to the middle. She studied the listings, gave a slight shake of her head, and then flipped back toward the front section. "Ha!" She waved the little blue book in triumph. "Just as I thought! Dunne, Bridget!"

All three males looked puzzled, but I practically jumped up and down. "Bridget Dunne Nyquist," I cried, for the elucidation of Milo, Ben, and Adam. "Is there an Alpine address?"

"No." Vida offered the book to Milo. "It looks like a Seattle number, no address. But one—or both—of these girls knew Bridget."

"Of course," I said, squeezing in between Vida and Ben on the sofa. "They went to high school together. I wonder if Kathleen Francich went to Blanchet, too." I poked my brother. "Call Bill Crowley. He'd know."

"Now?" Ben regarded me with reluctance. I poked him again, harder. He got up and went to the phone, then turned back to look at me. "I don't have his home number. He used to be in residence at Christ the King, but I'm not sure he's there anymore, with priests being moved all over the place lately. I'll call Mrs. McHale. My address book is at the rectory.''

Teresa McHale, however, did not answer. Ben remembered that she was taking Father Fitz's Volvo out for the evening, to visit an elderly shut-in. He promised to call the Blanchet chaplain first thing in the morning.

Milo was going through the little blue book page by page. I told him to check on a listing for Rachel Rosen. Ever methodical, Milo told me to hold my horses; he was only as far as the Gs.

He'd gotten to M by the time I announced that dinner was served. Speculation was rampant, but I must admit we didn't get much beyond what we already knew or guessed. There were so many *ifs* in the case. *If* the other dead body was Kathleen Francich. *If* one or both of the young women had been prostitutes. *If* Carol had maintained contact with Bridget Dunne Nyquist. *If* Kathleen had gone to Blanchet.

We ran out of conjecture about the same time I ran out of chicken. By then, everyone was full, sleepy, and content to stare into the fireplace. Milo offered to drive Ben back to the rectory. Vida wanted to help clean up, but I told her to head home. It was starting to snow quite hard. Adam could lend me a hand.

Adam, however, had dozed off on the floor by the hearth. Apparently, his exertions on the ski slopes the previous day had worn him out. After throwing an afghan over him, I went out into the kitchen. I was emptying the second load of the evening from the dishwasher when I realized that I hadn't finished my editorial, let alone even begun to lay out the newspaper.

It was after eleven. I dithered briefly, then decided it was better to get off to an early start than to make a late finish. I put the last of the silverware away, wiped off the counters, and headed for bed.

I stopped at the Nativity scene to add the second Wise

Man. The first was hiding behind a palm tree, peering out like a German spy from a bad World War II movie. Adam was still asleep in front of the dying fire. I left him there, offering up a prayer to keep him safe and happy. As I kicked off my shoes, I wondered if Carol Neal's parents had ever said the same prayers for her. If they had, their supplications had been stamped denied. Of course Ben would tell me it didn't work that way. Prayer acknowledges faith; it's like sending a thinking-of-you card to God. And sometimes even that gets returned to sender.

Chapter Twelve

We can't turn back the clock. But neither can we turn our backs on history. Washington State was built on a firm foundation—of logs. Trees are still our major crop. Scholars and scientists tell us we can have both a healthy environment and a prosperous timber industry. People must remain our top priority. We can keep the spotted owls in the trees, but let the logs keep rolling. And let the good times roll again in Alpine, and in other logging communities of the Pacific Northwest.

I hit transfer, save, and print. The editorial was finished, though my day had only begun. I turned my attention to Vida's story on Oscar Nyquist and the Whistling Marmot Movie Theatre. It was long, and, as was Vida's style when she got her teeth into a meaty feature, a bit rambling. She started with the theatre's early history in the social hall under the reign of Lars Nyquist, moved up to the new building site, mentioned that the Marmot had been designed by Isaac Lowenstein, a well-known West Coast architect specializing in movie houses, and then jumped to the postwar renovations and the most recent updating in the 1960s. The exterior had been repainted last summer, another product of the film location company, but with happier results than our garish yellow facade. The quotes from Oscar were mundane, but Vida had done a telephone sampling of local Marmot aficionados, who had waxed eloquent over such varied historic occasions as the first talking picture, a visit by Betty Grable on the vaudeville circuit, Bing Crosby passing through on a fishing trip during World War II, and the crush of females who had showed up for Elvis's movie debut in *Love Me Tender*. Amazingly enough, Vida had managed to track down Mabel Hubbert Bockdorff, who had played the piano for Lars during the silent-screen era. Mabel was ninety-seven yeas old, but still sharp and living on her own in Wenatchee.

Only in the next to the last paragraph did Vida allude to the Nyquists' recent rash of pesky problems: "Running a movie theatre isn't all roses and popcorn," wrote Vida. "Oscar Nyquist and his son, Arnold, have experienced their ups and downs, including an outbreak of vandalism on both their private and professional properties. The elder Nyquist has expressed a strong desire to see these culprits apprehended, but so far no arrests have been made." Vida summed up with a lengthy paragraph about all the excitement and romance and laughter and thrills the Marmot had brought to Alpine. She gave credit to Lars for being farsighted, to Oscar for his perseverance, and to Arnie for bringing a bowling alley to the town. I suspected that the last remark was made tongue-in-cheek, but I let it ride.

"Nice work," I told her, as Carla handed me the pictures of Evan Singer in his coachman's costume.

Vida made a harumphing noise. "I wasn't exactly interviewing Sol Hurok. If Lars Nyquist had owned an insurance agency, Oscar would have peddled policies door-to-door. If Lars had been a blacksmith, Oscar would still be pounding on the forge, and never mind that the horse and buggy has been gone for three generations. Oscar has no imagination. I doubt that he ever watches the movies he shows. At least Lars had enough emotion to get a crush on Greta Garbo."

Carla was looking at the photos Vida had selected to go with the story: the social hall, the Marmot's opening night, an amateur production of *You Can't Take It With You*, a head shot of the late Lars, and three generations of Nyquists standing under the marquee with *It's a Wonderful Life* in big block letters.

"When did you take this?" I asked Vida.

"Yesterday, while you were out gallivanting. See, Travis has thrown his crutches away, just like Tiny Tim."

I edged closer to Carla and scrutinized the photo of Oscar, Arnie, and Travis Nyquist. I noted Oscar's bald head, Arnie's receding hairline, and Travis's wavy brown locks. "I wonder how soon Travis will start losing *his* hair," I mused.

Carla gasped. "Don't say that, Emma! He's so cute!"

"Knock it off, Carla," I said, trying to keep my tone light. "It's a shame my son is too young for you." Of course it really wasn't. The role of Carla's employer was bad enough; being her mother-in-law would be worse.

Carla gave me an irked look. "You're a washout when it comes to helping me meet men. Adam's still a college kid and your brother is a priest. Don't you know any eligible guys?"

"If I did, I'd have first dibs," I replied, shoving one of the Evan Singer photos in her direction. "Here, don't you think he looks dashing in that coachman's rig?"

Carla's dark eyes grew very wide. "With a whip? Why not shackles and chains, too? I told you he was weird, Emma. You were pretty brave to go out to his cabin the other day. I would have taken Milo Dodge along."

Milo, in fact, was entering the door. He looked very purposeful this snowy December morning. "Things are beginning to hum," he announced. "The King County people are sending up one of Carol's co-workers to officially identify her. Whoever it is knows she had a tattoo on her backside."

If Milo was expecting congratulations, he got more than he'd bargained for. Carla zipped across the room, grabbed the sheriff, stood on her tiptoes, and kissed him soundly. "Mistletoe!" she chirped. "Hey, Sheriff Dodge, *you're* eligible!"

Milo reeled "For what?"

"Never mind," I sighed, shaking my head at Carla. "The sheriff's taken. Honoria Whitman, remember?"

Vida, who had removed her glasses, drank from a mug of hot water. "How is Honoria? I haven't seen much of her lately."

Milo was pouring himself a cup of coffee. "She left for Carmel Saturday. She isn't used to the snow and doesn't like to drive in it. And I've been pretty tied up. I wasn't able to get down to Startup last week."

I made sympathetic noises. The sheriff's current lady-love was hampered by more than a lifetime in California's warmer climate: Honoria's ex-husband had taken out his rage against the world by throwing his wife down a flight of stairs. Mr. Whitman had paid for his temper tantrum with a bullet fired by Honoria's brother. He'd served ten years, but had told his sister it was worth it. Honoria's sentence was longer—she would never walk again.

We were expressing our admiration for Honoria's independence and spunk when Arnie Nyquist stormed into the office. I'm used to irate readers, so I braced myself for a tirade. Arnie's target, however, was not me but Milo Dodge.

"That's it! You're a waste of the taxpayers' money, Dodge! Haven't you ever heard of patrol cars? Not only are those morons still screwing up the Marmot's marquee, but my house has been robbed!" Arnie Nyquist flailed around the office, gesturing wildly. I had a perverse wish for him to stand under the mistletoe so Carla could kiss him.

Keeping calm, Milo held his coffee mug in both hands. "Have you reported this?"

Carla jumped in between the two men. "I should take a picture! What does the marquee say this time?" She could hardly contain her glee.

Arnie glared at her exuberant form. "What the hell difference does it make? Some damned fool silly thing—'*Under A Low Stiffel*.' Jesus!"

Carla clapped her hands. "Cute! A Stiffel's a kind of lamp, get it?" She dashed to her desk to grab her camera.

"No, you don't!" yelled Arnie. "My dad and I don't want you poking fun at the Marmot!"

I shook my head at Carla. She hesitated, then docilely put the camera back on her desk. "You've got to admit it's clever," she muttered with a flash of dark eyes for Arnie.

Arnie ignored her, turning his ire back on Milo. "I reported it, all right. The robbery, I mean. That's how I knew you were here." He was still barreling around, bumping into Vida's desk. She gave him a frosty stare.

The sheriff had kept his expression bland. "The robbery happened this morning?"

Arnie finally stood still, just as Ed Bronsky came in, grumbling and brushing snow off his overcoat. "The mall! How can those merchants want all that advertising next week for end-of-year clearance sales? The paper will come out the day before Christmas Eve! Nobody'll read the damned ads!"

I would save my lecture on the importance of post holiday bargains in a depressed economy until after Arnie finished pitching his fit. And Arnie was indeed blustering away: "The robbery was last night, while Louise and I were gone. We drove down to Sultan to visit some friends. It was late when we got home, almost midnight. We went right to bed, and didn't notice we'd been robbed until this morning." He shot Milo a defensive look.

Ed was pouring coffee. "Robbed, huh?" he said over his shoulder. "You know, Arnie, if you didn't take out those two-inch ads every week for Nyquist Construction, nobody'd know who you were. Then they wouldn't realize you had anything worth stealing. You plaster your name all over the paper, and there you are—a sitting duck."

Not for the first time did I resist the urge to strangle my advertising manager. In fact, I secretly hoped Arnie Nyquist would do Ed in and save me the trouble. But Arnie chose to ignore Ed, which was probably what I should have done, had he not been on my payroll.

Milo raised his sandy eyebrows. "So? What was taken?"

A slight flush enveloped Arnie's round face. "Priceless stuff. Keepsakes, two cartons of 'em. How do you put a value on a lifetime of memories? They're irreplaceable!"

Milo's beeper went off. He gave Arnie a cool look, started to pick up the phone on Carla's desk, changed his mind, and announced he'd better go straight back to the office. He took our coffee mug with him.

Arnie was now leaning on Vida's desk. "Well? Aren't you going to put this in the story about our family? About how we're being persecuted?"

I watched Vida gaze up at Arnie. She looked a bit owlish. "I could. What's actually missing?"

Momentarily appeased, Arnie began to tick off items on his thick fingers. "A lot of family pictures, especially from when Travis was little. Maybe our wedding album—Louise isn't sure, she's been too busy crying. My discharge from the army, my diplomas from Alpine High School and the University of Washington, my yearbooks, and Travis's baby book. Letters, postcards, invitations, announcements—all the stuff people save. You know."

Vida gave a curt nod. " 'Arnold Nyquist—The Early Years.' Yes, I've got it." She put her glasses back on and blinked twice.

Now that Arnie had quieted down a bit, I posed a question of my own: "How did they get in?"

Arnie looked exasperated. "Walked. Louise forgot to lock the basement door." His voice dropped to a mumble.

Carla made a clucking noise with her tongue. "Oh, gee, that's not too smart, especially with a murderer on the loose. You know, Mr. Nyquist, you can't blame the sheriff for everything, not if you don't take precautions."

I felt like applauding Carla; Arnie Nyquist looked as if he wanted to slug her. But he refrained. Instead, he heeled around and slammed out of the office. We were not sorry to see him go.

"Neener-neener-neener," chanted Carla, putting her thumbs in her ears and waggling her fingers. "What an oaf!"

Vida snorted in apparent agreement; Ed shrugged and took a bite out of a sweet roll he'd picked up from the bakery. I retreated into my office to lay the paper out on the computer. The Pagemaker program has simplified my life, though sometimes I miss the immediacy of hot type and cold sweat. I was never very good at translating words into inches. Translating other people's incoherent words was more my line.

I had finished the front page when Milo called. The summons he had received had not only gotten his day off to a jolt, but also upset my carefully computerized Page One. Duane Gustavson, a shirttail relation of Vida's on the Runkel side, had been out fishing at first light on the Tye River at the mouth of Surprise Creek, near Scenic. He had caught an eleven-pound steelhead, a worthless white fish—and an arm. Duane had netted his dinner, but he'd lost his lunch. Or, in this case, his breakfast.

And I had another piece of the story. So to speak.

Doc Dewey and his wife had gone into Seattle to attend a conference and to visit relatives. Doc wasn't due back until Wednesday night. He had delegated Peyton Flake to take over as medical examiner, should the need arise. It had—unfortunately.

Dr. Flake cruised into his private office, sangfroid intact. Milo and I didn't share his equanimity, though, as professionals, we tried. The sheriff had studied Flake's impressive credentials; I had admired his collection of duck hunting stamps. The ducks were another matter: there were six of them, stuffed and glassy-eyed, with handsome plumage and unfamiliar pedigrees. I suppose they went well with the moose, stag, cougar, and lynx heads. I half-expected to see a couple of his patients mounted on the wall, but I was probably letting my imagination get the best of me.

"I don't like guesswork," Peyton Flake announced flatly. "It's going to take a while to get all the lab results back. But if you want my *opinion*"—he stressed the word, curling his lips over his teeth—"I'd say the arm went with the leg."

Milo nodded. "Do you think it had been in the river a long time?"

"Definitely. Two, three months." Flake fiddled with the rubber band that held his ponytail in place. "Unfortunately, from your point of view, there were no rings, no watch, nothing identifiable. You want a look?" He gazed at me, and I could have sworn that he was trying to keep amusement at bay.

Milo, of course, had already seen the arm. He was dutybound. I wasn't. I shook my head. I didn't even want to think about where Dr. Dewey and Dr. Flake filed spare appendages.

Dr. Flake had leaned back in his chair, putting his hiking boots up on the desk. "Interesting," he mused. "Amateur at work. A saw, I'd guess."

"Gack!" I closed my eyes and shuddered. Then I berated myself. It was all part of the job—the reporting of news, the discovery of facts, the search for truth. "Gack," I repeated, with less force.

Milo's suggestion of going to lunch fell on deaf ears. Not only had I lost my appetite, but I was up against a deadline. Milo didn't press; Carol Neal's co-worker was supposed to arrive at the sheriff's office around one.

Carla was out, Ed was working on his advertising layout, and Vida was munching carrot sticks between spoonfuls of cottage cheese. Ben had called while I was gone. Vida relayed his message.

"He talked to the chaplain at Blanchet. There is no record of a Kathleen Francich attending the school."

Somehow, I was disappointed. But the information goaded

me into calling Rachel Rosen at the University of Washington. I went into my office and closed the door, not to keep secrets from my staff, but to avoid distractions. I had the feeling I would need full command of my wits.

Luckily, Rachel had not gone out to lunch. She answered in the same manner as she had done the previous day when I called from the Villa Apartments. I wondered if she would remember my voice.

"Ms. Rosen," I began, using my most professional tone and trying not to jar Rachel too badly, "I'm the editor and publisher of *The Alpine Advocate*, on Stevens Pass. We're running a missing persons story about someone you know. Her name is Carol Neal. Could you tell me when you last saw her or talked to her?"

"Carol's missing, too?" The words were blurted out.

"You're referring to Kathleen Francich?" Milo should be doing this, I thought. Maybe he was, through the auspices of the King County Sheriff.

"Yes." Rachel Rosen paused. I could imagine her sitting at a desk, pondering the disappearances of Carol and Kathleen. When she spoke again, there was a note of caution in her voice. "I haven't seen Carol or Kathy in a long time. But I did talk to Carol a month or so ago. She was worried about Kathy."

"Worried because she'd disappeared?"

"Yes. It wasn't like Kathy to be gone so long. Excuse me, Ms. Lord, I have someone in the office here." Rachel had become brisk.

"Ms. Rosen—where did you go to high school?" The question flew out of my mouth.

"Seattle Hebrew Academy. Why do you ask?" Rachel sounded suddenly tense.

I ignored her query. I was a journalist; I could ask whatever I damned well pleased. "And Kathy?"

"Kathy? Holy Names, I think. Goodbye."

The phone clicked in my ear. Holy Names was a private

all-girls' Catholic high school at the north end of Capitol Hill. The Seattle Hebrew Academy was coed, but also private and located not far from Holy Names. What was the link between Blanchet's Carol Neal, Holy Names's Kathleen Francich, and the Academy's Rachel Rosen? Was there any link, other than all three young women had gone to private schools? And where, if anyplace, did Bridget Nyquist, also of Blanchet, fit in? I ignored my computer screen and drew strange rectangles on a piece of scratch paper. I wished I had been able to keep the little blue address book. But of course Milo had confiscated it, along with the mail I'd brought from the Villa Apartments.

A firm knock on the door jolted me out of my reverie. "Well?" Vida stood on the threshold, her green cloche hat askew, though with a cloche it's hard to tell. "Who have you been grilling?"

I told her, adding that while Rachel Rosen hadn't exactly been a font of information, she had made one telling remark. "She said Carol was worried about Kathleen because she was never gone for such a long time. That tells me Kathleen occasionally took off for a few days. I assume she went with a man."

"A fair assumption," said Vida, nodding. "It's also fair to assume that if Carol called Rachel a month or so ago, it was more likely back in October, not November. People lose track of time. And that could mean that the other body is indeed Miss Francich."

"Ugh." I put a hand to my head. "I hope somebody in Seattle is going to question Rachel. I got the impression she wasn't real eager to share what she knew."

My phone rang before Vida could comment. The call was from the sheriff's office, but it was Vida's nephew, Bill Blatt, not Milo.

"Sheriff's interrogating this Desmond woman," Bill reported in his youthful tones. "She positively IDed Carol Neal. Then she fell apart. But Sheriff Dodge said you'd want the information right away, because you've got to get the paper out, right?''

"Right." And God help Billy Blatt if he didn't deliver the goods to Aunt Vida and company first. "Does this Desmond person know the other girl, Kathleen?''

"Couldn't tell you," said Bill Blatt, then, lest his aunt and I accuse him of keeping secrets, quickly added, "That is, I don't know. I imagine Sheriff Dodge will ask her. We'll keep you posted."

I thanked him and hung up. It was an easy matter to add Carol Neal's identity to the story about the discovery of her body. We were a week late with the news anyway, having missed last Wednesday's deadline by a matter of hours. I'd already inserted Duane Gustavson's grisly catch on the Tye River. The front page of *The Advocate* was turning into a gruesome travesty. The lead story of a double murder juxtaposed with a picture of Fuzzy Baugh in a Santa suit wasn't going to make for the jolliest of holiday reading.

Vida was lingering in my doorway. "We've got to talk to Bridget again," she announced flatly. "We can't leave it up to Milo. He's too busy following *procedures*." She made a face as she spun out the word.

"Bridget doesn't want to talk to us," I pointed out.

Vida sniffed. "Of course she doesn't. But she will."

"How?"

"I'll think of something." Vida finally started toward her desk, then turned back to face me. "Say—if you need more filler for next week, I've got some fascinating background left over from the Marmot piece. That Lowenstein fellow designed several of the old movie houses in the Pacific Northwest, most of which have been torn down. The Marmot is the only one left on this side of the state. Besides, he lived in Alpine for a time, while the theatre was being planned.''

I considered Vida's suggestion. "Sounds good to me. But it might fit better in the New Year's edition.''

"Fine," Vida agreed. "That will give me time to see if I

can track down any old coots who might have known Low-enstein. Besides Oscar Nyquist, of course.''

For the rest of the afternoon, I tried to put murder from my mind. It wasn't easy, but by five o'clock the paper was ready to roll. Milo stopped in just as Carla and Ed were leaving.

"Lila Desmond," he said, sitting on the edge of Carla's vacated desk. "I hope I never see her again."

"Carol's colleague?" I signed my initials to the note for Kip MacDuff, who would truck the paper to Monroe in the morning. "What happened?"

Milo was looking bemused. "She cried, she got hysterical, she threw up. Trying to get any genuine information out of her was like walking in a swamp. All she could say was that Carol was a sweet kid and lent her a pair of earrings. Hell!" Milo made an impatient gesture with one hand, as close to anger as I'd seen him in ages.

Vida pursed her lips. "Now, now. Surely this Lila knew when she'd last seen Carol?"

"Sort of." Milo gave Vida a disparaging look. "She was vague about that, too. But she thought it was over the Thanksgiving weekend. I gather table-dancers don't keep to strict schedules. And no, she wasn't acquainted with Kathleen Francich. She knew—vaguely—that Carol had a roommate. But that was all." The sheriff now wore a disgusted expression. Alpine is not without its depravities, but table-dancing isn't one of them. Milo could cope with drunken brawls, domestic S & M, drug addicts, and even grisly homicides. But scantily clad young women bumping and grinding for bug-eyed lechers was beyond him. His idea of an evening on the wild side was four beers and a bowl of popcorn at Mugs Ahoy.

"What about Kathleen?" I asked. "Has anybody in Seattle come up with news about her?"

Now solemn, Milo nodded. "She hasn't shown up at work since October the sixth. She had a couple of days off at the bar and never came back. Nobody got excited. It happens, I guess.'' His hazel eyes suddenly sparked. ''But on October fifteenth, Carol Neal reported Kathleen missing.''

''Ooooh!'' Vida whipped off her glasses and rubbed frantically at her eyes. ''Why didn't you say so? Honestly, Milo, you are as slow as mold!''

Milo resumed his stoic expression. ''One thing at a time. The bottom line is that Kathleen never turned up.''

Vida stopped rubbing. ''So Carol went looking for her?''

''Maybe.'' Milo shrugged. ''Carol probably hoped the police would find Kathleen. Or that she'd show up on her own. What I want to know is why did she come looking for her in Alpine? If, in fact, that's what Carol did.''

''We can't know that,'' I murmured. ''And yet . . . If that other body is Kathleen . . . The tennis shoe fits, should she wear it?''

''Carol gave a description of Kathleen as five-six, a hundred and twenty pounds, light blonde hair, deep blue eyes, a small scar above her left eyebrow. Doc Dewey and Peyton Flake can figure out height, maybe even weight. But not much else. Yet.''

I grimaced at Milo's implication. Vida, however, appeared composed. ''Well. If Carol was out searching for Kathleen, Alpine may not have been the first place she went. But I have a feeling it was the right place, don't you?''

Milo nodded slowly. ''I'm afraid so. It was also the last place she looked.''

From that point of view, it was the wrong place as well.

Milo was taking his leave when Cal Vickers came into the office. ''Just the man I want to see,'' said Cal to Milo, after acknowledging Vida and me with a tip of his greasy duckbilled cap. ''Bill Blatt said you'd be here.''

''What's up?'' inquired Milo of the strapping gas station proprietor.

Cal was the sort who liked to spin out a tale, a habit forged while standing next to an open hood and putting off the moment when the car owner learns that it's going to cost him dearly to have his vehicle repaired.

"I got a call yesterday from Clancy Barton at the Bootery. You know Clancy, he's a fussbudget. The mall was busy over the weekend, and at one point they ran out of parking places. Clancy and the rest of the merchants wanted the sheriff to impound those old heaps that have been sitting there for weeks and have me tow 'em away." He stopped, taking off his earmuffs. "Actually, there were only two cars. Dodge here said fine, go get 'em; he had other fish to fry. So did we, with all the jackasses sliding into each other or landing in ditches. You'd think people around here would know how to drive in snow. Anyway, we finally got down to it this afternoon. The old Malibu belongs to some kid from Gold Bar. Starter went out, near as I can tell. You know kids, they'd rather give up on something than take the trouble to fix it."

Behind me, I could hear Vida emit a low, impatient sigh. I, too, wished Cal would speed his story along. Milo, however, appeared unflappable.

"Then we checked out the Barracuda. Man, it had been there a *long* time. Everything's froze up, no antifreeze, but almost a full tank of gas." Cal shook his head.

"Stolen?" The word was Milo's mild attempt to hurry Cal along.

Cal Vickers shrugged. "Could be. I figure you ought to run it through the computer." He removed his cap again and brushed his stubby fingers through the fringe of dark hair that grew from ear to ear. "The car's from Seattle. It's registered to a Kathleen Francich."

Chapter Thirteen

THERE COULDN'T BE much doubt that if Kathleen Francich's car had arrived in Alpine, so had Kathleen. How her car had ended up at the mall while she seemed to be appearing in various other places remained a mystery. Maybe Milo could wave his forensics wand over the Barracuda and come up with some answers. Meanwhile, I was going to rely on intuition. Sometimes it actually worked.

I had been bothered by Louise Bergstrom Nyquist ever since I'd run into her and Arnie at Barton's Bootery. Maybe I'd imagined that she had wanted to talk to me; maybe I'd misread the appeal in her eyes.

Nevertheless, on this snowy Tuesday night I felt compelled to talk to Louise. The timing was good: I'd put aside the cares of *The Advocate* for another week, and the planning commission met on the third Tuesday of each month. Arnie Nyquist was on the board. Louise would be home alone.

I arrived shortly after seven, my nerves frayed by the brief but treacherous drive up First Hill. Arnold Nyquist had built himself a house on Icicle Creek. Two stories of brick and cedar, the showpiece dwelling was set among the evergreens, but commanded a ravishing view of the town and Mount Baldy. Everything seemed to fit, from the cathedral ceilings to the Aubusson carpets. Everything, that is, except Louise Nyquist, who looked as if she would have been more at home with faded mohair and braided rugs.

"This is a surprise," she said in apparent pleasure. "I

was just going to bake some Christmas cookies. Would you like an eggnog?''

I said I would indeed, but to skip the rum. I had to face the tricky downhill drive to get back home. ''I wanted to tell you how sorry I was about your burglary. It's one thing to have VCRs and CD players stolen, but it's terribly sad when keepsakes go. Arnie said your wedding album might have been taken, too.''

Louise beamed at me from across the kitchen island where she was pouring homemade eggnog into tall mugs. ''I found the album, thank goodness. It had fallen behind a box of Travis's high school mementos. But you're right,'' she went on, leading me back into the living room. ''Those were treasures we can't ever replace. Now why would anyone take them?''

I was sitting in a tapestry-covered armchair; Louise was perched on an amber brocade sofa. Even with its cheerful Christmas decor, the room seemed stiff and formal. But it was also very beautiful. I wondered if the same person had done both this house and the younger Nyquists' decor.

''Mischief, maybe,'' I replied, taking in a Lalique vase, a Baroque mirror, and a brilliantly colored bowl that might have been crafted by Dale Chiluly. If the thief had had a pack like Santa's, he could have thrown in those three items and made off with six figures worth of goodies.

''Drugs,'' Louise was saying. ''That's what Arnie suspects. Whoever it was thought we might have some—or cash lying around—and when they couldn't find anything, they just grabbed the first thing that came to hand. You know how those people are. They don't think rationally, like the rest of us.''

I tried not to look dubious. But I recalled that Vida had said that Louise was no dope. Perhaps I could trust to be candor. ''You know, Louise, that doesn't seem likely. If the burglar was a drug addict, he would steal something he could sell or pawn.'' I waved a hand to take in the vast living room with its many-splendored things. "You have some valuable pieces. Sterling, too, I'll bet. Who designed all this? It's lovely."

Louise's gaze wandered around the room, from the demilune-inlaid console table to the satinwood urn filled with holly. "Designed it? We did. I mean, Arnie, really. But we always discuss what we're going to buy. Once in a while he comes up with a clinker."

I gaped at Louise. I couldn't imagine that Tinker Toy could possess such elegant tastes. But of course the houses he built—at least the ones that didn't fall down—were handsome structures. I had assumed that he used an architect. I said as much to Louise.

"Sometimes he does," she said. "He did for this house. But Arnie has quite an eye. He has to, since there's no real architect in Alpine. He couldn't be running into Seattle all the time for consultations. Besides, talented architects are very expensive."

It seemed to me that if Arnie Nyquist was going to spend money, he preferred to do it on himself. However, Louise and I had strayed from the point of my visit. If there *was* a point— Louise wasn't exactly pressing confidences on me.

I steered the conversation back to the burglary, but Louise dismissed my remarks with a small smile and a shake of her head. "What's the use? Maybe it's just mischief, like stealing Christmas lights and rearranging the Marmot marquee. I have to be honest, except for Travis's baby things, I won't miss any of it. Who really looks at old birth and wedding and engagement announcements after thirty years? As for the rest—it was Arnie's, and I don't think I ever took the trouble to go through his Tyee yearbooks from the UDUB in my life. I went to Pacific Lutheran." Her smile grew quite merry.

"But your M.A. is from the UDUB?"

Pride surged through Louise's plump body. "I wanted to do that for years. Arnie couldn't see why. But nowadays you have to have a master's to teach in most districts. The truth is," she went on, lowering her eyes, "I enjoyed my time in

Seattle. Being in the city was an adventure. Of course I would never admit that to Arnie."

I could see why not. "You went to high school together, right?"

Louise abandoned her memories of independence and nodded complacently. "I was two years behind Arnie. We didn't date until he graduated from college. It was cute, really." She settled comfortably onto the brocade sofa, looking more at home with her memories than with her furniture. "It was summer break, and I came back home to work at the Marmot, taking tickets. Grandpa Lars was still alive, and on weekends he liked to get all dressed up in a suit and tie so he could greet the customers as they came in the door. We were showing a Paul Newman film that night—I forget which, I think his wife was in it, too—and I just adored Paul." She emitted a girlish sigh, and I responded with a flutter of my own. I was not immune to Mr. Newman, either. "Grandpa Lars teased me about my crush and said if I wanted to meet a handsome young man, why didn't I come to dinner at Popsy's on my night off ? Popsy—Oscar, I mean—and Mother Nyquist had huge meals—courses, really—with soup and salad and fish and meat. Everyone said they ate like kings and queens. I wasn't as anxious to meet a handsome young man as I was to see the spread they put on. And they did." Louise rolled her blue eyes. "Gravlax and sweet soup and butter dumplings and veal sausages and potatoes cooked with anchovies and onions— oh, it went on and on. I was such a skinny little thing then, but I ate until I almost passed out. Then Grandpa Lars said, 'See this wee one. She can eat like a logger, ya? Maybe she can cook, too. You better marry her quick, Arnold, before she gets away.' " Louise's laughter bubbled over.

"That fast?" I asked, eyebrows lifted.

"No, no. I'd barely noticed Arnie, poor dear. And to be frank, he wasn't exactly bowled over. But we did agree to go to a church picnic, and the next thing I knew, I was having dinner at the Nyquist house whenever I had a free evening. I still had to finish college, but we wrote letters. Arnie was quite a good correspondent. We got engaged the day I graduated. His family welcomed me as if I already was their daughter.'' She gave another little shake of her head, apparently still overcome by the memory of such familial warmth.

"That's a charming story," I remarked, now racking my brain for a way to get Louise Nyquist to open up. I must have been mistaken. The pleading look I'd seen in her eyes at the mall had sprung from an urge no more specific than a need for female companionship. I'd risked my neck and my Jaguar for nothing. Except, of course, to be kind to another human being. Sometimes I'm surprised by my own crassness.

"We've done the same with Bridget, I hope." Louise had gotten up, going to the kitchen to refill our eggnog mugs. I followed, with an eye on my watch. It was almost eight, and planning commission meetings seldom lasted more than an hour unless there was something controversial on the calendar. According to Carla, who was covering the session, tonight's agenda was pretty tame.

"Bridget could use a maternal figure," I noted, admiring if not particularly liking the stark black and white modernistic design of the kitchen. "Her own mother and father are dead, I hear."

"Yes, very sad." Louise handed over my replenished mug. "She never speaks of them. I must say, it hasn't been easy. Making her feel loved, I mean. Oh, she's agreeable enough. I was so afraid she might put up a fuss about being married in the Lutheran church." Louise kept talking as we headed back into the living room. I noted with some alarm that the snow outside the tall windows was coming down so thick that I couldn't see anything but a film of white. "She was raised Catholic, you know. That can cause problems. That is,'' Louise went on, a bit flustered, no doubt because she suddenly remembered that I was one of Them rather than one of Us, "it *used* to be that way. Things have changed, I'm told. Bridget didn't protest at all."

Frankly, I wasn't surprised. Catholic education has become so ecumenically-minded since Vatican II that the younger generation has problems telling the difference between a Christian and a Jew, let alone understanding the finer distinctions between Catholics and Protestants.

"But you're fond of Bridget," I said, allowing only the hint of a question in my voice.

"Oh, yes," Louise replied quickly. "So is Arnie." She hesitated, caressing her eggnog mug. I had noticed that while my portions were as pristine as I'd requested, hers contained a fair dollop of rum. I wondered if the second shot would make Louise more prone to revelations. "The truth is, she's not an easy person to get close to. I suppose losing both parents while she was still young has made her a bit guarded. And I can be *too* affectionate. Or so Arnie tells me. He insists I spoiled Travis. But what could I do? Arnie was always so busy and Travis was our one and only."

"So's my son," I remarked. I didn't add that Adam wasn't spoiled, at least not as far as I was concerned. I'd had enough trouble just keeping up, financially and emotionally.

"Once the babies start coming, I'm sure we'll grow closer." Louise's expression was now sentimental. "Babies have such a way of bringing people together, don't you think? If you want to know the truth, Arnie and I never had a lot in common until after we had Travis."

I murmured something inane about babies, but my thoughts were wandering. Louise Nyquist had a lot of love to give—I didn't doubt that for a moment. But Arnie's courtship of her sounded oddly perfunctory, as if it had been orchestrated. Not once had I heard exclamations of "love at first sight" or "mad about the man" or any such indication that Arnie and Louise had been drawn together by a strong romantic attraction. The beautiful house with its handsome furnishings suddenly spoke volumes. Under that brusque, burly exterior, Arnold Nyquist aspired to champagne and caviar. Louise was satisfied with eggnog and cookies.

I hadn't worn out my welcome, but the Baccarat clock on the mantel told me that it was time to go. Louise protested, insisting that I have one more eggnog, a piece of homemade fruitcake, a taste of her Mexican wedding rings. I demurred, and after nervously negotiating the steep curves that led down First Hill, I slowly drove home through blinding snow.

Adam and Ben surprised me. They had brought my tree inside and set it up in the sturdy cast-iron stand fashioned by my father thirty years ago.

"It's been out there for a week," Ben said as Adam turned the tree to display the best side. "We thought we'd start decorating it."

I had planned on leaving work early Wednesday to put up the tree, but as long as my son and my brother were willing to help, there was no time like the present. Having decided on the fir's best angle, Adam began testing the lights, while Ben unwound the tinsel garlands and I opened the first box of ornaments. I had four cartons of them, each individual piece wrapped in tissue paper. Every year, I went through the same ritual, smiling and sighing over the ornaments' history: "This bell belonged to my parents . . . That reindeer came from Aunt Rylla in Wichita . . . The skinny Santa was a freebie at a toy store . . . Adam made this one with his picture when he was in first grade." Naturally, it took a long time to trim the tree, but every ornament was like a present, a gift from the past, a garland of memories. My son thought I was a real sap.

The topper went on first, an angel from Germany clad in blue velvet and silver tissue, with spun-glass hair and a golden halo. My grandmother had bought her over fifty-six years ago for three dollars, ignoring Adolf Hitler and his schemes to conquer the world. Hitler was gone and so was his ruthless ambition. Germany had been conquered, divided, reunited, and gone on to produce copies of this same ornament at twenty times the price. No wonder my angel looked a little smug.

The lights were next, no easy task. Adam didn't start them up high enough. Then he left gaps about a third of the way down. One of the plugs wouldn't reach the outlet to the previous string. The white electric candles tipped every which way. The last set, miniature colored bulbs, went out as soon as it was connected. Like the lights, Adam also blew up.

"Jeez, Mom, you're so picky! You've got six strings on the tree already! You want to blow a fuse?"

"I always have seven," I said doggedly. "Try plugging the little ones into the wall."

Muttering, Adam did as I suggested. Nothing happened. Ben intervened, fiddling with the plug. No luck. "I think these are shot, Sluggly," he said. "You got a spare?"

I did, but it was old, another hand-me-down from our parents. Some of the wires were frayed. I was a bit nervous about using them, but Ben assured me that there was no danger as long as we didn't keep the lights on too long at a time.

The silver tinsel was next, wound carefully around the tree by Ben and me. Adam had decided to take a break and watch TV. I would lure him back with popcorn later. We were halfway through the first box of ornaments when Vida called. She was practically chortling.

"I figured out a way to get Bridget Nyquist to talk to us," she said.

I was momentarily distracted from admiring a bright pink pine cone made of glass. "How?"

"We tell her that Evan Singer has been asking impertinent questions about her." Vida sounded as smug as my angel looked.

"Vida!" I protested. "That's unethical! You'll have to come up with something better than that. It's not worthy of you."

Vida harumphed into the phone. "It most certainly is. I

don't need anything better." She paused just long enough to speak sharply to her canary, Cupcake, who apparently had not settled down for the night under his cloth-covered cage. "It's true, Emma. Evan Singer left here not five minutes ago, on his way back from the lodge. He made some very strange remarks about Bridget. I wouldn't like to repeat them over the phone. We'll talk more in the morning." On an imperious note, Vida hung up.

Ben, who had been inserting a Jessye Norman Christmas CD into my player, stared at me. "What's up?"

Jessye's rich voice filled the room with the strains of "The Holy City." I tried to explain. "This is all very strange. What did your buddy at Blanchet have to say about Carol Neal and Bridget Nyquist?"

"Bill Crowley?" My brother turned Jessye down a notch. "Not much. He remembered them both, but they weren't very active in school. He wasn't even sure if they were friends. Or if they *had* friends."

I had resumed decorating the tree, clipping on a red and white mushroom, Santa climbing down a chimney, and a bird with a silvery tail. "If Bill Crowley was the chaplain, why didn't he help Bridget and Carol fit in?"

"Probably because they didn't ask him." Ben had joined me, hanging a yarn snowman with ebony eyes. "I got the impression they went their own way and were perfectly content. What are you getting at?"

I put up a gold glass rose, a silver pear, and a purple cluster of grapes. "I don't know, Stench. I really don't. But it can't be a coincidence that Carol Neal came to Alpine and got herself killed. I mean, why come here except to find Kathleen Francich, who probably was also murdered?"

"But Kathleen didn't go to Blanchet," my brother pointed out. "Why would she come to Alpine?"

I gave my brother a blank look. Somewhere, there was a common denominator. Was it Bridget? Was it the private school connection? Was it someone or something else we hadn't thought of?

"Let's face it," I said, opening another box of ornaments. "There are only four thousand permanent residents in this town. Oh, sure, people come here to hike and ski and fish and camp. Maybe that's what Kathleen Francich did. But Carol Neal didn't think so. Otherwise, she would have reported her missing to the Forest Service or to the sheriff up here. I figure that in the beginning, Carol didn't know where Kathleen went. But six weeks later—more or less—Carol comes to Alpine, too. Why? What did she learn in that time period that led her to believe Kathleen had come up here? And why didn't she go see Milo?"

My brother knew my questions weren't idle speculation. "If those two girls were engaged in prostitution, Carol may have been chary of contacting the police. Oh, sure, she called King County to report Kathleen as missing, but she waited quite a while, right? Maybe she was going to see the sheriff here after she saw somebody else."

"Somebody like Bridget?" I raised my eyebrows over a pair of turtle doves.

"You keep harping on Bridget," Ben remarked, getting on his knees to hang some of the heavier ornaments down low on the sturdiest branches. "Are you sure she's the only Blanchet High grad in Alpine?"

"She's the only one who went to school with Carol Neal," I replied. Seeing Ben look up at me with a mildly incredulous expression, I waved a plastic Rudolph at him. "Vida would know. She keeps track of every newcomer, every bride, everybody who arrives in town other than on a slow freight. It's not just being nosy, it's watching out for a story angle."

Ben stood up, rustling through the ornament box. In the background, Jessye Norman put her heart and soul into "I Wonder As I Wander." I wondered, too, about many things. So, apparently, did Ben. "Did Vida do a story on Teresa McHale when she took over at the rectory?"

"No." I set Rudolph on an inner branch, his red nose poking out between the thick green needles. "We ran a paragraph in our Community Briefs column about her." I paused, fingering my upper lip. "You know, that's kind of odd—as I recall, Vida wanted to do more, but Teresa said she wasn't interested."

Ben had resumed crawling around on the floor. "Not everybody is keen on publicity. Some people like to keep their private lives private." He put a plush calico cat on the lowest limb just as Adam resurfaced, seemingly refreshed by his thirty-minute break in front of the television set. My son admired the tree, hands jammed in his pockets. It was, I thought, an unconscious attempt to pretend he didn't have hands and thus avoid work. "Hey, cool! You're almost done."

"Guess again," I replied, nudging an unopened carton with my foot. "Get with it, Adam my son. The hour grows late and the old folks grow weary."

With a heavy sigh, Adam unwrapped a crystal snowflake. I wasn't kidding about being tired. It was after ten, and we were an hour away from completion. A glance out the window showed me that the snow was still coming down hard. I could barely see the outline of the Jag in the carport, a mere four feet away. Ben was going to have a difficult drive back to the rectory.

"Why don't you stay here tonight?" I suggested.

But Ben declined. "I don't want to take a chance on being marooned and missing morning mass. Besides, I walked. Teresa needed the car."

Thinking of my brother blinded by snow and lying half-frozen somewhere along Fourth Street, I started to protest. But St. Mildred's was only a half-mile away. Ben could practically slide down the hill from my house to the church. Instead of arguing, I shrugged, and ditched another one of Aunt Rylla's homemade concoctions close to the tree trunk, out of sight. Somehow, sequin-spangled furnace filters don't appeal to my Christmas spirit.

But one big bowl of popcorn and an hour later, I rallied. After a quick pass with the vacuum cleaner to pick up spare needles and spilled icicles, we switched off the living room lights and turned on the tree. Ben chuckled; Adam whistled; I gasped. As always, it was a miracle: Magic lights and glittering balls, silver garlands and shimmering rain, old memories and renewed promises. The tree was cut fresh each year, yet never changed. I glanced at Adam, at Ben. We were together. Christmas was nigh. I felt peace wash over me, and let out a weary, happy sigh. The moment was sufficient unto itself. Tomorrow and its troubles would have to wait.

I had no idea that they were only a few minutes away.

I had just put my book aside and was about to turn off the light when I heard the sirens. Shortly after midnight, by my bedside clock. My first thought was of Ben. The weird little fantasy I'd had of him struggling through a snowbank had come true. An ambulance was pushing up Fourth Street, desperately trying to rescue my brother.

But I can differentiate between the sounds of the various emergency vehicles. This was a fire truck—*both* fire trucks, in fact, and farther off, perhaps over on Alpine Way. It was hard to tell, with the wind blowing the sirens' wail in erratic directions. I settled down into bed and drifted off to sleep.

It might have been the middle of the night, it could have been early morning, but it was really only one-fourteen. Fumbling for the phone, I managed to knock my book off the nightstand and hit my elbow on the headboard. My brain was fuzzy with sleep.

"Emma?" It was Milo Dodge. His voice was tense.

"What?" I finally managed to turn the light on.

"Sorry to bother you, but I **know** you're sending the paper to Monroe first thing in the morning." He paused, and I heard shouts in the background along with the grinding of wheels.

"Right, right," I muttered, fighting to get my eyes open in the brightened room. "What's going on?"

"We're at Evan Singer's place. It burned to the ground. No known cause yet, no damage estimate."

I sat up, feeling a draft around my shoulders. "How sad!" In my mind's eye, I pictured the dreary exterior, the bizarre artwork, the strange Christmas tree. With candles. Maybe that's what had started the fire. The rickety old shack would go up like kindling. Even if Alpine had more than four full-time firemen and a dozen volunteers, there probably would have been no way to contain the blaze. In ten-degree weather, the water in the hoses would no doubt freeze. "How is Evan taking it?" I asked.

Milo expelled a little grunt. "I don't know. We can't find him."

My knees jackknifed as I clutched the phone. "What? You don't mean . . . Was he in the cabin?"

"We don't know yet." Milo's voice was grim. "I've got to go, Emma. If we have anything new, I'll call before you ship the paper out."

Clumsily, I set the receiver in its cradle. With a groan, I fell back onto the pillow. Surely it wouldn't take long to determine if Evan Singer had died in the fire? The cabin was small; the furnishings were sparse. The image of his Christmas tree with its dangerous candles and grotesque ornaments wavered before my eyes. Evan Singer was odd, maybe even unbalanced. But he shouldn't have been foolish enough to set his home and himself on fire.

Then, as I switched off the light, it dawned on me that maybe he hadn't. Perhaps someone else had done it for him.

Chapter Fourteen

I SLEPT FITFULLY, upset about Evan Singer, and aware that the phone could ring again at any minute. Milo, however, didn't call back until after six A.M. I was already up and dressed, having decided that as long as I wasn't going to get any more sleep, I might as well start the new day.

Milo reported that no remains had been found in the ruins. I heaved a sigh of relief, then asked if they'd figured out how the fire had started. They hadn't, but it had originated inside. His voice foggy, Milo announced that he was going to bed.

Vida was an early riser, so I had no compunction about calling her. She would want to hear the news, and for once, I had scooped her. Or so I thought.

"My nephew Ronnie called an hour ago," she said, sounding vexed at my insane notion that she should be uninformed. "He's my brother Winfield's son and a volunteer fireman, you know. It's all very peculiar. I think we should run out there. We'll need a picture, though I suppose we couldn't make the deadline for this issue."

We couldn't. But I was faced with an editorial problem. On page four I had a photo and a feature on a young man who was apparently missing. I had to pull the whole spread and move something from page one to fill up the hole. The cabin fire was late-breaking news and took precedence over everything except our female body count. *The Advocate*'s front page was getting grimmer and grimmer. As for going out to Burl Creek, a peek through the window revealed that we had at least another eight inches of snow. It wouldn't get light for two hours, and the county road probably hadn't yet been plowed. Nor would there be time to take the picture, get Buddy Bayard to develop it, and run the thing in the paper.

"Damn!" I exclaimed. "I wish we knew where Evan Singer was. We could fill up that hole with quotes from him." Only fleetingly did I chastise myself for my callous attitude. At six o'clock in the morning of press day, I tend to let a crisis make me a journalist instead of a human being.

Vida, however, understood. "We could hold off sending Kip to Monroe until eight or nine. Wouldn't you rather be late than inaccurate?"

Of course I would, but the printer would hate me for it. *The Advocate* had a specific time on the press. Missing it screwed everybody up, and cost me money. "We've got over an hour to hear anything new," I pointed out, trying to keep panic at bay. "I'm walking to the office. I'll be there in twenty minutes if I don't fall down and break my neck."

Vida said she'd come in early, too. Hurriedly, I drank a cup of coffee, ate a piece of toast, and bundled myself up for the foray out into the snow. Peeking in on Adam, I saw only a patch of dark hair etched against his old Superman sheets. It occurred to me that I should replace them. Maybe bedding could be added to his Christmas gifts.

It was still dark, still snowing, but the footing was decent. A few cars were plodding along Fir Street. I crossed it carefully, noting that several houses along my route had left their outdoor lights on overnight. They provided cheerful beacons as I made my way down Fourth, mentally waving to Ben as I passed St. Mildred's and the rectory.

Except for a couple of delivery trucks, Front Street was virtually deserted this early. By the time I got to the office, I was stiff with cold. It didn't seem much warmer inside than it did outside. I turned on the heat, made coffee, and didn't take off my coat. Vida arrived before I could switch on the computer.

"Where do you suppose Evan Singer is, if he wasn't at home last night?" Vida demanded, yanking off her heavy knitted gloves. "Ronnie told me the fire probably started around eleven-thirty. Nobody would have noticed it way out there if Sue Ann Daley Phipps at Cass Pond hadn't gone into labor. She and her husband saw the flames on their way into the hospital and called from the emergency room."

"What time was Evan at your house?" I asked, staring stupidly at the computer display of page one.

"About nine-thirty. The snow got so heavy that he couldn't get the sleigh through it. Henry Bardeen had to use a four-wheel drive to haul the diners back to the parking lot." Vida gave me a flinty look. "Don't say it. No, Evan did *not* tell me where he was going after he left my house. If he had, I would have told you already."

I fueled myself with more coffee and wrote the sketchy story about the fire. It filled up a scant five inches. I needed twenty. I could run Evan's photo with a new cutline—but only if I knew whether he was dead or alive. I scowled at the layout. It was after seven, and Kip MacDuff would be along any minute. To my astonishment, Vida was emptying a string bag on her desk. At first, I thought it was our mail, but the postman doesn't usually show up until around ten. Then I recognized the bag of letters and bills and circulars I'd brought from the Villa Apartments.

"How'd you get hold of that stuff?" I demanded.

Vida gave me a superior look. "Billy let me borrow them. He and the rest of those dimwits haven't had time to go through them yet. They only opened a couple of bills. Now that we know Kathleen Francich was in Alpine—or that her car was—we can proceed without further doubts." She waved a green-edged piece of paper at me. "See this? It's an oil-company bill with a charge for the BP station in Sultan, October seventh. I do hope Milo is going over that car with a fine-toothed comb.''

I stared at the list of billings; Vida was right. The Sultan charge was also the last one made on the account. The bill itself was dated November the first. Vida held up another BP invoice.

''December. No payments, no charges. Nothing on any of her credit cards since early October, either.'' She was haphazardly organizing the mail into categories: catalogues, circulars, bills, and personal mail. ''They both have a lot of creditors, their bank cards are up to the limit, and neither seem to make many payments. Dun, dun, dun—done.'' Vida pushed the bills to one side. ''There are some Christmas cards, but no letters. Most of the cards are absolutely hideous, as you might expect with a person of Kathleen's low morals. Vulgar, too. I really don't care to see Santa exposing himself. There are some for Carol, too, but read this one.''

Vida handed me an envelope containing a card that didn't seem to bear out her assessment. The return address, in Redmond, was for one Murray Francich. The card itself was a handsome cutout of a dove with an olive branch in its beak. Unless it produced bird droppings when I opened it, Murray Francich's greeting seemed to be the exception to Vida's rule.

Inside there was a note: ''Kathy,'' it began, ''it's Christmas, let's try to be a family for a couple of days. I'm heading for E. Wash. Dec. 21. Why don't you come with me? No matter what you may think, the folks want to see you. Call me. Love, Murray.''

I hazarded a guess. ''Her brother?''

''That's what it sounds like. Their parents must live on the other side of the mountains.'' Vida gazed down on her untidy stacks of mail. ''Frankly, that's the only one of real interest I found. The rest are signed with names and at best—or worst, considering—the occasional ribald remark.''

''Milo has to get hold of Murray,'' I said. ''Maybe the

parents, too. And Carol's. It sounds to me as if those poor girls had problems with their parents."

"No wonder." Vida grimaced. "Carol's background sounds unstable, but that's no excuse to sell herself into prostitution. Imagine! Private school backgrounds, good educations, a bright future—and now this." She slapped at the pile of allegedly obscene Christmas cards, symbolic of depravity. "What could have made them ruin their lives?"

I lifted an eyebrow at Vida. "What? Or who?"

Vida regarded me with approval. "A good point."

The door opened, and of course I expected to see Kip MacDuff. Instead, Oscar Nyquist blundered and thundered into the office. This day was definitely not off to an auspicious start.

"Now this! What next? Who do I sue?" Oscar was one of the few octogenarians I knew who could still jump up and down. His bulky body made the furniture shake.

Vida, however, was unmoved. "Sue the ACLU. Claim you're a minority and then get them to represent you against themselves. It should be an interesting case." She gave Oscar a tight smile.

As usual, her irony was lost on Oscar Nyquist. "I'm not kidding!" he bellowed. "I get down to the Marmot first thing, like I always do, never mind four or forty feet of snow. And what do I find? A trespasser, that's what! I made a citizen's arrest. It's come to that, I tell you!"

I edged a bit closer to Oscar. "You actually took this person to the sheriff?" Why did I doubt it? Oscar Nyquist looked as if he could have hauled off the entire loge section of the Marmot.

"You bet." He nodded vigorously, the tube lights lending a jaundiced cast to his bald head. "They'd better lock him up, too. He's dangerous. He was smoking dope!"

My heart gave a lurch. "Who? Who was this trespasser?"

Now Oscar shook his head, just as vigorously, but from

side to side. "That punk, you know, the one who drives the sleigh. Henry Bardeen must have been nuts to hire him."

I slumped against Ed's desk in relief. "Evan's alive, then?"

Oscar's bushy brows drew close together. "Evan? Is that what he's called? What kind of name is that? Only my sister could come up with such a silly moniker! She called her kid Norman!"

"It's no worse than Travis," Vida pointed out. She saw Oscar start to boil over again and shook a ballpoint pen at him. "Simmer down, Oscar. Haven't you heard about the fire last night?"

Oscar hadn't, though he recalled sirens somewhere between dusk and dawn. The burning of Evan Singer's cabin didn't faze him, however. "No wonder," he muttered. "He was probably smoking that dope and set it off himself."

It took some doing, but eventually we got a rational account out of Oscar Nyquist. He had come to the Marmot shortly before seven. Walking through the auditorium, he had noticed what he thought was a coat that someone had left on a chair in the third row. Upon closer inspection, he discovered Evan Singer, slumped down and fast asleep. Irate, Oscar had bodily hauled Singer out of the theatre and down the street to the sheriff's office. Trespassing charges had been filed with Deputy Dwight Gould, though Oscar didn't doubt for a minute that they'd be dismissed and that Evan Singer would be merrily on his way to go off and smoke more weed. Would we put the story in the paper? Oscar assured us that we needed to run this kind of publicity. Vida informed him that we didn't—at least not in this week's issue. We'd have to see the formal charges, talk to Dwight Gould, get a statement from Evan Singer, and take another picture of Oscar the Valiant Hero. Since the paper was due to leave for Monroe at any moment, our hands were tied.

Amazingly, Oscar seemed to understand. What was even more amazing was that after only another outburst or two, he left. Frenzied, I called the sheriff's office to make sure that Evan Singer really was alive and reasonably well, then redummied the front page, threw in Evan's picture, and added a semi-happy ending to the fire story. Three minutes later, Kip MacDuff was on the road to Monroe.

As for Oscar's prediction, he wasn't entirely wrong. Given the circumstances of the fire—which was news to Evan— Dwight Gould showed mercy, asked for a five-dollar fine, and tore up the charge.

"So where is he going to live?" I asked Carla, who had done the legwork on the latest developments.

"Evan doesn't know," she said, "and I didn't want to get close enough to ask. He's really upset. His artwork was destroyed, you know. I gather he figures Henry Bardeen will give him a room up at the lodge. Of course the cabin is owned by somebody else." She threw an inquiring look at Vida.

"Elmer Tuck," Vida responded promptly. "He lives out by the fish hatchery. Retired from the Forest Service. Originally owned by an offbearer in the old Clemans mill. Bachelor. Went up for auction in 'thirty-four and Elmer's dad, Kermit Tuck, bought it for two hundred dollars as a retreat from his wife, May. Awful shrew, but a fine cook. Kermit drank, but only on weekends." Vida summed up several lives without glancing away from her typewriter.

Wednesdays are usually slow days at *The Advocate*. Next week, however, we were aiming for forty-eight pages, which meant that there was a lot of copy to write. Now was the time to get a jump on it. I culled the wire service for anything that might have a local angle. Timber industry, ski resort, environment, state department of highways—often there was a tie-in. I handed several items to Carla and kept a couple for myself. By the time the AP got to business news, I gave the stocks and bonds my usual detached glance. But a dateline out of Seattle startled me:

The State Attorney General's office today announced the indictment of Seattle broker Standish Crocker on unspecified charges of gross misconduct. Crocker is the president and CEO of Bartlett & Crocker, a local investment firm. Pending further investigation, all activities of the firm have been suspended. Crocker, who lives at Hunts Point, refused comment.

I read the item to Vida who wrinkled her nose. "Hunts Point? Isn't that where all your rich city people live across the lake?"

It was. Or at least it was an enclave where many wealthy persons had palatial homes. Hunts Point spelled prestige, exclusiveness, affluence. And, in the case of Standish Crocker, gross misconduct.

"I wonder how Travis Nyquist feels about this?" I mused. "Shall we get a comment from him regarding his former employer?"

Of course, Vida agreed, and a moment later, I had Travis on the line. He was shocked; he was incredulous. Standish Crocker was the soul of integrity. There must be some mistake.

"Cutthroat," asserted Travis. "That's what the financial business is like. I'm glad I'm out of it. Poor Mr. Crocker— he's obviously got some sharks swimming after him. He'll be fine, trust me."

I didn't, of course. Not with a stakeout in a PUD truck sitting across the street from Travis Nyquist's house. I wondered how deeply Travis was involved. We were a week away from the next edition, but I felt a sense of urgency. It wasn't yet noon. Milo Dodge was probably still asleep. I called his office and left word for him to get in touch with me as soon as he checked in.

Ed Bronsky was moaning over a double-truck co-op ad from the mall. "Look at this! Every store there is wishing our readers Merry Christmas! And after gouging us for presents! That takes nerve!"

It also took money, which I was only too glad to accept. I

let Ed groan on while consulting with Carla about a feature
she was planning around holiday reunions. To my pleasant
surprise, she'd gone to the trouble to track down several Alpiners who were getting together with relatives they hadn't
seen in years, either here in town or some place else. If she
could carry through with her writing, the story should make
heart-tugging, tear-jerking Christmas copy.

Ginny had just delivered the mail, which was late and not
of much interest. Having skimped on breakfast, I was thinking about lunch when Vida announced that it was time for
us to leave.

"For where?" I asked, startled.

She gave me a look of exasperation. "For Bridget's. I told
you we were going to talk to her this morning."

"But . . ." I started to protest, watched her shrug into her
tweed coat, and gave up. "I mean, I thought that after the
fire, you might want to lay off Evan Singer."

Vida gave me a hard stare. "Why? He's not dead, is he?
Let's go."

We did, taking her big Buick up to The Pines. The snow
had let up a bit as the morning moved along. As difficult as
it may be to conduct modern life in a world of perpetual
winter, it is always beautiful. Each new fall obliterates the
blemishes, accentuates the magic, and enhances the peace.
Christmas lights, indoors and outdoors, sparkle all the
brighter against a backdrop of white. No wonder the old
pagans lighted bonfires for their winter festivals. Even less
surprising is our modern urge to tear the rainbow apart and
fill our homes and hearths with twinkling lights and dazzling
baubles. We have not come so far from the barbarians; we
merely have more means.

Bridget and Travis were both at home. Neither was pleased
to see us. "I just talked to you," said Travis, as if once a
day with Emma Lord was quite enough.

"You didn't talk to *me*," Vida asserted, breezing past our

host. "The truth is, you might want to make yourself small, Travis. We've come to call on your wife."

If Vida had used a lasso, she couldn't have come up with a better way of ensuring Travis Nyquist's presence. He still wore the walking cast, and though he limped, I saw no sign of a cane. Reluctantly, Travis offered us seats in the living room, where a graceful blue spruce had been added since our last visit. Its gold, silver, and red decorations harmonized with the rest of the holiday accents. I marveled anew at the Nyquist family's good taste.

Bridget perched on the arm of a chair, as if she weren't quite sure if she intended to stick around. "I told you, Mrs. Runkel, I don't know anything about this Evan Singer. From what I hear, he's totally strange." Bridget's voice had grown very wispy.

Unwinding her muffler, Vida made a clucking sound. "Strange or not, Evan says he knows you." Her gray eyes darted in Travis's direction. "*Both* of you, from way back."

Travis threw back his handsome head and laughed. "Poor guy! He's probably in shock. My dad said Singer's cabin burned and he had to spend the night at the Marmot."

That was a different twist to Oscar's version, and not necessarily an incredible one. But while Travis looked more amused than concerned, Bridget was wriggling nervously on her perch.

It was my turn to play interrogator. "Bridget, where did you work before you were married?"

I caught the swift exchange of glances between Bridget and Travis. Still, the answer came promptly enough. "I was a temp. I met Travis when I was working as a receptionist for Bartlett & Crocker."

I noted that Bridget seemed oblivious to having contradicted herself about Travis's place of work. There was no point in chiding her; obviously she had been protecting her husband from a possible scandal.

"Could Evan have met you there, too?" I asked.

"No." Bridget shook her head emphatically.

Travis, however, fingered his square chin and tugged at one ear. I was reminded of a third-base coach giving signals. Was Bridget on first? "You know," Travis said amiably, "Evan might have come through the office while you were there, honey. He was never a client of mine, but he could have consulted someone else. Didn't you have a nameplate on your desk?"

Bridget's eyes grew wide. "Did I? Maybe so, I don't remember." She grew more flustered. "I worked at a whole bunch of places."

I saw Vida draw herself up to imperial proportions. The moment had come. I braced myself for her next query: "Bridget—what about Carol Neal? When was the last time you saw her?"

The color drained from Bridget's face. Travis merely looked puzzled. "Who?" he asked.

Vida's lips were clamped shut. With a mighty effort, Bridget regained some of her poise but none of her color. "Carol Neal!" she echoed in wonderment. "Now there's a name from out of the past."

"Yes," agreed Vida, her fingers playing over the surface of the twining vines that adorned the armchair. She didn't speak again, allowing the sudden silence to fill the living room like the aftermath of a death toll. I was tempted to prod Bridget, but I understood Vida's tactics.

"At commencement, I suppose," Bridget finally said in a small voice. "The cruise, I mean, afterwards. It's been a while."

Vida nodded once, her buckled boots planted firmly on the tiled floor. "You didn't see her last week before she died?"

Bridget's mouth opened; Travis let out a short exclamation. Their surprise seemed genuine.

"Carol Neal *died*?" Bridget slipped off the arm of the

chair and fell onto the upholstered seat. "How? A car accident?"

"Why do you ask that?" Vida inquired, sounding bemused.

Bridget's hands fluttered. "Why—a lot of people do. Young people. What was it?" Her voice had taken on an edge.

Having failed to elicit more than shock, Vida grew impatient. "She was murdered. So, I fear, was Kathleen Francich. You can read all about it when *The Advocate* comes out today." She stood up, seemingly oblivious to the horror on Bridget's face. I couldn't see Travis's reaction; Vida was standing in my way. "I don't suppose you've seen Kathleen for years, either?"

"Kathy! Oh, no!" Bridget reeled. Travis rushed to her side.

"Please leave," he said, very low, very tense. "Why did you come?"

"We're going," Vida replied blithely.

We didn't need to be shown out, but when Vida turned the brass doorknob, Bridget called after us: "Wait!" She was pushing at Travis, scrambling to get out of the chair. "It must be him! Tell the sheriff! I need protection!"

Vida and I had turned around in the foyer. Bridget stood under the archway that led into the living room, trembling and distraught. Travis had moved toward her, but stopped short, favoring his bad leg. He, too, looked stunned, but another emotion played across his handsome features. Fear? Anger? I couldn't be sure.

"It must be who?" asked Vida, her voice more kindly. "Protection from what?"

Bridget was making short, chopping motions with her right hand. "From whoever killed Carol and Kathy. He must be going to kill me, too." She was starting to cry, her pretty face crumpled like a mangled Christmas ornament.

"Who?" repeated Vida.

Limping, Travis stepped up to Bridget, putting a firm arm around her shaking shoulders. "Calm down, honey. You don't know anything of the sort. Terrible things happen in the city. You know it. You were raised there."

Slowly, Bridget turned to look up into her husband's face. "In the . . . Oh!" She gulped and pressed her face against Travis's chest. He looked at us over her head. His curt nod indicated that we should be gone. I half expected Vida to linger, to ask more questions, to raise more cain. But she didn't.

"I'm a monster," she muttered, trooping down the walk to the drive where we'd left the car. I noticed that the PUD truck was gone. "Think of it, Emma—Bridget could be innocent!"

I stared at Vida through a fitful fall of snow. "You don't seriously believe she might have killed Carol and Kathleen?"

Vida had to jiggle the handle on the car door to open it. "No, I doubt that very much. Of course, all things are possible. Certainly we learned that Bridget and Kathleen knew each other, even if they did go to different high schools. But didn't you notice Travis's coaching? About *the city*?"

I broke my stare only long enough to get in on my side of the car. "He assumed Carol and Kathleen were killed in Seattle. He couldn't know—yet—that their bodies were found so close to home."

Vida gunned the engine, craning her neck to reverse down the drive. "No, no," she said impatiently. "Just because *The Advocate* isn't in the mailboxes doesn't mean the whole town doesn't know. You realize what gossips these people are. I mean that Travis wanted us to think he and Bridget didn't know anything about Carol and Kathleen. Now why, I ask you, is that?"

My guess came promptly. "Because Bridget knew they were in town? But even if Bridget had heard from one or both girls, that doesn't mean she did them in."

"True. But she's got something to hide, and that's what I

mean about her innocence, or lack thereof.'' Vida cornered in front of a greenery-topped mailbox on a red-and-white peppermint stick stand. "Vice, its various forms such as prostitution and drugs. Or whatever Travis was mixed up in. Gross misconduct, in Standish Crocker's case. What does it mean?''

I didn't know. "My guess is that it's financial misdeeds. You know, inside trading or embezzling clients' funds. Why are you suggesting something more seamy?''

Vida was keeping her eyes on the road, which was a mercy, since the chains on her car didn't seem to have too firm a grip in the snow. "How long did Travis actually work? Four years? Five, at the most. Now how many brokers or investment advisors or what have you make enough money in that span of time to retire? And why retire at all when you're only thirty? You don't think there's something fishy about it?''

I had to admit that I hadn't thought much at all about Travis's life decisions. "Maybe he wants to take over The Marmot when Oscar pops off,'' I suggested. "Or go in to the construction business with his father. It's possible that he burned out early in the financial world.''

"Oh, yes, anything's possible,'' Vida conceded as she pulled onto Alpine Way. "But I'm definitely dubious.''

Vida had a point. Certainly there was something suspicious about Bartlett & Crocker; ergo, there was something suspicious about the firm's former employee. Milo must know who had been keeping an eye on Travis Nyquist's house. But I doubted that he'd tell Vida and me who or why. Yet. I wouldn't underestimate Vida's powers of persuasion over Milo or his deputy, Billy Blatt.

Front Street was freshly plowed and sanded. "Vida, you've never told me what Evan actually said to you about Bridget.''

Vida inclined her head. We were passing City Hall, a refurbished red brick building of two stories with swooping strands of gold Christmas lights draped across the facade. "It didn't make a lot of sense,'' she admitted. "He called

Bridget and Travis a pair of selfish philistines with no sense of loyalty. Bridget was a parasite, an interloper. Evan had some harsh words for Arnie Nyquist, too. He called him a despoiler of the earth. He said the Nyquists in general had betrayed their trust. The line was diluted. Or was it deluded?'' She glanced in the rearview mirror, preparatory to backing into her usual parking place. "Really, he did go on."

I didn't doubt it. But I still couldn't see any connection between Evan Singer and the Nyquists. Why pick on them? Until Oscar had ejected Evan from the Marmot, there had been no encounters between the family and the newcomer.

Ben was waiting for us in the office. In truth, he wasn't exactly waiting, but in the process of writing a note to me.

"Aha!" he exclaimed as Vida and I trudged inside and stamped snow off our boots. "I'm taking in the homeless. Evan Singer is going to stay up at the rectory."

I shook out my car coat, which had accumulated a few snowflakes in the walk from Vida's car. "How does Mrs. McHale feel about that?"

Ben shrugged. "I didn't ask, I told her he was coming. There's plenty of room with Father Fitz gone. The place was built for at least two priests. What's the problem?"

I heard Vida sniff loudly, and knew that her thoughts were running parallel to mine. Occasionally, my brother's priestly naïveté gets the better of him. "Teresa McHale doesn't strike me as the Hospitality Queen of Alpine," I said. "I don't see her opening the rectory door to anybody, let alone a non-Catholic."

Ben tipped his head to one side and ruffled his dark hair. "Well, well. Then I guess I won't tell her that Evan was raised in the Jewish faith. Not that he follows it, being a freethinker and a world-class loony. For Teresa's sake, we'll pretend that Evan is something more ordinary." Ben glanced at Vida. "A Presbyterian, maybe."

Vida groaned. "He could never be one of my brethren. We only have *sensible* people in our congregation."

I was about to remind Vida of some of the less sensible—and more insane—members of her church when Evan Singer ambled into the office. He was unshaven and hollow-eyed, but the leather jacket he wore looked expensive, as did the calf-high snakeskin boots.

"How," Evan Singer demanded of Ed Bronsky's empty chair, "do you place a value on art? Insurance people are number-crunchers. They just don't understand."

I gathered, rightly, that Evan had been with the State Farm people in the Alpine Building. As it turned out, he had no insurance of his own, but was expecting his landlord to cover his losses. I wished him well, but had the feeling that Elmer Tuck, retired, wasn't about to reimburse him for the loss of his paintings.

Bill Blatt, however, wanted to be helpful. His eager face appeared in the doorway, greeting his Aunt Vida, nodding at Ben and me, swinging a plastic Grocery Basket sack at Evan Singer.

"We may not have saved your picture," said Bill, his cheeks pink with cold, "but we got the frame. Maybe you can clean it up. It looks like real silver."

Evan Singer, along with the rest of us, stared first at Bill, then at the charred object he was taking out of the sack. It was indeed a picture frame, eight-by-ten size, the glass blackened by fire and the silver melted around the edges.

Evan glared at Bill. "That's not the picture I meant! This is commercial trash! You savage! I was talking about my paintings! My artwork! My life! Up in smoke! Gone! Destroyed by the gods who envy mortal talent! A pox on them all! I'm going to a higher authority!" He yanked the frame out of Bill Blatt's hand, stared at it malevolently, then dashed it to the floor. The glass shattered into tiny shards. Evan Singer ran out through the open door.

"Well, there goes your houseguest," I said to Ben. "Now where did we put the office broom?"

Ben, however, was undismayed. "He'll show up." He

saw my skeptical look and gave a short nod. "He has no-where else to go."

"The lodge? A motel?" I was at the little closet in the corner, getting out the broom and a dustpan. Vida had come around from behind her desk and was inspecting the charred silver frame.

"Now where did he get that?" she murmured. Carefully, she picked up the frame, shook off a few bits of glass, and began to rub at it with her handkerchief. "That's a Buddy Bayard frame," she announced. "They cost at least a hundred and fifty dollars. Two years ago I bet Buddy he wouldn't sell more than one. Why do I think he didn't peddle this to Evan Singer?"

"Why shouldn't he?" I asked, whisking up glass.

Vida took the dustpan from Ben, who was trying to be helpful, but managing mostly to get in the way. "Did you see that picture frame in Evan's cabin?"

"No," I admitted, "but I might have missed . . ."

"No, no, no," Vida interrupted, dumping the dustpan's contents into Ed's wastebasket. "It was one room. You said you saw all those peculiar things stuck around. You'd have noticed something prosaic—like that frame. What would be in it? His parents? If so, wouldn't that have struck a normal note among the discord?"

"Vida," I inquired, a trifle annoyed, "what are you get-ting at?"

It was Bill Blatt, not his aunt, who answered. "Arnie Nyquist's van! He said a framed photo was taken with all that other stuff. It was a picture of Travis and Bridget."

Vida nodded in approval. "Very good, Billy. A photo Evan wouldn't display, for obvious reasons. He stole it."

Bill's deep-set blue eyes widened. "Wow! You mean he was the one who broke into Tinker Toy's van?"

"It wouldn't surprise me," his aunt replied, and then scowled at no one in particular. "Wait—what time did Arnie say the break-in occurred?"

Unfortunately, Bill Blatt couldn't remember the specifics. His round, freckled face grew troubled. Felons were a cinch compared to Aunt Vida. "Jack Mullins took the report. Do you want me to check the log?"

"Well, certainly," Vida said, though she softened the response with the hint of a smile. "You weren't going to rush out and arrest Evan on my say-so?"

Judging from the startled look on Bill's face, that was precisely what he'd been prepared to do. At least until he thought twice about it. Ben and I exchanged amused glances as Bill Blatt dutifully headed for the door. He almost collided with Carla. She took one look at his youthful, engaging face, glanced up at the mistletoe over his head, and planted a firm kiss on Bill's lips. The young deputy staggered, stammered, and blushed furiously. Carla released him and swished over to her desk, long black hair swinging under her red ski cap. Bill Blatt stumbled out the door.

She beamed at Vida. "He's eligible," said Carla.

"You're crazy," said Vida.

"So?" Carla was still smiling as she took off the red ski cap and shrugged out of her quilted parka. "Couldn't your family use a little loosening up? All the inbreeding that goes on around here must be producing a lot of idiots."

Vida's eyebrows lifted above the rims of her glasses. "So that's what causes it," she murmured. "Now why didn't I think of that before?"

Chapter Fifteen

WEEKLY LULL OR not, the season brought its fair share of news that Wednesday. Trinity Episcopal Church had collected two hundred pounds of clothing and four hundred pounds of food for the needy of Skykomish County. A California couple had gone off Stevens Pass four miles below the summit and were being treated for minor injuries at Alpine Community Hospital. Two Sultan residents had been arrested for cutting Christmas trees on U.S. Forest Service land near Martin Creek. The number three lift at the lodge had broken down, stranding a half-dozen skiers for almost an hour. Mayor Fuzzy Baugh's Santa Claus suit had been stolen from his office in broad daylight. The usual number of outdoor lights, none of them at properties owned by the Nyquists, were reported as broken or missing.

Returning from a late lunch with Ben and Adam at the Burger Barn, I had just waved my companions off when I saw Arnie Nyquist getting out of his van in front of the bank. I paused at the corner, and he waved me down.

"Hey—you heard the news?" he called, causing a half-dozen shoppers to turn and stare.

"What news?" It wasn't a response to add luster to my reputation as a journalist, but it just sort of tripped off my tongue.

Arnie approached, jerking his thumb in the direction of City Hall, two blocks down Front Street.

"Fuzzy's suit. What did I tell you? This town's going down

the drain. Now the crooks can walk into the mayor's office and steal the clothes right off his back!''

I gave Arnie my most ingenuous look. "Fuzzy was *in* the suit? Funny he didn't notice."

"No, no!" Arnie waved a hand, batting at a few drifting snowflakes. "It was hanging up. He was in a meeting with the Chamber of Commerce. But what's the difference? Milo Dodge has a crime wave on his hands. Murder, arson, robbery, vandalism—what's next, riots, like L.A.?"

Since the racial mix in Alpine is virtually nonexistent, and a Welshman is defined as a minority, I didn't bother to attempt reasoning with Arnie Nyquist. His remarks, however, had given me an idea.

"Say, speaking of clothes, what did you do with that stuff you found last week at the bowling alley site?"

Arnie looked momentarily blank. I waited, gazing at the city's Christmas decorations, the garlands and bows and bells and candy canes touched with snow. The lone traffic light blended in: red, green, amber-gold.

"Oh, yeah!" Arnie finally responded. "I tossed them in the Dumpster. Any floozy who uses my property to make out doesn't deserve to get her stuff back. I hope she froze her butt off." He stopped, suddenly embarrassed. "Sorry, I got carried away. These kids nowadays, all they think of is sex, sex, sex. In my time, a fellow might sow some wild oats, but he didn't hop into the sack with every girl he dated. He had some respect for her. And she respected herself. Now that's the way it ought to be."

Arnie Nyquist was only a decade or so older than I, but his romantic experiences were a world apart. The men I'd known in my younger years had used every ploy imaginable to get a female into bed. By my junior year in college, I'd heard everything from the possibility of facing certain death in Vietnam to suffering from hypothermia. A member of the Husky varsity crew had told me that sex would keep him from catching crabs. Justifiably confused, I had refrained, not realizing it was a rowing term.

I had not stopped to talk to Arnie Nyquist about sexual mores, however. At least not about the philosophy thereof. "Were you able to pin down about what time your van was broken into?" I asked.

Again, Arnie's expression was temporarily blank. "Heck, that was a week ago. I was at Travis's place for an hour or so. Eight, nine o'clock, maybe." His eyes narrowed as he looked down at me. "Say, are you deputized or something? Why do you want to know?"

I gave Arnie a big smile which seemed to thaw him a bit. "No, it's just that if we do this in-depth piece we mentioned to your father, we need to know details. Besides, I think we've got a picture frame of yours at the office."

"What?" Arnie would have jumped up and down if he hadn't been mired in six inches of slush. "How come?"

I explained that it had been recovered from the rubble at Evan Singer's cabin. Nyquist's reaction was less than I had expected. His high forehead furrowed, and he gave a little shake of his head. "Singer? That goofball who drives the sleigh for Henry Bardeen? He may be nuts, but he doesn't strike me as a thief."

My assessment of Arnold Nyquist shifted yet again. Originally, I had considered him a typical rough-and-tumble small-town builder, shrewd, but not smart; cunning, but not canny. Yet he was a UDUB graduate, which didn't stamp him as a genius, since I knew several people with college diplomas who could barely tie their own shoes and wouldn't qualify for anybody's brain trust. However, he'd gotten through the school, and that meant that he wasn't as dense as I'd figured. Then I had discovered that Arnie was blessed with inherent good taste. That had come as something of a shock. Now, it seemed, he wasn't entirely a things-oriented person as I'd suspected, but was occasionally given to accurate perceptions of people. Tinker Toy was full of surprises.

"I agree with you," I said, because it was true. "Evan Singer isn't a thief. Maybe he was looking for something." I watched Arnie carefully.

But Arnie merely shook his head. "Like what? My granddad's fountain pen? Or those photographs? How would he know what was in the van in the first place?"

"I take it you don't know Evan?"

"Heck, no," Arnie replied, looking mildly aghast at the mere idea. "In fact, when I heard he was out of work after he got canned at the video store, I was on my guard. I thought he might come around and ask to go to work for me. No thanks. I know trouble when I see it. I'd heard enough from Dutch Bamberg. If you ask me, Henry Bardeen made a big mistake hiring him. You hear how he dumped all those folks out of that sleigh the other night and they ended up in the emergency room at the hospital?"

"Not quite." I didn't want to press the issue. It's useless to try to squelch rumors in a small town, either in print or in person. Besides, Arnie Nyquist had told me what I needed to know for now. And a good thing, since I had a feeling that when Travis revealed how Vida and I had barged in this morning up at The Pines, Arnie might close up like a clam.

"Scratch Evan," I said to Vida as I entered the news office.

She glanced up from a spread of engagement photos. "I know, Billy already told me. According to the report, Evan Singer would have been driving the sleigh up at the ski lodge when Arnie's van was broken into." She looked vexed. "So how did he happen to have that picture frame? Is Arnie going to come get it?"

"I don't know—to both questions." I got out of my car coat, which had grown quite damp and even frozen in places while I had stood on the street corner jawing with Arnie.

"Unless the fire was set, and whoever did it left the photograph at the site."

Vida rolled her eyes. "Honestly, Emma, that makes no sense! I expect better of you!"

So did Ed Bronsky, who all but begged me to call the mall owners and ask them to cancel a full-page ad for a three-hundred-dollar shopping spree drawing to be held on New Year's Eve Day. "Now why would they go and do a thing like that?" Ed groaned, wringing his hands. "Are they so rich they have to *give* stuff away? Why not just donate it to the poor and keep quiet?"

His rationale sent me to the phone, not to call the mall, but Milo Dodge. The sheriff was back on the job, but sounding harassed. I hesitated briefly, but went ahead with my suggestion. Milo's reaction was predictably grudging.

"The Dumpster? What if it's been emptied since then? What do you think we'll find?"

"I told you, clothes. Carol Neal's, maybe. It's worth a try, isn't it?"

Milo started to mutter, mostly incoherently: ". . . Other agencies . . . Seattle . . . Damned computers . . . The brother, he's not so surprised . . ."

"Stop!" I ordered. "Whose brother? Speak up, you're talking into your socks, Milo."

"What?" Milo seemed to get a grip on himself. I could picture him behind his cluttered desk, his skin a sickly green under the fluorescent lights, his bony hands delving into his pockets for a roll of mints. "You mean Murray Francich? I talked to him about thirty minutes ago. He works for some software company on the Eastside."

"And?"

"He was afraid of something like this. He hadn't heard from Kathleen for six months. He figured some crazy john did her in."

"And?"

"It's possible."

"You're waffling, Dodge." I could picture him squirming in his fake leather chair. "You don't really believe that."

"We can't discount it, not with either of the girls." Milo sounded slightly affronted.

"So Murray knew his sister was hooking?"

"He guessed. They haven't been close for years." Milo paused, and I heard papers being shuffled. "Kathleen was the youngest of a family of four, sort of an afterthought. Murray is closest to her in age, some seven years her senior. The other brother and a sister live out of state, California and Illinois. The parents, who are retired, moved to the Spokane area a couple of years ago. I gather they wrote Kathleen off."

I waited for Milo to go on, but he didn't. "That's it?"

"What else? He hasn't seen Kathleen in over a year. They talked on the phone last spring. We're *presuming*, remember? We can't ask this guy Murray to identify limbs. But finding the car is pretty conclusive." Again, Milo sounded put out that I wasn't waxing enthusiastic over his disclosures. "I got some background on Evan Singer, too."

I decided it was time to give Milo a verbal pat on the back. "You've been busy. I'm surprised you've gotten so much done, after being up all night."

"Hey, Emma, this job's a backbreaker. We're understaffed, underpaid, and with jerks like Arnie Nyquist, underappreciated. Now Fuzzy Baugh is on my trail because his damned Santa suit got swiped. I told him to go ask his elves about it."

"Hmmmm. Good for you, Milo. What about Evan Singer?"

"What about a drink? I'm not officially on duty, wouldn't get paid for it if I were, so why don't I meet you at the Venison Inn? I could go for a hot toddy about now."

I started to say yes, then went into a stall. "Give me twenty minutes. Say," I added, apparently as an afterthought of my own, "what's Murray Francich's phone number?"

"Why?"

"Why not? Vida will get it if you don't give it to me."

Milo heaved a deep sigh, but capitulated, relaying both the work and home numbers. As soon as he hung up, I called the software company in Redmond where Francich was employed. It took three transfers, but I finally got him on the line.

I introduced myself, offered condolences, and explained that we were planning to do a background article on the murder victims. This was not a favorite part of my job. Murray Francich and his sister may not have been close in recent years, but he was obviously shaken.

"I was about to go home," he said a bit curtly. "I'm going to leave tonight for Spokane to see my folks. This is a hell of a thing to happen at Christmas."

"I suspect it actually happened back in October," I pointed out, wondering how families could become so estranged that one member could be missing for months and the rest wouldn't notice. Or give a damn.

"Kathy was too trusting," Murray Francich's remark came out of nowhere, except some sad corner of his soul. Was he making excuses for Kathy? Or for himself? "She was such a cute little kid, dimples, big eyes, curly blonde hair. But shy. My brother and I used to tease her about . . ." He stopped abruptly, aware that somebody was actually listening to his reminiscences. "What do you need to know, Mrs . . . ah . . . ?"

"Lord," I filled in quickly. "She went to Holy Names, I understand. How did she get off track?"

Murray let out an exclamation that was part snort, part hiss. "How do *I* know? She was the baby, and my folks spoiled her. No, that's not fair—they were older when they had her. They couldn't do what they'd done for the rest of us, like driving to music lessons and soccer practice and debate team meets. So they made up for it by sending her to private school—the rest of us went to public—even though they weren't well off. They tried to give her the right clothes and all that fad stuff, whatever was the craze that particular year. But Kathy never had many friends. She didn't date much, either. And then . . ." His voice faltered. "Is this what you're after? I don't like it."

Neither did I. "We're not a tabloid, Mr. Francich. We probably won't use most of what you're telling me. Does it help to talk?"

He sounded bleak. "I've tossed this around a hundred times with the rest of the family. What good can it do now?"

Of course he was right. I shifted to different ground. "Was Kathy a good student?"

"Oh, yes." His voice brightened a bit. "At least until her junior year. That's when she changed. But she did graduate."

Ginny Burmeister appeared with a bundle of *Advocate*s, fresh off the press. I signaled my thanks, then glanced at the grim headlines:

**SLAIN WOMEN FOUND
IN ALPINE AREA**

**ARSON DESTROYS
SECLUDED CABIN**

As always, bad news looks even worse in bold, black type.

"What happened when Kathy was a junior?" I asked as Ginny discreetly made her exit.

Murray Francich sighed. "That's it—we never knew. At first, my mother thought she had a boyfriend, some creep who wouldn't make muster with my folks. Kathy started wearing a lot of makeup, flashier clothes, keeping odd hours. My folks confronted her, but she wouldn't tell them anything. There were some godawful fights. I was still living at home, and it got pretty ugly. Kathy moved out for a while— with a friend, I guess—but my mother was so frantic that she begged Kathy to come home. Then Kathy bought a car, with her own money, and more clothes, and she was gone every weekend. It was hell, I can tell you. I got an apartment that winter, and as soon as Kathy graduated, she was gone. The next day, in fact. She came home once, to pick up some tapes she forgot. My folks were heartbroken.''

My own heart went out to Mr. and Mrs. Francich. How do children go wrong? Where do parents fail? Who's to blame? I may not be my brother's keeper, but I am my child's custodian. Still, I don't like pointing the finger at parents who haven't been as lucky as I have.

"What about drugs?" I knew I was pushing my luck with Murray Francich. He'd been far more loquacious than I'd expected. Maybe he'd underestimated talking through his sister's troubled life.

"It's possible. I wondered at the time. I know there was alcohol.'' Murray was beginning to sound weary. It was going on four o'clock, and he'd had a terrible day. The trip to Spokane still lay ahead.

"One last question.'' My tone had turned ingratiating. "Did you know Carol Neal?''

"No. She'd been Kathy's roommate for quite a while, but I never met her. I don't know how they teamed up. A mutual friend, maybe.'' He gave a sudden, harsh laugh. "They weren't good for each other, I guess.''

They certainly weren't. And someone had been very bad for them both.

Milo's generic hot toddy turned into his standard Scotch. I, however, kept to the season and drank what the Venison Inn called a Yule-a-Kahlua. It tasted better than it sounded.

"Who gets these girls together?'' Milo mused after he'd scanned the front page of *The Advocate* that I'd brought along for him. "How many were there? So far, we've culled four out of that address book, which, by the way, must have been Carol's. There were no Franciches, but there's a Burt Neal in Grants Pass, Oregon. Her dad, it seems, but there's no answer.''

Burt Neal didn't interest me as much as the four culls. "What do you mean? Who are they?"

"Rachel Rosen. Bridget Dunne, now Nyquist. Tiffany Matthews. And April Johnson. Tiffany went to Bush, April to Seattle Lutheran." Milo was reading from his notebook. "Tiffany overdosed two years ago on Christmas Eve. April married a soldier and is living at Fort Hood, in Texas."

Bush was an exclusive private school near Lake Washington. I didn't know much about the Lutheran setup, except that it was over in West Seattle. "Has anyone contacted April?" I inquired.

"King County did, this afternoon. She hung up on them. They also tried to reach Rachel at the UDUB but they've gone on Christmas break. There was no answer at her home number." Milo regarded his Scotch as if he expected it to elude him, too.

I was silent for a bit. The sound system played "The Little Drummer Boy." Pah-pah-pah-pum . . . Pah-pah-pah-pum. "How about Tiffany's family?"

"Kid gloves," Milo replied, again on friendly terms with his Scotch. He signaled for the waitress to bring another round. "The Matthewses are very rich, very influential. Old money, big house on Lake Washington Boulevard. To complicate matters, they're in Europe."

"Swell." I gazed around the room, with its red and green streamers, big paper bells, and real stockings affixed to the fireplace's temporary cardboard brick mantel. Half the tables were occupied, and a handful of customers sat on stools, joshing with each other and with Oren Rhodes, the full-time owner and part-time bartender. It was too early for any of the clientele to be drunk or unruly. Serious daytime drinking in Alpine was reserved for private homes and the Elks Club.

Oren himself brought our drinks, ribbing Milo about having his hands full. His attitude toward our recent tragedies was detached. Like all good bartenders, he took death, divorce, and other debacles in professional stride.

"Why single out these girls?" I asked after Oren had re-treated to his post behind the bar. "That address book had a lot of names."

Milo nodded. "They'll all be checked out. But a red flag went up at King County on anybody with a private school background. It may mean nothing, but it's the only link we've got between Carol, Kathleen, and Bridget. And Bridget is the only Alpine link to Carol and Kathleen."

"Bridget's scared," I admitted. "Or pretending to be. But she denies seeing Carol and Kathleen recently. I have a hunch she's lying. I don't suppose you want to tell me who was doing the surveillance at the young Nyquists'?"

Milo grimaced. "I don't know why, but I could say who. It'd be off the record, though."

I hate off-the-record information. If I know something, I feel that the public ought to know it, too. But I can keep a confidence when necessary. "Who, then?"

"State police," said Milo Dodge. "They went home yes-terday."

"Having been successful?"

"I wouldn't know." Halfway into his second Scotch, Milo had visibly relaxed, although he still looked tired. "Evan Singer went to Lakeside."

I wasn't surprised. "Rich, huh? Lakeside costs a bundle. Where does the money come from?"

Milo again consulted his notes. "Father is Norman Singer, a prominent plastic surgeon. Mother, Thea, is a rabid patron of the arts. Grandfather was an architect. One sister, dab-bling in the New York theatre scene. Varied academic career, no degree. Arrested twice, once for disturbing the peace, the second time for disorderly conduct. Plea bargains, fines, but no jail time." Milo closed the notebook.

"Spoiled rich kid," I murmured. Evan's claim to have lived all over the world was probably pure hokum, invented to add exotic zest to his suburban upbringing. "Has he ever invested with Bartlett & Crocker?"

"His money's tied up in trusts. Dr. Dad apparently realized Evan wasn't stable." Milo was grinning at me. "Well? Have you and Vida solved the case yet?"

I sniffed at Milo. "All this stuff is interesting, but not very helpful. Evan's too old to have known any of these girls in high school. We need some serious leads."

"We need another drink." Milo waved his empty glass at Oren Rhodes. I, however, demurred, and urged him to do the same.

"You're still beat, Milo. Go home, eat something, watch TV until you fall asleep." I stood up, ready to head back to the office to see if the place had gone to hell in a handcart during my absence.

Milo was gazing up at me with an off-center grin. "Emma, are you mothering me? Haven't you got enough men in your life at the moment?"

With Adam and Ben around, I certainly should. But without Tom, all the men in the world weren't enough. The ridiculous thought crossed my mind in a haze of rum and Kahlua. "I'm a jackass," I announced in my best imitation of Vida. "Go home, Milo."

He was still grinning as Oren appeared with another Scotch. But before Milo could take a sip, Bill Blatt hurried into the bar. I stepped aside as the young deputy nodded at me in greeting and addressed his boss.

"We found the clothes, Sheriff. They're girl's stuff. Jeans, sweater, jacket, and . . . ah, bra and panties." Bill blushed, though not as deeply as he had when Carla had kissed him.

"Damn!" Milo drained his glass and got up. "Back to work. We need the lab to check the stuff out, match it with the victim, see if . . ."

Milo and Bill had outdistanced me. I shrugged and wandered out through the restaurant. Oscar Nyquist was sitting alone at a corner table. A napkin was tucked under his chin, and he was engrossed in the *Advocate* story about the Marmot. I hesitated, then saw the waitress approach with his order. Oscar put the paper aside and began to eat.

"How's the story?" I asked, resting a hand on the vacant chair across from Oscar.

He looked up from his meatloaf, his blue eyes wary, his bald head shining pink under a grouping of red Christmas lights. "Okay, so far. That Vida writes like she talks. A lot of words, blah, blah, blah. It sounds like that architect fella built the Marmot instead of my father."

"Lowenstein? Vida wanted to make sure he got credit because the theatre is such a structural gem. Apparently he was well known for his work all over the West Coast."

Oscar speared a chunk of over-browned potato. "Yeah, sure, he was clever. That's how he got rich. My father paid him a bundle." His wide face turned sullen, making him look like a big wrinkled baby due for a crying spell. "Better to have run him out of town."

I shifted in place, wishing Oscar would ask me to sit down. "Why is that?" I asked.

Oscar waved his fork. "Never mind. What's done is done. I'm too old for grudges. You eaten?" He pointed the fork at the spare chair.

I rested one knee on the seat cover. "No, I still have some work to do. I'll eat later at home."

Oscar nodded. "I always eat early, except on Sundays. For forty-eight years, my wife had supper on the table every night at five. Then I'd go to the Marmot to open the doors at six-fifteen. Astrid's gone, but I still eat at five. And I still go to the Marmot at six-fifteen." He spoke with pride.

"Let me know what you think of the rest of the story," I told Oscar with a smile. I almost wished I could join him. How many nights did he eat alone? I was feeling sorry for him as I walked up the street with my head down to ward off the wind and snow. The Burlington-Northern whistled as it started its climb to the summit. There was more traffic than usual on Front Street, caused by Alpine's usual exodus from work and the Christmas shoppers returning home. The amber headlights glowed in the scattered snowflakes. I glanced up, seeing the town perched on the mountainside, windows shining, trees lighted, decorations ablaze. The sight cheered me. Oscar Nyquist not only had family, he was probably the object of many Alpine widows. He was also the type who enjoyed his solitude. I realized that he hadn't exactly jumped for joy when I showed up at his table.

Everyone was gone at the office except Ginny, who was finishing the weekly mailing to out-of-town subscribers.

"I'll just make it to the post office by five-thirty," she said, dumping the last bundle of papers into a mailbag. "We had more calls than usual after *The Advocate* came out. They were mostly people upset about the murders, but some of them phoned to say they liked your owl editorial. Then there were some who didn't."

I laughed. "I expected that. If it weren't the Christmas season, I might get bomb threats."

Ginny, always serious, gazed at me from under her fringe of auburn hair. "You think people really behave better this time of year?"

"No. They're just too busy to make mischief." I glanced at the old clock above Ginny's desk, with its Roman numerals and elaborate metal hands. It was 5:24. "You'd better hurry, Ginny. But be careful."

She was putting on her blue anorak. "I'll get there. I made one trip already. I couldn't find our mailbag. This is a new one I got from the post office this afternoon." She hoisted it over her shoulder, looking from the rear like a small Father Christmas. "See you tomorrow."

"Right. Good night." I went into my office, swiftly sorting through the phone messages. Nothing urgent, nothing startling. Ginny had made notes on some: "Green River killer loose again?" "Saw stranger Monday night in Mugs Ahoy. Saw man from Mars there last week." "Owls have big hooters." "Bride wore teal going-away suit, not *veal*." "Buckers got robbed on charging foul in last twenty seconds against Sultan." "You're an idiot."

It was the usual assortment, many anonymous. The only one that held my attention read, "Ask Oscar Nyquist about Karen." The space for the caller's name was blank. I wondered if Ginny had recognized the voice. She often did.

Karen, I thought, as I started my uphill climb for home. Who was Karen? The name rang a bell, but I couldn't place it. Vida might know. I'd call her after Adam and I had dinner. Ben was dining with Jake and Betsy O'Toole. The zealous Teresa McHale couldn't coax him out of eating with the owners of the Grocery Basket.

My son, however, had spent the afternoon with my brother. To my amazement, Adam had helped Ben with some fix-up chores around the church. They'd repaired pews, shored up the confessional, replaced light bulbs, and gone through the decorations which would be put up on Christmas Eve Day.

"Tomorrow we're going to do some stuff at the rectory," Adam declared matter-of-factly as we dined on pasta, prawns, and cauliflower.

I couldn't help but stare. Here, in the home I'd created for the two of us, rafters could fall down, sinks could overflow, walls could collapse, and Adam would wander through the rubble, looking for the TV remote control. "Gosh, Adam, what happened? Did your heretical Uncle Ben introduce you to the Protestant—gasp!—work ethic?"

Adam didn't get the joke—or didn't want to. I dished up tin-roof-sundae ice cream for him and listened to his account of Ben's Tuba City chronicles.

"They've got all these great Indian ruins around there, way back to the Anasazis. There's Betatakin, with dwellings just like big apartment buildings carved into the cliffs from over eight hundred years ago. It's real green at the bottom of the canyon, not like the desert up above. Uncle Ben says there's aspen, elder, oak, and even Douglas fir. I want to go there next summer.''

I gazed fondly at Adam, who was finishing his ice cream. Over the years, he had seen Ben an average of once, maybe twice a year. They rarely wrote and never talked on the phone. Yet there was a closeness between them, born of a solitary man's need to love and a child's instinctive response. Adam had only recently met his own father. They had started to forge a bond, and I was glad. Typically, my son hadn't regaled me with details, but his attitude toward Tom seemed friendly. And now, he was seeing Ben, not just from a nephew's point of view, but man-to-man. I was pleased by that, too.

"You ought to go down there," I agreed. "Maybe you could get a summer job."

Adam nodded, a bit absently. "That would be so cool— archaeology, I mean. Or is it the other one—anthropology? I wonder how long it takes to get a degree?"

I said I didn't know. I refrained from adding that it probably wouldn't take as long as it had for Adam to declare a major. At twenty-one, it seemed that it was time for him to decide what he wanted to be when he grew up. Or, having grown up already, he might consider his future in terms of . . . a job. I would say this later. Maybe it would be better coming from Ben. Or even Tom.

I caught myself up. For over twenty years, I'd never delegated an ounce of my parental responsibility. I wasn't about to start now. I rose from the table and went to call Vida.

She wasn't home. I'd forgotten that she was going to her daughter Amy's house for dinner. The question about *Karen* could wait. So could relaying Milo's various pieces of information. I settled down to watch a video that Adam had picked up earlier in the day. It was the remake of *Cape Fear*, and it scared me witless. How could anyone be as evil as the Robert De Niro character?

"Hey, Mom, it's only a movie," Adam said, laughing at my dismay while he rewound the tape. "Lighten up."

Adam was right. It was only a movie.

But out there in the drifting snow, among the festive lights, with the sweet strains of carols in the air, evil, real and terrifying, was on the loose. *Who was the killer?*

The only thing I knew for sure was that it wasn't Robert De Niro.

I would do Elvis. And the Wise Men. Ben had to attend the St. Mildred's Christmas Pageant, so I decided to join him on Thursday night and cover the event. Adam was noncommittal. He had met Evan Singer's replacement at Video-to-Go, and her name was Toni Andreas. I vaguely recognized her from church. She looked as if the wattage in her light bulb was pretty dim.

The day had dawned crisp and clear, with the wind blowing the snow clouds out over Puget Sound. Alpine sparkled in the early morning sun, and I could have used my sunglasses. Native Puget Sounders are like moles—for nine months of the year, they see the sun so seldom that their eyes can't take the glare.

The first thing I noticed downtown was the Marmot's marquee. It was the last day for *It's A Wonderful Life*, which was just as well, since the letters had now been rearranged to read *A Wide Full Fir Stone*. The Nyquist staring up at the scrambled title wasn't Oscar, but Louise.

"Now why do people do things like that?" she asked in exasperation after hurrying over to meet me at the corner. "Popsy will be wild."

"Where is Popsy?" I asked, as Louise fell into step beside me.

"He slept in," she replied, her brown boots mincing through the rock salt. "He needed his rest after last night." Her profile was uncustomarily grim. When I made no comment, she turned to give me a sidelong look. "You haven't heard? It's that same demented young man, Evan Singer. Two nights in a row he's caused problems for Popsy! Really, something's got to be done about him!''

"What now?" I asked. Trucks from UPS, Federal Express, and the U.S. Postal Service were already out and about, making early deliveries of Christmas presents and mail order gifts. Something about the vehicles rattled my brain, then melted away. Maybe I'd forgotten to mail a parcel. Or a greeting card. It'd come to me, hopefully before Christmas.

"It's crazy, just crazy," Louise was saying. "He came to see the movie—again—but this time, he was dressed as Santa Clause, complete with a pack over his shoulder. That was strange enough, but then he got into an argument with somebody because he insisted on sitting in their seat. The usher came, then Popsy, and finally the other person moved, just so they could start the movie. It's not as if there was a full house—the picture's been showing for over a week—but Evan Singer wouldn't back down. Popsy should have thrown him out, but he didn't want to upset the other customers.''

We'd reached *The Advocate*. I invited Louise to come in, but she said she was going to the bakery. "We're having Travis and Bridget to dinner. Travis is so fond of the Upper Crust's sourdough rolls. Maybe I'll get a dessert, too." She gave me a faintly wistful smile. "I *could* make one. But the last few days have been so upsetting. Arnie thinks Evan Singer stole that Santa suit from the mayor. If he did that, then I think he was the one who robbed our house and van. But Arnie doesn't agree with me, he says just the suit. I think." Louise looked confused over her own words, and I could hardly blame her. Confusion seemed to have the upper hand in Alpine these days.

I said as much, and Louise heartily agreed. Certainly anything was possible with Evan Singer. I had to talk to Ben, to ask if Evan had showed up at the rectory. But it was eight o'clock, and my brother would be saying the morning mass.

Louise scurried off to the bakery. Inside the office, I found

Ginny and Carla, both still wearing their coats and fiddling with the thermostat.

"No heat," Ginny announced, pulling off her white ear-muffs. "It's freezing in here. The pipes are okay, though."

"I can't type with my mittens on," Carla complained. "I'll make a lot of mistakes."

I suppressed the obvious rejoinder. But she and Ginny were right about the heat. The electrical unit wouldn't turn on. Otherwise, we had power.

"Call Ross Blatt over at Alpine Service and Repair," I told Ginny. Ross was, of course, a nephew of Vida's, and thus Bill Blatt's first cousin.

"How old is Ross?" asked Carla, loading her camera. "Is he married?"

"Yes," I replied. "He's got a couple of kids. He must be ten, fifteen years older than Bill. Why? Are you giving up on the local lawman?"

Carla shrugged, heading for the door. "Maybe. You did." She left.

"I never . . ." But there was no one to hear me. Ginny had gone into the front office to call Alpine Service and Repair. It was useless anyway to point out that Milo Dodge and I had never been a romantic item. Everyone assumed that because we were peers, single, and enjoyed each other's company, we ought to fall in love. Everyone, that is, except Vida, who knew better, and who was crossing the threshold carrying a Santa Claus suit.

"I found this in my front yard," she announced. "I'll bet it belongs to that old fool, Fuzzy Baugh. Why is Carla taking a picture of the Marmot's marquee? Haven't we given the Nyquists enough coverage?"

I thought so, too, but apparently Carla couldn't resist cap-turing for posterity one of the scrambled movie titles. It was the kind of photo we could use as a novelty: "Alpine Out-takes," or some such filler feature for a slow news week.

"Vida, what do you know about somebody connected to the Nyquists named Karen?"

Vida was taking off her coat. She cocked an eye at me from under the brim of her red veiled fedora. "Karen? She's Oscar's sister. Why?"

I told Vida about the anonymous phone call. Vida put her coat back on. "Oooooh! It's like ice in here! What happened?"

My explanation was brief. Vida gave a curt nod. "Ross knows his craft. It's too bad he's such a noodle otherwise. Now what's this about Karen Nyquist and asking Oscar? What's to ask? She moved away from Alpine when she got married back in 1938."

I sat down on Ed's desk. He'd be in late, this being the morning of the Chamber of Commerce's Christmas breakfast. "You mean she never came back?"

"Of course she came back." Vida yanked the cover off her typewriter. "She and her first husband, Trygve Hansen, and Oscar and Astrid were all close to Lars and Inga. Then the war came, and Trygve got a patriotic urge to serve. Maybe it was because Norway was occupied or some such silliness. He and Karen had no children yet, so the army took him just like that." She snapped her gloved fingers. "He was killed in North Africa. Karen went to work for Boeing, where she met her second husband, a scientist. He was a Jew. I told you that already." Vida fixed me with a reproachful look.

"I forgot." Vida was right. She'd mentioned that someone in the Nyquist family had married a Jewish man. But their genealogy, like that of so many Alpiners, was too complicated for a poor city girl to follow. "What happened then?"

"Nothing." Vida sorted through a stack of news releases, discarding most of them in the wastebasket. "Old Lars disowned Karen, more or less. He never mentioned Karen's new husband by name. Oscar went along with it like the lump of a lamb he is. Arnie was still a boy. Goodness, I was in high school at the time." She rolled her eyes at the marvel of her youth.

"So you don't know what became of Karen Nyquist Hansen after that?" I saw a note on Ed's desk from Francine Wells; she was having a pre-Christmas clearance, with twenty-five to fifty percent off on all designer dresses. I winced inwardly, trying to calculate what I would have saved if I'd waited to buy my green wool crepe. It had certainly been wasted on Milo.

"I know she and her second husband had a family. Karen hoped that the children would soften up old Lars, but of course he wouldn't give in. Finally, she stopped trying. I hate to admit it, but I lost track of her." Vida looked uncommonly rueful. "I suppose everybody else here did, too. Including the Nyquists."

I was lost in thought. Vida had begun hammering on her typewriter, having better luck with her gloves on than Carla would with her mittens. Or without. "I wonder who called," I finally said aloud. "And why."

Vida looked up but didn't stop typing. "Some busybody the Marmot story set off. You know how that goes. Shouldn't we call Milo about that Santa suit?"

Since I was still wearing my car coat and it wasn't any colder outside than in, I carted the suit down the street to the sheriff's office. Ross Blatt honked as he passed in his repair truck, presumably headed for *The Advocate*.

Milo shook his head as I handed him the suit. "Let's see if it's got a Fantasy Unlimited label. Irene Baugh remembered that much, even if Fuzzy wasn't sure which parts were red and which were white."

The suit indeed bore the proper label. Milo had heard about Evan Singer's latest escapade at the Marmot, courtesy of Sam Heppner, who had been in the audience. Deputy Sam had not wanted to interfere, since he was off-duty as well as loaded down with popcorn, soda pop, red licorice, and Milk Duds.

"The question is, did Evan Singer swipe the suit," said Milo, offering me some of his dismal coffee. "If so, why?" He bit into a glazed doughnut, which I presumed was breakfast.

"Because he's nuts?"

Milo wasn't amused. "First the Nyquists on my case, now the mayor. Who's next? The KKK and the ACLU?"

I got serious, too. "Do you think Bridget Nyquist needs protection?"

"She hasn't asked for it." Milo poured himself another mug of coffee. I realized he was using *our* mug. Maybe this wasn't the time to request its return. "Let's face it, Emma, we've got zip. Oh, those were Carol's clothes, hair and fibers match, right size, all that. But so what? The killer dumped the stuff at the construction site, and any traces have been covered by snow." He paused, rummaging through the file folders on his desk. "Here—how's your stomach? I got some details from the M.E. in Everett. Are you up to it?"

I blanched, then lied. "Sure. Go ahead."

Milo perused the typewritten form. "First victim, presumably Kathleen Francich, was dismembered with an axe. Do you want to know how?"

I told the truth. "No. I mean, I can guess. Do I need to know?"

Milo shook his head and finished his doughnut. The man had nerves of steel and a stomach to match. I had to give him that. "But consider what a mess it would make. Where does the killer do it? Outside, where the snow will eventually cover the blood? Off on some logging road? A hiking trail? How do you transport the remains to the river without staining your car or truck or whatever? In a sack? Maybe. Still, I think you're taking a big chance. There are too many people out roaming the woods, especially in early October."

"Stop saying *you*. I feel as if I'm about to be arrested."

Milo gave me a thin smile. "Okay. But what do *you* think?"

I preferred not to think about it at all, but just to sit in Milo's crowded office, feeling the warmth of his space heater and drinking his dreadful coffee. However, I was a journalist with an obligation. "If it was an inside job—literally—where? A private house? If you could be assured of privacy and then clean up like mad, maybe so. But that's risky, too."

An enigmatic expression crossed Milo's long face. "What if your place was secluded and you burned it to the ground?"

Milo's theory had some merit. It also had some flaws. "Why wait two months? Kathleen Francich was killed in October. And, if the same person killed Carol Neal, why not dispose of her in the same way?"

"No time. There was a rush on with Carol. If we knew why . . ." He let the thought float away.

"Motive," I said, looking into my coffee mug as if I were reading tea leaves. Maybe it *was* tea, not coffee. That would explain why I could see the bottom of the mug with an inch of liquid left. "If Carol and Kathleen were hookers, was Bridget, too? What about the others? It sounds as if you're envisioning a ring of private school prostitutes."

"I am." Milo didn't look as if the idea agreed with him. "Carol, Kathleen—and Bridget—all suddenly had money to burn in their junior year. Drugs or prostitution? Both, maybe, but I lean toward the sex angle. If we can nail Rachel or April, we may find out."

"Tiffany was rich already," I pointed out. "Why would she get involved? Drugs?"

"That's a decent guess," Milo replied. "Nobody's ever rich enough to afford a serious drug habit. Especially not a young woman who was probably on an allowance."

Milo made sense. "How did they get together? Carol and Bridget went to the same school, but not the others." I frowned at the mounted steelhead behind Milo's desk. He had decorated it with a strand of green tinsel. "At dances? Football games? Summer camp?"

"Hey!" Milo grinned at me. "You're sharp. We'll see if

King County can find out if they were counselors. Going into their junior year, they'd be sixteen, seventeen, too old to be regular campers." He scribbled a note to himself.

"I still think Bridget may be in danger," I said, swallowing the last of the ersatz coffee.

Milo's phone rang; he ignored it. The caller persisted, which meant that Bill Blatt wasn't intercepting in the outer office. Resignedly, Milo picked up the receiver. His indolent form snapped to attention.

"Is that right? . . . I'll be . . . Yeah, right, we figured that much. . . . Oh? . . . Well, now . . . When? . . . Sure, okay. . . . Thanks. By the way, here's something you might want to run through the . . ."

I stood up, now too warm in my car coat but unwilling to take it off when I knew I was on the verge of leaving.

Milo continued to give instructions to the person on the other end of the line. At last he hung up, and gave me a self-satisfied look. "Standish Crocker is being charged with racketeering, money laundering, and drug dealing. He used that investment firm as a front for providing cocaine and call girls to businessmen from Seattle to Singapore. What do you think of that?"

I sat down again. "Whew! That's incredible! I thought Standish Crocker was some stuffy old Brahmin. What'd he do, go into his second childhood?"

"He died. Standish Crocker II, that is, in 1989. His son, Standish Crocker III, is only thirty-four, a real swinger. But he swung too far. Maybe Travis did, too." Milo was still looking pleased. "He's being taken into Seattle for questioning today."

My first, irrelevant, thought was for Louise Nyquist and her dinner party. I didn't admit as much to Milo. "So maybe that's how Travis met Bridget? She was one of the call girls?"

"*Was*. Maybe." Milo was now frowning at his hastily scribbled notes. "Bridget Dunne, Carol Neal, Kathleen Francich, Rachel Rosen, April Johnson, and Tiffany Matthews all have arrest records for soliciting. But only Kathleen and Carol have been busted during the last year and a half. That figures—Tiffany died, April and Bridget got married. Rachel . . . maybe she reformed and went to college.''

"Let's hope. All of them had some advantages. It would be reassuring to think they didn't have to come to a tragic end." I suddenly felt weighed down by Milo's news. It was one thing to make suppositions; it was quite another to be confronted with the bald truth. Six girls, from decent families with good intentions, sent off to private schools to develop their intellectual and spiritual potential—and they'd ended up selling themselves to international thrill-seekers who hid behind three-piece suits. "Is Standish Crocker in jail?" I hoped he was hanging by his thumbs.

"He was released on his own recognizance." Milo saw my disappointment. "No doubt he's languishing in the quiet splendor of his Hunts Point mansion."

I stood up again. I felt a perverse need to make Milo feel as glum as I did. "You still don't know who the killer is."

Milo's hazel eyes studied my gloomy face. "No. I don't. But we can start grilling Bridget Nyquist. With Travis gone, she'll be vulnerable."

She would indeed. And not just to the sheriff. Bridget would also be vulnerable to the killer. I was sorry I'd taunted Milo. Most of all, I was sorry for Bridget and the other five girls from fine private schools. Three of them were already dead. Was April Johnson safe in Texas? Where was Rachel Rosen?

Bridget Nyquist was in Alpine, and everybody knew it. Including the killer.

Chapter Sixteen

THE REST OF the day was not nearly as eventful as the first hour on the job. It took Ross Blatt less than ten minutes to restore our heat. The bill came to $87.34, a cut-rate bargain, Ross asserted, due to the presence of Aunt Vida. I hated to think what it would have cost if there had not been a blood relative on hand.

There was more reaction to this week's edition of *The Advocate*, with two dozen letters to the editor arriving in the mail. Eleven upheld my stand on the spotted owl, two denounced it, four criticized the sheriff for not having arrested the murderer or anybody else, three had their own memories of the Marmot, and the rest were miscellaneous. As usual, I'd run them all.

The fire department and the insurance people still hadn't decided whether or not Evan Singer's cabin had been burned deliberately. Evan had admitted that he didn't always lock up when he left. This revelation was made to Ben after Evan arrived at the rectory around ten o'clock the previous evening. He was not wearing a Santa Claus suit.

If Milo had learned anything new about the murder case, I didn't hear it. The details of the charges filed against Standish Crocker III came over the wire, but they didn't provide further enlightenment. Bill Blatt had called around eleven to say that Travis Nyquist had been taken into Seattle. He had put a good face on it, claiming he was being summoned merely to help out with the investigation. To my relief, Bridget went with him.

The pageant was scheduled for seven P.M., but Ben suggested that I join him for dinner at the rectory. Teresa McHale was leaving for the evening, but planned to put out what she termed *a cold collage*. Adam's date with Toni Andreas was on, though he allowed that they might show up at the school hall later. Toni's brother, Todd, was playing Colonel Parker.

I left work early, arriving home in time to go through the mail and check in with Adam. He had spent the afternoon at the rectory again, but hadn't accomplished as much as expected.

"Mrs. McHale insisted we work on the front porch," Adam said, haphazardly unsorting the laundry I'd set out for him that morning. "She's really picky, and insisted the porch was rotting and somebody would fall through and sue the church. But Uncle Ben and I couldn't figure out where it had gone bad and even with the sun shining, our fingers got so stiff we had to quit. We ended up hauling a bunch of junk from the church basement."

I had been in St. Mildred's basement once, when I had volunteered to help set up for Easter. If the bowels of the Marmot contained a history of Alpine entertainment, the church vault was a religious museum: the purple draperies that once shrouded statues during Lent, a set of wooden clappers used on Good Friday in the pre–Vatican II millennium, a carton of outmoded Baltimore Catechisms, and an actual nun's habit, complete with wimple. Relics, I'd thought, not in the true theological sense, but certainly of a different era in the Church. I suspected that the first item that Ben threw out was the Baltimore Catechisms.

I left before Adam did, again walking. The sky was still clear, and the stars were out. Almost every house now had its tree—fir, spruce, pine; tall, bushy, angular; flocked, artificial, traditional. Christmas trees are as individual as the people who decorate them. Mine was as big as the room could hold; its branches were as loaded as they could bear. Was I compensating for a hole in my life? Probably. Weren't we all?

When I got to the rectory, Teresa McHale was about to leave. "There's ham, macaroni salad, bread, sweet pickles, and cheese," she told me, jiggling a set of car keys. "I may be late. I'm meeting an old friend in Edmonds."

"What about Evan Singer?" I asked. "Is he eating here, too?"

Teresa bent down to pick up a large canvas shopping bag that bore a recycling logo. It was crammed with red tissue paper. Maybe it was recyclable, too. Fleetingly, I wondered if Teresa was one of the environmentalists who disapproved of my stand on the spotted owl.

"Evan Singer!" she exclaimed. "Really, that man is deranged! I'm all for being a good Christian, but there *are* limits! Your brother is very naive about people. He's spent too much time with all those blacks and the Indians." With a nod, Teresa exited the rectory.

Ben popped his head around the corner of the pastor's study. He was grinning. "Do you think I'm naive, Sluggly?"

"Eavesdropper! Yes, in some respects. Or maybe it's just that you're not a complete cynic like most of us."

Ben led me into the parlor, which was aptly named, because it was right out of a 1930s time warp. Overstuffed mohair furniture, solid but dull end tables, a glass-fronted bookcase, and a cut-velvet side chair with curving wooden arms were crammed into the room, along with a somewhat newer TV console of bleached mahogany. The brown wall-to-wall carpeting dated from the 'Sixties, and was worn but curiously unfaded, as if the drapes were seldom opened. It was a room more suited to listening to Notre Dame football than to the tribulations of a troubled soul.

Since liturgically the Church was celebrating Advent, rather than Christmas, the only holiday concession was a velvet-covered wreath with an electric candle, which glowed in the front window. The walls were covered with religious art of the sentimental school—a proud-as-punch Virgin Mary and St. Joseph showing off the twelve-year old Christ as if He'd just won first place in a debate contest (come to think of it, He had); St. Cecilia, with plucked eyebrows and marcelled hair, being showered with roses as she played her harpsichord; the Holy Family on the flight into Egypt, a term that has always thrown me since they couldn't possibly have gone more than three miles an hour with that plodding little donkey. My favorite, however, was the one picture that attested to Father Fitz's humanity and to the fact that somewhere, at some time, the man had possessed a sense of humor: The art work dated from the turn-of-the-century and showed two red-robed altar boys hiding behind the corner of a huge stone church, about to launch snowballs at an unsuspecting young lad in civilian clothes. I loved the scene. I loved Father Fitz for displaying it.

"We can't eat in here. Mrs. McHale is afraid we'll ruin the furniture," Ben said wryly, opening the cupboard doors on the TV cabinet. He got out a bottle of Canadian whiskey, two glasses, and a bucket of ice. "Father Fitz was down to his last drop of Bushmills. No wonder he had a stroke. It's a good thing I like rye."

"Where's Evan?" I asked, accepting a glass from Ben. It was Waterford crystal, cut like diamonds, and felt good in my hand.

Ben sat down in the other overstuffed chair. "Who knows? He's been gone since noon. He didn't get up until eleven."

"Did you talk to him much?"

Ben shook his head. "Last night I got him settled down in Father Fitz's room. He acted upset, tired, so I didn't push it. Of course I didn't know about the latest incident until you told me this morning. Evan was out of here before we could have any meaningful dialogue."

"Will he be back tonight?" It was chilly in the rectory, and I eyed the empty fireplace with longing.

"Who knows?" Ben followed my gaze. "Forget it. Mrs. McHale says fireplaces are a bother. Now you know why Father Fitz wore two sweaters."

Teresa's cold collage was adequate. The pageant was endearing. Elvis learned much from the Wise Men, despite Colonel Parker's lousy advice to ignore them. But even the colonel capitulated at the end, joining the rock 'n' roll shepherds in a stirring version of "O Come All Ye Faithful." Elvis, as it turned out, was a girl.

After partaking of refreshments, Ben and I returned to the rectory. There was no sign of Teresa McHale or Evan Singer, but it wasn't yet nine o'clock. The clouds were rolling in again from the north. Ben and I had a dollop of brandy before I headed home. Adam and Toni hadn't showed up at the pageant, which didn't come as a surprise. It did, however, present a new set of worries. When Adam was away at school, I had put his love life out of my mind. But while he was under my roof, I fretted. I was visited by visions of an irate Mr. Andreas, who grew taller and broader with every passing minute, pounding on the door and demanding that my son make an honest woman out of his daughter.

But Adam was home when I got there, comfortably ensconced on the sofa, watching *Cheers*. "Toni's brain is unfurnished," he said at the commercial break. "What's with people around here? Some of them think the big city is Monroe."

I was about to explain small town mentality to my son when the phone rang. It was Ben.

"I found a mailbag under Evan Singer's bed. It's got a tag on it that says it belongs to *The Advocate*. You want it?"

I frowned into the phone. "Sure. But . . . I don't get it. Why did Evan Singer steal our mailbag?"

Ben chuckled. "He needed something to put these old film cans in. You ever heard of a movie called *Gösta Berling's Saga*?"

I had—and recently. "Listen, Stench, don't you read *The*

Advocate?'' I heard Ben squirm at the other end. He'd read *most* of the paper, at least the front page. But a pastor's life was busy, especially when you were new in town, and it was Advent . . .

I cut Ben off. "*Gösta Berling's Saga* was Greta Garbo's first big hit. It was also the film that Lars Nyquist used for the grand opening of the Marmot. Now what the hell are you talking about?"

Ten minutes later, I was back at the rectory, this time driving my car, which took five minutes to warm up. Four big round tins of film lay on the parlor floor, clearly marked in English and in Swedish. "Where," I asked in amazement, "did Evan get these? They must be worth something."

Ben got out the brandy again. "Think about it," said my brother, his usually crackling voice slowing to a drawl that he might have picked up in Mississippi. "Evan Singer spends Tuesday night at the Marmot. How long is he there? What's he doing? We don't know, Oscar doesn't know. Oscar finds him asleep in the theatre's auditorium. Cut to Wednesday. Enter Evan dressed as Santa, suit stolen from the mayor, mailbag taken from your office. Now why does he need the sack?"

I eyed my brother in the dim amber light of a three-way lamp, conservatively set on low. "To carry something . . . And," I added, suddenly remembering Vida's barbed remark of the previous week, "because Fuzzy Baugh didn't use a pack. He has lumbago."

We were silent, both of us staring at the film cans. "Evan found the tins Tuesday," my brother speculated. "Where?"

"The basement?" I had been down there, but Ben had not. "It's full of old stuff, but I didn't see anything like this." I closed my eyes, trying to picture the clutter. Oscar had shown Vida and me almost every nook and cranny. Where had the film cans been stashed? "The rain barrel! Lars saved it from the old social hall. It was probably empty, and somehow these cans were put in it after the movie ended its run.

Lars Nyquist was a great fan of Garbo's. Maybe he wanted a souvenir."

Ben nodded. "Could be. It was illegal, unless he worked out some kind of deal. In any event, I'll bet Evan Singer found these cans and took them up to the auditorium, ditched them under the seat—and fell asleep. Oscar found him and threw him out before he could get away with the reels. So he had to come back—and sit exactly where he was the previous night. That's why there was the ruckus. Somebody else was already in that seat. During the movie, Evan slipped the cans into the mailbag. Who would stop Santa with his pack?"

I had to laugh. Evan Singer might be crazy, but he wasn't stupid. "How did you find these?" I asked.

Ben lighted a thin, black cigarette, one of his rare tobacco indulgences. He knew better than to offer me one. I would have accepted. "Teresa McHale will kill me for smoking in here, but I'll remind her I'm the pastor. How, you ask? Same reason—Teresa. She's so damned fussy, and I was afraid Evan might have trashed Father Fitz's room, so I went in to check. It was tidy enough, he hasn't got much left since the fire, but when I looked under the bed, I found this." He waved his cigarette at the mailbag and film cans. "Now what do I do? Confront him?"

I didn't like the idea of Ben confronting Evan Singer. My brother was a big boy, and reasonably fit. But he had no killer instinct. I was beginning to think that I couldn't say the same for Evan Singer. "We'd better find out if these reels came from the Marmot."

"Where else?" asked Ben.

"Right." I watched Ben's cigarette smoke spiral upward toward the ceiling, drifting into the old-fashioned light fixture of orange bulbs shaped like candle flames. "Ben—we're asking the wrong questions." My brother blew a smoke ring, forming his unspoken *oh?* I stood up and began to pace the room. "It isn't enough to know how Evan Singer stole this movie. We need to know why. We need to know how he knew it was there in the first place. Most of all, we need to know who in hell *is* Evan Singer?''

I lingered at the rectory, unwilling to leave Ben alone. At last, I openly questioned my brother's safety. He might be sleeping under the same roof as a known thief and a possible killer.

"I'll admit I can't see why Evan would kill those two girls," I said as the old marble clock on the mantel chimed eleven, "but I'm worried. Maybe you should put those film cans back under Evan's bed before he gets in."

Ben shook his head, his customary indecisiveness coming to the fore. "I can't. If Evan's got the nerve to ask for them, we'll talk it over. But I need to think this through. Now go home, you're stalling to give me protection. I don't need it. Teresa McHale is strong as an ox. She could put Evan Singer on the ropes in the first twenty seconds of round one."

"But she's not back, either," I protested. "Where are you going to put those film reels?"

Ben picked up the four cans, placed them in the mailbag, and pulled at the sleeve of my red sweater. "Come on, Sluggly, I'll show you."

The rectory was built on a simple, practical floor plan. The parlor and study were at the front; the housekeeper's room and bath were separated from the two priests' rooms by the kitchen, dining room, and another bath. The long hall gave the impression of a dormitory.

The priest's guest room was spartan, with a twin bed, a bureau, a desk and a chair. A crucifix hung above the bed, but otherwise the walls were bare. Ben opened the closet to reveal his limited travel wardrobe. He put the mailbag on the floor at the rear of the closet, then set his ski boots at such an angle that the sack was obscured.

"Okay?" He gave me a tight smile. When I didn't respond, he sighed. "All right, come here. I'll show you my life insurance policy." He went over to the bureau and pulled

out the top drawer. Socks and underwear were folded neatly.
Ben reached under a pile of T-shirts. I waited. Ben reached
some more. I glanced out the window to see if it was snowing
yet. It wasn't, but the clouds were low and seemed to press
in on Alpine.

Ben swore. I jumped. Under the tan, his face had lost its
natural color. "It's gone, Emma," he said hoarsely. "God
help me, it's gone!"

"What?" Ben's reaction baffled me. It annoyed me, too,
since he seemed to think I knew what he was talking about.

Ben slammed the drawer shut, rocking the rickety bureau.
"My gun. The Browning high-power. It's gone."

I was adamant. Ben was either coming home with me or
I was staying at the rectory. He refused to leave. So did I.

"You're irrational, Emma," said Ben, sounding angry.

"You're a fool," I countered, dialing my home. Adam
answered, half-asleep. I wasn't sure my message sank in, but
maybe he'd figure it out when he woke up in the morning
and found me gone.

At last, Ben gave in, but insisted that I take his bed. He'd
sleep on the davenport in the parlor. We'd just settled this
minor dispute when Teresa McHale came in. Seeing her solid,
no-nonsense figure made me feel a bit foolish.

Ben, however, took command. "Please sit down, Mrs.
McHale," he requested, indicating one of the mohair chairs
in the parlor. "I want you to tell me who has called at the
rectory this past week."

Teresa was still wearing her handsome plum-colored wool
coat. She set her handbag down on the floor next to the chair.
"The last week? Really, Father, I don't know if I can remember
everyone. The entire school faculty and staff at some point.
Most of the parish council. Mary Beth McElroy, the CCD
teacher. Annie Jeanne Dupré, the organist. Oh, the choir, after
practice Monday night. Mrs. Nyquist from the Lutheran Church.
The eucharistic ministers. The dishwasher repairman."

"Mrs. Nyquist?" I interrupted. "Which one?"

Teresa eyed me with distaste. It was one thing for a new pastor to invade her domain. It was something else for the pastor's lippy sister to butt in. "Mrs. Arnold," she replied coolly, turning to Ben. "Louise Nyquist. She came by Monday, after you attended the St. Lucy service. You forgot the Swedish Christmas chimes they presented to the clergy, Father."

"Oh. Right," said Ben. "Who else?"

Teresa continued her list of names, which made up most of Catholic Alpine and a dash of Separated Brethren thrown in for good measure. At last Ben revealed the source of his anxiety. The housekeeper was appalled.

"A gun? You carry a *gun*, Father?"

"I need it in the desert, believe me," Ben replied, a trifle testily. "I've got a permit. I brought it with me because my quarters are being renovated while I'm on vacation. The workmen had to pull the safe."

Teresa did not look appeased. "I see," she said between taut lips.

I dared to interject myself once more. "Mrs. McHale, when Louise was here Monday was she ever alone in the rectory? Waiting for you or something?" Louise Nyquist wielding a Browning high-power seemed incongruous, but so were a lot of other brutal truths.

"Certainly not," Teresa answered, taking umbrage at my suggestion that she somehow might have been derelict in her duties. "I let her in, we chatted, she said she'd never been in the rectory before. Mrs. Nyquist joked that her parents had told her horror stories about the place. You know, the usual Protestant mumbo-jumbo—orgies, Black Masses, human sacrifice, all that nonsense. She seemed interested, so I showed her around. She stayed so long that I thought she was thinking about converting." Teresa laughed softly at her own small jest.

Ben and I exchanged glances. I knew we were thinking

alike: while Louise Nyquist detained Teresa, someone else
might have sneaked into the rectory. It could have been pre-
arranged; it could have been by chance.

Teresa still seemed unconvinced about my reasons for
spending the night. Indeed, I was beginning to change my
mind. But when the housekeeper headed for bed and Evan
Singer knocked at the door, my resolve was renewed.

"I've been out to the cabin," he announced, looking
mournful. "It's all gone. Everything. I communed with the
spirits. They told me to go to Hoquiam."

"Hoquiam?" Ben and I chorused. There's nothing wrong
with Hoquiam, which is a small city in the Grays Harbor
area out on the coast. Still, it struck both of us as a strange
choice by the spirits.

"I leave tomorrow," Evan said, drifting down the hallway. "My task here is finished." He went into Father Fitz's
room and quietly closed the door.

I grabbed Ben's arm. "What if he sees the film reels are
gone?"

Ben shrugged. "He'll ask. I'll tell him. Stop fussing,
Sluggly. It's after midnight. Go to bed." He kissed my forehead.

It was very chilly in the rectory, so I slept in my clothes.
I didn't have much choice, unless I borrowed one of Ben's
sweatshirts. As late as it was, I couldn't settle down. The
bed was too narrow, too hard, too unfamiliar. I wondered
how Ben was faring on the davenport.

I tossed and I turned. I thought I heard a wolf howl. Was
Adam okay? Should Ben have reported the missing gun? Or
the discovery of the film reels? Maybe I should call the sheriff's office. Dwight Gould was on night duty this week. But
I might wake Ben if I went down the hall to use the phone in
the study.

A frantic knock sent me bolt upright. Evan Singer demanded to be let in. On stockinged feet, I hurried to the
door. Evan flew into the room, wearing jeans and a T-shirt.

"They're going to kill me!" he cried. "It's horrible! The rack, the boot, the Iron Maiden!" He fell on his knees, wringing his hands. "Save me, Queen Isabella! Tell Torquemada I'm innocent!"

"Oh, jeez!" I rolled my eyes, then collected myself. "Okay, I'll send Ferdinand. Get up, you're safe. Hey, Evan, come on. You've reached sanctuary."

Slowly, Evan Singer got to his feet. He gave me a pathetic, grateful smile. "You're a good person," he said, sounding almost sane. "I know the Inquisition is passé, but that room scares me. Think of it, a priest occupying it all these years! Do you think he wore a hairshirt and flogged himself?"

Evan might like to think so, but I didn't. Such extreme penitence wasn't Father Fitz's style. He'd be more inclined to give up fudge for a week. But I didn't expect Evan to believe that.

"You want to trade rooms?" I inquired.

He considered the offer carefully, then accepted. Ben was at the door, looking bleary-eyed. Teresa McHale, wearing a brilliant satin quilted robe, stood behind him. Without makeup, she more than looked her age. She also looked upset.

"Really, Father," she murmured to Ben, "didn't I warn you?"

Ben ignored the remark. He stood by while Evan and I switched sleeping quarters. Teresa padded off down the hall.

"Well?" I whispered to Ben after Evan had closed the door to the guest bedroom. "I don't think he noticed that the film was missing."

Ben gave a little smirk. "That's not all that's missing," he said, starting back toward the parlor. "And I don't mean the Browning."

"Hmmmm," I said, and yawned. Evan's outburst had broken the spell. It seemed normal for him to be crazy. I went to sleep almost immediately.

Chapter Seventeen

BEN WAS STILL hemming and hawing over telling Milo about the missing gun. As for the film cans, my brother would hide them in a safer place. Evan wasn't going anywhere. Milo had seen to that. He had arrested Evan first thing Friday morning for the theft of Fuzzy Baugh's Santa suit.

"Honestly," Vida exclaimed as Milo joined us in the news office around nine o'clock, "you can't hold him long on such a flimsy charge!"

"It's Friday," Milo replied. "We'll be able to keep him over the weekend. Besides, he's got nowhere else to go unless he wants to stay on at the rectory and get himself harassed by Torquemada and the Spanish Inquisition." Milo gave me an amused look. "By the way, Travis and Bridget are back."

I turned away from the AP wire, which was spewing out national news. "What happened?"

Milo took a maple bar from the sack of goodies Ginny Burmeister had brought for a special Friday treat. "Not much. Travis insisted he didn't know what Standish Crocker was up to. They didn't charge him, so I have to figure the surveillance team didn't turn up much." He dug inside his down jacket. "Except these."

I took the four photographs from Milo. They showed a man standing in the driveway of the younger Nyquists' residence, then on the snow-covered lawn, leaning against the gnarled cottonwood tree, and finally up against the side of the house. Although the pictures were fuzzy, there was no mistaking the tall, thin figure of Evan Singer.

"The guys in the PUD truck took these shots a week ago Tuesday. I guess I was wrong about the lurker's intentions. Or was I?" Milo looked bemused.

I handed the pictures to Vida. "Bridget and Evan as lovers? Well . . . maybe."

Vida huffed as she studied the photos. "I don't call this *lurking*. He's bold as brass. The least he could do is hide in the shrubbery or climb up that tree."

I practically fell over Vida's wastebasket. "Let me see that again!" Puzzled, Vida handed the pictures back to me. I scrutinized all four in turn. The big tree at the edge of the front yard was prominent in each shot. "Isn't that a cottonwood?" I asked.

Vida didn't bother to look. "Certainly not. It's an oak. George Jersey, who felled the first tree when Alpine was still called Nippon, planted it back in World World I."

I felt half-silly, half-euphoric. I described the gnarled tree Evan had sketched, told how he had said his entire life was pictured there. A *family* tree, I realized, with its roots in Alpine. It was the same tree that grew in the front yard of Bridget and Travis Nyquist's house.

"Vida, think—is there any way Evan Singer could be related to the Nyquists?"

I heard Milo guffaw. But Vida merely adjusted her glasses. "Now that's an interesting question, Emma." She picked up a pencil and began to draw lines on a blank piece of paper. "Let's see—Arnie's sister, Thelma, had twin girls who must be in their late twenties. Thelma and her husband, Peter, live in Spokane—he works for a packing company." Vida drew another line, in reverse. "Oscar's sister, who is, of course, Arnie's Aunt Karen, had no children by her first husband, Trygve Hansen. But as I told you, she had three by the second marriage to Mr. . . . Well, if that doesn't beat all! I never knew his name! None of the Nyquists would mention it because he was Jewish.'' She looked to Milo for confirmation.

''Hey,'' said Milo, holding up a big hand, ''I was a baby when all that happened.''

I turned to Milo. ''Can you find out what Karen Nyquist's married name is?''

Vida was dredging up the Seattle White Pages. ''I can. If I'm following your thoughts.'' She dumped the book back on the floor. ''I don't want that, I want the Eastside, don't I?''

''I don't suppose,'' Milo said in his laconic voice, ''that anybody's going to tell me what's going on?''

Vida looked up from the Eastside directory. ''Oh, hush, Milo! It's obvious.'' She bent her head over the pages again. ''There are four of them in the Bellevue area . . . ah!''

''You found Karen?'' I asked eagerly.

Vida regarded me with dismay. I felt as if she were about to crown Milo and me with dunce caps. ''Don't you pay attention either, Emma? I'm not looking for Karen Nyquist, I'm looking for her son: Norman Singer.''

I had forgotten that Oscar Nyquist had told us that his sister had named her son Norman. Vida, naturally, had absorbed that piece of knowledge like a sponge. Milo and I waited quietly while she dialed the Bellevue number. We were as fascinated by the excuse she would come up with as we were by the possible confirmation of my theory.

''Mrs. Singer? Yes, this is Vida Blatt, from West Seattle. I understand your son, Evan, is an artist. . . . Oh, really? No, it doesn't matter if he's sold previously. I was thinking of a commission. A mural for my backyard fence. Your mother-in-law suggested it. Karen Singer, is it? I met her at Bel-Square a while ago. . . . Confined to a wheelchair? Since when? Goodness, maybe it's been longer than I thought. You know how time flies. . . . Oh. Oh, that's a shame. I'll have to find someone else. Thank you so much.''

Vida put the phone down and smiled in triumph. "Now you see how easy that was? The personal touch. No computers, no data whazzits, nothing but pure human communication. Thea Singer, Mrs. Norman, says her son has moved out of town. Surprise. Grandma Karen has been stuck in a wheelchair since she had a stroke a year ago. What else do you need to know?"

Milo grabbed a cinnamon twist and started for the door. "Plenty. Evan Singer's got some explaining to do. We may have cracked this case." He left.

Vida snorted. "This case isn't cracked. Milo is." She dropped the Eastside phone book back into the pile of directories.

I'd sat down at Ed's desk. He was breakfasting with the Rotarians this morning. Ed Bronsky might not enjoy selling advertising, but he certainly relished the job's fringe benefits. "Listen, Vida—Evan shows up here in early October. Kathleen Francich is murdered about that same time. Then Carol Neal. Evan is photographed hanging around Bridget's house. He said he knew her in Seattle. Now how much more . . ."

"That's not what he said," Vida broke in. "Evan was never clear on that point. It *sounded* as if he'd known Bridget and Travis for some time. And he had—not personally, but as his long-lost relatives."

"True." My hypothesis wasn't totally destroyed, but it certainly had suffered some dents. "I suppose we could ask Evan."

Vida looked as if she considered the idea worthless. But before she could put her reaction into words, Ginny Burmeister appeared with the mail. I remembered to ask her if she had recognized the person who had called with the message about Oscar and Karen.

But Ginny had no idea who it was, other than that it was an adult female. "I don't think I ever heard her voice before," said Ginny, filling Vida's in-basket with an assortment of items addressed to the House & Home editor. "She was brief. Businesslike."

I sighed. It could be anybody. But it wasn't Evan Singer. "Okay," I said to Vida after Ginny had finished her delivery chores and returned to the front office. "With or without Evan Singer, we need a motive. Why kill two out of five prostitutes—the sixth one being dead already?"

Vida looked up from the typewriter. "Blackmail. There's no other reason, except a mania. This is not a maniac, not in that sense. A true sociopath would have killed any young woman he encountered. She might be a prostitute, she might not. But Kathleen and Carol had something in common. They were chosen deliberately. And before that happened, they chose to come to Alpine. Deliberately. Carol probably came looking for Kathleen. Why did Kathleen come here? Why has nobody come forward saying they saw her?"

Vida had made some good points. I decided to tackle the last one. "As far as we know, Kathleen didn't check into either of the motels, the hotel, or the lodge. Her car ended up in the mall parking lot, but the killer might have driven it there. Where did Kathleen go after she got to Alpine? Where did Carol go? Did they call on Bridget Dunne Nyquist?"

Vida was sitting with her hands folded under her chin. She seemed to be staring at the opposite wall, where Carla had hung a cardboard cutout of a jolly gingerbread man. "Of course they did," she said in a hushed voice. "Where else would they go?"

Evan Singer had come down with a case of Constitutional rights. He demanded to call his attorney, who turned out to be a senior partner in one of Seattle's most prestigious law firms. He was also Evan's uncle, on his mother's side.

I felt my breath catch as Milo Dodge finished his recitation. Another piece of the Singer-Nyquist puzzle might be falling into place. "What's the uncle's name?" I asked, leaning on Milo's desk.

Milo looked down at his notebook. "Benjamin Stern. You know him?"

I felt deflated. "Mrs. Singer was a Stern before her marriage? Drat! I was sure it would turn out to be Lowenstein."

Slouching against his imitation leather chair, Milo frowned at me. "Lowenstein? Who's that? Composer? Third baseman? Furniture-mart mogul?"

I bit back the urge to ask if *he* ever read *The Advocate*. "I had this crazy theory—except it wasn't so crazy, since I figured out that Evan Singer was related to the Nyquists—that somehow the guy who designed the Marmot was also a relative. Evan's maternal grandfather, maybe." I saw Milo lift his bushy eyebrows. "Hey, it's not so weird—it would explain where Evan got his interest in art and how his sister ended up in the theatre back in New York."

Milo gave me a patronizing look. "His mother's a big art buff, remember?"

"Patroness of the arts. It's not the same." I turned mulish, reluctant to let go of my idea.

Milo ambled over to the hook that held his down jacket. "Let's eat," he said. "It's almost noon. I suppose Evan Singer is halfway to Monroe by now."

"Heading for Hoquiam," I said with a sigh. We started through the reception area only to be confronted by Carla, who flew in the door. She was coatless, and her long, black hair was dappled with snowflakes.

"Emma, your brother is on the phone! He needs to talk to you quick!"

Running in the newly-fallen snow was prohibitive. All the same, the three of us hurried as fast as we could, covering the block between the sheriff's office and the newspaper in less than a minute. I took Ben's call in the front office, where a startled Ginny Burmeister was waiting on a customer who wanted a classified ad.

"Emma," said Ben, his voice crackling more than usual, "those film cans are gone! Mrs. McHale thought she saw

Evan Singer rushing out of the church about ten minutes ago!''

"Out of the church?" I stopped myself. There was a covered walkway that connected the rectory to the church. I'd momentarily forgotten. "Evan's still in Alpine then." I turned to Milo, my comment as much for him as for my brother. I put my hand over the receiver so Ben wouldn't hear. "I have a confession to make, Milo. Evan stole an old movie from the Marmot. He's got it with him."

"An old movie?" Milo looked unimpressed. "The guy steals Santa suits and old movies? Whatever happened to bearer bonds and diamond rings and *money*?" All the same, Milo was out of the office like a shot, presumably to launch a manhunt.

Ben had lost Evan Singer, and I'd lost my lunch date. I went into the news office, where Vida was munching on a carrot stick, Carla was brushing the snow out of her hair, and Ed was getting ready to go to the Kiwanis Club Christmas lunch. The bells went off on the AP wire, signalling a late-breaking bulletin. We all ignored the sound. It was hardly unusual.

"Santa Claus," chuckled Ed, letting his belt out to the final notch. I didn't know if he was referring to the AP bells or his ever-expanding girth. "I'll be late getting back. If Gus calls from the Toyota dealership, tell him this isn't the right time of year to sell cars."

I tried to coax Vida into going to the Burger Barn, but for once she was adamant about sticking to her diet. "There are too many temptations this time of year. If I eat my carrot and celery sticks and hardboiled egg and cottage cheese, I'll be able to have two pieces of Grace Grundle's pecan pie at the John Knox Christmas Fun Fest on Sunday."

I started to remind Vida that John Knox had been virulently opposed to the celebration of Christmas in any form, but decided against it. If we Catholics had survived Vatican

II, there was no reason the Presbyterians shouldn't have their own share of revisionism, too.

Takeout was the only answer. Carla said she'd go fetch me a hamburger, fries, and a Coke before she and Ginny went to lunch up at the lodge. "It's our pre-Christmas treat," she explained. "We might be a little late."

Absently, I nodded. It was, after all, the last Friday before Christmas. I wasn't in a position to hand out holiday bonuses, only modest presents. Why not offer the hired help a gift of time? Carla scurried off to pick up my meager repast. I dialed the rectory to check in with Ben. Teresa McHale answered.

"Father is counseling an engaged couple," she said smugly. "His afternoon is quite full. He plans to join the school faculty's Christmas party, then he meets with three sets of new parents to give Baptismal instructions, and this evening, he intends to start going over the parish books for year's end. May I give him a message?"

I was hungry, frustrated, and annoyed. "This is his sister, not somebody selling a new format for the parish bulletin." I paused, seeking a more conciliatory note. "I'm upset. Teresa, what happened with Evan Singer?"

Teresa McHale also became more human. "Evan Singer! What did I tell you? Now he robs us blind. See how much good it does to extend charity to people who don't deserve it? I can guess who stole Father's gun."

I could, too. Probably. Except that if Evan Singer had taken Ben's Browning, Milo would have found it on him. At least that was a plausible scenario.

Ed left for Kiwanis. Carla returned with my lunch. Vida snapped off more carrots and celery between bouts with the typewriter. I worked on my next editorial, which would be benign and brief. It didn't take many words to wish our readership a Merry Christmas. They could save their eyes and I could spare my brain. I polished off my hamburger and fries, then went out to check the wire. It shut off at two P.M. Carla had let about two hours worth of news pile up on the floor. That wasn't so strange. Most stories that come in after eleven are late-breaking developments from earlier pieces, sports summaries, stock market reports, and other details that don't suit a weekly's needs. Indeed, I often wonder if we could get rid of the wire and save some money. The only time we really need it is on Tuesdays, when we might otherwise miss a hot story with a local angle. The rest of the week, it's just a legacy from the Marius Vandeventer era.

Still, I always scan the long strip of paper to see if we've overlooked something. Once in a while there's a feature on Fridays that's aimed for weekend editions that we can pick off for filler on Wednesday if *The Times* and the *Post Intelligencer* don't use it first.

"Oh, my God!" My jaw dropped as I clutched the long ream of news. Vida looked up from a set of contact prints. I ripped the paper midway off the wire and brought it over to her. "Standish Crocker is dead! He died in a fire last night at his Hunts Point home! Are you thinking what I'm thinking?"

Vida took off her glasses, regarding me with unwavering gray eyes. "Of course. Shall we go see Bridget?"

"What about Milo?"

Vida was getting into her tweed coat. "Milo's out playing sheriff. Let him have his fun. Meanwhile, let's go catch a killer."

Travis Nyquist met us at the door. His handsome face looked tense. The walking cast was gone, but his limp was more pronounced. He didn't ask us in.

"Bridget's not home," he said curtly. "Excuse me."

For once, Vida's protests went for naught. We were left staring at the red and gold wreath on the front door. Vida frowned at the two-car garage. It was closed on both sides.

"No fresh tire tracks in the new snow," she noted. "Don't tell me Bridget walked. It's not her style."

We had started down the drive to the road where I'd parked the Jag. "You think she's home?"

Vida didn't answer. I glanced back over my shoulder. The big oak's branches framed the front window. Travis was looking out, watching our progress.

We got into the car. "It's just a matter of time," said Vida. "Travis is as guilty as sin."

I gave a little jump and accidentally hit the brake instead of the accelerator. The Jag stuttered, then eased down the winding road. "Of what? Murder?" I sounded incredulous.

"Maybe. Certainly of other things, à la the late Standish Crocker." Vida twisted around in the passenger seat, trying to look out through the rear window. The Nyquist house had disappeared from view. "If only we knew where Bridget is . . . I feel as if I'm swimming in cheese soup."

Vida insisted that we stop at the sheriff's office. Milo was still out, looking for Evan Singer. Bill Blatt was manning the front desk. His aunt had orders for him.

"Billy, I want you out there combing this town for any sign of Bridget Nyquist. *Any* sign. Do you understand me?"

Bill's freckled face grew distressed. "But Aunt Vida, I can't leave until Sam Heppner comes back from highway patrol!"

"Radio Sam and get him over here right now. Hurry, Billy, this is a matter of life and death. Start with Travis Nyquist's house."

Torn between his appointed duty and his aunt, Bill Blatt naturally gave in to Vida. After a few more instructions, Vida led me back outside. "That's all we can do for Bridget. Let's hope I'm wrong."

We left my car in front of the sheriff's office and walked to *The Advocate*. It was snowing harder, and the air felt raw. "Do you really think Travis killed those girls? And set fire to Evan Singer's cabin and Standish Crocker's house?"

Vida was trudging along in her flat-footed manner. "Heaven help me, I don't know. But the killer is somebody close to Bridget. I'd stake my soul on that. Who could it be but Travis? Oscar, Arnie and Louise wouldn't want it known that their daughter-in-law is a former prostitute and their son is a crook, but none of them strikes me as a killer. As for Evan Singer . . .''

Across the street, Evan Singer was coming out of the Marmot. He wasn't alone. Oscar Nyquist was at his side, an arm draped around the younger man's shoulders. My first reaction was that Evan was being forcibly ejected. Again. But as Vida and I plunged across Front Street, we saw that the pair was engaged in deep, intimate conversation.

Most people wouldn't have dreamed of intruding on Oscar and Evan in what was clearly a private moment. Vida, however, was not most people. She was Vida, and she marched straight up to confront the two men.

"Oscar," she nodded her cloche, then jabbed a finger at Evan. "Milo Dodge is scouring the town for you, young man. You stole something besides a Santa suit."

Evan, looking bewildered and very young, started to answer, but Oscar broke in: "He didn't steal anything. He borrowed it. Come here." Oscar led us back into the empty Marmot, which would be showing *Fantasia* that evening. I glanced at the lobby's sidewalls, divided by art-deco columns, and featuring individual murals of forest creatures in sylvan settings. We climbed the half-dozen stairs to the upper foyer where the auditorium was dark behind the parted velvet curtains. "In there," said Oscar, his voice unusually hushed, and his eyes never leaving the blank screen, "we watched greatness. Greta Garbo in her first important moving picture. It runs three hours. My father, Lars Nyquist, ran it every year on his birthday. He was Garbo's biggest fan. I haven't seen it since he died."

The words were spoken simply, and I felt slightly embarrassed. Oscar Nyquist was not given to emotional outbursts, except anger. Yet he could not have made more of an impression had he wept and wrung his hands.

Some of the steam had escaped from Vida. "Well, now." She turned to Evan Singer. "You returned the reels to Oscar?"

Evan took his time replying, and when he did, his voice was very thin: "I wanted to see it. This is the only full-length copy of *Gösta Berling*. The director, Maurice Stiller, died in 1928, and his assistant cut the movie by half. A few years ago, the Swedish Film Institute tried to restore it, but some of the footage was lost. Only the Marmot has the complete motion picture."

"It must be worth a fortune," I remarked, noting Vida's frown. "How did you know it was here, Evan?"

"My grandmother told me." He darted a look at Oscar Nyquist. "May I, sir? What difference does it make? It all happened almost seventy years ago. Your father and Mr. Lowenstein are both dead."

Oscar's barrel chest lurched as he emitted a big sigh. "My sister talks too much. I always said so."

Evan's usual gawky animation began to return, but he seemed oddly in control of himself. "Isaac Lowenstein came to Alpine to design a new movie theatre. He was brilliant, but like a lot of creative people, he short-circuited now and then." Evan gave us a self-deprecating smile. It was obvious that he considered himself both brilliant—and short-circuited. "Lowenstein had a passion for beauty. He also had a yen for little girls. My grandmother was eight years old, golden-haired and pretty." He looked at Oscar for confirmation; the older man gave a single nod, his eyes half-shut. Evan continued in quiet lucid tones: "Lars Nyquist, my great-grandfather, caught him in time. He told him to leave Alpine and never come back. But Lars had already paid a portion of the money for Lowenstein's work. He'd bragged to everyone that Alpine would have a theatre designed by the great Isaac Lowenstein. So he ended up paying Lowenstein off to *not* design the Marmot. Lars Nyquist did it himself, creating one of the first art-deco movie palaces in the world. He was very talented, don't you think?''

My eyes scanned the graceful columns, the elegant arches, the charming frescoes. Lars Nyquist was indeed a talented man; he might have been a genius. I was flabbergasted. But Evan's story explained a great deal, at least about the Nyquist family's inherent good taste. It was in their blood. Arnie, perhaps Travis, and now Evan had all come by their artistic talents naturally.

Vida wedged herself between Oscar and Evan. "Honestly, Oscar, after all these years you're going to acknowledge Karen's family as Nyquists? What's come over you?''

In the lobby's soft blue lights, Oscar's face flushed. One bearlike hand gestured at the classic flocked wreaths that adorned the walls. "It's Christmas,'' he muttered, then added under his breath, "it's about time.''

Vida spent the rest of the day fuming over Oscar's change of heart. "Why wait so long?'' she'd say at intervals. "Karen is an invalid, Norman and Thea have never known the rest of the Nyquists. What a waste!'' Or, "Stubborn Norwegian. Oscar wouldn't have caved in now if Evan hadn't played on his sympathy by showing an interest in that old movie. But Lars was such a sap about Greta Garbo—and Oscar fell for the soft soap.''

In between grousing about Oscar, Vida fussed over Bridget. By late afternoon, Milo and Bill hadn't turned up any trace of her. They had finally obtained a search warrant and showed up on Travis's doorstep. Travis told them that Bridget had left Alpine. He also told them to go to hell, but Milo wasn't listening. He and Bill went through the house, finding nothing. Some of her matched luggage was missing, as was a chunk of her wardrobe. The lawmen began to wonder if Travis wasn't telling the truth.

"I hope Bridget is far from here,'' Vida said as we prepared to close up for the weekend. "I don't like it, though.

It's easy to ditch some clothes and a couple of suitcases. Of course it's not so easy to ditch an entire person.''

I shared Vida's concern, but I had no idea what to do about it. Finding Bridget was up to Milo. Perhaps a check of the airlines, trains, and buses would turn up a lead.

"With both cars in the garage, how did she get out of Alpine?'' I mused, looking up and heading into the heavy snow.

Vida's car was parked in front of *The Advocate*; mine was still down the street, in front of the sheriff's office. Vida gazed into the flying flakes, chewing on her lower lip. "I called Louise Nyquist. She said Bridget went to Seattle with Travis yesterday. She never came back.''

Chapter Eighteen

I CONSIDERED STOPPING in to see Milo before I got in the Jag, but Peyton Flake was coming out of the sheriff's office, carrying a sleek medical bag.

"Why don't they deputize me and get it over with?" he grumbled. "Dodge and Blatt are out, Heppner's off-duty, Gould's on the desk, and Mullins is trying to break up a fight at the Icicle Creek Tavern. Your editorial pissed off some people." Behind the wire-rimmed glasses, Flake's eyes were gleeful.

"My editorials are often controversial," I sighed, then pointed at his case. "As you off to patch up the losers?"

Flake shook his head, the ponytail swinging under an Aztec print wool cap that matched his fleece pullover. "I'm rescuing Durwood Parker. He took that freaking snowmobile up to the ranger station and ran over himself. Let's hope I can find the old fart in this weather. If not, I can cut some firewood." He pounded on the rear door of his Toyota van. I could see a gun rack, an axe, a maul, and a brown paper bag that may or may not have contained a fifth of Wild Turkey.

I wished Dr. Flake well, musing on how different he was from his predecessor, the late Cecil Dewey. Or from Gerald Dewey, who was almost as tradition-bound as his father. Maybe Peyton Flake's brand of medicine would eventually catch on in Alpine. Certainly he seemed to have the skill and the dedication. I watched the rust-colored four-wheel drive pull into Front Street and wondered why the forest rangers hadn't brought Durwood back to town. Probably, it dawned on me, because Peyton Flake relished taking off into swirling, hip-deep snow with his medical case and a mission. He might not seem suited to Alpine, but Alpine was certainly suited to him.

At home, I discovered that Adam was going night-skiing with Carla and Ginny. I shuddered at the lack of visibility, but he laughed at my fears. Then I shuddered at the thought of my son in Carla's clutches. But this was a buddy event. They were a threesome. Surely Adam would be safe. Carla was two years older. Nineteen months, actually. Put like that, I shuddered some more.

The lamb steaks went back in the fridge. I wasn't in the mood to cook for myself. Maybe Ben wasn't as busy as Teresa McHale had let on. I dialed the rectory; there was no answer.

Adam came into the living room, carrying his skis. He saw my worried look. "I forgot to tell you," he said, running a finger up and down one of the skis to test the surface, "the phone's out. Or some of them are. I got disconnected from Carla, and when I called back, it rang and rang, but she didn't answer."

I sighed. First the electricity, now the phones. It was annoying, but it wasn't unusual, given Alpine's hard winters with so much snow, ice, and wind. I decided to walk down to the rectory after Adam left.

I felt restless. Anxious, too. Vida's concern for Bridget Nyquist was contagious. I wondered if Milo had made any progress. Maybe Vida was right—Bridget had never returned to Alpine. She was in Seattle, staying with friends.

But Bridget had no friends, except for the girls who had formed the ring of hookers. Three were dead, one was in Texas, and the other's whereabouts were as big a question mark as Bridget's. My anxiety mounted. Irrationally, I started to worry about Ben.

But at the rectory, all was well. Ben was in the study, poring over Father Fitz's files. He wasn't aware that the phone was out; he was merely thankful that no one had called to distract him from his duties. Teresa McHale was in her room, watching television.

"This isn't your responsibility," I told Ben as I sat down in the room's only other chair, a straight-backed oak number that probably had been part of a dining room set sixty years ago.

"I know, but somebody's got to do it. Peyton Flake told me today that Father Fitz isn't rallying. He may have to go to a nursing home."

I sighed. "I'll miss him. We all will. He's a good man." I gazed around the small study with its open bookcases, filing cabinets, and more religious artwork. Our Lady of Mount Carmel, holding Baby Jesus, stood on a slim wooden pedestal. *The Agony in the Garden* was painted in murky colors above the desk. "Can I help?" I asked.

Ben shook his head. "I'm not balancing the books or anything like that. The parish council can do it. Mainly, I want to make sure all the masses have been said by people requesting them, that any queries from potential converts or fallen-away Catholics have been answered, that I'm covered on weddings and baptisms—you know, all the usual parish stuff. Bridget Nyquist, by the way, put her father's name in for All Souls' Day masses. She was generous—fifty bucks."

"I'm surprised," I admitted. "Given what she's been through and her marriage in the Lutheran church, she might have given up on Catholic trappings."

"Old ideas die hard," Ben muttered, checking names off a list. "Bridget's been a Catholic for a lot longer than she's been a Lutheran. Or was a whore."

"Right." I sat back, watching Ben go through file folders.

"Gripes," he said, putting one aside. "Kudos," he said, setting down another. "Crackpots," he said, fielding a third.

Ben kept at it. I felt useless. After ten minutes, I saw a

well-worn book of devotions on top of the nearest filing cabinet. I got up and flipped through the pages. It was very old, with fragile paper and heavy ink. Red rubrics and line engravings decorated the beginning of each section. Prayer cards, mostly for deceased priests, marked favorite passages.

"Father Fitz's?" I asked when Ben reached a lull.

He smiled and then, surprisingly, turned quite serious. "I was looking at that this morning after Evan Singer vacated Father Fitz's room. You know, I shouldn't be surprised when I discover that every priest has suffered some pretty severe temptations. Nobody knows it better than I do. But with an old guy like Father Fitz, it still brings me up short."

I gave my brother a curious look. "Temptation? Like what? Wild women?"

"Worse. Determined women. Or just one." Ben opened the middle desk drawer. He took out a single sheet of pale blue stationery. "This was stuck to the back of the prayer book. Look at the date. Father Fitz must have been in his late fifties. I guess that's not too old for midlife crisis, especially for us socially retarded priests."

I took the flimsy paper from Ben and began reading the close-knit handwriting. It wasn't easy to decipher.

May 23, 1960

My darling:

I can't believe you don't [won't?] love me. I saw it in your eyes. I felt it in your arms. No matter what else you are, you're still a man! Act like one and defy old laws [?]. Why should you care about generations of cold-blooded robots who blindly obeyed instead of following their hearts? Why does religion have to put up barriers [farriers? fanciers? financiers?] between people? Isn't love [?] everything? Please! I'll wait forever, if I have to!

With all my heart,
Your loving MA

"*Ma?* Isn't that carrying the Irish mother bit too far?" I handed the letter back to Ben.

"It must be initials. I wonder what happened to her?" My brother looked wistful as he studied the letter again. "He must have thought something of her, or he would have thrown this out." Ben returned to his file folders. My watch told me it was almost eight. I hadn't eaten dinner and was suddenly ravenous. I asked my brother if he might be hungry, too.

Ben shook his head. "Mrs. McHale fixed me a crab omelette and a green salad. Delicious." His puckish expression showed that he still delighted in taunting me.

I waited until he seemed absorbed in his work. "Any leftovers?" I, too, could be a pain.

"What? No, I ate the whole thing." Ben looked very pleased with himself. "The salad, too."

I got out of the chair. "In that case, I'll go forage for myself." I headed for the kitchen.

The rectory refrigerator was not only immaculate, but virtually empty except for the usual dairy products, condiments, and a crisper drawer full of vegetables. Except for a wedge of cheddar cheese, there wasn't much with which to make a meal. The freezing compartment was small and looked as if it had been recently defrosted.

"Try the big one in the basement," said Ben, lounging in the doorway. "But don't let Mrs. McHale find out I said it was okay. She lives in mortal fear that somebody will screw up her food-filing system."

"She files food?" I wrinkled my nose. "What is she, a frustrated Department of Agriculture clerk?"

Ben chuckled. "She's the most organized woman I've ever met. Peyton Flake keeps telling me how Father Fitz tries to give orders and practically gets himself worked up into another stroke. The poor old soul needn't worry—Teresa McHale will keep this place running like a Swiss watch."

We headed out the back door. The basement stairs were at the rear of the house, off the small porch. "Father Fitz is lucky to have her," I noted, as a blast of snow and wind hit us. "He ought to stop fussing and put his energy into recovering."

"I know," Ben agreed as we carefully trod the dozen wooden stairs that led to the basement. Although the steps were covered, snow had drifted onto them, making the descent treacherous. I worried about Adam skiing. Then I worried about Adam *not* skiing. But if he was sipping mulled wine in the lodge with Carla, Ginny would be there, too. Somehow, I wasn't consoled.

Ben tried the door; it was locked.

"Damn," he muttered, unhooking a set of keys from his belt. "Which one is it? I've never been down here before. Front door, back door, church, garage, car ignition, car trunk . . . here, it's got to be this one. . . ."

It was. The hinges creaked, and we couldn't see a thing inside. Ben felt for a light switch, but couldn't find one. At last he made contact with a thick string. One pull illuminated the unfinished basement. The usable area wasn't much bigger than the parlor. Above four feet of concrete and several beams, we could see piles of dirt and some large rocks. The mountainside pushed up beneath the rectory. It was no wonder that the basement smelled damp, even rank.

"This place needs airing out," Ben remarked, grimacing. He moved toward the old freezer, which was wedged between a large fruit cupboard and a stack of cartons tied with twine. Next to me was an ancient, black steamer trunk with rusted locks. I wondered if it had made the original crossing from Ireland with Father Fitz. Like its owner, it would probably never see the Emerald Isle again.

Ben put his shoulder to the heavy freezer and lifted the lid. I was wrinkling my nose. The basement really smelled terrible, an odor I couldn't define. Ben bent over the freezer. And let out a horrible cry. I think I made an exclamation, too, of shock. Ben allowed the freezer to slam shut. He reeled, then stumbled toward me and held on for dear life.

"Ben . . ." He was clinging to me so tightly that I could scarcely speak. "What . . . ?"

Taking deep breaths, Ben kept his arms around me but steered us to the door and onto the stairs. The snow swirled around us; the wind howled in our ears. Ben's face was in shadow from the basement light, but I could see that he was pale under his tan.

"It's a body," he finally gasped, then groaned. "*Some* of a body . . . Oh, God!" He let go and crossed himself.

I fell back against the side of the house. "Ben . . ." I couldn't think clearly. Had he said it was *somebody* . . . or *some body*?

My brother put his hands over his mouth and took more deep breaths. Then he squared his shoulders. When he spoke, his voice had lost its usual crackle. Indeed, he sounded faintly giddy. "Oh, Emma—I think we found the rest of Kathleen Francich!"

Maybe I always knew we would. Or that someone would. My knees turned to water. I kept leaning against the house, oblivious to the snow that blew in under the overhang, impervious to the sharp wind that came off the mountains. In truth, I was turning numb, and that was just as well. Maybe I could go to sleep and not have to deal with what was left of poor Kathleen. . . .

But Ben rallied. "Come on, let's call Milo." He snatched at my hand, which hung limply at my side.

"Milo?" I spoke his name as if I'd never heard of him. "Oh. Milo." I felt Ben tug at my hand and I gave myself a shake. "Yes . . . Milo." We started up the stairs but I stopped behind Ben at the door. "Wait—the phones—maybe we'd better drive over and find him in person."

Ben's brown eyes darted this way and that, indicating he was considering our options. "Right. But we'd better tell Teresa. What if she happens to go down to . . .'"

He saw the awful look on my face and his jaw dropped. "Oh, Jesus . . . Emma . . . What are you thinking?"

My voice came out as a rasp. "Ben—that letter. Quick, let's take another look. Please."

Furtively, we moved through the rectory, past Teresa's room, which was now ominously silent. Ben closed the study door behind us and locked it. I grabbed the blue sheet of stationery and put it directly under the desk lamp. The cramped handwriting wasn't improved by the illumination, but my brain was illuminated instead. "Oh, Ben—this doesn't say *defy old laws*—it says *defy old Lars*."

"*Lars?*" He sprang toward me, reaching for the single sheet. "Let me see!" Scanning the page, Ben was incredulous, then puzzled. "So what does it mean?"

A kaleidoscope of seemingly unrelated bits and pieces of knowledge spun in my brain: Bridget's mother's suicide, Arnie Nyquist's former girlfriend, Teresa McHale's desire for a public swimming pool, Francine Wells's remark about Teresa seeking a job, Ben's comment about Bridget's request for masses for her father, and now, the letter signed *MA*.

"This wasn't written to Father Fitz," I said in a hushed voice. "It was sent to Arnie Nyquist, from his Catholic girlfriend. Who, I might add, was quite a swimmer." Ben's puzzlement deepened, but I rushed on; there wasn't time for detailed explanations. "This woman was begging Arnie to defy his grandfather, Lars Nyquist, and not let religion stand in their way of getting married."

"I don't get it." Ben's forehead wrinkled. "What's it doing in Father Fitz's prayer book?"

"It wasn't in the book, remember? You said it was stuck to the bottom. I'm guessing there were more letters, which have been destroyed." I swallowed hard, trying to figure out what to do next. "They were stolen from Arnie's house, along with his UDUB-yearbook and that other stuff. Ben, let's get out of here."

But my brother was still looking baffled. "Hold it, Emma. Are you saying . . . Oh, come on, Sluggly, you don't think . . ."

A noise in the hall made both of us freeze. Ben's face turned grim as he positioned himself at one side of the door. "We've got company," he whispered. "Do I attack first and ask questions later?"

Frantically, I shook my head. "She may have your gun," I whispered back.

"Oh, God!" Ben glanced at the doorknob and recoiled. Maybe he thought that Teresa McHale was going to blast her way into the study. Maybe he was right. "The window," Ben breathed, shoving me across the room. "It opens. I smoked one of Flake's cigars in here today and had to air the place out."

It was only a two-foot drop into the snow. A last look over my shoulder caught the doorknob turning. Of course Teresa had a key. Ben and I ran as fast as the snowstorm would permit. We were on the side of the rectory directly across from the darkened church. To our left was the garage and woodshed; to our right, the street. Teresa hadn't followed us through the window. My guess was that she was going out through the front door. Ben was already heading that way.

"Wait!" My voice sounded hoarse. Ben turned, cocking his head. "Let's go the back way and around the church," I urged, shivering in my green sweater and flannel slacks. "We can get to Fourth Street. There's bound to be some traffic there."

Looking as chilled as I felt, Ben followed my lead. As I fought through the snow that had drifted up against the sanctuary, I kept looking back. To my relief, there was no sign of Teresa. Maybe she had decided to make a clean getaway. Maybe she didn't feel threatened. Maybe my hypothesis was dead wrong.

There wasn't time to open the garage and get out the old Volvo. Across the empty church parking lot, Cascade Street was obscured by the blowing snow. A dash for the nearest house might be smarter than trying to get down to the intersection. I felt Ben at my elbow as I tried to make out any nearby lights. My face stung from the cold, and my feet felt numb. We pressed forward, and I uttered a sigh of relief to find that the snow was only a few inches deep in the parking lot. Apparently some Good Samaritan was keeping it plowed.

But nobody could keep it from icing up under foot. I slipped and would have fallen had it not been for Ben. We teetered, then started forward again, moving at an agonizingly slow pace. On any given Sunday, the lot always seemed too small; tonight it was vast, windswept, like the frozen Arctic tundra.

The voice came out of a void. Or so it struck me at first. Then, when I turned, I realized it had come from the rear entrance of the church. Teresa McHale's shadowy form was barely perceptible through the flying snowflakes. She had used the covered walkway between the rectory and the church. No wonder we hadn't seen her.

"Come here," she called, her voice strong and steely.

I glanced at Ben. He gave a faint shake of his head. We plunged forward. Teresa called out again. We kept going.

The single shot ripped past us, maybe between us. It was impossible to tell. We were both jarred, and fell against one another.

"Stop." Teresa's voice now sounded very near. I looked around Ben to see her approaching, the Browning high-power clutched in both hands.

"Is that what you used on Standish Crocker before you set his house on fire?" I had no idea what prompted me to make such an inquiry under the circumstances. Begging for mercy would have been more appropriate, but a journalist's quest for truth dies hard. Right along with the journalist, it suddenly occurred to me.

Teresa was now within ten feet of us. Still, I could barely make out her heavy orange jacket and brown slacks. "You don't need to know about Crocker. Get inside the church."

Priest or not, this was one time Ben didn't seem drawn to the altar. Neither was I. Our only hope was for someone to drive by, realize something was amiss, and bring help. But Cascade Street was obliterated by the snow, and seemingly untraveled. On this stormy Friday night before Christmas, Alpine's residents must be keeping cozy at home, wrapping gifts, sipping eggnog, listening to carols. There was no reason to expect them to cruise the town in a blizzard, looking for a homicidal housekeeper and her would-be victims.

"Listen, Mrs. McHale," Ben began, the crackle back in his voice, "you're going to get caught. If you shot Standish Crocker, the police have found the bullet. The law will exact its price. But you *are* a Catholic. What about the higher law? Have you thought about your soul?"

I couldn't see her expression, but I could hear the contempt in her voice. "My soul died with my heart a long time ago. What did being a Catholic ever do for me? If I'd been something else—or nothing at all—I wouldn't have lost the only man I ever loved. I've been dead for thirty-two years. The only pleasure I've had is watching Bridget marry into that stiff-necked bunch of Lutherans. That, and making money by making fools out of men. Don't give me a homily on the state of my soul, Father. I've been in hell since I was a girl."

Despite the imminent danger of dying in the freezing snow, I was aghast. "You turned your own daughter into a whore just to avenge yourself on the Nyquists?"

Teresa gave a little snort. "On *all* men. A woman has the power to reduce any man to the status of an animal. But I did it for the money, too. My husband ran his trucking business into the ground. He'd even let his life insurance lapse. When that oaf died, I had nothing. I couldn't make ends meet as a sales clerk in a boutique." She gave a toss of her head. "So I put Bridget and the others to work. They loved it. It was party time, 'round the clock. Young ladies of the finest backgrounds, groomed to please silly businessmen. Catholic, Protestant, Jew—take your choice. I was sorry I never had a real minority. That was my goal, but the girls graduated first."

For someone who didn't want to tell us anything, Teresa McHale seemed to be revealing a lot. And why not? Where else could she brag about her brilliant call-girl scheme? Maybe she wasn't going to shoot us; we could freeze to death instead.

But I was too optimistic. Teresa gestured with the Browning. Maybe she was cold, too. "Enough. You're trying to stall. Let's get on with it."

An even stronger gust of wind blew down from Tonga Ridge. Briefly, Teresa disappeared in a flurry of snow. Siblings have their own wavelength. Ben and I ran for the street. We slipped; we slid. Teresa screamed at us to stop. The gun fired again, not quite so close, but near enough to make my heart skip. No doubt she was right behind us, more than halfway across the parking lot. Or maybe we'd reached the sidewalk. It was impossible to tell. If there was a streetlight in the vicinity, we couldn't see it. Teresa shouted another warning. The people who lived in the houses across the street didn't hear a thing. The sound of the wind muffled not only her voice but the shots from the gun.

I turned to see if she had us in range. She did. I made a misstep, and fell off the curb. Ben reached down to help me. Teresa stopped at the edge of what must have been the sidewalk.

"I'd rather not do it this way," she said grimly, "but you're giving me no choice. Maybe it's just as well. The snow will cover your bodies. I'll have left the country long before the thaw sets in." She laughed, a hideous, grating sound.

Ben got me on my feet just in time to see Teresa aim the Browning at us. I was so cold, I could barely react to the incredible notion that my brother and I were about to die. My heart was pounding, and a strange rumbling sound assaulted my ears. Teresa seemed to appear and disappear between flurries of snow. I heard a click; the safety? Ben would know. I gazed up at him—my brother, my friend, my only close family besides Adam. . . . How ironic that we should die together.

The large black form seemed to rumble out of nowhere, sailing along the sidewalk and striking Teresa with full force. The gun went off, and this time I saw its flash. I also heard a masculine voice, letting out an obscene exclamation. I gasped; Ben swore. Teresa lay on the ground, writhing in pain. A thud echoed on the wind, then more curses. Dazed, I grabbed Ben's arm and followed him to where Teresa lay. The Browning was a couple of feet away, already dusted with snow.

"My back!" Teresa groaned. "I can't move!"

Ben was kneeling at her side. "We'll get help!" He put a hand on her forehead. There was blood along her hairline and a gash in one cheek. Her left leg protruded at an unnatural angle. "Mrs. McHale, would you like me to hear your confession?"

The laugh was twisted, agonized. She stared up at Ben, her eyes glassy. "You're incredible, Father." Her face was wrenched with pain. "You really believe all this swill, don't you?"

Ben nodded, an offhand response. "So do you. The day Father Fitz had his stroke, you went to confession. Why?"

Teresa let out a series of little keening cries before she answered. "Habit, I guess. What difference does it make?" Her eyes closed and her body went limp.

Ben made the sign of the cross on her forehead. "It made a difference to Father Fitz," he muttered, sounding angry. "Her confession probably gave him the stroke."

"Is she dead?" I was shaking all over, from relief, shock, and the aftermath of terror.

"No." Ben was standing up again, peering into the snow. "Now where did . . . ah!" His shoulders slumped as he waved a hand. Peyton Flake was limping toward us, looking furious.

"What have we got here? I told that goddamned old fool

he ought to let me drive that snowmobile.'' Flake, his vocation as automatic as my brother's, bent down to examine
Teresa McHale. "She's a mess. We'll have to get an ambulance. I feel responsible. I was supposed to be rescuing one
patient and now I've got another one. Shit.'' He turned back
in the direction he'd come. "Hey, Durwood, let me see if I
can get a can-opener and pry you out of that freaking snowmobile.''

"Actually," I said, trooping along after Dr. Flake like a
pet pup, "you saved our lives. We'll explain all this later,
but now I'll go see if the phones are working.''

Flake didn't seem to hear me. Or at least he didn't seem
to understand. He tripped over the Browning. "Hey—is this
yours, Ben? What happened, did your housekeeper make you
a crummy casserole?''

Ben's smile was thin. He was still standing next to Teresa's
inert form. I was struck by the irony. She had tried to kill
us, had murdered at least three other people, had corrupted
six young women, including her own daughter, and yet my
brother wouldn't abandon her. Peyton Flake and Durwood
Parker might have saved our lives, but for me, Ben was the
real hero.

Chapter Nineteen

THE WHISTLING MARMOT Movie Theatre's marquee had again suffered at the hands of pranksters. Overnight, *Fantasia* had turned into *Ana is Fat*. I'd seen the rearrangement on my way to the sheriff's office Saturday morning. Milo Dodge had put off taking depositions from Ben and me due to our half-frozen, totally exhausted state.

Teresa McHale had been transferred from Alpine Community Hospital to Harborview in Seattle. She was in critical condition, but despite internal injuries, a concussion, and broken back, ribs, and leg, Peyton Flake thought she would recover to stand trial. Frankly, it was a good news/bad news prognosis.

Of course she wasn't Teresa McHale, but Mary Anne Toomey Dunne. Vida was still shaking her head over the events of Friday night when she approached the impromptu buffet supper I had prepared the following evening.

"It's bad enough that I never knew Lars Nyquist had designed the Marmot, though I still can't imagine him being so clever. He certainly hid it well. But I'm ashamed of myself that I didn't figure out Teresa McHale," she complained, spearing slices of ham and roast beef. "Of course, I'm not a Catholic." She managed to say the words with a mixture of accusation and relief, as if she was sorry that I had a venereal disease but thankful that she didn't.

"You never heard her make a fuss over Alpine's lack of a public swimming pool," I pointed out, handing Milo Dodge a paper plate etched with boughs of holly. "You never saw the letter she wrote to Arnie Nyquist. And you didn't know she'd applied for a job at Francine's Fine Apparel."

Ben looked up from his mound of potato salad. "If I'd known that about Francine, I might have wondered. I assumed she'd been sent up here by the Chancery. But of course she was already in Alpine and only needed an okay from the Chancery office. It was just a coincidence that Edna McPhail died not long after Teresa followed Bridget to town."

Milo dumped horseradish on his beef, tossed two dill pickles onto the plate, and scooped up a spoonful of black olives. "This has been the damndest case I ever saw. Jack Mullins threw up when he opened that freezer in the rectory basement."

Ed Bronsky nodded from his place in my favorite chair. The springs would have gone if he'd had any more food on his plate. "It was pretty bad, I guess. You'll have to get a new freezer, Father. Alpine Appliance is having a sale after New Year's. If they get pushy, you'll see the ad in next week's paper." He sighed with resignation.

Shirley Bronsky, who was squatting on the floor at her husband's feet and revealing a great deal of fat white thigh in the process, clasped both hands to her bulging bosom. "Honestly, what's this world coming to? A mother who turns her daughter into a prostitute? But I still don't understand why Mrs. McHale—or whatever her name is—had to kill those poor girls!"

"Simple," said Milo, sitting down next to Vida on the sofa. "Blackmail. Once Bridget got her hooks into Travis Nyquist, Teresa figured it was time to retire and gloat. She staged her own suicide with that phony cancer story, jumped off the Bainbridge Island ferry coming into Seattle, and swam over to the Smith Cove marina. It's not that far, at least not for a strong swimmer."

"Which," I noted, "Teresa was. Olympic class, in her youth. It appears that without Teresa running the show, the two girls who wanted to continue hooking didn't do so well on their own. Until Teresa comes around—or Bridget opens up—we won't know exactly what happened, but one theory is that Kathleen came to Alpine to hit Bridget up, and Bridget panicked and told Kathleen to go to the rectory. I doubt that Kathleen knew Teresa was still alive, so imagine her shock at discovering Mary Anne Dunne taking care of a small-town parish and a deaf old priest. I can imagine how Teresa met a demand for money." Sadly, I shook my head.

Milo made a crunching sound with one of his dill pickles. "The body had to be disposed of. Father Fitz apparently never went in the basement because of his arthritis. There was an axe in the woodshed which has bloodstains on it." Milo glanced at Ben. "Didn't you say something about how she wouldn't let you use the fireplace? She didn't want you near that woodshed, just in case there were some incriminating traces left."

Ben ran a hand through his dark hair. "There I was, eating omelettes and oyster stew and oven-fried chicken, and meanwhile Teresa had already confessed to my predecessor that she was a murderess." He pulled his hair straight up on end.

Vida wagged a finger at him. "Now just a minute, Father Ben. I thought you priests weren't allowed to tattle about what you heard in confession. Don't tell me that old fool of a pastor *blabbed*!"

Ben gave Vida his most somber expression. "Mrs. Runkel, how could you? An upstanding Presbyterian gossipmongering? Tut! I can only speculate on what Teresa said to Father Fitz in confession. But a few minutes later he suffered a stroke. And then Peyton Flake said Father's been acting agitated, passing on instructions. I wonder if he wasn't trying to give a warning instead. Without naming names or deeds, of course."

"Poor old guy," remarked Milo. "He was oblivious to everything that happened. Not that you could blame him, given his age and health problems. Teresa sure took her time to hack up. . . . ''

Shirley Bronsky let out a squeal. ''Stop! We're eating! Please, Milo, I have a very delicate stomach.''

I tried not to lift my eyebrows. Shirley's stomach looked about as delicate as a blast furnace. Ben came to Milo's rescue. ''Teresa had the luxury of time with Kathleen. But then Carol Neal came along looking for her friend. We assume she went to see Bridget, too. And got the same response: head for the rectory.'' He shrugged. ''Same result, except that I showed up, neither deaf nor feeble. Teresa must have put Carol in the freezer for a couple of days and then used the Volvo to transport the body to the river, at which point the temperature rose—which explains why Doc Dewey noticed some signs of thawing.''

Carla flipped her long, black hair over her shoulders. ''Really, it's too dumb! Why not get another pimp or madam or whatever? I mean, it's totally weird to expect somebody to hand over money for nothing.''

There were days when I felt as if I were doing the same thing with both Carla and Ed, but this was hardly the time or place to say so. ''It wasn't that simple,'' I pointed out. ''Kathleen and Carol were over their heads in debt, and they'd have a tough time finding anybody as efficient as Teresa. Remember, she was a terrific organizer. She booked her stable with several different businesses at first, then got in thick with Standish Crocker, who was also peddling cocaine. So was Travis, which is what made him wealthy, if nervous. He didn't get out of the investment business because he was tired of making money. He was afraid he'd get caught. And, along with Crocker, he did.''

Adam, flanked by Carla and Ginny, brought their plates over to join the circle. ''So Teresa bumped off Standish Crocker with Uncle Ben's gun and set his house on fire because she was afraid he'd squawk about the call-girl ring?''

Milo nodded. "You bet. And he would have. Travis will do it now instead."

Ginny, with her usual serious mien, fingered her small chin. "How can Travis do that when his own wife is involved? And why didn't Mrs. McHale get rid of Travis, too? Then Bridget would have been a rich widow."

Milo sipped from his tankard of ale. "Travis might have been next, but I think Teresa was hoping he'd never have to testify. As for Travis and Bridget, that marriage was doomed from the start. Bridget dazzled Travis, and of course Teresa egged her on. It was the perfect revenge, full circle on the Nyquist family. But let's face it, I wouldn't call it a love match. Bridget is better off back in Seattle with Rachel Rosen."

Vida heaved a sigh. "Thank God Rachel and Bridget are safe. Where did you say Rachel had gone for a few days? Portland?" The question was for Milo.

"Eugene. But she came back a day or so before Bridget went to Seattle with Travis," Milo explained. "At that point, Bridget suspected what was going on with her mother. I don't think she knew—or would believe—that Teresa had killed Kathleen and Carol until she couldn't duck the truth any longer. Bridget had to get away. She used the trip to Seattle with Travis as an excuse. She told him she wanted a trial separation."

My idealist's scenario called for Bridget to follow in Rachel's footsteps and go to college, to put Travis and prostitution and even her mother in the past, and to try to pick up the pieces of a life that had been broken at seventeen. It could be done, but the realist in me painted a grimmer picture.

Adam had gotten up to turn the CD player on. The Mormon Tabernacle Choir sang "Hark the Herald Angels Sing" at less than the usual ear-shattering decibels my son preferred.

"It was the masses," Ben said, seemingly apropos of nothing. We all looked at him. "For All Souls' Day. Bridget had asked Father Fitz to remember her own father among the dead. But she didn't request any remembrance for her mother. That made Sluggly here wonder why. The answer was obvious. Mrs. Dunne wasn't dead.''

"That and a lot of other things," I said, "including all those trips Teresa kept making with the Volvo. She didn't appear to have any friends in town, and yet she went out quite a bit. As it turned out, she was disposing of bodies, setting fires, and shooting people.''

Carla leaned back in her folding chair, the long hair dipping toward the carpet. "Talk about a hectic holiday season! Wow!''

Ed, however, was once again looking puzzled. "Now wait a minute—you mean Mrs. McHale set the fire at Evan Singer's place? Why?''

Sometimes Milo's patience astounds me. Maybe it wouldn't have been so exemplary if he'd had to work with Ed on a daily basis. "She was trying to divert suspicion. Evan was a likely target because he's a bit strange. She also needed to burn all that stuff she stole from Arnie Nyquist's house and van. The old letters he'd saved, even the college yearbook with her pictures and inscription had to be destroyed, just in case anybody ever found them and made the connection. I don't think she and Arnie ever ran into each other, but if they had, the middle-aged Teresa McHale didn't look much like the young Mary Anne Toomey. I figure she hoped Arnie's van was unlocked with the keys in the ignition. She probably wanted the one for the house. Teresa couldn't count on Louise Nyquist not locking up. The picture of Bridget and Travis was a bonus. It was the sort of thing a lovesick swain would take—and burn.''

I was gazing into the fire, listening to the Mormon rendition of "Away In A Manger." "I feel sorry for the Nyquists. Travis is a terrible blot on the family escutcheon. Poor Louise. But maybe reconciling with Evan's side of the family will help.''

"Evan will help," Ginny announced, surprising all of us. "I hear he's going to stay in Alpine and work at the Marmot. He's nuts about movies. After all, Oscar can't live forever."

"He's working on it," Vida said without enthusiasm.

I got up to get the dessert out. The Upper Crust had provided me with a *buche de Noël* that looked too good to eat. Almost. To my surprise, Adam came out to help me. To my amazement, Carla and Ginny tagged along to help Adam.

Ginny and Adam busied themselves with plates, forks, and more napkins while Carla lounged against the counter. "Now why couldn't Travis turn out to be a good guy so he could dump Bridget and become eligible?" She uttered a dramatic sigh. "He was handsome, rich, charming."

"And a crook," I noted, carrying cups and saucers back into the living room. I checked my big pot that stood on the dining room table; the coffee had finished perking. Vida would probably want tea. The phone rang on my desk across the room. Ben volunteered to answer it. There was no one at the other end, but the answering machine clicked on.

"The phones still aren't working quite right," I said. "If there's a real message, I'll get it later." It couldn't be an emergency affecting anybody I cared about, since they were all under my roof. If it was for Milo, his beeper would have gone off. I went back into the kitchen.

Adam, Carla, and Ginny were clustered together like a baseball conference on the mound. They were laughing and whispering in a conspiratorial manner.

The only words I caught were Ginny's: ". . . *Bugsy* starts next . . ."

All three jumped at my intrusion. I stared. They grew awkward. I frowned in puzzlement. And then it dawned on me. I dove for Adam, grabbing him by the front of his beige sweater.

"You! I don't believe it! How could you?"

"No, hey, really, I only . . . uh . . ." My son tried to

escape my clutches, his eyes darting back and forth between his accomplices.

Carla doubled over. "I can't help it! It's too funny!" She held her sides, giggling and jiggling away.

Ginny was the first to regain her composure. "Carla's right. It *is* funny. And what else is there to do around this town in the winter? What's the harm? It's good publicity for the Marmot. Who can resist checking out that marquee every day?"

I released my son and bit at my cheeks to keep from smiling. My gaze remained on Adam, who was adjusting his shirt collar and straightening his sweater. "When did you join this merry band, my boy?"

"Uh . . . last night. We couldn't ski. The weather was too crummy."

I gave a shake of my head. "I can't condone this."

Carla had gotten her giggles under control. "You don't have to. Would you rather we shot out Christmas lights or stole wreaths off doors?"

I sighed. I would rather they acted like responsible adults, but that was expecting too much. At least Carla and Ginny weren't selling themselves to the Alpine Kiwanis Club and Adam wasn't hustling crack to the Rotarians. Maybe I ought to count my blessings. I started back into the living room, made a quick change of direction, and went into the bathroom.

And laughed my head off. Carla could spell! Ginny had imagination! Adam wasn't rolling around with either of them in the snow!

Or maybe it was Carla's imagination and Ginny's spelling. It didn't matter. At least I might be right about Adam. Then again, we don't always get our wishes, not even at Christmas.

By eleven-thirty everyone had gone home, and Adam was in bed. I started the dishwasher and put on a German boys' choir Christmas CD. Except for the tree, the living room was dark. No, I was mistaken. The answering machine light was on. I turned the volume to low and played the tape.

"You must be out reveling," said the mellow voice of Tom Cavanaugh. "Sandra and I are leaving for London tomorrow. She's always wanted a Dickensian Christmas, so I'm going to let her shoplift Royal Doulton at the Olde Curiosity Shoppe. I'll be back in San Francisco the twenty-seventh. Sandra's going to spend a few days with her sister up at Lake Tahoe. Any chance you and Adam could fly down to welcome Baby New Year? The trip's on me. Merry Christmas." There was a pause, then Tom's voice deepened. "Every Christmas I miss you like hell. Now that I've finally met Adam, I miss him, too. Damn and double damn. Why is life such a pain in the ass? I'll call you the twenty-eighth."

I replayed the tape three times, foolishly drinking in his voice, savoring his sentiments, wishing I weren't such a sap. There would be no New Year's party for Tom, Emma, and Adam. Ben would still be in Alpine, and I couldn't run out on him. Oh, he'd try to make me go if I told him about the call. But I wouldn't. Tom had his principles, which some might call excuses; I had my own sense of honor. And I'd call it what I pleased.

I hung the last angel above the stable. All the sheep were on their backs, looking as if they'd been mowed down by an outbreak of anthrax. I righted them, then adjusted the angel who seemed intent on flying off to the port side. Through the speakers came the pure, youthful voices of the boys' choir. *Stille nacht, heilige nacht*. I stood next to the tree, the lights shimmering, the icicles dancing, the ornaments sparkling. Outside, it was still snowing, though not nearly as hard as the previous night. *Silent night, holy night*.

Christmas was five days away. There was one more Sunday to go in Advent. The last ten days had taken a terrible toll. I realized I was exhausted. But tonight I felt contentment wash over me. I unplugged the tree, but paused again by the crèche. The tiny manger was still empty. Baby Jesus wouldn't bide there until Christmas Eve. I smiled and headed for bed.

Sleep in heavenly peace.

Life in a small town tucked away in the foothills of the Cascade Mountains is supposed to be tranquil and safe. So why does Emma Lord, editor-publisher of the local paper, keep getting mixed up in murder? Read all about it in the novels of

MARY DAHEIM

Published by Ballantine Books.
Available in your local bookstore.

CHRISTMAS CAN BE MURDER.